A STORY OF PILEAUS

THE UNMADE MAN

D.T. Gooden

THE UNMADE MAN: A STORY OF PILEAUS
Copyright © 2019 Daniel Tyler Gooden & Jeremy D. Mohler. All rights reserved.

Published by Outland Entertainment LLC
3119 Gillham Road
Kansas City, MO 64109

Founder/Creative Director: Jeremy D. Mohler
Editor-in-Chief: Alana Joli Abbott
Senior Editor: Gwendolyn Nix

ISBN: 978-1-947659-50-6
Worldwide Rights
Created in the United States of America

Editor: Gwendolyn Nix
Cover Illustration: Chris Yarbrough
Cover Design: Jeremy D. Mohler
Interior Layout: Mikael Brodu

Printed and bound in the United States of America.

Visit **outlandentertainment.com** to see more, or follow us on our Facebook Page **facebook.com/outlandentertainment/**

Sometimes, when part of a man is lost, the rest seems in ruin.
Sometimes, it's the unknown that binds him together

CONTENTS

- I -

THE WAITING BOY

T
he boy felt the man descend from the ridgeline like his own hand held out into a numbing cold and now returning as a stranger to the warmth of his pocket. He was glad. The Fae had searched long for them both, reaching out with eyes and whispers from their home in the Dreaming Lands. Now the boy would journey home, if this new man could bear the weight of the burden he'd come to carry.

The boy listened to his grandfather's last breath as the man and his three riders broke through the jungle's edge. He held his mouth shut and watched them ride into the field. When they were halfway across the thin valley the child inhaled again, no longer fearing that his grandfather's last dead breath would be sucked into his own body. In life the old man would never have done the boy harm; he was a protector. In death, the boy knew, spirits tend to do odd things.

He laid his small hand on the dead man's chest, feeling the heat slip from the corpse. He felt his grandfather's magic fade too. The ties snapped like a broken spider's web. The strands began to sever and would soon wipe clean what life he knew in this hidden glade.

The riders came to a halt before the porch. This is where his life would now go. His grandfather was gone, and he'd taken the protection of the valley with him. The boy thought little of that, noticing only the runes tracing down the arm of the man standing before him. There was much power there. A keen few would see them: those that still knew the smell of old magics, those that heard the hum of coarse power even trapped in script. Why did the man risk laying that secret bare for those watchful few? The boy gazed at the others in the group. There was much strength here, almost as much as there was weakness. He rubbed his palm against his grandfather's chest, one last goodbye and a measure of what little time they had left for introductions.

Boruin ran his hand through his short gray hair, deciding what to make of the scene. The smell of the dust rising up where his boots stirred the earth was too sharp. His scabbard smacked against his leg louder than it should have. He could feel it all changing. The jungle around them was coarse as rock salt rubbed into a wound; this place was smooth and fine, but it was cracking. The dead man's magic had polished down this deep valley. He had held the land in check, held his valley in a chosen image. Now he was gone, and this place was on its way out.

Boruin could feel Pile's eyes pricing the items on the porch, peering through the open door into the gloom. He didn't have to see the young man's hands to know they were already twitching, ready to take his share. They had all been relic hunters in their own way and time, but it was engrained in Pile, part of the young man's fabric.

Wraethe kept Pile in check with her imposing presence alone. She stayed wrapped in her shadowy cloak, her raven hair and pale skin hidden from the sun. Only her blue eyes appeared under that dark hood as she dreamed of the day and waited for night. She could wake now, if needed, and come forward into the world, but rarely did those eyes rise into the bright sunlight without riding on a wave of rage.

Toaaho showed no sign of eagerness, no pleasure at finding the boy. Perhaps the mask of tattoos laid across his face kept his emotion hidden as well. The broad strokes covering his sun-darkened skin seemed overdone as just decoration, but they kept the Mana'Olai hidden from more than just his emotions.

Boruin stepped forward, and the boy took his hand off the dead man's chest. He did not shy away, did not run and hide from the four strangers. The old man watched the boy's eyes dart across his left arm and it made him nervous. His tattoos were not visible to all—to very few, in fact—and for a child to see them meant something. The boy was not what he expected, much like this whole contract. Every time he swore off that damn Nefazo merchant, the next job was doubly strange.

The boy reached out to touch the black runes, and Boruin almost stepped back. He took the small hand and dropped to his knees before the boy.

"Do you know me?"

The boy shrugged.

"You know why I'm here, or who sent me?"

The boy nodded yes. He stood up and walked to the horse as if he had expected a ride. The stirrup hung shoulder high. Though the steed stamped about him, the boy did not flinch. He placed his small hand on the horse's flank and it quieted.

"Do you have anything to take, anything you need? You won't be coming back," Boruin said. The boy pointed south, where the jungle closed in to swallow the valley at its needle point. A brown cloud had stirred up—dust, probably. The wind had begun to descend out of the hills. Wind didn't suck the thick grass down into the ground, though.

"Time to leave," Toaaho said in his quiet, ever undisturbed voice.

Pile spat in anger and the wind blew it back on his jungle-stained pants. "What about all this? You promised us some treasure! I didn't hack through the Fae-cursed jungle to leave empty handed." He sidestepped his horse closer to the porch, and Wraethe's black shift rustled in response. His eyes darted toward the shrouded woman. "Come on, Boruin. I'll be quick. Anything will do. It'll just go to waste."

"I see wooden bowls and a dead man, Pile. Search for more if you want," Boruin said, placing the boy on the horse and vaulting up behind him.

"The time is almost past," Toaaho said, turning his horse to the north.

Boruin followed and shouted over his shoulder against the rising rush of the wind. "Half the valley is gone. Take what you can if you wish to join it!" Pile looked back and saw the valley behind him was now a whirlwind of destruction. The air sucked down out of the hills, pulling the soil toward the pocket storm. Pile's mouth snapped shut as a heavy gust made his horse stumble backward toward the swirling mass.

"Have it your way!" the young man shouted as he spurred his horse into a gallop after them.

Pile hurried his mount forward and soon led the galloping riders through the field. The grass lay flat before their horses' hooves. They all leaned close to their mounts, save for Wraethe, who seemed to flow as part of the gale.

The moisture drained from the dirt and great cracks split through the soil. Boruin glanced back and watched as the storm engulfed the small cottage. The old man's body rose into the air, or maybe it was the ground collapsing beneath. It hung still and then pulled apart as if made of dust.

Boruin drove his horse on harder as they crashed back into the thick jungle. The horses did not slow and their riders did not try to rein them in. They plowed along a shallow stream and stayed low, ducking under the trees. The wind continued to blow down off the ridgeline, whipping the tangled branches and vines across their skin.

"Up! Up!" yelled Boruin as he felt the first tremor. The horses staggered as the earth began to shift, and the riders turned up the slope. Toaaho led them, switching back and forth up the steep walls of the valley.

Pile swung free from his saddle, leaning off the side of his horse as a boulder burst from the underbrush. It passed behind his mount's head and flew down into the valley.

"I'm going to pass you if you don't flog that beast!" Pile yelled at Toaaho. He dug his spurs in and his horse tore forward. Wraethe followed after, and Boruin pushed his steed onward, cursing from the rear.

The horses halted as a great tremor shattered half the valley. The bedrock snapped with a loud groan and the shelf sagged beneath them. A cleft in the hillside, virgin gray of exposed stone, ran upward from their feet. Toaaho did not hesitate to gallop up this strange track. The others followed. Boruin could smell the sharp spice of sparks as iron horseshoes clattered against the tilting rock. The trail canted steeper as they rushed on. The valley was dropping away and soon there would be nothing but air under their feet.

As the gray stone began to crumble, Boruin felt a wet mist blow from beneath them. The top of the ridgeline was right there, and he stopped cursing the gods to offer one quick prayer. Perhaps it did them good; perhaps the crash of water and splinter of stone drowned it out. Regardless, Toaaho reached the top just as the stone began to slide. Boruin saw Wraethe's horse slip, so he rammed it forward with his own. It was enough to drive them both up off the tipping stone and onto the stable ground of the jungle above.

Pile leapt, wide-eyed, from his horse. "Yuin's whores, what a ride!"

Toaaho turned to watch as a great geyser of water shot out from below. The sliding walls of the valley had uncovered a deep river, and the wash now vaulted into space and tumbled into a bottomless cavern. The valley was gone, swallowed by the earth. The dead man could have received no deeper grave.

The horses pranced about, their blood still churning in excitement. Pile dropped to his knees, panting. He searched through all the hidden pockets of his red vest. On finding a charm, idol, or trinket he kissed each in turn as thanks and then tucked it away again. Toaaho soothed his horse, whispering quietly into its flickering ears.

Boruin wiped the sweat from his neck as he watched Wraethe's horse back into the shadows of the nearest tree.

In the full light of the sun Wraethe seemed weak, and to an extent she was. She sat still in her shadows, never seeming to move in the light. Still all of them feared her, even in day. Boruin would deny that, but in day and certainly at Diuntyne, he was as wary as any. Wraethe was like the trained war cat; fierce, loyal, and just wild enough to never take your eyes off of completely. Her nature was more cruel than kind. And at Syan, at full night… she could be pure nightmare.

The boy alone turned his back on the valley. He sniffed at the air, his tongue licking out as if he were catching a scent the way a northern boy would catch a snowflake. When he had smelled enough, he turned to catch Pile's attention.

"Father of Yuin!" Pile yelled when the boy placed his hand on the back of the man's neck. "Don't sneak up on me like that, boy! I'm a trained killer and I almost did you in!" The boy did not flinch at the barrage, but held out a strand of beads and tied rocks. "What's this for?" The child shook it, as if enticing a baby.

"Treasure," Toaaho answered, his face motionless.

"Kind of worthless."

"Only kind you'll get today," Toaaho replied, his eyes sparkling.

Boruin pulled himself to his feet, laughing. "He's right, Trained Killer. Better hold on to your share."

He left Pile to grumble at their teasing and stepped to the edge of the valley wall. The rock had shorn clean off, and a new granite cliff followed the waterfall down into the deep gloom. Boruin wondered if he could have seen the bottom even with the sun directly overhead. He looked up, checking its position, but it was lost above the thick jungle canopy.

Boruin turned his gaze to Wraethe. Only her eyes were visible behind the veil of shadow. They watched him back, dark as Diuntyne's setting. They would brighten nearer sunset when she would come forward. She was mostly asleep and that meant it was still afternoon. Wraethe would follow and she would flee, but she would remember little of the day except as fading dream. This was her slumbering hour, her weakest hour when he watched out for her. At night she returned the favor.

"It may not be wise to linger here longer," Toaaho said, stepping beside Boruin.

The older man nodded. "There is more magic to that man than the valley. I felt it, too."

"I would guess more protection," Toaaho replied. "Something ranging that let us pass before."

"Why did it drop? Why so much magic here? Do you think he was Fae?" Boruin asked. Toaaho shrugged and did not answer. "Well, Belok better have more of an idea than you. I knew I should have sent him to peddle his contract elsewhere when he offered so much gold."

There was nothing but brush in the deep jungle, but Pile found some way to lead them on. Smart-mouthed, selfish, shallow, and short, Pile was more annoyance than good companionship, but he had his uses. Boruin kept him around mostly because he could swallow a joke. They tried at least once a day to get him riled, but Pile could take it as well as he could dish it out.

Pile could also find a trail, even if there wasn't one, and he could see far. Despite the brush, despite the sun hidden behind the thick leaves, Pile could see what was coming.

So, when the dead man's guardian found them, Pile had long seen it on its way, and they were as ready as they could be for a twelve-foot construct of mud, rock, and wood—the life of the jungle—twisted into new form by strange magic, sentient and seeking them out.

Boruin was not worried about Wraethe. She would wake if she felt the need, but the boy was going to be a complication. They hunkered down, waiting while the monster sniffed them out. The boy stepped lightly around Boruin, looking up at the trees, waving at colorful birds. The old man took his hand and hid him behind a thick tree root. Soon the child was back on his feet, undisturbed, unafraid, and unaware of the rising tension.

Toaaho disappeared into the brush, his movements slow and perfect. Years in slavery had not dissolved his training, and he'd had plenty of time to develop his skill since Boruin had purchased his writ. Pile watched the creature come and tapped his fingers across his axe blade. It echoed out a light ring, a tinny reverberation that sounded eager to be put to work.

Boruin licked the fingertips of his right hand and considered a small prayer. Maybe his last had delivered them out of the valley, but he decided against another. No reason to make a habit of it.

His fingers grazed the tattoos on his left forearm. He tried to forget about the creature, forget about the boy prancing in circles around him. The old man flicked his fingers over the dark runes, spinning them like a street shark's gambling wheel. He felt the pull on his flesh as the line began to move.

The runes curled over his shoulder and down his bicep. They turned under his arm and over his wrist, climbing back up his forearm. The line crossed his shoulders and dropped down his back. They twisted around his chest and down across his hips, a long line of black characters that made no sense to him at all—at least very rarely. Boruin dragged his fingers across a choice few as they spun across his wrist, pulling them out of line and into his palm where they settled like fallen leaves. He had created spells before, finding the right arrangement, or right match, or right sub-category, something right— but it was rare. Working combinations came to him in odd moments of inspiration, and he was hoping for one now.

The guardian was bigger than he had first figured. The hard rock spikes shoved into its shoulder blades and forearms did not mark it as a peaceful creature. Its body was clay, with part of the forest shoved into the wet mass to give it more strength. Heavy limbs jutted out of its thighs and vines bound its chest into a dense and solid torso. Briars wound about its lower legs, placed there on purpose or mindlessly collected as it roamed about the forest.

Boruin had selected four runes when the boy sat down beside him. The child watched the symbols flip by and examined the ones on the skin of his hand. The old man was sliding the fifth into his palm when the boy stopped him, motioning that it should be returned and the search should continue. Boruin would have ignored anyone else, but that the boy could even see them was odd. He slid the rune back onto his wrist and moved the line along. The boy's pointed finger followed a sharp-cornered rune down from Boruin's shoulder, snaking around his arm, to his wrist. Boruin pulled it onto his palm, though he did not recognize it, and the boy clapped silently.

The old man stood behind Pile and tightened his left hand under a growing burn. He felt the runes heating up in his hand; he felt their combination mixing. He wasn't sure how effective it would be, but he knew it would create something. There was a feeling about a rune combination, a power that radiated when they matched. At times they matched too well and Boruin let them run back up his arm for fear of their strength. This time they felt just right. As the creature stepped out of the brush and turned to look at him, Boruin flung the runes out of his hand.

The magic sliced through the air and hit the clay monster with a wet smack. The flesh of its body rippled back as the spell hit, forming a crater on its upper thigh. Blood red flowers erupted from the hole. They sprouted out of the clay and ran across the beast's dark, muddy skin. The monster froze, watching the old man with his arm still outstretched. The matched gaze held until the flowers opened and all burst at once, gold pollen showering out from the wide blooms. They shone like stars where they crossed the thin shafts of sunlight piercing the canopy.

"The rutting Mother!" Boruin cursed. The boy clapped out loud and squealed in glee. Pile laughed through the horrified look on his face. Toaaho dropped out of the trees and drove his dagger into the creature's back.

The monster roared and twisted, flinging the Mana'Olai off its hump. It tore at the flowers, dragging them out by their roots. It did not clear them all before dashing forward at Boruin. Pile met it halfway, swinging his axe up into its kneecap. The blade hit with a dull thud, and Pile dragged it out covered in mud. The creature came on, undeterred by the blow.

Boruin pulled his sword from the scabbard on his back. "Go!" he shouted at the boy. The child dashed off behind a tree, peeking around the other side as if in play. The guardian swung, the rock barbs severing the branches and scoring tree bark as its heavy fists came down.

Dancing aside, Boruin flicked the tip of his sword up under the beast's arm and into its armpit, through where its vital organs should have been. The blade came back out of the monster's body with nothing but clay streaking the well-oiled metal.

Toaaho drove his blade into its back again, trying to sever the beast's spine, if it had one. The dagger opened a great gash, but no blood welled out.

The three fought fast, circling, turning the beast like a bull on festival day. They fought and tired and the creature raged on.

Pile stumbled back, trying to catch his breath. "Köpeka's bloody sons, Boruin! You got more than flowers for us?"

"Now would be the time," Toaaho agreed, dropping below a thundering punch that felled the tree behind him.

Boruin glanced back down at his runes. The growing gloom left little to see. The thing was big but not slow. They were tiring, and in the dark there would be little chance of blindly outrunning it.

The light was still low and tinged orange with sunset, but Boruin knew that day was gone and Diuntyne was upon them as a flash of black swept out of the jungle.

With shadows trailing behind her, Wraethe vaulted up the creature's body, climbing the protruding rocks and shattered branches. Thick clay fingers dropped severed to the jungle floor as the creature's hand tried to close about her. She rose fast and graceful up its body to perch on the golem's crown, like a crow on a gargoyle. The creature groaned as Boruin saw her white hand wipe the creased clay smooth across its brow.

The monster's knees shook and buckled. Pile dove out of the way as the mountain of clay came down. Wraethe stepped free from the softening creature. Her body shivered and her hands clenched. She leaned her head back, lungs sucking in the moist air as if she were drinking in the night to wash down the taste of battle. Boruin and the others held still until her breathing steadied. They knew better than to rush her out of a fury. Fighting always gave rise to her blood, and it was unwise to approach her even after the heat of it had passed.

In the darkness her face glowed like the great moon, her skin pale. She drew back her black hood, swinging the cloak over her shoulders, and seemed to step fully out of shadow. Wraethe tugged a red bloom from the dead clay and rubbed the mud from her hands with the petals.

Her eyes flashed like sisters of the moons and she turned to Boruin. "Your work?"

"Mine and the boy's," he said.

"The boy helped?" she asked. "When almost no one can see them, the boy helped?" Wraethe frowned. "I've warned you about fooling with what you don't understand."

"Yes. You have."

"But we did find him, then," she said, turning to the child. "I dreamt we had." The boy stepped out from behind his tree and came forward. He bent to grab a fallen red petal and took her hand in his. The red leaf wiped the last smear of mud off her wrist, leaving her skin as pale cream.

Wraethe smiled and smoothed back his wild hair. "You are a good boy, aren't you?" The boy nodded. "Learn no lessons from these three and we will get along brilliantly," she continued. The boy widened his grin until it outshone her pale shimmer.

"How did you beat it?" Pile ventured to ask.

Toaaho answered for her. "The sigil. She saw the sign on its head that bound the material animate."

Wraethe nodded. "Some details stand out in my day dreams better than others. The sigil on the beam of the porch shone like a dying star."

Pile shook his head in exasperation at Toaaho. "Why didn't you do that if you saw it?"

"Didn't see what it was," Toaaho said calmly.

"What's done is done," said Boruin. "Now we know what to watch for. If there are others, hopefully they will be the same."

"Are they ever?" Wraethe asked.

"Never," he replied.

UNDER THE SHADE
OF A TRAVELING TREE

Boruin tossed the bones of his dinner into the fire and looked in disbelief at his companion. "An Aiemer flow?"

"That's right," answered Wraethe.

"You're saying that the man, after he was dead, somehow drew upon a fable to destroy his valley?" Boruin said.

"No. That is impossible," said Wraethe.

Boruin raised his hands in exasperation. "Exactly!" He opened his mouth to continue, then stopped, confused. "Then what are you saying?"

Pile pulled a stick from the fire and held it above their cooking stone. "She's saying the valley was torn apart by the Aiemer after the old fellow died." He dashed the ember against the rocks and let the rising sparks of the dead coal serve as example.

"When you know more about any subject than I do, I'll ask your opinion," Boruin said, giving Pile a sidelong sneer.

Pile saw an opening, and his teeth shone in the firelight. "Like who your mother is?"

"Or where you were born?" Wraethe added. Her rare smile matched Pile's in its eagerness.

"Like why every time we drink, you slip into some northern sailor's accent?" asked Pile.

"And why, for as long as you and I have traveled together, neither of us remember where we started or anything before," said Wraethe, her right eyebrow cocked.

Boruin knew that look. He didn't remember any more of his past than she of hers, and now was not the time to get back into that saga. They had the best of him, and it was either time to storm off or to give in. Boruin leaned back against the high tree root and sighed.

"Fine, so what do you know about the Aiemer?" he asked.

Pile played stubborn, his lips twitching to turn up into one of his wide, lop-sided grins. "Nothing."

"Pile, what do you want to enlighten us about?" Wraethe asked.

Pile held back his smile at her firm tone. "You know, your good moods are too short lived," he replied, waving off her sour look. "I know a few things from back when I worked the old mah'saiid ruins with Graemer. He could translate the old glyphs and he told me some of what he'd read," said Pile.

"Like what?" Boruin asked.

Pile poked around in the fire, uncomfortable as Boruin and Wraethe turned their full attention to him. "Here's how I understand it. The Aiemer comes from the second realm of Baeg Tobar. Though the two realms of this world are split, the Dying and the Dreaming, the Aiemer can move freely between both. In the Dreaming Lands, the Aiemer saturates the land like it's a sponge. It is part of everything and everything exists because of it. Maybe some of that is bedtime tale, maybe not."

"All things in the Dreaming Lands originate in the Aiemer?" asked Boruin.

Pile leaned forward as if giving his mind a push before it stalled out. "No, and don't stop me; I'll lose my train of thought. In our mortal realm—the Duine Lands, as the mah'saiid called them—the Aiemer is untouchable; unseen, unsmelled, untasted, unheard. That's really the main thing. I mean, it still influences things, but mostly it is very subtle, and we don't see it. Here, Aiemer moves of its own accord, like tides in an unseen sea. Where it does slow and pool, it saturates the ground and changes it. Maybe in the image of the Dreaming Lands. I don't know."

"That's the children's story part," said Boruin.

"Fingle and the Floating Mountain of Emeralds," offered Wraethe.

"Imber's Ocean of Glass," added Boruin.

Pile waved his finger in agreement, but kept his attention in the fire as if the flames were spelling out his tale. "There is little that affects the Aiemer, and even less that can harness it. Graemer thought though that the Aiemer was where all magic rises from. The sorcerers, the priests, the bards—they all draw from the same source. It seemed to him that the Aiemer must touch everything, and those that make magic use the Aiemer that has touched and settled in their bodies as fuel. We Duine, then, are limited in power, as we can only draw from the Aiemer inside us. It's not like the fables that tell of the Fae's direct control of the Aiemer turning mountains into emeralds." His glazed eyes rose from the fire, and the return of his smile told them he'd reached the end of his speech.

"But again, the guy in the valley was dead. There is no controlling anything after you've gone under," said Boruin.

"Right!" Pile agreed. "The Aiemer didn't destroy the valley after his death. The Aiemer *was* the valley. He held it in place, controlling it until he was gone. That's the problem, and that's big." There was no trace of humor left on his face.

"Give me your idea of big," Boruin said.

"That kind of power could have brought down the whole nation of Nefazo, turned them all into goats and their shit into gold. But instead it was providing a safe place for a mute, near-mindless kid," said Pile, digging around in the coals of the fire. He held up the glowing brand and pointed it at Boruin. "What is with this kid?"

Boruin stood up from the dirt and looked around. "Where is he?"

Wraethe pointed off into the darkness to some hidden spot in the murky gloom. "Keeping watch with Toaaho."

"Well, he can keep him. That boy has been nothing but trouble. I'm going to sleep," Boruin said.

"He does make a nice bouquet of flowers," Pile offered, regaining his humor. Boruin ignored this and lay down with his back to the fire. They would begin moving again in six hours, and he needed to sleep. He was sure it wouldn't happen, but he could lie still and think. Pile was right about the boy; there was more to him than there should be.

Boruin wondered why Belok had offered them this job. The man had a habit of profiting well on a contract, and Boruin wondered who was behind this one. He turned the events of the day over in his head. Pile was right about the Aiemer and the valley–he had to be. Boruin knew of no magical crafts that would bring down that valley. Certainly no mortal ones.

The boy was special.

Belok had passed the job off as a retrieval and escort, but it was more than that. Though his mind kept churning, Boruin slipped away into the darker field of sleep. He slept lightly, still bothered by Pile's reminder that the details of his own life were more of a mystery than any of this mess.

Every night as Diuntyne arrived, silver Diun breached the horizon like a titanic ship entering the open sea of dark sky. The stars were smothered under the polished light of the moon's swirling gas surface. It lost little of its size as it arced above the land. To hold one's fist up against it was to see it well around like liquid spilling over the brim.

In the jungle west of Nefazo, Diun seemed to illuminate Wraethe no matter what shadow she led the horses through. After their dinner and mid-night sleep the woman glowed even in the moon's absence, when Diun dropped behind the horizon and Syan, the moonless, star-filled cycle of the day was upon them. Boruin watched her skin dimly shimmer in this jungle darkness where the starlight refused to enter. It was almost as if she gathered the cool light of the moon about her as armor against the blackest night. Even her coal-black hair shone, dark blue flashes reflecting out of the loose coils.

Pile ambled before Boruin and Toaaho followed behind, but in the darkness, he only made them out by the sound of their horses' hooves on the trail. They all followed the woman, because at night her vision was as bright as her skin.

"It's Diun, I'd wager," Pile had once ventured. "She shares its eye as her own. If the great orb beholds it, I'd lay coin that it's known to Wraethe. It's unnatural."

Boruin did not dispute it. Wraethe's uncanny nocturnal senses had often kept their hands out of the irons and their feet off the branding plates. It wasn't natural. The lij had spread wide across this massive continent and there were all sorts of people different from another, but Wraethe compared to none Boruin had met. The alternative—that she could be from the Dreaming Lands—was not something that he liked to think of.

Boruin heard the boy sigh and felt him lean back against his chest. As mixed as his feelings were toward the boy, Boruin held him tighter. The kid slept, his hands wrapped in the mane of Boruin's horse, his heels bouncing against Boruin's thighs as they rode. They continued through the night, stopping only once as Pile dozed and slipped from his horse. He woke, cursing the fall, and climbed back into the saddle to sleep until dawn.

Wraethe stepped down from her horse at the first sign of twilight. A faint blue line, heavy like a welling tear, rose from the edge of the horizon. It would be another few hours before the sun would break that same edge, its light washing out to burn off the thick mists. Its bright wink would soon tease the great flowers, dangling as ornate tapestries from the tall trees, into opening again and paying homage to its brilliance.

Pile stretched, hands on his hips and leaning as far back as he could without tipping over. "Time for a rest?"

"Could use one, huh?" Boruin asked. "Snoring take a lot out of you?" Pile raised his thumb and clucked through the side of his mouth in his sarcastic "you got it boss" fashion. Boruin let him be and stretched his own tired limbs.

Toaaho tethered their horses and set to breaking out his equipment. First, he'd rub oil into his leather scabbards and harnesses, then he'd check his knives for rust and sharpen them. Black tiger stripes of whetstone grit stained his leather pants where he constantly wiped the blades clean. It was a morning duty that the Mana'Olai attended to better than a Yuinite priest to his prayers. He didn't even budge as the boy, weaving half-asleep toward him, curled up behind him to share the heat of his broad back.

Pile had his own routine when they ended a ride. He'd check that damn red vest for tears, pockets and all, and sew it back into shape. Only Yuin knew who he was trying to stay presentable for. All Boruin knew was that faded, blood red fabric wasn't the best camouflage in the jungle. Just as routine as his sewing, Pile's head would soon be nodding, and they'd find him asleep between stitches with a shirt or pants in hand. He'd finish that jacket first, though; he was enamored with the damn thing.

"We've made good time," Boruin said as he felt Wraethe walk up behind him. She joined him in peering back along their route. They had followed a ridgeline up to this small peak, perched like a watch-tower over the next valley. There they would wait for dawn.

"The other guardians?" he asked.

She pulled her cloak around her shoulders as if she could already feel the touch of the sun. "I saw nothing of them, though a large cat tracked us for an hour."

"That would have been nice to know," Boruin responded.

"Toaaho handled it when it got too close," Wraethe replied. Boruin grunted his acceptance. It didn't surprise him that he had heard nothing.

The sky brightened, and the wind teased the fog pooled in the valley below. It swirled and rose as if the ridge were a sleeping giant, slowly pulling its white comforter over its shoulders.

A great tree in the center of their small hill had grown wide, its branches hanging over the crown like a wool cap stretched too big.

Wraethe followed Boruin to its massive trunk and they sat facing the brightening horizon. They discussed the coming day, where they were, and where to go. It was a pre-morning ritual as much as the other's.

The changing of the guard came at dawn as Wraethe retreated into sleep, her sharp senses blinded by the hot light. They watched in silence until the first edge of the sun broke over the jungle.

"Keep an eye on that boy, Boruin."

"I will."

"He's different, and I like him," she added, her voice lighter, sounding tired.

"I know you do. You've always had a soft spot for the odd ones," Boruin replied, but Wraethe was already asleep. He watched as her hands pulled the black hood over her head. Her blue eyes receded into the darkness from where they would gaze outward without seeing.

"HUMBRUEWUM," a rumbling sound like grinding rock shook the hilltop. Boruin rolled out from under the tree, standing on guard and searching for the source of the sound. No other creature stood on the hill; Boruin and his companions were joined atop it only by the bright sun. He dashed around the other side of the tree as the sound rumbled out again into the morning air.

Pile circled the tree, peering down into the morning mists curled about the base of the hill. "Another guardian! Sounds bigger, too." His axe swung back and forth beside him. It was a nervous twitch Boruin had seen before. He wondered how long it would be before Pile swung the weapon a little too close to his thigh and shaved off a strip of meat.

Toaaho gazed out from under the tree's wide branches. The old oak had long lorded over the hilltop, smothering the rest of the undergrowth with shade and giving a far view on all sides. "No guardian. There's nothing moving at all."

"Maybe it's not a guardian, but moving or not, something is here," Boruin replied. He turned back to the tree and ran his hand along its bark. The rumbling had quieted to a deep chanting. It moved in a strange, melodic murmuring, reminding him of a contented house cat and its purring sigh. Boruin could barely hear it, but the vibration tickled his fingertips through the bark.

"It's below us," he said, dropping to his knees to press his hand to the ground. The whole hill reverberated with the chanting. It rumbled through the rock and up into the leaves above. The hill began to heave; little tremors bounced them on their feet as if the ground was trying to break free. Boruin turned to see the boy standing on its tiptoes, his ear pressed against a knothole in the tree.

The child's face was crunched up tight, his lips pursed as if deciding whether he liked a particular spiced meat or not. He decided he did not and stepped back with his arms crossed, his face a mix of contempt and impatience.

Like he's the adult, and whatever this may be is being childish, Boruin thought.

Toaaho stepped up beside the child and placed his ear over the hole. He motioned to Boruin, but Pile rushed up to put his ear there first. Boruin pulled him back and listened.

From deep somewhere in the roots the voice rose as a mix of echoes bouncing around inside the hollow trunk. "Boombruem wholiday. Fineriy, fine certainly fair morning to hill."

"Fae, if I've ever known 'em," Pile said.

"Oh, that's your expert opinion?" Boruin replied. "Then it must be."

"It is," Toaaho added.

Boruin grabbed the boy up around the waist. "I know, damn it. Let's get out of here." They turned, but there was no leaving. Their horses were gone, their small campfire distant and the ridge slipping out from under them. Boruin's head snapped around to find Wraethe, but she was still leaned up against the trunk, rolling lightly with the motion of the hill. The boy wriggled out of his grasp. Never good with ships, Boruin sat quickly, cursing his wavering feet and his turning stomach. Though he knew this was no boat, his body had yet to arrive at the same conclusion.

"Yuin, hear my prayers," Pile said, his hand tracing the god's sigil in the air as his mother had taught him long ago. Toaaho moved back to the knothole, his ear listening while his eyes watched the moving landscape. Boruin just sat, nauseous, watching the land slide by as the hill moved off the ridge and into the valley. The boy had taken to the front of the tree to watch the jungle break before them.

Pile sat by the boy to watch and shouted back in amazement. "This is not normal, Boruin! Not normal at all!"

"Great Mother, damn the Fae," Boruin whispered as the hill turned to ride up a shallow crest and roll down into a neighboring valley. He watched the dense jungle part before them. It slid around their hill and then came back together as smooth as if there had been no great mound of rock plowing through. The hill and the tree meandered about and then headed south, back over the ground they had spent all night covering. Boruin took a deep breath to calm his rolling stomach and climbed next to Toaaho.

"Listen," the Mana'Olai said. Boruin pressed his ear next to the hole and heard the voice again. It thrummed and piped and hummed and gurgled, a mix of noises that betrayed only childish play.

"It's definitely Fae. Doesn't sound too civilized, and the wild ones are usually the most troublesome," said Boruin. "Any ideas?"

Toaaho shook his head. Wraethe was still leaning against the tree trunk, though now on the opposite side of the sun. She would be no help.

Well, when in doubt for the right idea, try what's probably wrong, Boruin thought to himself. He placed his mouth over the knothole and hollered as loud as he could. "BY THE MOTHER, HILLS AREN'T SUPPOSED TO MOVE!"

"No?" bubbled up the answer through ground. "I'm moving quite nicely."

Boruin grabbed tight to the knothole as the hill rolled down a steep trench and back up the other side. "You're not a hill, though."

The burbling echoes bounced up from the deep roots. "I look like a hill."

"And I look like a lij," Boruin retorted.

"You're not a lij?" the voice asked. "You look like a lij."

Boruin's chest rose as he summoned as much commanding impatience as he could. "I'm not a lij! I'm your uncle, and I demand to know what you are doing out here milling about with this hill!"

"Do Fae have uncles?" Pile whispered.

"Careful," Toaaho cautioned.

The hill ground to a halt in the middle of a wide stream. Fish flopped downriver as the water began to back up on the other side of the mound. The boy pointed upward, and they all turned to stare as the branches above wove into a new shape. After a few moments a face began to appear out of the layers of leaves and limbs. Boruin leaned to one side and the face disappeared; he stood straight again and the face reappeared. It was like teasing your eye into seeing shapes in the clouds, except this shape moved as the voice boiled up through the ground around them.

"Which uncle are you: of the dew or the mid-month morning mist? For no uncle of mine ever dressed so lij-like," the voice said, now deep, stern, and doubtful.

"Of the tides of Diun's dawn, and I have my reasons for being shaped as such. It is not for you to question," Boruin answered, trying to stare down the illusion of a face above him.

The eyes, blue from the sky behind them, squinted back in consideration. "Curiosity is our vice of choice," the hill said.

"And its consequences our bane," Boruin responded in turn, the words snapping into place. The phrase was new to his lips, and Boruin could not remember where it came from. It rose from that place still lost in his mind, but he pushed wondering away for after this bluff.

"Humbreuwum… fine, Uncle Lij, what do you wish of me on my day of play?"

"Just to give you a gift, is all. You have caused all this… bruhuumbrum for nothing," Boruin chided.

Pile leaned close and whispered to Toaaho. "What is he talking about?" The Mana'Olai shrugged. The tree began to shiver in anticipation, the leaves flipping about as if a storm gust had blown down upon them. Burbling rumbles shook the ground around their feet. Boruin grabbed Pile's hand and slipped the silver charm bracelet off the young man's arm before he could even look down to see it disappearing.

Boruin broke off one of the silver discs, caught a sunbeam on its polished surface, and let the light flash up toward the makeshift face. The leaves forming the lips pulled back in an eager grin as the reflection danced about.

"Oh, ew, ew, a present not past, but all not part," the hill said childishly. Boruin agreed and slipped both the disc and the rest of the bracelet down into the knothole.

Pile jumped to the trunk, his arm down the hole to the shoulder. "Those are my charms!"

"Snap it shut," Boruin ordered.

"But I've been collecting them for years!" he replied, turning to Toaaho. There was no sympathy behind the mask of tattoos.

"You find the gift to your liking?" Boruin asked the Fae in the hill.

"Flitty pretty little meetel metal," the voice burbled. "I do, I do. For two or three I'll beg and plea," the hill answered.

"A gift's a gift and a favor owed is a favor owed," Boruin said.

"Aye, and a trick is a trick," the hill said. Boruin crossed his arms and sucked up his chest as if to holler. "But the rights have been met, and I've accepted your bauble and grant your favor," it continued.

"It's not so bad," Boruin said. "Continue your day of play, but let us ride along. I hear there is great hilling to be done in the northwestern jungles. If you know the Mountain of Three Hands, take us there," he ordered.

The hill roared in laughter as if it had gotten the best of its uncle. "I do and will, and yes, it's no great favor you've asked." The branches rustled and the face disappeared as the hill turned back north. The river rushed back into its stream, covering the flapping fish none too late. The hill moved up a steep ridgeline, and Boruin's stomach lurched again.

"How did you know it would buy into all that nonsense?" Pile asked softly.

Boruin sat and tucked his legs under an exposed root as the hill tipped down the other side of the small mountain. "You know a little about the Aiemer, and I know a little about the Fae. Now tie me down."

"You owe me for my charms," Pile said.

"You cheated a half-drunk whore out of those at Tragle's Tavern. I watched it happen," Boruin said, and Pile cursed under his breath.

As the hill pushed up steeper hills, Toaaho lashed down Wraethe as well. "Do you think it will really take us into Nefazo?" Toaaho asked.

"That'll be a relief. I forgot how much I hate this jungle," Pile said.

Boruin spat and held his stomach. "Be happy while you're here. We've got some answers to beat out of Belok, and that, my friends, will take a con from Apros L'eure himself."

"Or just Wraethe's godawful stare," said Pile.

- 3 -
HOSTILE RETURN

Boruin wavered, still feeling the rocking of the hill even as he watched it drift back south into the jungle. He had saved his breakfast, which was a better result than what would've happened if they had actually been aboard a ship.

"Damn Fae," he cursed again, though he could not deny that his crew had gotten the better out of their deal. It had taken weeks of searching the jungle before they found the boy. It would have taken two more to make it back without the bumbling little creature piloting that hill. The Fae had cut straight cross-country, though at times tipping over the steepest cliffs and climbing up the highest peaks. It was a path Boruin did not wish to take twice, even if they had made it in a day. Beyond that, he was looking forward to Wraethe's waking remarks. She would, of course, deride his decision and method of dealing with the Fae, but she could not dismiss the results.

They set to trekking down the western shoulder of the mountain, the ridges below them spreading and splitting until they formed three separate hands pointing out from the large peak. At one time, it might have been the Mountain of the Four Hands, but the northern side of the peak had sheared off long ago. The locals claimed that the mah'saiid had carved a massive city into that fourth ridge. The drunken ones would whisper low over the table that it had been the capital of the secretive race's ancient civilization. The Purahd, that unknown plague that 3000 years past had torn body and soul out of the mah'saiid and the land they lived on, had not taken the city. Instead, rumor said that it was moved when the Nefazo crossed south over the Monahdriachean Range. It was all ale-soaked nonsense to Boruin. Perhaps it had never been there, or perhaps the Purahd had taken it, but the city sure hadn't up and moved, no matter how powerful the mah'saiid were. To the locals, though, every twisted tree, box canyon, and unexplainable cosmic event had something to do with mah'saiid secrets. Pile led them down the mountain along game trails and forgotten paths. Few would expect a tired and worn group to come out of the jungle, climbing up the mountain just to walk back down, but Boruin was careful. They avoided the main roads and stepped down the ridge without incident.

Boruin spat, almost at the same time as Toaaho, as the jungle cleared and the city became visible below. The heart of Terre Haute had the makings of a beautiful town. Resting on the upper slope between two of the main ridgelines, the old settlement sat above the swamp where the breeze washed away the smell of wet decay and the hungry midges.

The North Quarter was one of the birthmarks of the Nefazo nation. Those old stone buildings, with their squat towers and wide arches, bore the look of distant northern cities. Their builders had been the first families of the great caravan sent south by the high merchant houses of northern civilizations. Two hundred years prior they'd traveled south, seeking a trade route through the wild center of the continent. Those that survived refused to risk the death that would come of returning. Instead they carved out a new country in the jungles and lowlands of the south.

The Nefazo nation was born of merchants weighing chance against risk. Modern Nefazo continued in the same vein. The merchants were generally a lot fatter than their ancestors, and the chances they weighed were of sly sales and trades rather than survival in a wilderness. Regardless, all Nefazo were merchants right through to the juice of their bones. That was one trait that had never been bred out of the Nefazo. They worshiped the art of the trade, and its laws, the L'Traie nu Duoit, were their scripture.

Terre Haute crumbled into ruin as the nation expanded toward the southern coast to take advantage of oceanic trade routes. When the mah'saiid ruin of Trilaeta was found three weeks' hard journey northeast, eyes turned again to the northern borders. The mah'saiid had long ago withdrawn from the world, their civilization dwindling down to nothing, but their ruins remained. An ache for artifacts from that mysterious race had long infected the modern Nefazo like a slow fever. Terre Haute returned to life and growth, but it took on a new character.

Down the slopes below the North Quarter, new merchants built their quarters. They flocked from Ouilainne to buy cheap from those foolish enough to enter the jungles and sell the newfound treasures back to the capital. Between them and the swamp, ramshackle inns and cane and leaf huts were tacked together to house those fevered relic hunters who came to Terre Haute with their eyes set on the wealth lying hidden under the blanket of jungle growth. Illusions of gems nestled among the river stones and vaults of gold under each northern hill swam through their minds. Some returned south with the treasures and stories for which they came. Most entered the jungle and stayed there, rotting in the swamps under blood-letting plants or in the bellies of hungry creatures.

Worse were the seekers of darker items. Crossbreeds of magic and metal would purchase entire kingdoms. Unlike the stories of unlimited gold and silver, these artifacts were more than just rumors. Too many had been found to deny their existence. Most were carried out of the jungle in disrepair, sitting too long under the humid press of mist and mold. A precious few survived intact, their metal untarnished, their workings unmolested by time. Their workings were often as mysterious as their purpose: devices that changed river mud into chalky stone, drove veins of metal into wood, thickened water until it sat like a ball inside its bowl. Some simply killed; others just healed. Typically, neither were precise. Rarely were these finds carried out of the jungle without a dark smear of new blood staining them—a sign of a double cross, an ambush, or an amateur hand too eager to test the uses of its hard-won treasure.

The buyers of such things were cautious ones. They bartered for other, more powerful, men unknown and carefully hidden. It was these rich proxies that now inhabited the North Quarter. Belok had taken a shop on the outskirts, though he could only wish for the influence and wealth of these elite merchants. It was for them that Boruin's spit had left its mark in the dirt. If anything had caused the legendary Purahd, Boruin guessed it had been machines like the ones they sought. If any man was further removed from the proud merchants that had conquered the continent by crossing it, it was a merchant willing to pay any price, in gold or blood, for those vile machines.

Yet, Terra Haute was home. It was no great city, but neither was it a backwater slum. It was somewhere between, like the prospectors and relic hunters, whores and reputable merchants that all shared shoulder space between the middle and western hands of the mountain. And where there is wealth—or even just imagined wealth—there is thievery.

Boruin had caught Pile's hands in his pocket here, a skinny boy hardly older than nine years that could turn sideways and almost slip between a door and its jamb. He'd put the kid to work for one week as punishment, and Pile liked to joke that the week was now fifteen years long.

"Watch for them," Boruin whispered as they stepped onto the city bridge that stretched over the mountain stream and into the small clothing market on the west side of North Quarter. A boy lifted his eyes from his small blanket of wares and tracked their crossing. He wrapped up his things, threw the load over his shoulders, and bounded off through the crowd.

Pile chewed on his thumb to cover the movements of his lips. "That's one."

"Two more," Toaaho added.

"The one in the swamp waders?" Pile asked.

Toaaho stooped to pluck a stone out of his boot and, with his back to the market, thumbed toward a stall covered in stacks of brightly colored bolts of silk. "Yes, and the one in the red trousers," he replied.

Boruin saw another man look up from his drink, his ornate earrings sparkling brightly across the fine weave of his robe. The merchant tipped back the mug and left the patio for a refill at the bar. Boruin knew they'd been marked. No rich merchant gets his own drinks. He'd look too eager and unable to barter for a lower price. He memorized the man's high sideburns, light scar near the hairline, and long stride before turning back to his crew.

Boruin gathered them in a close circle. "At least four. Our contract may have caught someone's attention," Boruin said. "Pile, work the taverns. Find out who's looking, which ones were looking for us, and which were just the regular purse cutters." Pile smiled too broadly, and Boruin reminded him to listen first and drink second. "Toaaho, check the hotels and the gaming houses. See who's in town."

"What about the boy?" Toaaho asked.

Boruin looked to the sun. It wasn't as low as he'd like, but dusk was close. "I'm quite capable, and Wraethe will be up soon. I'll make the evening's arrangements. You know where. I expect you back at a decent hour." Boruin faced Pile for that last statement. The short man winked and bounded off with his hand already in his coin purse.

Toaaho tightened his black silk scarf to keep the wind from pulling it free from his face. There were plenty other slave tattoo masks in Nefazo, but Boruin didn't chide him for his need of secrecy. He knew well enough when to leave a man alone.

"Here, boy. Come on, now," Boruin called, trying to command the child away from a horse trough. The boy continued to scoop the water up and hold his cupped hands under the horses' noses. Boruin slid between the drinking beasts and bent to the boy.

"There will be plenty of time to play," he said, "but there are times when we must be serious. I'll need you to listen closely and act quickly. Can you do that?" The boy looked hard into the man's eyes, as if deciding. He wiped his wet palms on Boruin's vest, leaving a stained print, and wrapped his fingers around the man's hand. "I guess that's the way it'll have to be—but the left hand, son."

Boruin led with his right thumb resting in his belt, close to his sword's hilt. Wraethe walked just behind and beside the boy. Her stride was long and smooth, and she seemed to glide over the cobbled street. Those that recognized the dark shade stepped lightly out of her way. He hoped her senses were near the surface of her sleep now that the sun was dipping close to the horizon. Walking into town with a contract completed was not the time to let your guard down. More than once a crew had been waylaid just as they returned for their pay. Disreputable merchants would leak their contracts and pay a street thug half of the amount they'd offered the relic hunters. Thieves in the home stretch were almost more dangerous than the creatures abroad.

Belok was not one to be trusted. Boruin had no love for the man and that certainly went both ways. The skinny bastard always tried to renegotiate after completion, but he had yet to seriously cross Boruin. Belok knew that the old man could handle any job faster and more discretely than most. The merchant had promised to pay dearly for this one, but not what it was truly worth—not by far if Pile's theories were right. Boruin wondered if he knew whom he had sent them for.

Boruin moved quickly through the streets, sticking to the shaded side of the avenues in hope that Wraethe could come forward sooner. He watched every passing face, marking any that gave him consideration. He moved fast but not so quickly as to draw extra attention. He relaxed, and his breath deepened as he reached Simonez's curio shop. They would be safe for the night, at least.

"Baelly'o, here's your man, back aga'n!" Pile slurred as he waltzed into his third bar. His rowdy hair was smoothed down to one side, probably with some of the ale that had drenched the front of his red vest. The keep looked up with half a wince and half a smile as

Pile plopped himself down on the nearest stool. It was the kindest response the short man had received all afternoon, though he knew Baelly liked him less than most.

"Back from the graves, me boy'o?" the bartender asked.

Pile placed both hands on the bar and carefully climbed up on top of the stool. "Aye, and your coldest mug from the coldest tap would just quench my thirst," the young man answered.

Baelly made no move to serve him. "Not a chance, sonny. I got no help today, and I ain't climbin' down the cellar stairs with hands such as your's about."

"Fair enough. Then I'll take whatever warm, swamp-stale pot of piss I can afford," Pile said.

Baelly pulled out a mug and poured a deep red draught from his tarnished pitcher. He held the mug just behind the bar as Pile wet his lips and reached out with two hands for the drink. "And that's the key, ain't it? What you can afford."

It was Pile's turn to wince, but he followed through with a flip of his thumb and a silver coin spinning on the bar top. "One for yourself out of that," Pile said as he took a long swig of the hard ale. "I need more than just your drink today," he added.

"Never known anyone that comes only for that," Baelly answered.

"Right you are, and so then: any word on me and my crew?"

"You mean the ghost and her crew?" Baelly asked.

Pile leaned back, ignoring the insult. His hands snapped to the edge of the bar as he remembered at the last moment there was no back to the stool. "Well, call it what you must."

"I've heard nothing in terms of your work, but that gentleman's been all over town asking if you've come in," Baelly said with a wide grin and a nod over Pile's shoulder.

Pile turned to follow the bartender's glance and saw five fingers plowing him out of his seat. The short man sat up and shook away the stars, his eyes clearing to see a man bowing his head just to fit under the rafters.

"Mother had a giant fetish, didn't she?" Pile coughed as the enormous man picked him up and slung him back across the room. The man ground his teeth and held his tongue, but drove down with his heavy boot to crush Pile in the ribs. The thin relic hunter rolled under the man's wide stance and sliced out with his knife. The sharp edge bit above the hard leather of his opponent's boot and split a chunk of his huge calf. The man roared and pinched his feet together, but Pile was already moving. The unexpected punch had knocked the afternoon's drunk right out of him, and he was ready now.

"All right, tall and dim, you want to start this over?" Pile asked, his short axe swinging lightly in his hand.

Splitting up hadn't done them any good. The four that scrambled to pass word of their arrival weren't just on the lookout for any returning contractors. The people now following Toaaho were very professional. They worked as a team, taking turns tailing him every few blocks in the hopes they'd go unnoticed. Toaaho hoped the others were facing better odds.

A thin alley appeared as he passed the next merchant's cart, and Toaaho ducked inside. The walls tapered closer, and the Mana'Olai pressed himself against either side, climbing quickly between the small, squat houses surrounding the square. He vaulted over the short mud wall around the roof and landed motionless, one leg passed through the ties of a hammock. The man stretched out in his nap did not move as Toaaho silently stepped around him.

The three men who had been following him were still in the plaza, idling between the carts, looking across the merchandise and around at the crowd. They converged slowly at the head of the alley and whispered through their thick veils before separating once more. Toaaho watched them mingle again, deciding which to follow. As he rose to trail his target, the sharp whistle of a feathered shaft slicing through the still air caused him to throw his body back, leaving him leaning dangerously far over the edge of the building. His foot hooked into the base of the small mud wall and held him as the arrow passed just across his chest. He rolled to the side and watched the round clay tip burst. Its contents swirled in dark blue vapors across the sleeping man.

Toaaho held his breath and lunged into the cloud, grabbing the edge of the hammock. He felt his skin start to go numb as he dumped the sleeper uncaringly out of the net and down the hatch that lead into the house below. He heard the man hit the floor with a thump, but it couldn't hurt more than the gas, had it gotten into the man's lungs and blood.

His knife sang as it deflected the second arrow, this one tipped with iron and ready to kill. The third flashed in the setting sun, dropping down from a high tower across the plaza. It buried deep into the mud wall where Toaaho had been just moments before he'd dropped to the street.

The Mana'Olai ran down the alley, holding his breath until his lungs burned like white embers. The vapors released by the exploding arrow would cling to fabric, though such a small amount would not knock him unconscious. He could not afford his mind to slow; his tingling hands would be problem enough.

The alley opened into a cool garden backing the small houses built shoulder-to-shoulder against the surrounding streets. Toaaho did not break stride, hearing more footsteps than his own echoing between the mud walls. He tore into the next alley, continuing even as a dark silhouette raced toward him with a silver blade extended. The two closed fast, and Toaaho did not change his pace until he saw the man would not feint, but intended to drive him through.

The Mana'Olai vaulted again, cartwheeling above his attacker. His short knife parried his opponent's blade down as he bit into the walls with his knee and shoulder, bracing tight. He hung there for a moment, his knife drawing blood under the man's neck as his other hand ripped the cloth from his attacker's head.

Toaaho searched the face, ignoring the fear and the sudden surprise that always comes before death. A quick glance was enough to confirm this man did not know who he was after, not truly. The men that would come for Toaaho, son of Anitelu, would come prepared to die, as the Köpeka did not die well.

Two hands grabbed him from above and Toaaho was flung back toward the garden. He fell hard, and the man charged again, but the Mana'Olai was already rolling to his feet and back out of the alley. The two men above dropped from the roof, and Toaaho could feel others filing in from the other streets. He pulled free his robe, his fingers still numb but able to hear them tap at the blades in his belt.

The assassin's dart passed through Wraethe's shadowy form before it struck the door of Simonez's shop, Boruin was sure of it. He could still see the thin hole and the loose thread torn from the fabric of her cloak. He pulled the boy behind him as a second and third were thrown through the woman's body. They stuck shivering beside the first in Simonez's door. Boruin looked for a seizure of pain, the hurt of the needle-sharp metal puncturing her body. He saw instead her eyes appear, the blue coming forward like a down rushing storm.

If they had thought to catch Wraethe asleep, they'd come too close to Diuntyne's dawn. The sun still covered the threshold of the shop, but Wraethe woke all the same. Her robe swirled about her like overlapping shadows, and Boruin heard the twang of her bow from somewhere beneath. The assassin doubled over and then whipped backward as the first shaft caught him in the gut and the second through the skull.

"Inside," Wraethe commanded with a whisper, rationing her strength. Boruin threw his shoulder against the wooden door and pushed the wide-eyed boy into the shop. He turned and guarded the opening as they came for her.

A second man stepped out of the thinning crowd, thrusting his knife from behind. The blade passed in and out of the darkness of Wraethe's robe. He slashed across, cutting only fabric as the iron tip of an arrow stabbed out of the shadows to pierce his throat. She let him fall and stepped back into the deepening shade of the building as if the dimming light smothered her and the growing darkness was air she could breathe. Archers let fly from the rooftops. Wraethe held her ground as the shafts broke on the hard brick behind her. She slung her own upward, the feathers screaming their high-pitched whistle until throttled out by their smash into meat.

The street emptied quickly. Citizens disappeared around corners or forced their way inside through quickly closing doors. The few left—assassins, all—charged forward in their mission, none noticing that Diun was now sharing the sky with the sun, pressing it deeper into the horizon.

The dark woman began to move as the harsh, hot light dimmed and a pale silver glow replaced it. The veil of shadows around her solidified as Diun's light brought her to full strength. She shot the last of her arrows across the rooftops and into those stupid enough to come running at such a skilled bowman.

Wraethe prowled the street, pulling the dark shafts from the dead to refill quiver. The crash of iron-shod horses echoed around the corner. Four strong horses followed the deadly tips of four polished pikes, all lowered toward her breast.

One last beam of sunlight cut between the clay buildings. Wraethe stepped into it at the last second. The outlines of her shape blurred back out of definition before the pikes cut through her. They passed on, the black strips of cloth clinging to the shafts the only trophy of their marksmanship.

The beam of sunlight dropped below the horizon, but it did not matter. Diun hung full above the city and Wraethe was angry. She cast aside her tattered cloak, revealing pale skin that glowed in the moon's light.

Her eyes burned bright blue as two of the four riders turned quickly and charged back for a second pass. She lunged toward them, catching the left pike in her hands and rolling right, across the other rider's path. She dug her feet in and wrenched backward like an angry sailor digging her oars into a crashing wave. The animal went down, throwing its rider across the hard cobblestones. Wraethe came up with the pike and held it just long enough to aim and throw. The second rider went down in the dust, his hands clutching the wooden shaft now sticking out of his guts.

The horses of the last two riders stood stamping at the end of the street. Wraethe watched her enemies make a quick decision before one turned and disappeared around the corner. The last turned his steed in a circle so tight that it brought the charger up on its hind legs. The man cried a war curse and drove the animal back down at the stone. Sparks exploded from the horse's shoes as they scrambled forward. Wraethe's tongue traced the edges of her lips, tasting the cruel smile that formed there.

The pale woman leaned easily aside as the head of the long pike passed by. Her body then blurred in motion as she caught the horse's neck between her arms and twisted. The animal's shoulder dropped as its head turned too far around. It tumbled, sliding hard across the street and through the front wall of a cobbler's shop.

Wraethe stepped out of the cloud of dust, her hands covered in the bright blood of the dispatched horsemen. She stepped lightly down the street, her stride more as if she were late for dinner than thirsting to find their merchant boss and spin his head off like a child's top.

Boruin left the open door of the curio shop from where he had watched Wraethe's furied battle. Brought awake early, she was more deadly than usual, and though terrified, he placed himself in her path, squared his shoulders, and barred the woman's way. Her eyes burned brighter than Diun's shine, almost casting his shadow across the cobbled avenue. She moved to pass him, but he caught her hand, mindful that he could not hold her. Wraethe leveled her eyes into his, but Boruin did not flinch. Her breath was still frantic, but she did not pull away.

"You have your rites to give," Boruin said.

Her voice was firm, but just barely. "Some business comes first." Boruin knew she was being pulled in two directions. Her will was strong, but her desire for more blood was fierce.

Boruin let go of her arm. "I will have words with him, if needed. You have your rites to give." She stepped back, her angry eyes still flooding his face with their light.

Wraethe turned and dropped to the first of the dead, and Boruin could hear the quiet whisper of her words. Whether they were prayers or some older magic, her words gave the fallen redemption for their sins. The rites also removed some measure of corruption from her own actions and lessened the price of the death on her hands. The killing and the rites were a balance on the thinnest edge. Death brought something true out of Wraethe; what that was, Boruin couldn't guess. He only knew to thank the Mother for the rites that released her war-rage and kept it from consuming her entirely. Who knew what she would become if left solely to killing?

Boruin watched until he was sure she was again calm, that her prayers were solemn, driven neither by the sins of the dead nor her own rage. Only then did he turn back to the darkened shop. His own anger settled under his skin as he thought of the words he would indeed have for that bastard Belok.

- 4 -
CHANGE OF COURSE

Pile rushed Boruin almost before he made it through the front door of Simonez's shop of Dry Goods and Assortments. "We got trouble, boss."

"Where's Simonez?" asked Boruin.

"Taking the boy upstairs. Haven't seen Toaaho. I think he's in trouble," said Pile. He paced down the aisles as he talked, his hands unconsciously touching the wares: bits of nails, screws, bundles of thread, rolls of wire, leather string, iron pots, barrels of sweet syrup. His thieving fingers seemed to run on habit as his mind ran in circles. Boruin ignored him and climbed over the old man's counter.

"No, really. Big trouble—and I mean big!" Pile added. Boruin sorted carefully through the merchandise stacked on the rear shelves. There were small bags of powders for a woman's makeup, bottles of pills and alchemist's mixtures. He found the switch he was looking for under a velvet box of Mana'Olai healing stones. The bottom panel of the counter unlocked with a snap, and Boruin pulled it open with the edge of his knife. It was unwise to carry all your valuables out into the wild, and Simonez had long been trusted with his Terre Haute stash.

"I'm talking huge! This guy was a giant, or at least a half-breed. Anyway, he got the drop on me at first," Pile continued as Boruin fished around under the counter. There was only one thing he really needed. When his hands closed on the rolled document, a mean smile, much like Wraethe's, formed on his lips.

"So he goes for me while I'm down—"

Boruin speared out a finger, pointing angrily at his partner. "Can you shut your mouth, Pile?" Boruin asked, his ability to ignore such annoyances now fully spent.

Pile could not. His eyes widened in exasperation. "But boss, I'm trying to tell you we got huge guys out for us!"

"Huge guys, as in more than one?"

"This guy alone was twice—if not three times—my size."

"I seriously doubt there is a band of abnormally huge guys after us. Besides, everyone is twice your size," Boruin added. He looked up as the jibe somehow shut the short man's mouth. Instead it was Wraethe. She stood in the middle of the room, and she did not look well.

Exhausted, Wraethe rocked unsteadily on her feet. Blood dripped from her pale hands, creating petal-like stains on her dust-covered clothes. "People after us, Pile?" she asked with tired sarcasm.

For a moment he stood amazed at the gore covering her exposed skin. "Were they huge?" he finally whispered.

She leaned heavily against the counter. "No, Pile, they weren't huge. Just men. Simple men." Wraethe's energy was almost gone, even with Diun shining above. Had she rushed to Belok's, she would have fainted at his door. Boruin knew when the attack began outside Simonez's that she would be useless after. It took too much for her to wake in the daytime. The energy she spent there would leave her weak for the rest of the night.

"Pile, take her to the apartment," Boruin ordered.

Wraethe moved toward the back of the shop, her steps slow as she carefully placed one foot in front of the other. "I can make it. You should take Pile with you," Wraethe countered, her voice softening with each word.

"What for?" asked Boruin.

She leaned heavily against an open barrel of dried beans. "You'll need help—and he knows Belok."

"If he can keep his mouth shut." Boruin had no doubt that Pile had taken his attacker. The kid was fierce like a whirlwind when the odds were against him, but pride drove his tongue like a flag in the same gale.

"Wraethe is next, Sim," said Boruin as the merchant appeared from the back of the shop.

The elderly merchant clutched at his fading hairline as he rushed to her. "Oh, my lady, what have they done to you?"

"Not me, Sim. Not mine," she whispered. Though the man was thin and his muscles slight, Simonez easily lifted the taller woman and laid her gently across two bundles of soft cotton. Years of rolling barrels of iron nails and tossing sacks of flour about the shop had kept him strong, even in his declining years. He busied himself by wiping the blood from her arms. His white apron was soon a mess of red.

"We'll get you all cleaned up and in some new clothes. Don't you worry."

"It's you that needs the worrying," said Boruin. "When they come, tell them we went in the front and out the back."

Simonez tossed the ruined apron to Boruin. "Spread that around the courtyard. They'll see the blood and know you've fled. And don't you worry," he added as Boruin pulled Pile toward the door, "this won't be the first time I've forgotten knowing you."

As they walked uphill toward the North Quarter, the cool night air came down from the mountaintops and pushed the city's heat into the swamps. It did nothing for Boruin's anger, though. The thought of Belok's betrayal and Pile's inexhaustible moment-by-moment tale of the bar fight kept him livid.

Belok's shop was dark, but oil lamps still burned in the upstairs office. Pile picked the lock and Boruin chose their steps, his long familiarity with Belok's ways giving him a leg up on the tricks and traps inside. They arrived upstairs without being detected and hit the door with both their shoulders.

"BELOK YOU son of a..." started Boruin, but the office was destroyed. Belok's large print of the beggar Apros L'eure had been pulled from the wall. The scene of L'eure's famous trade that had turned him from beggar to merchant king and crowned him the patron saint of all aspiring traders was scattered in fragments across the room. Bits of crockery from the jungle ruins were smashed against precious carvings from the tribal Dalam. Leather bindings were torn from old books and their pages scattered across the furniture like fallen leaves. Vials of costly perfume and bottles marked "Oil of Dridge Lily" had been upended and now mingled in the delicate Mana'Olai rugs that covered the floors. The combined vapors stung their eyes and almost drove them back out of the room.

"Watch out for that razor fern," Boruin said. The sharp-leafed plant had been tipped off its stand. No longer bound by its shattered pot, the fern had stretched its roots across the floor. It slowly inched out of the corner in search of dinner.

Pile leaned in close and whispered to Boruin, "The roots are reaching for that desk. There's something warm-blooded back there."

Boruin nodded his agreement. "Go take a—" His words were cut short as he slung himself to the side, dodging a thick copper basin pitched from behind the overturned desk. Pile only spun around, and the heavy pot caught him in the shoulder, knocking him back down the first few stairs.

Boruin returned fire, throwing a crystal vase that crashed against the ceiling above their attacker. The shards rained down and prompted a fierce return of a golden scale and its bronze set of weights. Boruin avoided all but an ornate two pound weight shaped in the lewd fashion of Belok's favorite possession. The bronze penis caught him in the head and turned him around on his feet. He shook his eyes straight in time to see the attacker shoving open a window. The orange light from the oil lamps sparkled off his ornate earrings and caught the strands of precious metal woven into his robe. *The rich merchant who fetches his own drinks*, Boruin thought, recognizing him from their first step into Terre Haute.

He vaulted the razor fern and lunged around the desk, but tripped on the form of Belok, tied and crumpled in his overturned chair. The attacker landed hard on the street, but he was off and running before Boruin could lay his hands on anything to throw.

"Your mother was a Fae whore!" Boruin yelled out of frustration as the man disappeared around the next corner.

"Thanks for the help there, Bucko," Boruin said, turning to find Pile back on his feet.

Pile's face grew red. "That pot really hurt! That metal is thick. It could have killed me!"

"Fast as lightning. Like the northern wind blasting down from the God King's own throne, isn't that how you described yourself not two minutes ago?" Boruin yelled back.

"Yeah, but—"

"Shut the brat up, will you Boruin?" Belok muttered from his chair.

Boruin kicked the merchant square in the gut. "Tell me you had nothing to do with today."

"Right, I confess. While strapped to my chair, in between punches I orchestrated whatever shit you're talking about," Belok replied. Pile and Boruin righted the chair. The merchant was bleeding from the mouth, and his always-immaculate hair bristled up like a turkey with its tail spread. Boruin stared at the man for a moment, considering whether one more kick would do him any real good or just be pleasurable. Instead he cut him free and helped him to his feet. Belok looked around and cursed slowly with as much vulgarity as Boruin had ever been privy to. He pulled the lines of his robe straight, a nervous habit of tucking each bloodied and wrinkled piece of fabric and sash back into its place.

"Just 'cause it's broken doesn't mean you can have it," said Belok, pointing at Pile so there would be no confusion. He turned to Boruin. "Keep his hands off my stuff. I told you never to bring him here!"

Pile's eyebrows narrowed in disbelief, and his lips pressed tight. "I can't believe I'm hearing this. I've brought you a lot of gear out of those jungles—"

"Whoresons, the both of you," Boruin yelled. "Pile, keep your hands in your pockets. Belok, who'd you tell about our contract?" Belok just stared until Boruin began to think he'd have to put the merchant back in his chair and resume the intruder's interrogation session.

"If I knew your mother's name, I'd curse it in ways more foul than you can imagine and less foul than she deserves. I am the most honorable trader between Terre Haute and the blessed Ouilainne. For you to have the gall to accuse me of Breach of Contract... I've... you'd ...if you think ..." Belok stuttered in rage before settling on something simple. "Screw you, Boruin!" he finished, sitting with a cold stare on the drawers of his overturned desk. Boruin leaned into the hard eyes and turned them back.

Boruin kept his voice cool and his tongue slow so Belok could not mistake the measure of his words. "Don't give me your bull about Breach of Contract. That charge might be the vilest for Nefazo's petty merchant kings. To me it's backstabbing and ankle cutting. Anyone tries to bring me down like that—bring down *my crew*—and there will be no punishment worse than my wrath. Is that understood?"

"Screw you, Boruin," Belok said again, but he dropped his eyes and breathed out deeply and in defeat. "I don't know who attacked you. I don't know who attacked me. But they must have contacts here if they caught you as you came into town. You trust your people?" he asked with a glance toward Pile.

"Yes," Boruin said without hesitation.

"You didn't take the main roads in, did you?" Boruin just stared until Belok continued. "No, of course not. I'll talk to some people tonight, but I'm not staying long. I don't intend to get attacked again. I'll leave as soon as I have your answers and you deliver on your contract. I assume you didn't bring it out tonight."

Pile huffed at the absurdity. Boruin silenced him with a look. "No," he replied.

"Well, we'll meet in the morning to make the exchange. After I'm gone you can burn this city down to find your attackers. It means little to me; all I have here is destroyed now, anyway."

Boruin looked out the window, wishing to see that damn merchant peeking back around the street corner. "And you'll go where with them chasing after? They're after the boy, Belok, not me." Boruin said.

"To Ouilainne."

Boruin smiled at Pile and turned to give Belok his casual grin. "Our next job is in the capitol. With things as dangerous as they are, it might be best we ride along," said Boruin.

"I've already hired an escort. Just give me what you brought out of that Fae-ridden jungle and you'll get your money. Complete your side of the contract and with any luck that'll be the last time I'll have to deal with you."

"I think I'd rather wait."

Belok rose from the desk. His fists pumped as if trying to squeeze some sort of help out of the perfumed air. "As much as you may think you're above them, you know the rules of violating the contract. You would not leave the city alive."

"I'm not in breach. Read it for yourself," Boruin said. He handed over his copy of their contract, the rolled parchment Simonez had hidden for him under his shop floor. "No time or place is specified for delivery, Belok. If I want to complete the bargain in Ouilainne, it's within my rights to do so. Hell, I'll finish my end north on the Pilean Emperor's palace steps if I choose to."

Belok smacked the parchment against the desk in frustration. "This was a contract written between friends. If I had known you would take liberties, I would have been more precise," Belok said.

Boruin's smile widened. "I know. Don't feel betrayed, Belok. I couldn't take the thought of it. Make your inquires and find out what we have before us. I'll take your package south of the city. Be on the swamp road to Ouilainne by daybreak. Either meet us there or catch us further down the road," Boruin said as he snatched the contract back out of the merchant's tight fingers. He pushed Pile out the door and left Belok staring about the broken room.

When Boruin and Pile stepped into the apartment above Simonez's shop, Boruin found the old merchant handling the longest needle he had ever seen. Toaaho sat silently as Sim stitched the deep gash along his shoulder. The curved needle caught the light of the room's single candle as it worked its way in and out of the skin like a silver fish diving in and out of the waves.

"Alright?" Boruin asked. The Mana'Olai nodded.

"Belok?" Wraethe asked. She slumped low in Simonez's reading chair with her eyes half closed. Ledgers and Nefazo books on merchant law rose around the chair as if attempting to slowly swallow the reader.

Boruin rearranged one of the stacks, looking for a stool to sit on. "And the rich merchant from the café."

"Talking?"

"Torture," Boruin replied.

"Traitor?"

"Definitely," Boruin said.

"Steal any of that broken shit? Come on, really?" Pile muttered. "There was nothing good in that whole shop. I thought Belok valued my business, knew my eye for artifacts."

Boruin smiled at the young man. "Pile caught it quick: not a thing of real worth in that whole broken office, and you know that worm's tastes," Boruin added.

"So what are you going to do?" Simonez asked. He cut the thread from the last stitch and wiped a greasy swab across Toaaho's wound.

"Show them, Pile," Boruin said. The thief drew out his newest hot-fingered treasure with a large smile hallmarked for such trickery.

Simonez unrolled a parchment. Dark valleys of wrinkles creased his stern face as he read it. "How did you find this?"

"It was hidden in the one chest not broken. Lazy son of a habback."

The master contract between Belok and the Undurland Trading Company was very specific. It required Boruin as subcontractor for the task of retrieving the young boy. The boy was to be escorted north, by Boruin and his crew, to Underland's door in Priyati, the capital of Easlinder. Boruin had no doubt that Belok charged double for that condition, even though they were neither the most expensive nor the largest outfit currently working out of Terre Haute. While the job was unequivocally meant for him, Belok had kept quiet about that fact while subcontracting it to them, certainly at a fraction of his quoted price. The master contract bore Undurlund's stamp and Belok had counter-signed. That was enough proof for the shopkeeper.

"You can take him to court on this," Simonez said. "There's no way he could disprove Fraud by Hostile Renegotiation."

"Yep, but Belok will get any trial deferred until spring, two years next," Pile pointed out. "So what do we do?" he asked with a look to their boss.

Boruin scratched out his decision with a quick scrawl on paper. "I claim Belok's prior agreement default through fraud." Simonez signed as witness with a tight grin and promised to deliver it, and copies of both contracts, to the merchant court personally.

"Now, we go north to Priyati," Boruin said. "We go north and see who knows my name." One by one, each looked toward Toaaho. "Are you prepared for that?" Boruin asked.

The Mana'Olai's lip slipped into a rarely glimpsed smile. "I have not been a fleeing child for many years, Boruin. I am no longer scared of what may await me at home."

They left Terre Haute before dawn, long after Diun had set and true night covered the jungle. Each took a different path out of the city, slipping though back streets past shops, then houses, then shacks, and finally trees. They met again where Simonez had instructed, tucked in a hollow just out of sight of the jungle highway.

"These horses are from my son's ranch. You won't find any stronger," Simonez said as Pile arrived last, creeping quietly down from the road.

Boruin rubbed the nose of his gray charger. The animal's hot breath warmed his hands as she took in his scent. "Thank you. This is more than I wanted to ask of you," he said to his friend.

The old merchant lowered his voice. "Nonsense. You know I owe you much." Boruin swung up onto the horse and felt her strong muscles dance for a second under his thighs.

"You've long paid any debt you think you owe, Sim," Boruin said, his hand on the man's shoulder.

"Regardless, it is my pleasure," Simonez said. He lifted the boy up and placed him before the aging fighter. "Here, little man," he continued, stuffing a small bag of sweets into the boy's shirt. "Eat slow, or you'll be sick." The boy reached out and tousled the old man's hair, an act of affection somehow backwards.

Toaaho twisted his dappled mare toward the road. "Riders! Their hooves are padded." Boruin felt the trembling of the air before he could hear the hooves, and suddenly horsemen were funneling off the road. Boruin wrenched his horse around and into the dense brush at the edge of the small bowl. The others formed up behind and beside him as the riders filled the opposite side of the hollow, closing off any escape.

"Pile, find me a way out," Boruin whispered as the riders rode in, five, ten, now fifteen.

Pile glanced about, but he had circled the hollow earlier. The swamp behind them was choked with thick mud and razor ferns. The horses would fall quickly if they retreated, with their riders soon following. Ahead, the ground rose to the road, and the horsemen were spreading out on that higher ground. "Rule 47 of Pile's Guide to Survival: don't trap yourself in a Fae-cursed hollow with no way out," Pile retorted.

The riders halted a stone's throw away. Their mounts' panting was the only noise in the hollow, save for the last horse making his way down slowly into the bowl. It arrived well after Boruin recognized its rider.

"South of the city, remember? We're going to Ouilainne, to Nefazo's great capital. Isn't that what you said, Boruin?" Belok called out into the lessening darkness. The sun was making its presence known, now painting the edge of the horizon pale blue. It would not be long before Wraethe would be asleep and useless for fighting. Boruin wondered if Belok knew to stall until they were one man short.

"At dawn, Belok. I had to rustle up some horses and then I was headed south. But it looks like you had enough for all of us," Boruin said.

Belok laughed. There was no trace of the beaten and humbled man from earlier in the night. "Right, right, my mistake. I should have waited for you longer, let you get farther away, isn't that so?"

"'I swear I had nothing to do with you getting attacked,'" mocked Boruin, "I guess we both had a couple of memory lapses tonight." His horse picked up on the tension and nervously stamped her front hoof. The hard iron shoe snapped a dry limb under the decaying leaves, and the sound brought the entire band before them to an attack position. "Friends no more, eh?" he asked.

"Not necessarily, Boruin. Just fulfill the contract. Hand over the boy."

Simonez pushed his horse forward, though Boruin could see his old hands shaking. "Coercion by force and attempts to undermine render a contract null and void," said Simonez. "It was invalid the moment you had your men attack the signed parties of the contract. Edict 4, sub—"

"—sub-rule 12, line 38 of the L'Traie nu Duoit," Belok interrupted. "No need to quote scripture. I know Avidade's founding rules as well as you, Simonez. It is you, isn't it, that half-wit dry goods shopkeeper? I don't know why they ask you people to swear to the nu Duoit. You're little better than the roadside farmer. What do you know about the sacred treaties of contract law?"

"Enough to know the Guild congressman will be overjoyed to hear of these breaches. You're not Terre Haute's finest as you've allowed yourself to believe."

Belok's horse stamped under him, feeling the man's temper rise. "The boy, Boruin. The boy and this beggar merchant," he answered gruffly. "Hand them over and the contract is completed. Hand them over and we'll be done. Let's make this an amicable finish to a fairly profitable history."

"You have my money?" Boruin asked.

"Of course. Let's go up to the road," Belok answered. The light was now bright enough that no one could mistake the false smile painted across the merchant's face.

"Alright, alright," Boruin said. "Move your men up the hill. We're coming." The horsemen shifted, but not up the hill. Instead Belok motioned them aside and opened a hole for Boruin's crew. They had clear passage to the road, but it was the riders at the sides moving further around the edges of the hollow that worried Boruin.

"Start slow, and rush them when I call," Boruin whispered. "They'll try to surround us. We have to break through—" A jangling chill ran up his spine as the boy's fingers slid the black ribbon of runes across his skin. He looked down at the boy guiding a single sigil into his palm. The spell reacted immediately, a single push of force. Boruin felt a buzzing in his body, like some great cathedral bell had been rung unheard next to his head. The boy rocked his body forward, motioning behind a great fire oak towering over them. Boruin flicked the reins in compliance.

"The road is this way. Up here, old man!" Belok laughed as he watched the two cross behind the tree.

They rounded the immense trunk. Boruin tucked his arms in as they squeezed between the tree and another oak growing under the shadow of its elder. His breath caught in his throat as he felt a rush of unexpected cold, like dunking one's face into an icy stream.

"Oh shit," Pile whispered as he watched Boruin disappear in the dim morning light. The space between the two trunks shimmered darkly. *As if he went underwater*, Pile thought. But it was a way out, and so he drove his horse forward with Simonez on his heels. Toaaho grabbed Wraethe's reins, now slack in her hands as the first true light of the sun broke over the jungle. Then they too rode through the wavering curtain between the two trees.

"Oh, rut..." Belok whispered as one, then two, and then the last of his quarry moved behind the oak and did not come out on the other side. Their hooves sounded distant, too far away. They were gone when he reached the back of the tree.

Boruin's horse leapt to the side as Pile and Simonez came at a full gallop through the strange curtain between the trees. As Toaaho and Wraethe followed, that massive unheard ringing rattling Boruin's body faded away. It carried with it the cold curtain. Where there had been two oaks and too many horsemen, only an empty trail remained. Toaaho reined in on a wide and obvious path. Packed dirt threaded through a jungle quiet with the morning. There was no sound of Belok and his riders.

"I'd have those back," Wraethe said. She tugged lightly at the reins stretching to Toaaho's hand. The Mana'Olai turned to see the woman's cowl off her head and her eyes a blue more brilliant than seemed possible.

He handed the reins over while he and Boruin watched in wonder at the sunlight dancing across her pale face. "Up late?" he asked.

"Seems so," she replied, spurring her horse forward to catch Pile.

They found Pile and Simonez dismounted beside their horses and staring open-mouthed through a break in the dense jungle. Boruin cantered up beside to see what held their attention.

"That was a trick," Simonez said as he pointed south toward the swamp plains below the city.

They looked down a long, slow hill and the brown gash of highway splitting the jungle. It climbed from the hollow they'd just abandoned to pass before their feet. Black riders spilled out of the jungle not a minute's hard gallop behind them, but they had walked no more than a hundred yards.

"There's that son of a whore," Pile said as Belok rode out and beat the nearest rider with his crop. The horseman turned north, and dust began to rise into the trees as they galloped up the hill and highway.

"Ride hard!" Pile shouted, but Boruin had turned his horse to block the opening where their trail and the highway touched boundaries.

Boruin looked again at the sun touching Wraethe's face. "Let's keep to the path for a while." This was one of those odd moments; things were about to go really well or really poorly for them. With Wraethe so awake and aware, in the daylight no less, he'd take the chance and follow this lead the strange boy had provided.

They trotted back down the trail and crossed a small stream gurgling and dancing down through its gravel bed. Downstream the water spread into a small pond. Insects dropped from the air, skimming across the surface for a taste of the sweet water. *That's not a dragonfly*, Boruin thought as he peered closer. The small, winged creatures looked curiously like tiny lij except for their long fingers and toes. One flitted across the water and cupped its hands down for a drink just as a fish breached the calm surface behind it. The trout's mouth opened wide as it leapt. The tail slapped the water into a brilliant burst of rainbow mist as the fish dropped back into the water with a mouthful of breakfast.

Fae be damned, Boruin thought, *it wasn't a bug*. He looked down to find the boy looking in the same direction, chewing slowly on a piece of salt taffy. Boruin wondered if he had seen the same thing.

Simonez reached the next opening in the trail first.

"The Three Hands," he said, running his hands though his hair. The mountain was south of Terre Haute, and not by a small measure. The great peak was hazy in the distance, a full day's ride behind them. Again, the highway and their trail brushed shoulders like two drunks stumbling along together. "I think I'd better leave your company here," he said.

"They'll be coming up this road," Toaaho said.

"Yes, but they'll be galloping hard for Easlinder. I'll have plenty of time to duck into the trees," he answered.

Boruin nodded his agreement. "I'm sorry you got involved in this, Sim," he said.

"Nonsense. Business is war, and war makes enemies. Don't think I am unprepared. I have more leverage against Belok than he knows."

"Alright," Boruin said. Simonez rode his horse off the trail and through the brush. He turned as he reached the highway. Boruin watched him scan the jungle as if they weren't a mere twenty feet away. The old merchant reached up and waved regardless, and the boy returned the gesture.

"Hell of a short cut, Boruin!" he shouted as he turned south.

"Hell of a short cut, indeed," Boruin replied. He wondered if they too should abandon the strange path. It wasn't natural, and it smelled of the troublesome Fae. Wraethe took the decision away as she popped her heels and drove her horse onward along the path. Boruin felt the boy relax and lean back against him. He reached into his shirt and drew out a piece of taffy, placing it in Boruin's hand.

"On we go, then," he said, edging his horse after Wraethe and down the odd trail.

- 5 -
THE MONARHIG

Boruin spent their afternoon rest spinning the line of runes across his torso. They moved like a snake around his chest, over his shoulder, and down his left arm in one long loop. He watched for the one the boy had chosen to open the pathway. A rough, winding symbol, like a whirlpool, caught his eye as it slid around his bicep and back down his forearm. He pulled the ribbon of sigils further down where the whirlpool crossed his wrist. There he slipped it from the line and into his palm. Some small magic was there, but it felt wrong. He released it and spun the line again, letting the runes run in circles before his eyes.

"Which one, for Yuin's sake?" Boruin muttered. "Damn boy."

Toaaho broke from his meditation and crossed the path to deliver Boruin's forgotten lunch.

"He used your runes?"

"Yeah, chose and cast one from my hand. Tell me how he did that," Boruin replied.

"Curious," Toaaho said. Whether to contemplate the problem or contemplate nothing, he went back to his meditation without another word.

The two sat as the others rested around them on the strange path. The boy picked rocks from the road and tossed them at Pile as the short man napped with his arm over his eyes. Wraethe was further down the path where a sunbeam had won its fight through the thick jungle canopy. She stood in the small ray of sun and rubbed her skin, feeling the warm touch as if it were a lost lover's. The woman stared upward at the shades and glimmers the light cast through the leaves, her face a richer, fuller beauty now than under the paler glow of Diun. They rested and did not worry, satisfied that the trail would move them quickly away from Belok and into Easlinder, however impossible that seemed.

Boruin crossed his arms behind him so he couldn't see his runes. They were only making him angry now. Any instinct of which rune had opened the shimmering curtain had faded to guesswork. He lay back on the edge of the dirt path and his mind turned to the fish he'd seen not long ago. *It ate a Fae. What kind of a fish eats a Fae? What kind of Fae gets eaten by a fish?*

"What time would you say it is?" he asked Toaaho.

Toaaho opened one eye and glanced at his shadow across the ground. "Midmorning, no later than three hours past sunrise."

"How far would you guess we've come?"

"Two hundred leagues, at least," Toaaho answered again, his voice calm despite this impossibility. The path was taking them to Easlinder almost faster than the sun could cross the sky.

Tired of his mind turning in circles, Boruin called them all to mount up. The break had not been restful for him. He took the lead, as watching Wraethe angle her face up into each sunbeam just brought on more questions.

This path bothered him greatly. The jungle was not without its own magic; he had spent enough time here to know that. Pile told stories that most would find impossible, yet Boruin knew the man's lies from his stretched truths. The treasure hunter had seen some strange things in the old ruins scattered about the land, but there was no magic he'd witnessed that explained this trail.

To their the left, the trade highway continued roughly parallel to the path, peeling away and leaving them alone, then returning to break though the dense brush. But after the fish and the Fae, Boruin had begun sneaking looks to the right. When the jungle opened there, it wasn't just giant trees and songbirds that appeared. In small windows, where the jungle allowed a far view of the distance, the landscape seemed skewed. Water was unbound from the earth and rivers ran in any direction they chose. The sky seemed to tease the horizon and twist against its constraints. Boruin glimpsed mountains built of fire and lightning, and spotted wind stripping trees bare only to replace their leaves with the next gust. It was all too odd to believe, especially when glimpsed between trees in the brief moments that passed with each step of his horse.

In other places, the jungle opened to shallow glades and hollows that seemed normal until one stared a little closer.

"That sure has weathered strangely," Pile said as the jungle opened on their right. The path took a wide circle around the west face of a natural stone tower.

Wraethe took her eyes down from the sun to look. "Almost like it was grown that way," Wraethe added. It unsettled Boruin that she was obviously right.

The rock was darkest at its root, a great hard stump from which the stone had grown in layers. Each rising segment grew thinner until the top, with its wide edges, sagged under the weight of the rock. Cracks appeared along the bowed crown and the boulders at its base suggested that cycles of collapse and renewed growth were not uncommon.

"It's an umbrella to shield those mushrooms," Toaaho ventured. Boruin had missed them before. The brown and black fungi were almost invisible in the folds of rock and deeper crevasses.

They had almost passed it and were entering the jungle again when the boy added his opinion. His shrill whistle startled Boruin. It took him a second of looking around to realize the noise came from the small boy, his fingers jammed between his teeth. Responding to his high-pitched call, the mushrooms on the rock face closest to them exploded into action. Spores jettisoned from the round heads bursting into the air. The event spread quickly through the small colony as if the whistle were fire set to their tails. The mushroom caps shot about, some firing straight into the forest, some looping around in tight circles. The child laughed so hard that Boruin tightened his grip around the boy's waist for fear he would fall from the horse.

The mushrooms raced about the rock, spores falling like sparkling snow behind. Boruin spurred the group on when he saw the herders. They were like hedgehogs or some similar small, short-furred beast. They flapped off the top of the rock, diving down on stubby wings. Their round nets cast out across the mushrooms and dragged them back into the shade of the outcropping. One flew in close beside them, chasing after a lively cap, and shook his fist as he passed. Boruin's crew had caught the small boy's laughter, and they roared as they left the small creatures to their flock and disappeared into the jungle.

Their delight was cut short as they found an impossibly tall man turning his steed across the path to bar their passing. "You find tormenting the Feirnann humorous?" he asked. *By Yuin, he's glorious,* Boruin thought despite himself.

The sun set the rider's face in a flawless glow as if it shone only to worship his glory. A pure smile curled at the corner of his lips so perfectly that each of the travelers returned the expression without realizing it. The tall man's horse too was of fine breeding, but it still probably cost less than the man's attire. As a cloud passed above, the sun still managed to sparkle in the white sapphires that were scattered across his loose shirt like stars. When the light returned in full, it was like flame rising to frame a god.

Somewhere under the swell of sudden affection for this man, Boruin noticed his high forehead. He pulled his head down, forcing his chin lower until finally his eyes broke from the rider's face. Then he looked for the man's fingers and found them too long for a lij. This was a Fae, and not a simple one.

Boruin tried to speak, coughed to clear his throat, and continued. "We did not mean to bother them."

"You will not speak to me, lij!" The final word almost spat off his lips as if the use of it brought him a foul taste. The Fae did not glance toward Boruin. Even his horse seemed to be purposely looking elsewhere. Instead he peered across the group and singled out Wraethe. "You, though, I would hear speak, for I imagine your voice would be as pleasant as the breeze across the Gathered Sea above my home."

Wraethe rode forward almost as if the man's bright lavender eyes drew her to him. "We meant no harm to the land shepherds. We will apologize to them if you wish," she said.

The man laughed, swinging his head back so his white hair flowed in waves down his back. Boruin rolled his eyes, and he heard Pile gagging behind him. The Fae's flip from sweet to sour seemed to have broken his effect on the crew; now they, the men at least, felt a little sick at the sight of him.

"One does not apologize to the Feirnann. They are the lowest of us Fae, merely clever pets," he said once his light cackling finally ceased. "Do you know who I am?"

"You are a Monarhig, my lord. A prince of the Dreaming Lands," Wraethe answered.

"The Prince of Winds, to be precise, but what are you? Curious, as you are not Moir. Though if I saw you in a dream I might well swear on my grandfathers' stone beds that you were a sister of mine."

"That is kind of you, my lord, as I know your sisters are of remarkable beauty."

"Now I know you are not Moir, for no Bragheayn queen would regard any more beautiful than she. But you are not Duine, though I smell their world on you. It is not a spice that suits you. Should I ask you to a bath, would you agree? There is one not much further along my path. It is not as fine as the springs in my manor, but I'm afraid you would not pass the gate into my world." The Fae prince set his charger to walk, taking Wraethe's reins to guide her beside him. Boruin felt angry heat rise to his face, but he made no other sign of his growing dislike for the Monahrig as he and the others followed behind.

"Your world? I had thought we were there already."

"No, my lovely, this path is constructed in your world. It rubs against mine, but you are still far from entering the lands of the Fae."

"And yet you, my lord, travel here lightly."

"I hand the trophies of my visit over to a certain Riddari for his study. Of course I can't name names, you understand, but he is a keeper of no small secrets," the Monarhig said, tugging at his fine lace cuffs.

"What trophies are these, that are worthy of your attention?" Wraethe asked, her coquettish smile a small upturning at the corners of her mouth.

"Here, let me show you a few. I think you will find them to your liking," he said, slapping Wraethe's horse to send her up the trail before him.

"Fae-damned… Fae," Pile muttered, his eyes on the prince and his voice low so as not to catch his attention, not that the Monarhig had once turned his eye toward them. Boruin agreed but did not answer. His mind was turning over what the man had said. The trail was next to the world of the Fae. That explained the strange landscapes he'd seen, but was that why Wraethe was still awake in the daylight? If so, it made no greater sense to him. If anything, it added another layer to the old questions of his life that he couldn't answer. There were scant clues in the world about Wraethe and him, about where they had come from, about what she was. He had ideas, though, and he liked where they pointed today even less than usual.

"Churly! Where are you wasting my time?" the Monarhig yelled as they climbed towards the top of a high crest. The Nefazo highway again appeared on their left, but on their right the land dropped off a sheer cliff. Boruin never expected to see a sight such as what was below them. He heard even Toaaho gasp at the eight crudely cut wedges of strange land over which the sun and all Baeg Tobar's moons, at once and always, spun tightly. The spheres, never leaving the sky, seemed to have come to an agreement. In even parts, the land was split into the dark night of Syan, cool Diuntyne, and hot day. There was no dawn or dusk to be seen. The divisions turned about the dark hub in the center as if the land were the face of a clock and the heavenly bodies its guiding hands.

"Yuin's teats, we must be miles up! I can't see the bottom." Pile crept forward slowly to spit over the edge and watch it drop out of sight. He looked up and wiped the saliva off his lip. "What the hell is that? Easlinder?" he asked.

"Easlinder?" Boruin asked. "Seriously? Pile, for a man so stoked in tales, secrets, and myths of the Fae, how is it you can't tell the Dreaming Lands when they're laid out like a map in front of you?"

Pile scoffed. "You know the tricks of Fith's whorehouse in Ouilainne, but I doubt you know all the ladies' birth names, now do you?" He took a second look at the legendary realm. "Why does it look like a pie?"

Boruin glanced at the Monarhig. It might be unwise to watch the scenery instead of the prince. He was still enthralled with Wraethe, though, and was leading her about his camp, presumably in search of the creature called Churly. They were laughing as they turned over chests, opened wide the silk tents, and looked under plush couches. It was ridiculous.

"They were divided long ago by the Iraemun, gods and grandfathers of the Fae," said Boruin. "Each Iraemun's sphere of influence reigns inside their talamhs: Action and Consequence, Creation and Craft, Magic and Fire, Time, Vision, Water, Death, and Air." Only after naming each slice of land did Boruin realize how easily their titles sprang to mind. His head seemed so clear here, and if Pile had challenged him, Boruin wasn't sure he could say where he had learned so much about the Dreaming realm.

Pile pointed north, to the border between the mist-darkened talamh of Magic and the great ocean of Water. "And they war against each other?" Pile asked. Water was driving into the mists, pushing the fog back like one great army routing another.

"Look," Toaaho replied, "it is a dance of balance." Farther along their borders, almost out of sight, the dark mists became the invader. The talamh of Water shrunk under Magic's attack and the shifting borders stilled. A moment later the sound of the great battle of waters and mists rose on the wind as a whisper of distant surf. There were no straight borders between the talamhs; each looked to have been pulled and pushed. The talamh of Death, for instance, was pinched by its neighbors so it looked like a great hourglass.

"Their lands war, it seems, but the Iraemun sleep," Boruin said, answering Pile. "Their children begged the Great Mother to bring them slumber. She bound them in sleep, but I think they murdered one, too."

"Why was that?" asked Pile.

"Polorun was the Iraemun of Vision, master of dreams and nightmares. I would guess trapping his siblings in a realm under his control turned out to be a poor idea."

"No, why were they put to sleep?" Pile corrected.

"The Iraemun's arguments built and broke Baeg Tobar more times you'll breathe in your lifetime. Their first children, the Nai'Oigher, now rule their realms. 'Sixteen twins, and a tower for each,' I think it is said. That could be false, though. I see only one tower in each talamh."

Boruin's eye drifted about and caught at the center, where all the talamhs tapered together into a single point. A shadow sat where they met, like a sooty smudge on a windowpane. He followed a road leading away from the center and realized that a city had appeared in the corner of his eye. It was like spotting some dim star; it hid from the sunburned center of his sight, but it crept in around the edge of his vision when he glanced just beside it. Eight high palaces, near twins to their rural cousins, rose where the points of the Talamhs met. Boruin strained to look closer, to see more, but doing so brought the center of his eye to bear, and the city blurred over. The city did not wish to be seen so casually, but that mattered not. Boruin knew it. Though he couldn't remember having heard it before, the name rose right to his tongue.

"Maeda Criacao," he whispered to the wind.

The Monarhig turned suddenly from Wraethe. His eyes narrowed and swept up and down Boruin for the first time. The prince started to step forward, but Churly suddenly burst onto the hilltop carrying the head of a huge snake on his shoulder and dragging its half-cleaned body behind him.

The servant's long Fae fingers had managed to wipe the gore of the snake across most of his white tunic. There were even streaks of red where he'd slapped at the sweat on his elongated forehead. His eyes were large like walnuts under wire-thin eyebrows. His pants were a mess of mud, as if he'd had to wrestle the dead snake through a swamp before cleaning it. He did not convey the glorious image of a Fae quite like his master.

Churly's shoulders hunched as he spoke, as if he were used to taking a blow regardless of the worth of his words. "Sorry sire! Sorry!

I was by the stream, cleaning this most magnificent catch. It is truly stupendous, and the way you dispatched of—"

"I know how great it is, Churly. I slew it myself. Quit your babbling and bring us some wine," the Monarhig commanded. The servant dropped the snake and headed behind a tree, skidded to a stop to return and keep the snake from rolling down the steep hill, then dashed back behind the tree again. He reappeared moments later with a jug of chilled white wine.

"Could be a hell of a swamp runner-dodger, if you could stand to ride the fat man," the Monarhig said, again tossing back his head to laugh. Wraethe joined in the laughter. Pile moaned, and Boruin and Toaaho traded a look of confusion at her gaiety. The boy cackled lightly in a near perfect imitation of the Monarhig. The prince took notice of none of it.

"We might as well not even be here," Boruin said.

"Look," Toaaho said. Boruin followed his gaze upward. He almost rolled defensively to the side at the sight of the thul bear dangling from the tree above them. If it were still alive, the bear would have already leapt, crushing them both under its 500-pound mass. A second one, even larger than the first, hung on the next branch. Hundreds of animals were roped into the tall tree above them, some harmless, but most Boruin recognized as very, very dangerous.

The Monarhig and Wraethe stood under another tree full of the prince's trophies. They drank their wine as he continued to praise himself as she twirled her hair and smiled.

"These two were bound together after the rutting season. It seemed silly not to put them out of their misery," he explained. The two black deer hung with their immense antlers crossed and tangled in their fight over some mate now lost to the both of them. "Now, about that bath," he said, his smile flashing and beautiful.

"I really couldn't. We are needed in Easlinder, and I couldn't ask my companions to wait."

"Yes, about that," the Monarhig began. "I really can't have these creatures wandering on these trails. I am To'Sidhe'Lien, and our half of the Courts of Twilight supports strict isolationism when it comes to the mortal races. Really, how would it look if I let them continue?"

"Surely there is some compromise we could come to? Behave!" she said as the Fae's lip curled up to forecast a lewd suggestion.

"Humm," he said, tapping his finger to his lips and walking around Wraethe. His eyes never left her body, and Boruin's never left the killing spot on the back of his neck. "I did happen to see your bow. It is not a bad weapon—certainly not the quality of mine—but fair," he said. Churly had foreseen his master's command and was there with his case. The Monarhig drew out his ivory hunting bow and turned it about in his hands. "How is this? You shoot for your passage, should you win. I shoot for a bath if I win." Wraethe stared long at the man, and Boruin eagerly awaited the tongue lashing he knew she was about to deliver.

"Passage and the bow," she countered. The Monarhig smiled his approval. Boruin spat in the dirt.

They lined up along the cliff to watch the prince. The high-born Fae drew a cloud from his pocket—something no one understood, but something they all accepted as the oddest part of a strange afternoon. He folded it in his hands, and then out it sprang in the shape of a fish. The fish swam over the cliff and out into the sky. When he shot, his eye and hand were fantastic, the arrow arriving to burst the cloud in a puff of glittering scales.

Wraethe held her bow in position. She raised it before her and inhaled slowly as she drew. The next cloud, this one shaped as a star, was now far over the edge and beginning to dance in the winds that rolled up the face of the cliff. Wraethe's pale arms glowed in the noon sun, and Boruin heard her gently exhale. He knew she was then ready to fire. A second later her arrow arced up and out. It spun as it flew, the feathers twirling in a black blur. It began to fall, starting that long downward plunge toward the distant ground. It sliced through the small pocket-cloud on its way, perfectly splitting the target as it turned its iron head lower and dropped.

"Well done," the prince said with a clap of his hands, his white shooting gloves softening the applause. Wraethe curtsied deeply. The prince took his bow from his servant and pulled another cloud from his pocket. It sailed out on his breath. The prince took aim, and then lowered the bow as if something important had just caught his attention.

"Do you prefer soap or sand? I have the finest bathing sands. They were given to me by Lady Freinlass of the Stropping Ferns. She has the smoothest skin, you know," he said as he returned the bow to a full draw. The arrow was unleashed almost before he had finished speaking. It rocketed out into the air, carving an almost flat plane on its way to the target. The cloud burst into tatters as the wooden shaft split it and continued on out of sight.

Boruin took a step back and massaged his shoulder. A muscle had started jumping, and he rubbed the spasm to get it to stop.

Wraethe exhaled slowly and was near the end of her breath before she released. The arrow slung out fast, quivering as if eager to make its mark. It reached its apex and arced down, losing strength but passing through the target cloud at the last moment. Boruin knew that was the last one. Wraethe would never admit to it—she was better than any he had seen with a bow—but she could shoot no farther. *Stupid girl. Challenging a Fae, and so near his realm.*

The Monarhig set a small cloud in his palm and blew it out into the void. He turned to take a glass of wine from his servant and continued to gab about perfumed oils and intoxicating candles. The others watched as the cloud drifted farther and farther, now knocked about by the distant winds. The prince took his bow and almost without looking let the arrow fly. It shot out, seeming to follow the cloud like a falcon after some fat pigeon. When it pierced the cloud, Pile sighed and walked to his horse. Toaaho watched without emotion, and the boy continued picking flowers in the grass and chasing the odd bug under the horse's hooves.

Boruin barely noticed. That spasm had turned into a fierce itching. Again, he rubbed at the spot. This time his runes rolled over his shoulder with the motion. The uncomfortable sensation shifted. Boruin dragged it down his arm, and suddenly there was a rune he recognized. *Shem'broun,* he thought, confused again as to how he knew its name, and why his head was so clear. As Wraethe drew her bow, he pulled the rune onto his wrist and traced the design with his finger. *As fast as sure, as quick as true.* The traits sprang into his mind from somewhere lost, but he knew how to use the rune and what it did. He could not believe it.

Wraethe's arrow tumbled down to earth. They watched it go, falling short of its target as the winds continued to pull the little cloud out into the distance.

"Well done all the same. Truly a good show, truly. But I must say you do have fierce competition. I am regarded as the top..." the Fae bragged on, but Boruin was not listening. He pulled the rune down into his palm and lifted the prince's bow from the hands of his dumbfounded servant. The cloud was now almost beyond sight. It danced in the distant winds, whipping around like a child spinning in the arms of a playful father.

Churly stumbled back wide-eyed and sputtering as Boruin drew his master's bow and the rune exploded into use. The prince's words fell silent from his mouth as the bowstring hummed with its release. Boruin felt the hot release of the spell in his hand, saw the blue burning flame licking out between his closed fingers, but did not regard them as the arrow screamed through the air. He watched it shoot true, unaffected by the gusting wind. It traveled out into the deep blue sky, a straight unwavering line. The cloud danced until the arrow caught it, exploding in bright purple flame.

Stunned silence reigned on the hilltop for a moment until Boruin heard soft applause. The boy danced about in a small circle, doing a funny little jig while clapping and grinning huge at him. He almost smiled back, but the fuming Monarhig wrenched the bow from his hands. Boruin stepped away and wondered if he hadn't made a mistake.

"LIJ!! YOU PUTRID SACK OF DYING MEAT!!!" the prince screamed with a voice louder than possible for his thin frame. "That you would presume to come close to me! That you would presume to even touch my servant, let alone my own bow! It is tainted by your stink!" He broke the ivory shaft in two and cast it over the cliff. "I will flay your skin from your bones and leave them to bake in the Sunken Desert! Your cries I will bottle so your agony will ever amuse me! Your head will be preserved in your ass so you will ever feast on your own foulness!"

Boruin suddenly realized that the spell he'd used was not the only one he knew. Two more runes sat on his shoulder, and he knew the third was somewhere across his back. He spun the line and stacked the runes into his palm as they passed. His hand burned with power. The knowledge that he'd formed it right sent an unexpected rush through his body. Brun'gordhiem could stop a tidal wave; it could halt the rush of a mudslide; it would sheer a hard granite peak from its mountain—and it would certainly kill a lij. A Monarhig prince would only find himself knocked off the edge of the cliff and fending for himself in open air. *Probably*, Boruin thought.

The spell blossomed in his hand, the prince's eyes opened wide at the raw magic streaming from the old man. He had misjudged the travelers, and the woman was not the only mystery in their band.

The spell slammed against the Monarhig like an iron hammer swung by a god. The Fae tumbled back, but to Boruin's despair the prince lowered his shoulder and dug in his toes. He slowed to a stop just before the edge of the cliff. A moment of assessment passed between them, and then the Monarhig inhaled.

Afterwards, Boruin wasn't sure if the wind came from the prince's mouth or from over the cliff, but the gale roared across them all and they were blown back down the hillside. Jungle flashed by as they were whipped by swirling leaves and loose brush. Boruin felt himself sliding to a halt and tasted dirt.

"Nice move, boss," Pile said as he untangled himself from the branches of a small tree across the Nefazo highway. Boruin rolled over and squinted at the bright sun in his eyes.

"Son of a whore," he muttered as he pulled himself to his feet. Toaaho rode down two of the horses as Boruin fetched the boy, sitting pretty as if they had still been on their leisurely ride, off the third.

"How did you fair so well?" he asked. The boy was still smiling, and Boruin noticed he too had dust in his teeth. The boy's small hands pulled the runes down his arm, faster and faster. "Not a toy, son. Not a toy."

Boruin knew Wraethe would repeat the same to him come nightfall. She would wait until then, though. The strange trail was gone, and Wraethe was at the road's edge, tucked under the dark shade of an encroaching rock. Her cowl was low over her face, and there was only darkness beneath it.

- 6 -

AN ILL MOON'S CROSSING

The enormous silver moon lit the highway and the jungle glowed beside them. Bluestar ivy winked from its perch high in the trees, its phosphorescent flowers fluttering in the breeze. Diuntyne cooled the hot jungle and they rode on at their leisure. When Wraethe woke, she'd noticed immediately that a week had passed them by on that strange trail. The Monarhig had done more than banish them from his path; they had fallen back on the highway days later. It was as if they had stuck to the trade route to Easlinder and only dreamt the rest. Hoof marks of tired horses told that Belok had rushed past them in his haste, so it was a boon in a way. With luck, he'd gallop all the way to Priyati.

"Since when do you curtsey?" Boruin asked Wraethe as they continued north up the trade highway.

"Since when are you jealous?" she shot back. Her voice was teasing, an edge of pleasure in the retort. Boruin had expected her usual berating when Diun rose and the sun had finally fallen. Instead he had to bring up the encounter with the Monarhig while she rode on, staring up at the sky.

Boruin waved off the possibility. "I'm not jealous. I'm merely saying that I wouldn't have had to try the runes if you hadn't been so—"

"So what?"

"So girlish," Boruin said.

Wraethe snorted. "I did exactly what you would have, had it been a Moir."

"I don't curtsey. I don't prance, giggle, twirl my hair, or flutter my eyelashes," Boruin said.

"I didn't giggle," Wraethe said sharply, turning her face down from the moon.

"You did so," Pile retorted. "Giggled, pranced, twirled—and you couldn't keep your hands off him."

"You too, Pile? How about you, Toaaho? Are all of you adopting Lakshi's green face?"

"Horseshit! I'm not envious, not of that flouncing court nancy," Pile said before Toaaho had time to answer.

Wraethe pulled her horse close to Pile's. "Come Pile, tell me the truth. You're a little jealous. No more than Boruin, certainly," she said. Her voice was smooth like the pale moon's glow gone liquid. She reached out, and her fingers brushed across Pile's neck and under his chin. The man's jaw bounced, his tongue only stuttered, but his feet worked and he kicked his horse ahead. Wraethe laughed, and Boruin favored her with a hard stare.

"What is going on with you?" he said.

"It's a nice night, that is all," she said, turning her head again to the blue-black sky. "The day was pleasant for a while, but you know the night is my favorite."

"It might have been pleasant, but it had an odd effect on you," he said. Wraethe smiled impishly, and it caught him in the gut like it always did in the rare times she got this way. He put the feeling aside before it could stir more trouble and broke from her eyes.

Diun was now high above them. Boruin wondered how long it would be before the Trickster would appear beside it, how long then before Nurom Misuer would also follow. How much worse would she get before the three moons ended their strange dance? Boruin knew the answer to all three questions, but managed to put them out of his head until they reached the foothills of the Monahdraichean Mountains.

A cat's scream echoed off the ridges above the camp, alerting Boruin that someone had made another kill.

"Wraethe or Toaaho?" Pile asked.

"Wraethe. Toaaho knows better than to mess with anything that bites back, if he can avoid it," Boruin answered. He slid forward to join the boy by the fire. The flame warmed his fingers as he flicked gristle and fat into the coals, cleaning his hands after finishing another skin. The boy poked at the red embers with a long stick, laughing at the ones that popped and shot sparks up to dance briefly with the swirling snow.

The air had gone cold quickly as they climbed from the jungle and into the mountains below Po'o'La'aei Pass. It was hard to imagine winter while among the hot swamps of Nefazo, and Boruin remembered why he preferred the milder climes. His hands stiffened as he scraped the skins their two hunters had already dragged out of the forest. It was messy work, but the furs would be welcome as they trudged through the snow-filled peaks in the high winds. Pile was ahead, his hides clean and the man already cutting the leather into cloaks and leggings.

"Do you think Belok made it over?" Pile asked.

"Could be. It's early in the season. Depends on how much snow has filled the fields above and how loud his riders are," Boruin said. He threaded a thick needle and started stitching through the soft leather while the boy squatted to study his work like a tiny apprentice. "If he did make it and can't find us in town, he'll try to catch us between the pass and Priyati." The boy nodded his head in agreement before jumping up to chase a pair of large moths fluttering on the night breeze.

Boruin was not worried about that yet. It did no good to think of Belok until they too had crossed the snowfields. If they could manage that, then he'd consider Belok a problem again.

Po'o'La'aei was known for its vile winter temperament, the name a regular curse word among the Nefazo merchants. The pass narrowed as it snaked between three peaks, just wide enough to move two wagons abreast. The slopes above held their snow, but only baring any whisper. More than a few eager traders had died in avalanches while trying to move their great wagons, full of wares, between markets in the off season. Boruin and his crew would have to leave the horses, but there were a few higher trails that would take them above the great snowfields. It was a harder climb, but better then dying under a smothering blanket of snow.

"That should finish my coat," Wraethe said as she slung the heavy cat into the middle of the camp. Pile rolled back with his knife poised as the dead beast sailed out of the shadows beyond the firelight. "That going to protect you from this feline?" Wraethe asked as he moved back to working on his own hide. Boruin wondered if she meant the cat or herself.

Wraethe sat by the fire, her eyes glowing bright from her hunt. She refused the boy's offer of a rag, enjoying the smell and the slick feel of the blood still wet on her hands. Here was a true predator, more so than the beast she had stalked. Boruin watched her closely, measuring her smile and the fierce glint in her eye. She was near euphoric as the heat from the hunt bled out into the cold air. She tore into the cat, stripping the skin and cutting free what meat they would use before the long climb into the mountains. The steaks would be welcome, a better fare than the oily flesh of the thul bears she had brought in the night before.

The Monarhig's prizes had stirred the huntress in Wraethe. Boruin hoped that these animal kills would slake her need for bloodshed as Nurom Misuer continued to grow larger in the sky. Boruin watched her quickly debone the cat, her movements as fast and graceful as the feline's would have been. He looked up at Takata Shin and wondered if it would be enough. *No. Not enough by far,* he thought.

Takata Shin, the Trickster, was edging out from behind Diun, a bright earring now hanging beside its large companion. The small moon would peek out farther before the weight of Nurom Misuer's passing pulled it back again behind Diun. It was a rare dance, the three moons together, and one Boruin had learned to hate.

Nurom Misuer, the Envious, spent most of the year slung out into the black night, a distant red star at the far arc of its orbit. But twice a year it returned to fill Baeg Tobar's skies, coloring Wraethe's moods deadly black and furious red. The random appearance of the Trickster made it worse, an aphrodisiac to the woman so affected by the night skies. Gay and girlish was not in the normal range of Wraethe's emotions, but this little jewel of a moon brought it out like a ball gown thrown on a farmer's daughter. When Takata Shin disappeared she would plummet, the easy humor and flirtatious nature gone. Wraethe would sink low and in the bottom of that well would be Nurom Misuer's mad whisperings of rage and blood.

Above the tree line, the mountainside was bitter cold after dark. Diun hung heavy in the sky and lit the snow fields like day. At this height the flood of light from the massive moon seemed an added weight pressing on their backs. The winds licked about their bodies, trying to find a seam in the heavy furs that protected them. Wraethe forged ahead with her jungle cat coat white against the white beyond. Only the black collar, added from a small and unfortunate sable, was visible during the thicker gusts of driven snow. Somewhere farther on Toaaho scouted their trail.

It was Pile's turn to pull the boy's sled behind him, and again he cursed at the small weight as his feet sunk deep in the drifts. The boy did not seem to notice, sitting quietly and looking up at the jagged black stone rising out of the field above them. Boruin was glad they'd decided to avoid Po'o'La'aei. Perched high above it, he could see that the pass was a dead man's choice. The snowfields at either edge were like an ocean's wave frozen just before breaking. They hung fat over the pass, ready for the slightest cry to wake the crashing wave of snow.

Diun was far from setting when Toaaho appeared like a ghost out of the swirling curtains of snow. Ice clung to the fur wrapping his face, his moist breath freezing almost before it escaped his mouth. He leaned into Wraethe, and she nodded, then he walked back through her broken trail to Boruin.

He leaned in close and still had to holler over the wind. "Another cleft for shelter."

"It's early," Boruin shouted.

"Hard ground ahead," he replied before turning back up the mountain. Boruin staggered through the drifts and wondered what ground could be harder than this.

The Mana'Olai took Boruin forward to the end of the snowfield and for a moment he saw nothing at all. The wind changed direction, pulling the falling snow with it. The ground appeared, thousands of feet below his boots. Where their path ran, a great sheet of snow had been blown like mud against the mountain; caked to the stone, it closed their trail. Toaaho examined it a moment more before sliding into a great crack running up the mountain.

The split in the rock broke the wind, but snow continued to sprinkle down from above as they huddled in the smallest joint.

"Can we climb higher?" Pile asked.

Toaaho rubbed his hands to work the cold out of his fingers. "No easier. Cliffs above, cliffs below," he answered.

"Yuin's bastard daughters… we'll have to go back," Boruin decided.

Pile fought to turn around and face Boruin. "Back? Back where? We can't climb down half the places we climbed up."

"What would you have us do?" Wraethe asked.

"Use some of that damn secret magic you've got hidden in that arm of yours, Boruin. Burn a hole through the snow or something," he answered.

"Burn a hole? Why don't I just bring the Fae-damned moon out of the sky to cart us over the pass? Might as well level off the mountain tops and tip them into the valley so you could walk straight across into Easlinder, for Yuin's sake!" Boruin yelled over the screaming wind.

"Great! Get your hand off your shriveled tom and go to it!" Pile yelled back. Pain in the ass that he was, Boruin knew Pile was right.

"You don't have to," Wraethe whispered into his ear. "Those runes will take you apart, flesh from bone, if you're not careful."

Boruin pushed past her with a laugh, "Yuin's sake, woman! They frighten me enough without your encouragement." His smile dropped as he stepped into the wind, but not because of the cold. She'd berated him plenty for casting his spells blindly; this pleading in her voice, though, terrified him. It scared him because she was right. He had been using them more since they found the boy. It was only a matter of time before that burning power would rush inward instead of out.

The old man walked wearily back out into the snow. He pulled his cloak tight about him and surveyed the impasse. The snowfield tapered down to a thin line that ran through a stagger in the cliff face. The stone broke back to leave a ledge separating two towering walls— one above and the other below. The snow had filled that crack, wind packing it in to smooth the broken stone.

He drew his arm out of his cloak, his skin aching with the cold. The runes ran down his forearm as he looked and felt for some sign that one was right. The spells against the Monarhig had come to him from somewhere deep inside, but now there was no sense of recognition, no instinct that called out to him. This would be a blind cast, and the fear of it writhed in his stomach like a worm.

He pulled three runes down into his palm. One looked like a spike for cutting. The second had a long arm that spun out and away. The third one he pushed back. It just looked wrong. Sometimes Boruin chose the runes at random; other times he grouped runes with hard angles, or the ones that looked more fluid. This time he looked for a balance. The dark tattoos slid across his back as he spun the line, looking for the proper rune to complete the spell. He found a third with a central twist, opposite and maybe a good counter to the middle sigil. The choice was made, and he felt the three begin to agree. There was a spell there and it would work. *But how?* he thought.

The burning runes crushed together in his grip like brittle embers. Boruin raised the fist above his head. His hand opened, and motes of black dust spilled from his palm, the wind swirling them out above the abyss.

"Damn," Boruin said as he watched the dark cloud wash against the cliff above. "Spectacular job, you half-assed magician," he muttered to himself. The dust stuck to the cold rock and did nothing.

Frustrated, Boruin rubbed the frozen skin of his arm, flipping the runes again. He picked another three, this time at random, and looked up to see a shadow seething across the stone and snow. The runes slid back out of his palm, forgotten. The black mass congealed and snaked into the cracks of the rock as if fleeing from the cold.

Boruin watched, fascinated, as long spines grew out of the crevices, sharp and red-tipped like the poisonous blood orchids nestled high in the Kleas forests. A large bloom trimmed in red punched out of the rock, and the howling winds shredded it with their cold teeth. The bud opened wide in agony. Boruin stumbled back, falling into the drifts, as a howl exploded between the bud's long rows of teeth.

"Oh, Yuin! What the…" Boruin stopped speechless as the spell-thing burst upwards, growing through the rock. Shards of granite burst from the cliff as spines punched through, birthed from inside the rock face. Long vines, writhing like tentacles, spread from the crevices, bunching and wrapping together against the cold.

More mouths appeared as the thing spread outward, growing and howling in fury. More stone crumbled as if the monster Boruin had summoned was burrowing into the mountain, seeking to possess the great pile of rock. The vines stretched toward him, whipping out as if they would snap free just to reach and punish their maker. The mouths screamed wildly, their voices louder than the wind.

Boruin found himself back on his feet and running through the snow. He did not turn until he was almost back to the cleft. He saw the top of the cliff between gusts of snow. Ebony spires groped for the sky, thorn towers growing thicker. A raging mouth rose among them like the domed cathedral of some demonic church.

Boruin slammed his hands over his ears and screamed along with the great mouth. His knees gave way and he buried his head in the snow. The earth rumbled as the echo bounced off the mountains.

For a moment he was sure he was falling, sure he'd open his eyes and see the world racing at him. The ground bucked beneath him and he tore his face from the snow to see the high cliff exploding out into open air. The black plant, veins pulsing with freezing blood, rolled down the mountainside with broken granite. Thorns shattered and skin burst in the avalanche.

Boruin's ears were ringing, but he heard Pile shout, "What in the rut was that?"

The quaking had driven the others out of their safe harbor in the cleft, and they all watched the plant thing tearing angrily at the air as it fell. The sound of the impact was lost in the wind, but they could still see it moving at the battered foot of the mountain. The upper cliff was gone, a raw boulder field left in its place.

"Ruttin' moved a mountain! I didn't expect you to do it!" Pile said.

"And don't ask me again," Boruin replied. His eyes stayed on the monstrosity pulling itself down under the snow and rock to escape the freezing wind. Its howls continued to torture his ringing ears as the travelers picked their way through the boulders and down the side of the mountain. That worm in his gut continued to churn; the fear of the runes tearing him apart was now terror for the world he might tear asunder.

They shed their heavier furs as they hiked down into the wide valley that held, like a mother's cradling arms, the nation of Easlinder. Great blankets of bluestar vine burned brightly all around them. Boruin watched the flowers turn, sensing Wraethe's passing as if she were their moon now that Diun had dropped below the horizon.

They walked through the night, Boruin pushing them forward even though the beast of his construction was far off and walled in by mountains of stone. He said little, even once they regained the highway, somber and quiet while Wraethe oddly chattered and flirted with Pile and then teased him for his response.

Toaaho led them from the merchants' road when they found Belok's trail, backtracking to a thin logger's path that turned deeper into the forests to the north of Priyati. Their leader's silence seemed to infect Toaaho, who spoke less the further they traveled. Boruin had known the trip would be difficult for the Mana'Olai. Toaaho had not returned to Easlinder since fleeing as a boy.

Boruin did not confront him until he realized they had left the trail to wander blindly in the mountains. "Where are we going, Toaaho?"

"Priyati."

"This is the way?"

Toaaho did not respond and Boruin did not press him.

"This isn't a way," Pile muttered. "This is stumbling through the brush. A way was the road obviously going the right way."

Toaaho did not stop. The woods grew thicker until they were following game trails, ducking under the draping branches of

Easlinder pines and pulling thorns from their skin as they pushed through the brambles.

The sun began to drop, and Wraethe would wake soon. Boruin left her with Pile and the boy, hoping to pick Toaaho's mind before she woke and made a mess with her unfettered tongue. He shouldered into another hedge, plowing over a mess of branches as even the game trails had finally ended. He cursed as the brush scratched his face, but suddenly he was through. Then there was Toaaho, standing still for the first time all day. Scorched stones slumped in ruin among mounds of a fallen shale roof from some massive house. The ground was bare as if trampled by cattle, but no animal had visited the hollow. It was too quiet, too dead here.

"What is this?"

"My home," Toaaho replied. Boruin wasn't certain what to say.

"You were barely a child. How did you remember?"

Toaaho looked at the ground at his feet. "There is where my father was slain. My eldest brother fell beside him." The man began to walk. He pointed to the rubble of a barn, his voice calm as if he were a priest giving a tour in Pileaus's great cathedral. "My aunts died there, defending their children. They were left to burn inside."

The man strolled through the rubble, pointing out every spot where a family member had fallen. He named his uncles and brothers, his father's men. The Mana'Olai named each of his family and where their blood had soaked into the earth.

"And you?" Boruin whispered, his voice unable to rise any higher.

The Mana'Olai squinted through the last of the sun and pointed to the top of a tall cedar. "There. Hidden in the smoke as my home burned."

Boruin knew of Toaaho's loss, knew the death of his father's camp had turned him orphan and exile, but now the knowledge settled into a place that was real. His stomach took an ill twist. He could almost see the young boy holding tight to the high branches, the smoke burning his eyes, and then the smell of it turning sweet and sick as the bodies were cast on the flames.

Pile blundered out of the brush, the boy and Wraethe in his wake. "I'm not stopping here," he said. Boruin turned to see the short man's eyes wide.

"This is where… this is Toaaho's home," Boruin said. Pile grabbed Boruin's arm and dragged him off as Toaaho continued to stare into the tree.

"This place is not good. We need to go," he said. His eyes turned to check around him, looking up at the sky and then behind. Boruin knew Pile's fear. It was rare to find a man who made his living on the mah'saiid ruins and wasn't afraid of spirits, imagined or not.

"We have a moment for this, Pile," Wraethe said as she pulled her cowl from her head.

"Oh, Yuin!" Pile cried in disbelief. He looked again at the darkening sky that had woken her. Pile dropped his pack and dug into his things. "No amount of time spent in this place is good. I know, for Yuin's sake, and you know I do, Boruin!" he said, his fingers quivering.

Boruin felt small hands clutching around his thigh and looked down to see the boy standing very close. The old fighter's eyes snapped right as they caught movement, a running form on the dim edge of the tree line. It was too quick to be sure, but for a moment something was there and then not. *Shadows, Diun's dusk light. You're catching Pile's spooks,* he thought. But he still turned to Toaaho, the boy holding fast to his leg.

The Mana'Olai was sitting, his feet tucked under his legs and his hands out, poised in meditation.

"Maybe now is not the best time—"

Toaaho spoke softly. "Down the ridge to the south there is a spring. I'll meet you at its fount." Another glimmer at the edge of Boruin's eye, a woman running, struck and then falling into thin air. The sharp scent of smoke caught Boruin's nose. He tried to tell himself it was from the morning fire still clinging to his clothes.

"Boruin!" Piled pleaded. He could hear the rattling of the short man's bone wards and the pack thrown onto his back.

Boruin crouched before his man, forcing himself into Toaaho's glazed eyes. "I can't leave you here."

"You own my writ. Do you make this order as my master?" Toaaho answered.

"Of course not. I ask always as friend and debtor to you."

"At the spring," Toaaho said. Boruin knew it was final. He spotted a severed hand in the rubble of the house, and he heard the distant clash of steel, a death scream. Boruin knew now the ground was trampled bare by the feet of angry ghosts. He swung the child into his arms and fled, the others running behind him.

- 7 -
TOAAHO'S HAUNTS

The boy stood on a flat stone in the middle of the stream with his hands in his pockets, cringing when the screams floated down from the ridge and faces appeared under the pine boughs. Boruin wanted to go out to get him back, but the water was deep and the stones out of reach. He had turned his back for a moment and found the boy in the middle of the stream moments later, dry as dust.

Pile passed by Boruin again, pacing away his worry in circles. "You own his writ. Make him come down," Pile said.

"He's not my slave, Pile," Boruin answered.

"You own his writ!"

"Toaaho is not a slave!"

Pile stopped his feet, but his bone wards kept rattling on as if for emphasis. "You own his writ, Boruin. That means he is your slave!"

"I bought his writ, but that's all. He is no slave to me, and even if he were it would carry no weight in Easlinder. They'll stone a slaver, especially if he claims one of their own."

"Well, you still have to make him come down," Pile said. "He won't last an hour in a place like that. Yuin, the death there! I can't get it out of my nose." Another shade flitted past him, and Pile almost fell as he twisted about and flailed his wards at it. That was all he could take, and the small man began to wade out into the cold spring water.

"What are you doing?" Wraethe called after him.

"I'm sticking with the boy. He's no idiot. No ghost has touched him since he got out there."

Wraethe watched the shadows move around them. "He's right, Boruin," she said. "These are no kin of Toaaho's. Maybe the ones in the glade are, but the spirits here are something conjured, something set to keep us away." Boruin's fingers rubbed the back of his neck. He could feel the welts where dry fingernails had raked across his skin. These ghosts were spiteful, darting out of the dark to pinch and scrape, trip and cut. He felt another one close, smelled its sour odor behind him, and he began to turn. Wraethe caught his arm.

"You don't want to look. It's trying to scare you," she said. Her face wrinkled, horror and disgust appearing as the creature showed her something. Boruin could feel its cold breath on his neck and was glad he hadn't turned. "They are horrible. I'm for the stones," Wraethe said, lifting her skirt to step into the stream. As her toes reached the edge, the sparkle of Takata Shin rose off the water. She paused as the reflections of the night sky swam across her face and summoned a more entertaining idea.

Boruin, Pile, and the boy sat on the flat rocks in the pool and watched Wraethe spin in and out of the shadows. Her weapons slashed through the night, and Boruin saw her devilish grin wax under Takata Shin's diamond gleam. She could do no harm to those already dead, but it did not stop her from trying.

Pile continued to chalk wards into the rock, his back to the boy's as they shared a wide piece of shale.

"What's keeping them off us?" Boruin asked. The boy let his hand drop into the water and swirled it about.

"Running water, I think. Maybe that's why Toaaho wanted us here." Pile answered.

"He didn't mention being in the water. He figured we'd be safe this far off," said Boruin.

"Then Wraethe is certainly right. These ghosts aren't family; they're here to harm trespassers. All the more reason to drag Toaaho out of here."

"We will wait, and that means you," Boruin said.

Pile quit drawing his wards to raise his eye to Boruin. "Then tell me why. Why do you have a writ on him?" he asked. Boruin watched a pale face brighten out of the gloom across the pool; it tugged at its shirt tail and then ripped upward. The shirt and skin peeled from its body, pulling over its head. Wraethe appeared behind it, her sword cutting through the spirit. Blood that could not have been real splashed out over the water. Boruin took a breath with which to answer and locked his gaze to his feet.

"I met Toaaho on a slaver's trail in south Nefazo. I needed to avoid a few problems, so I sold myself into a slave caravan moving north," Boruin said.

"It was a long highway. The marshes made the road soft, water pooling where the ruts sunk in the low earth. The slaves dragged the wagons when the habbacks weren't enough. I spent most of my time strapped into the harness beside Toaaho.

"When we arrived in Ouilainne, Belok bought me out, as I'd arranged, and I bought out Toaaho."

"That had to be years ago. Why do you still own him?" Pile asked.

"I owe him for a few indiscretions that he pulled me out of. He won't leave until I've paid up."

"So pay up," Pile said.

"They're not that easy to repay. It's not coin that he's asking."

"Yuin, you're so damn cryptic! Can you give me a straight answer?"

"No."

"Then the Fae may steal it! You're like talking to a rock," Pile said. Behind him, the boy laughed softly. Pile turned his head to face him. "And you! It's like carting a monkey around, all tricks and trouble. At least quit talking all the time and give us a rest," he said, prodding the boy with his elbows. The child continued his giggling, and Boruin was glad Pile had chosen a different distraction from the ghosts. There were some secrets he could not easily divulge; his history with Toaaho was one of them.

Boruin laughed as the boy almost jostled Pile into the water, but he did not look up where the ghosts waited with spilling blood and torn limbs. They all kept their eyes down, nearly missing Toaaho stumbling among the horrid visions as he came down the ridge.

"You whoreson!" Wraethe shouted, pulling up her sword at the last moment. "Toaaho, I could just kill you!" she snarled, furious that she almost had. The man had stumbled down among the ghosts and the embattled woman had almost cleaved him in two. Diun had set, taking the Trickster with it. Nurom Misuer now reigned above, and Wraethe's mood was no longer giddy or fun.

Boruin dropped into the water and headed for shore. "Is he alright?" he called. He watched Toaaho tumble to his knees as a ghost, swimming in a cloud of long, blood-stained hair, launched onto his back. Gore flew as her fingernails cut into his flesh. Wraethe's steel split her from crown to breastbone and then the ghost was gone. The angry woman turned circles around the fallen Mana'Olai, daring any other to come close. They came and came fast.

"You wanted to go. Now's the time!" Boruin hollered back to Pile.

"Now? You want to go now?" Pile yelled back as more spirits spilled down off the ridge and into the valley. Boruin took another look at Toaaho and made up his mind. The Mana'Olai's back was shredded, as if in penance paid for a hundred men's sins. He could make out the flecks of white where Toaaho had been scored down to the bone. They had to move and get the man to safety.

"Dawn is not any time soon, and there's no guarantee it will be better. Let's go!" he hollered, ducking as Wraethe's blade whistled over his head and struck the spirit behind him. The ghost split and vanished, only to reform in the dark and come to crowd around again.

Pile made it to shore, but it was the boy who came bearing their way out. The small child darted into the darkness, slipping between the wisps of dark spirits as they reached out for him. He was gone only for a moment, but Boruin's heart was in his chest and his hands had forgotten tending to Toaaho's wounds.

A crashing came down the hillside as a shadow rolled out of the forest and splashed into the stream leaving the pool. The boy leapt behind, landing on the soft top of the giant mushroom cap. The thick wafer floated downstream toward them as Pile and Boruin dragged their friend out into the water. Wraethe moved even faster, a blur of blue eyes in the darkness. It reminded Boruin of Thilan flame dancers, visible only by the light of their fire coursing through the night.

Toaaho floated unconscious on the makeshift raft as the boy kept his head from falling into the water. Pile and Boruin guided them both downstream as Wraethe continued raging along the banks. The spirits continued to chase, but they were fading.

By the time the stream began to drop into deeper valleys, the ghosts had thinned to only screams and chiding threats. Wraethe disappeared into the forest, chasing down all she could, futile as the whole action was. Toaaho weakened until his breath was barely a whisper between his lips. Boruin knew there was little hope left if they did not reach Priyati soon.

"HE COMES!" Toaaho shouted, his back arching so sharply the spasm almost threw him from the raft. Pile dropped underwater, startled by the loud cry. The boy clamped his hands around the Mana'Olai's jaw, pulling his teeth wide and looking down his throat for the strength of the voice.

"COMING! ONE MORE... mpht!" Toaaho's scream rang out across the quiet hills until the boy clamped his hands over his mouth.

Pile floundered back to the raft. "Yuin, what's the matter with him?" Pile asked, once again clutching his wards tightly. Boruin had no answer. He grabbed the boy, trying to pull him free, but the child was suddenly strong. Toaaho gurgled, a choking gasp and a thrash that was too weak to break from the small hands.

"You're choking him, boy!" Boruin shouted. He yelped as the boy's teeth broke the skin of his hand and sent him too sprawling into the water. The boy pulled Toaaho's jaw wide again and leaned down as if to kiss him. Instead he screamed a high-pitched warble back into the Mana'Olai's mouth. The cry brought Wraethe rushing out of the jungle.

She moved to intercept the raft and the two men clinging to its sides. "What the rut are you doing to him?" she cried. Wraethe pushed Pile off and reached to drag the boy free, but halted as his small hands slid between Toaaho's teeth. The boy's face was of strained concentration as his fingers slipped and then found purchase on the wet tongue and began to pull. Boruin grabbed him again as Wraethe pulled the Mana'Olai in the other direction. There was no separating the two, locked impossibly by the boy's small-handed grip.

Toaaho's tongue began to slide free, and the boy reached deeper, grabbing the thicker root. Pile screamed with confusion and horror as it began to tear free. Boruin pulled but fell into the water as the child's jacket split. He did not want to renew his hold, but when the boy turned over his shoulder with a pleading look for help, he knew he had no choice. Boruin dragged the raft to the shore and braced his foot against the bank. He grabbed the boy and pulled up, putting all his strength into it. Then he saw what the boy was after.

What Boruin had thought to be Toaaho's tongue was a thick, black worm that writhed as it blocked Toaaho's throat. The boy pulled at the parasite and Boruin pulled the boy. They both screamed, the boy in his odd high warble and the man in frustration and fear. The false-tongue came free, long and sinuous like an eel.

Wraethe was on it even before it hit the ground, her blade cutting to no avail. The thing was not a spirit, but it wasn't real, either. It was impossibly thin and strong like a cord of gristle and thick as a habback's tongue. How it had fit in Toaaho, Boruin couldn't understand. It must have grown in his throat, growing there as the man stumbled through the woods to them.

The creature continued to scream as Wraethe smashed its mouth down into the dirt. The sound echoed on, and Yuin only knew what would come to its call.

The boy pulled at Wraethe's cloak. She nearly backhanded him, but he ducked and ran into the forest.

Pile jumped to follow. "After him!" he yelled. "He's the only one who knows what's going on!"

Wraethe dragged the flailing, screaming creature into the woods and found the boy at the base of a wide tree. He handed a round stone to Boruin and pointed to a rotted knot shaped like a mouth in the hollow trunk. Wraethe shoved the squirming thing into the darkness. Boruin drove the rock into the hole with the pommel of his sword. He leaned his ear to the bark and could still hear the parasite's screams, but far off like a distant horn through the fog. They could hear it scrambling up and down the trunk, beating itself against the wood as it tried to escape.

Pile dropped to his knees, head down like a man ready to pass out. "Anyone want to guess on that?" he asked.

"Not a ghost and not Fae," Boruin said.

They jumped as Toaaho stumbled out of the brush behind them. "Gruw-makken," he answered. His legs quivered underneath him, but his voice held steady. "It is a black thing, a flesh magic."

"Are there more?" Boruin asked.

"I don't know. It was not what I expected. I'm sorry."

"What had you expected?" Wraethe said, her voice cold and angry.

"Peace and understanding."

Pile made it back to his feet and walked a wide circle around a still agitated Wraethe. "Well, it's been a right good time here, but I'm bushed and would like to get to somewhere else soon." They followed him back to the stream. As Wraethe plunged on into the darkness, Boruin and the boy helped the Mana'Olai follow.

Near dawn, Nurom Misuer drifted over the horizon. Wraethe slowed with exhaustion, her anger spent with the setting of the moon. They camped above Priyati, the silver Oriune River visible as a thin line splitting through the city and jostling on in its liquid haste down the mountains.

"This thing isn't finished, is it?" Boruin asked as he pressed fresh dressings into Toaaho's wounds.

"No," he said.

"Did you find what you were after?"

"I was given this," he said, sketching a cruel sign in the dirt with his finger. The upturned curve could be mistaken for a smile, but Boruin recognized the down-rushing lines beneath for the hot blood of a cut throat. "It is my family name—as the Mana'Olai know us."

Wraethe kicked the foul sign out of the dirt. "And how did you come across this knowledge?" she asked.

"They whispered it in my ear to remind me of my shame."

"As they shredded your back," Boruin finished.

Pile spat in the fire, despite just getting it lit. He blew on the kindling and cursed. "Rutting ghosts. Always nasty business."

"They have only misery and shame to give. It is all they know now, all they are left with," Toaaho said in defense of his ancestors.

The Mana'Olai winced as Boruin helped the man pull his shirt back over his shoulders and down across his wounds. "And the tongue?" Boruin pressed.

"An alarm left to watch and wait—specifically for me."

"It could have been for anyone, just a precaution," Boruin said, sounding more convinced of that than he felt.

"Who knows you've returned to Easlinder? Are they now preparing for us?" Wraethe asked from across the fire.

Toaaho slumped low over his knees and grimaced as his shirt drew tighter across his back. "Had you not caught the gruw-makken, it would have betrayed me. Still, I don't know. Its voice might carry farther than we know."

"Spill it then," Wraethe snapped. "You aren't a talking man by trade, but you'd better catch us up. I don't want to be walking blind here."

"For Yuin's sake! Would you cut the man some slack?" said Pile. "You and Boruin ain't laid your past lives open for review." He dropped his gaze under Wraethe's stare.

Toaaho began to speak before she could continue her recriminations. The companions huddled close around the flame to listen. His words crept off his tongue and stayed close to the ground with their softness. Steam began to rise from their wet clothes as if to carry his story away, clouded from any hidden witness.

"My family name was cursed by our people. Köpeka now means deceivers.

"Before the Dabattu, the great exodus of the Mana'Olai, the immortal Kukane'Haku, the God-Kings, ruled. The gods had men for all tasks, from farming to ship building to earth moving to magic weaving. The Köpeka were the Kukane'Haku's most righteous followers. We were their chosen killers.

"We moved among our own people, seeking out the rebellious, removing those that spoke against the God-Kings, murdering those unworthy to pray. The Kukane'Haku were all-powerful, and we were their unseen hands.

"By the grace of a true god, Kahie'Hoku, we were also the betrayer of their secret. It was my family that discovered they were not immortal gods. The God-Kings were men, and our devotion was to a race no more holy than we.

"My family fled when God-King Hammeoto was killed. We hid in the masses of our people who chose to cross the sea. Few knew we had exposed the God-Kings and our name is still a curse to the Mana'Olai. We welcome their hatred until we have purged the last memory of the Kukane'Haku from our people.

"You say we, but aren't you the last? How can you do that?" Pile asked, breaking into the man's story.

"By killing the Makua'Moi," Boruin answered for him.

Toaaho nodded. "The Makua'Moi continue to worship the God-Kings while hiding among our people. They pray for their return, seek to bring them north across the southern sea. They are devoted to the false gods, and the Köpeka are devoted to their destruction."

"Seems the Makua'Moi are a little ahead in the tally," Pile said.

"Very much ahead. I'm alone, and they are strong," Toaaho said.

"Not so much alone, as few," Boruin offered.

"Right. There are four and a half of us, if you count the toddler there," Pile said, smiling in the dawn light.

"And he is our first concern," Wraethe added, bringing things back into focus. Her hands twisted her hood as she fought to get her last words out before sleep could claim her. "We are here to see the boy delivered. Him first, and then you can renew this blood feud. For now we have enough trouble with Belok. We don't need any extra work. Especially with you all beat to a pulp," she said. Her eyes disappeared into shadow.

Boruin agreed, but his mind was a mess of worries as they lay down with the sunrise. Wraethe was one to preach—she would be more threat than anything in the coming nights, and he couldn't afford to exile her to the jungle as they'd done twice before. The moons were peaking, the Trickster beginning to slip back behind Diun. Nurom Misuer was swelling red, a ripe belly full of hate. It was almost full in its orbit, and Wraethe was a volcano nearing the end of her warning steam. When the miserable moon swung close and rose in the sky larger than Diun, fire and ash would erupt and burn Priyati to a crisp if his grip on her was not firm.

Between Wraethe, Belok, and now the Makua'Moi, Boruin wondered if these weren't the last of his days.

- 8 -
BELOK'S PLAY

Boruin woke with a hot coal of fire in his hand. His eyes snapped open as he released the spell from his burning fist. He saw Toaaho turned away from him in sleep, but it was too late to stop the magic. The power rushed from the runes, breaking against his companion's wounded back. Boruin's breath seized up in his chest as if the strength of the spell had slammed the wind out of his lungs. It was a long moment before he could stop grimacing in pain and confusion and force himself to breathe.

In that moment the spell coated the Mana'Olai in a thick amber sap that sunk through the bandages like water into cracked desert earth.

The man spun to his feet, turning to face Boruin. "You have no right to work your spells on me without permission."

Boruin flinched from his friend's rare display of emotion. The boy walked past him and smacked Toaaho on the back. The Mana'Olai began to shoo him away before realizing he felt no pain.

"Did you do this?" Boruin asked, grabbing the boy's arm. The child smiled at him and reached up to flip the runes across his forearm. "Yuin's sake, boy! These are not toys! Not for you to play with! Do you hear me? Do you understand what's coming out of my mouth?" he shouted. The boy just smiled at everything he said.

Pile dropped his axe back into the dirt, his eyes still droopy after being startled from sleep. "The boy can work your runes?" Pile muttered as he collapsed on his bedroll. "Boy, I must be the street-card's mark. I can't even see them."

"You and everyone else. That's how I like it," Boruin answered. He caught Wraethe's eyes fading back beneath her cowl. She had nearly come out from her sleep, but had left the boy to play with his magic. *For Yuin's sake, what if it had been the toothy plant instead?* The fear of it drove him to his feet.

Boruin stormed off into the woods, leaving the boy and Pile to remove Toaaho's bandages. He knew the deep scores in Toaaho's flesh would be healed. He had felt that in the spell even before he had fully awoken. There were six or seven runes in that combination, he was almost sure of it. The power had been immense, and it had happened without him. Boruin stood on the ridge overlooking the distant capital. He counted the towers standing like guards over the garden parks, traced the lines of its boulevards, and watched the Oriune River flow through Priyati until his blood cooled. Then he went back to the camp and waited on sundown.

They entered Priyati one by one, appearing out of the forest on the edges of avenues, slipping in between houses. Boruin walked with the boy on his shoulders like a father out with his son to enjoy Diuntyne after dinner. If Belok was around he was watching the highway. Boruin saw no man note his appearance as he approached the market, but Priyati was a big place.

The Diuntyne market was full. The merchants had brought out their perishables, the moon's gaze less harsh on the meats, fruit, and fish than the sun's. Now that the heat of the day had lifted, Priyati's folk moved through the stalls, picking out greens and meats for the evening meal and collecting eggs and milk for the morning. Food wasn't the only fare for sale, though.

Boruin could hear Wraethe bickering in a nearby stall as she tried to trade their furs for finer apparel. In a brewer's stand, Pile had found his own method of shaking off the day's heat. He set a mug to his lips and winked over the brim at the boy as he passed atop Boruin's shoulders. The old man bought the boy a sweetstick and found Toaaho sidling up to buy his own.

"No troubles?" Boruin asked.

The Mana'Olai shook his head. "We need to find a place to stay."

"Done," Wraethe answered. "My young friend knows a fine apartment overlooking the Oriune River." They turned to find Wraethe had replaced her furs with a light cloak and leathers that seemed to trace her curves rather than cover them. The young man carrying her purchases stood flushed and open-mouthed.

Boruin eyed the dressings with a frown. "I hope you paid for that by the yard," he said. The woman smiled, but her eyes were cold toward him. She was not in a teasing mood. Pile wandered up from behind, smiling.

"Not bad, if you are going to whore it up toni—" Wraethe's quick slap snapped across Pile's cheek. His face burned red at the rebuke. "More right than I thought," he said, turning back to the casks of ale. Wraethe headed farther into the market without a word. Diun's pale light set her skin to burn lustfully as she passed each watching man. Her young attendant followed behind.

"At least we don't attract much attention," Toaaho said. They waited for Wraethe's admirers to turn back to their wares before heading after her.

Boruin stood on the balcony three stories above the Oriune where it raced through the southern end of the city. The river roared out of the mountains so quickly that the cautious Easlinders had set high railings along its banks. If you fell into the frigid Oriune, they might find your pieces days later where the river slowed at the Mana'Olai border.

The three-room suite was large enough to fit them all comfortably. White-washed clay walls had darkened to a hazy brown, but at least the dust in the corners betrayed no mice prints. The boy settled on a deep windowsill. He lay on musty sheets scrounged from the closet and watched out the window as men moved stone into boats with tall wooden cranes and lumbering habback. This block seemed to function as the border where the city's sprawling gardens deferred to its shipping interests. The old building loomed beside the river in the last of the ancient groves, while stone and ore yards shored up its back.

Though timber and mining had built Easlinder, the capital was kept as a showpiece of the country's wilderness. They'd followed Wraethe's man through prairie glades, primal groves, and strange flats where gardens of stone and water blended like twin elements. The trees were old men with sprawling, muscular branches. Homes and shops nestled under the knotted boughs. Some larger buildings rose around the trunks and into the crown, like a heavy winter coat sprouting branches out of buttonholes, pockets, and sleeves. The Easlinders had built the city into the land rather than across it.

The rilk, rock creatures still new to the Duine of the surface lands, had apprenticed them in that task. Their hard hands and graveled voices had shaped the rock gardens that rose in flowing forms to mirror the running water. The city's stone buildings were all shaped by the rilk's influence, built by their guidance. Tall towers and squat buildings alike were fluid, as if rock was a creature of motion somehow caught naked by one's eye and scared to move. It seemed likely that the soft lines had gradually shifted over time, growing fuller curves or longer cascades.

The people moving along the boulevards, and the rilk through the tunnels below, were another claim to harmony. Northern Yuinites walked with the Mana'Olai, their rejection of Pileaus, the self-proclaimed God Emperor, acceptable to the southerners, who had many gods already. The small peace achieved in the high mountains of Easlinder was a welcome change from bickering Nefazo.

Down on the street, Wraethe kissed her young attendant on the cheek. He almost tripped over his feet as he raced back to the market to find Pile and supply their address. Wraethe loped slowly along the cobblestones, giving a somber-robed Yuinite priest a wink and a long look as she passed. His fellow held him tight around his waist to keep him from following. Priyati was a prowling ground tonight; more than a few young men would fall into lust unimagined.

Boruin hoped they would tide her over until they could get out of town. Takata Shin was just caressing the edge of Diun and would not be visible much longer. It would be nice to have turned over the boy to the right people by then. Paid, gone, and Wraethe free to lay waste to an empty jungle would be best. But Boruin rarely achieved what was best, and he mulled over what he might have to do otherwise.

Wraethe's errand boy returned, hanging around the corner to watch for her. He lingered until Pile arrived and ran him off. Wraethe would be in no mood for the youth when Diun set and she returned. Boruin wondered if that was Pile's intention or if he simply disliked Wraethe's affections for anyone, feigned or not.

Boruin moved within grabbing distance as Pile stumbled onto the balcony and leaned back on the railing. "That contract house is east of the river near the rilk colony," he said.

"What's their business?"

"No news of that. It's a small place, a front for a company further north called Undurlund, I guess. Nobody knew nothin' else," Pile said.

Boruin snapped his fingers, and Pile's face came down from the sky to land on his eye. "Easy around Wraethe for a bit. She's a little on edge."

Pile pushed himself away from the rail. "Over, I'd say. Plummeting to rutting madness, *I'd* say," he slurred as he rambled back toward his room, dropping clothes as he went. The drunk collapsed onto his bed, asleep before he could get his other boot off. Boruin settled into a chair. He watched the moon drop slowly and fell asleep listening for the sound of Wraethe's long stride on the cobblestones.

Dawn found Boruin in his chair. He awoke with a start, shaking half-forgotten dreams into pieces. He spat the taste of stale wine from his mouth and took the cup of dark tea Pile offered him. The short man kept one hand over his squinting eyes as if the light were a liquid pain seeping into his head. He sat on the floor and leaned against the wall, sipping from his own cup. The boy and Toaaho played a game of sliding stones, though the boy kept getting up to watch the workers by the river as Toaaho considered his move.

"Wraethe?"

Pile's hand switched eyes. "Raced in with the first light like it would catch her on fire," he said.

"How'd she look?"

"Fine, I guess. What do you mean?"

Boruin didn't answer, and Pile's head was too thick to remember, or care, that he'd asked a question.

When he was ready, Boruin went to her room and checked Wraethe's hands himself. Her eyes rose as he looked for blood under her fingernails. He watched her watching him and waited to see if she would wake, waited to see if her anger would stretch into the daylight. Instead her eyes dulled back into distant sleep. There was no blood. *Must have found enough fun to tide her over*, he thought.

"You be good tonight. Try to behave," he said, though he was sure she wouldn't hear. He wondered what tonight would be like. Takata Shin would be gone either this evening or the next. Nurom Misuer would rule her house, and she would rage like the Emperor burning across the north. He wanted to rush to the contract house and deliver the boy, but he knew that was the wrong move. There had been no sign of Belok, but he had to be in town.

Boruin left Wraethe to her rest and returned to the main suite. "Toaaho, I want you to find the Undurlund trade house and a discrete way to get there and back. Camp out and see if it's being watched."

"Why not rush it? Get in the door and we're done, right?" Pile asked.

"No telling what Belok might have put together. I'd rather wait until Wraethe can join us."

"So she can seduce them to death?" Pile added.

Boruin smiled despite himself. "Whatever it takes."

Toaaho came back as the sun was setting and found the rest ready to go.

"Anything special?" Boruin asked. Toaaho had little to say. There had been two visitors to the contract house, but neither hung around. Patrons of the scant shops and bazaars nearby shopped quickly and moved on. The contract house abutted a cliff near the rilk colony. The stone face made for few places to watch from. It seemed safe.

Boruin slipped an extra knife underneath the back of his vest. "Doesn't mean Belok isn't there. He might know we wouldn't come without Wraethe awake this time. We'll just have to chance it," he said.

"I hope he's there. I could use something to get my blood up," Wraethe said. Pile snorted but did not say more and ignored her hard look.

They crossed the Oriune in a loose gathering. As he climbed the Iron Bridge, Boruin watched the shops that lined both sides of the wide stone arch. At the high peak of the bridge, the top flattened where four Easlinder commodity houses ruled the ore market that named the bridge. Far-traveled merchants traded wares, coins, and promissory bills for more ore than just iron. The relationship with the subterranean rilk had benefited Easlinder through more than just architectural aesthetics.

The Nefazo merchants yelling their bids above the Oriune paid no attention to anyone that wasn't a trader of the four main houses. So, when the boy pestered Boruin, pulling on his fingers, he gave in and lifted him up on his shoulders, hoping it wouldn't become habit.

Toaaho kept them away from the main avenues, leading them through small residential parks and thin streets just busy enough that they couldn't be attacked without witness. Boruin would have preferred empty back alleys.

Diun was fully borne over the eastern horizon, and Boruin saw that damn Trickster moon barely peeking out from behind its bigger cousin. This was the last day it would give that moon-spun woman satisfaction.

Wraethe attracted every man that crossed her path. Those that didn't see her at first found her sauntering close so they would. She flirted as she had for the last few weeks, but now it was desperate.

Her natural grace had devolved, her walk now a slink too wide in the hips. A few men responded to her advances with disgust, easily mistaking her for a wayward woman. Those she chided and chased with her cussing tongue down the street. One she slapped for being too embarrassed to look her in the eye. When Boruin approached her, she calmed, feigning a playful tease. Somehow, they reached the stone cliffs at the north edge of the city without incident.

They watched for men in the shadows, for streets too quiet, and for silhouettes on rooftops. Instead they found people hurrying home for the evening meal. Boruin looked up to see Pile standing on a merchant's step, "Undurlund" painted in faded blue letters on the sign hanging over the doorway.

"How's the evening, father?" asked a meandering man of Mana'Olai blood. He looked too young in the face to be a lawman, but the constable's crest on his breast said otherwise.

Boruin smiled but kept on toward the door. "Fine, isn't it?" he answered.

"Out with your son?" a second voice asked. Boruin turned to face the speaker. His deputy crest shined in the moonlight. Another man with the same crest strode out of a shop across the street. Pile stepped back down from Underlund's doorstep.

"Thought we'd stretch our legs before dinner," Boruin replied. "Turns out mine got all the stretching, though he's got the energy." He reached up to the boy on his shoulders and tugged a bit on his dangling feet.

The deputy smiled with a nod of understanding. "You from around here?"

"Visiting."

"From Nefazo?"

"Mana'Olai."

"Huh," said the constable. "Word is a small company came down out of the mountains."

The deputy jumped back in, still smiling. "You'd cross the pass in winter just for a visit?"

"I told you, we came from the south. No snow there."

Boruin wondered if he was in a juggling show as the constable took the lead again. "Pretty sure I heard you came from the west. That lady there traded a lot of furs in the market." He pointed to Wraethe. "These the others that came with you?" he asked as Pile and Toaaho started walking toward the group.

"We *four* have been traveling together. Does that concern you *three*?" Boruin asked. The constable shrugged and went to brush his hair out of his eyes. Boruin recognized the movement, knew it would be a truth ward, but it was too late. The man quickly sketched the Skuwari on his brow and the sigil caught Boruin's gaze. It spun on the man's forehead, pulled his eyes to the constable's and held them there. More men appeared out of the shops. Wraethe, Pile, and Toaaho stepped closer together.

"Why are you in Priyati?" asked the young constable. He, like his deputies, had tossed aside the smile. He stood rigid, his body tight with the strength it took to hold Boruin in the Skuwari. His face, though, was calm, his eyes cold like a deep well. The old fighter now did not think the Mana'Olai lawman was as young, or as green, as he'd hoped.

"I'm contracted to escort this boy here," Boruin answered, his lips moving even though his mind clamped down to try and hold his words.

"By whom?"

"The Undurlund Trade Company."

"Not with a Nefazo merchant?"

"Initially, but originating through Undurlund." *Rutting Belok. Here's the man's play*, Boruin thought.

"So you renegotiated your contract with the merchant?"

"For Yuin's sake, Boruin," Pile muttered behind him.

Boruin tried to bite his tongue, tried to answer that Belok had skewed the contract to try and cut him out, but he had to answer the question as it was. "No, we fled town."

"Do you know the penalty for breaking a contract and fleeing across borders?"

"Hanging," Boruin said, though he knew no trade court would support Belok's attempt to hijack the contract.

Fury twisted the constable's face. "And for slavery?" asked the constable. *Rutting son of Yuin's whore!* Boruin thought as the constable pulled Belok's trump. There was no worse crime among the Mana'Olai. Their civilization had escaped from ages of servitude not long ago.

"Flogging, hanging, burning alive."

"Yes, at our discretion," the constable said, his voice thin and hard. He pulled a rolled parchment from his vest. Boruin did not have to see the writing to know it was a copy of Toaaho's writ. Belok must have stored a copy away for good measure.

"Toaaho. That man there?" the constable asked.

"Yes."

"And he's from Priyati, as the merchant says?"

"Yes."

"He could be one of our brothers, you worthless rat! What's his whole name?" Boruin tightened his chest, willing his lungs to cramp and hold in the air. The veins in his neck throbbed as the words escaped.

"Toaaho Köpeka," he managed to whisper.

"What?" the constable asked. His eyes tightened, and Boruin could feel the Skuwari reaching down into his gut to drag the word out louder.

"Köpeka!" he shouted. The constable's eyes widened. The man at his side blanched, his face a ghostly white under Diun's shine. He stumbled back into another deputy, and they both began to run. Boruin heard the men's fleeing boot heels fade down the distant street and his heart sank. The constable did not notice. The name had stunned him like a child's nightmare climbing out of the shadows. Köpeka was a curse word to him–worse than the thought of a slaver. They were the deceivers, the betrayers of the Mana'Olai. His eyes broke contact for a moment as this feared name shook him. Boruin took advantage of the lapse.

No longer bound to the Skuwari by the man's eyes, Boruin slapped the constable across his brow, smearing the ward. He dropped the boy from his shoulders and drew his sword in one motion. His troupe was at his back in the same second. They faced outward at the constable and his men, a small circle of steel surrounded by an outnumbering wheel of opposing blades.

The constable swirled his arms as if spinning air into a vortex. Boruin felt the wind of it pass over him and then a frightening stillness. Their breath sounded too loud in his ears, and he reached out and jammed his finger on nothing. Pile thrust his sword, testing a near deputy, and his blade rebounded dangerously close to Toaaho's thigh. This new spell surrounded them, a sphere of dense air they could not see or pass. It held them trapped like fish in a tank on a butcher's live meat counter.

"A Wa'Ha'Wae," Toaaho muttered.

"A Waha what?" Pile asked.

"A sorcerer. We walked into magi," Wraethe said.

"You said nothing of a Köpeka!" the constable shouted over Boruin's shoulder.

"No doubt I would have told a more profitable party had I known," Belok said, stepping out of a dry goods shop. "All the same, I leave them to your care. I am just pleased to be able to fulfill my contract."

"I'm sure," the constable said with a snap of his fingers. Boruin had the sensation of slipping, as if he had blinked his eyes and stepped a foot to the side without realizing it.

"How did he do that?" Pile asked. Boruin turned his head to see the constable handing the boy over to Belok. He turned about, looking around him. His mind would not believe that the magi constable had snatched the boy away in some missing moment. He heard a rumble and knew Wraethe's short temper was long gone. She was winding up and being trapped inside the constable's spell with her was going to be bad.

"Hold yourself. We can't start murdering lawmen. I can still talk us around this," Boruin told her.

"Talk all you want, fool. It's done us so well already," Wraethe replied.

He held the original contract, lifted from Belok's office. "The boy is my ward," he said. "I've been contracted by this house. It's binding to my name and non-transferable." Another snap of his fingers, and the constable was glancing over the paper.

"Just like Tradesman Boruin's copy."

"Sorry, who?"

"Boruin," the constable answered, pointing at Belok. Belok smiled wide, trying to enjoy the moment while holding the squirming child to keep him from chasing a glow moth skirting the cobblestone.

"This guy right here is Boruin," Pile shouted. "That guy is Belok! He's the one cutting in on our contract!"

"Except he's got an Easlinder merchant pass in his name and a Nefazo trade guild card. Four other merchants witnessed him in my office just last week. You have your pass?"

"No," answered Boruin.

"Guild card?"

"No"

"Any respectable witness?"

"No."

"You're free to fulfill your contract, Tradesman Boruin," the constable said without looking at Belok. In his anger, the man kept looking between Toaaho and Boruin as if trying to weigh evils.

"Thank you for your assistance," Belok answered. "I'll sleep well knowing your justice has amended this situation." The boy walked into the trade house, his hand curled around Belok's, unconcerned. *Simple fool*, Boruin thought, though his anger was not really for the boy. He wasn't ready to let him go. There were too many questions left.

The invisible sphere pulled them into motion as the constable started walking. The fish tank was now on wheels; they'd been picked for dinner. "Toaaho isn't my slave. I bought his writ to get him out. He'll tell you the same," Boruin said.

"No doubt. I'm sure he's very well-behaved," the lawman answered. He turned down a long avenue and Boruin could see it end with the Iron Bridge arching high over the Oriune.

"Knock him down, and I'll let you have this," Wraethe said to the accompanying deputies, pulling aside her thin shirt. Though the men blushed at her display, they all sneered or looked away. She threw herself at the wall of containment, clawing out at the men.

"Can you make a separate spell for me, for Yuin's mercy?" Pile yelled at the constable, ducking as Wraethe's sharp nails sailed over his head. Toaaho snatched out and took her hand, holding it carefully. She calmed a moment as he whispered to her, and then they both threw themselves at the wall. The magi slowed, but the spell held.

"Would you just listen a moment?" Boruin yelled as he and Pile too shoved against the back wall of the spell. The four hit the invisible sphere together, stopping the magi constable short on the first step of the Iron Bridge. He spun with a curse.

"What can you say? You answered under the Skuwari. You could not have lied, and I know all I need to know. You can dispute Tradesman Boruin's accusations before the judges, but even if they dismiss the contract breaches and the slaver's charge, which they won't, there is still the Köpeka. I've never seen a less promising chance for defense."

"He can't be judged just on a name," Pile said.

"Not a name. *The* name. Those that kept us as slaves to the Kukane'Haku. The deliverer stamped them out. Alaka'i Mei destroyed them and led us from the God-Kings."

"Maybe I misunderstood," Boruin said.

"You would have not said Köpeka if you did not believe it."

"Then ask me why I believe it," Boruin said. The constable looked puzzled, but sketched the truth ward again across his forehead.

"How is he a Köpeka?"

"It is true they deceived their own people, but no less than they deceived themselves. They fled with the Dabattu, and when they found the Makua'Moi had followed, the destruction of that cult became their path to redemption. The Köpeka remained in secret to stand against the Makua'Moi, to destroy them and the last link to the Kukane'Haku. All but Toaaho died here, in Priyati, doing just that."

The constable turned his gaze to Toaaho. "Does he say the truth?"

"Yes. My family came soon after Priyati was founded, hiding in the flush of new migrants. They'd hoped to grow the family stronger, for their long war against Makua'Moi had as many losses as it had victories. It did not last. The Makua'Moi grew too strong in Mana'Olai, in our absence. When we were found, my family could not stand against them."

The young man looked away and wiped the ward from his skin. His shoulders sagged, but he still held the force sphere around them. "Your belief does not make truth. Tonight has brought too many of the old evils. I don't have the heart to hear more. It is not my place to weigh this. It must be decided before the judges."

"There is no trial needed." An old man stood leaning on his cane at the top of the arched bridge. The avenue had emptied, save for a few watchers peeking from shops and the ore houses on the bridge's back.

"Your honor, I was bringing these charges to the courthouse."

"I heard," said the judge as he walked slowly down the steps. Two deputies walked behind as if to catch the frail judge if needed. Boruin recognized them; they'd run from the constable's side at sound of Toaaho's family name. "A slaver, a thief, a whore, and a legendary Köpeka. Their fates are easily decided."

"They have answered under a ward of truth," the lawman said as he walked them up to meet the judge. "They should be reviewed before the council."

"Yes, the Skuwari. That has always been your specialty, Eloni. I have no doubt that you brought the truth out of them. Did they deny their crimes?"

"No, but—"

"No need for a courtroom," the judge said as he continued down the steps toward them. "These crimes are punished with death. They are dangerous. Look at how the whore paces. She'd tear your throat if given the chance. Tighten your spell, Eloni."

The constable stepped back. "Your honor, they cannot be put to death without trial."

"And who would seat the trial? I have made my decision. I will not change it," said the judge.

"I can't just kill—"

"Do it!" yelled the judge.

"But, your honor!"

The judge raised his cane and slammed it down on the stone. The bridge bucked, and the spell knocked the constable off his feet. His head slammed against the rock. Boruin felt the air relax around him.

The judge's tongue lashed out old words and a hail of burning stars rained down on the bridge. Pile dove through a shop window, and Wraethe followed. Boruin checked his run as Toaaho grabbed the constable. They rolled him under a stone bench before leaping into the storefront. Three deputies fell, struck down by the hot stones still burning inside them.

"Makua'Moi," said Toaaho.

"And not just one," said Wraethe, her cruel smile wide and joyous. She dashed up a ladder and onto the roof as a crowd swarmed over the arch of the bridge. Their eyes were wide and frenzied behind bloodied masks that hid their faces. Boruin heard Wraethe's feet running across the roof and then nothing as she launched into the air.

Wraethe came down in the mass of men, her sword slinging through flesh. Pile was out the door as the last stones bounced across the cobbles. His axe was buried in a man's chest before Boruin could draw his own blade. It had been awhile since last they'd fought so outnumbered, and Boruin felt the familiar rush of fear and desperation. His eyes widened with madness and he screamed as he entered the street.

Toaaho ducked the clawing grasp of a deputy. Fire filled the man, sparks flying from his mouth as he stumbled after the Mana'Olai. The three struck by the judge's brimstone had yet to die. The stones burned inside them, but the Makua'Moi sorcerer had kept them alive. Their bodies fought while their mouths screamed of their souls' anguish.

Toaaho darted in and cut, spinning out again as burning guts poured onto the bridge. The body lurched on, dragging its entrails down the rough street to collapse in the doorway of a tailor's shop and setting the building aflame.

A hard kick scorched Toaaho's boot but sent the second deputy tumbling back into the third. The dead, burning creature roared, the intense heat shattering its teeth, launching them out to skitter across the stone. Its lips peeled back in blackening curls from its steaming jawbone. The Mana'Olai danced around its groping arms and sliced through its cooking hamstrings. It fell back, and Toaaho turned over a stone bench to pin it as the coals burned its body down to cinders.

The last deputy sat on his knees, abandoned by the judge, and Toaaho left it retching fire out a hole burned through its throat. Tears streamed out of its baked-white eyes to rise into steam off the cheekbones. The night air caught up its flaming hair and lifted, the ash of it turning up into the sky, red cinders winking.

Toaaho ran up the bridge, leaping onto a stone lintel and vaulting over Wraethe's circle of enemies. The two fighters drove a wide berth around themselves, cutting open the tight knots of men that tried to overwhelm their position. They began to turn like dancers, their blades shredding those that dared close and attack. Blood ran thick down the cobblestones as the two worked through the mob.

The old judge, the Makua'Moi sorcerer, dropped to his knees. He cupped the blood in his withered hands and spread it across his face. When he looked up again his eyes were on Boruin and his hands flung the blood toward him.

The drops hardened into shards at the old man's hissed command. Boruin dropped to his knees to duck most and swung his sword in what he knew would be a vain attempt to deflect the rest. The shards exploded into dust as the constable's spell of dense air rose just before Boruin. The judge snarled at Eloni's interference.

Blinking back the dark tunnels before his eyes, the constable dragged himself out from under the bench. The lawman's legs shook as he stood, but he drew his sword as the judge's men turned toward him. The judge gathered two handfuls of blood and tossed them again toward Boruin. The force of the blood crashing against Eloni's spell knocked the lawman back on his heels, but the wall of air held, protecting his prisoner.

The constable's sword tip dropped off-guard and Boruin knew the man could not defend them both. *This is not enough*, Boruin thought. Pile swung out and caught one man in the back as he passed, headed for the lawman. The other bowled over the constable, and the shield faded back into nothing.

Pile stumbled as a pommel caught him in the head. He dropped, dazed, to his knee. Wraethe screamed with pleasure as a blade caught her thigh and pain lanced through her. Toaaho fell and rolled, cutting out wildly beneath swords and spear tips.

"This is not enough!" Boruin cried as the judge took another handful of his men's blood. The runes fell into his palm as he pulled on the long cordon of spells. He imagined the spell he wanted, willed the driving wind that would blow the judge off the bridge and into the Oriune. Boruin saw the Monarhig in his mind and prayed for that wind.

"I must be more," he whispered to himself and to the mass of burning runes crushed between both palms. He threw the spell outward, but his hands flashed into flame. The wind was dead calm as the fire walked up his forearms. The judge swung his handful of needled blood, and Boruin stood holding his flaming arms away from his body, roaring in pain. The blood sizzled as it fell on the fire and was devoured. The flames climbed higher, and Boruin held out his arms, watching the fire consume him. "Oh, Yuin!" he cried through grinding teeth. *I've finally killed myself*!

"By Hammeoto," the judge whispered. The fire burning across Boruin was not Wa'Ha'Wae magic. He could hear the flames whispering hungry words. With his sorcerer's eyes, he saw the flames for the summoned fire imps they were. Flickering and dancing across Boruin's skin, the creatures growled and gnashed their glowing teeth. This was a magic too strong and unknown to him. "Kill him quickly!" he roared. The Makua'Moi ran down the bridge in a wave.

Boruin forgot the searing pain as the first man drove his spear forward to impale him. Habit brought the old fighter's hand to his hilt. He drew the sword and sidestepped the sharp point. The flames ran down his fingers, running across his blade as he swung. The Makua'Moi's flesh sizzled and cauterized as the steel parted him in half.

The constable was on the ground, straddled by his attacker. As the man beat his fists against Eloni's face, Boruin cut through the top of his head with an easy swing. The blade carried around to parry the next man aiming for Boruin's heart. Landing in the flame, the attacker's sword began to glow. Before the Makua'Moi could drop his weapon, the fire licked over the hilt as if sensing dry timber. It lapped across the man's wrist, his skin seared, and the flame raced up his arm and over his face. The fire took him like he was a paper man with oil for blood and dry parchment bones.

Boruin began to swing again as the first wave of rushing Makua'Moi stalled before the flaming man. Those behind pressed them into stumbling forward. The eager flame ate flesh and Boruin's steel cut through what was left.

Wraethe and Toaaho fought to the top of the bridge and turned, driving the Makua'Moi down toward Boruin's fire. Several peeled away their masks, pleading not to be struck down. Wraethe pulled these closest to her and killed them as they felt her hot breath on their lips. Others dove through the shops, leaping for the cold hands of the Oriune rather than meet the pale woman or the flaming sword.

The ranks of the Makua'Moi thinned until Boruin pulled his sword up short on the judge. The suffocating man's face was swollen with blood, his lips blue. Boruin saw his hands weaving useless spells that swirled and mixed in a small pocket of used up air. Behind him, the constable was tightening his fists, the spell choking down around the judge's hands and neck.

Boruin rammed his sword back into his scabbard. As his mind turned from the bloodshed and threat of death, the flame sputtered out with a distant sigh as if its plate was emptied, its appetite sated. Boruin placed an easy hand on the constable's arm.

"Eloni, you'll do more damage to them if he lives," he said.

"They should not be here! We built Priyati as a place of peace with the rilk!"

"They came for the Köpeka," Boruin said.

"You see now, our belief is truth," Toaaho added. "The Makua'Moi fight against me, because my family was their enemy of old. They would have the God-Kings return, not the Köpeka."

"There will be more, Eloni. Killing him will only rob you of a chance to find them," said Boruin.

Silence held for a moment, then the constable dropped his spell. The judge gulped down hungry, ragged lungfuls of air. Eloni tied the judge's hands behind him, separating each sorcerous finger, and kicked him over into the gutter.

Dark bruises stained the constable's face, but this evening his heart had taken the worst beating. "So many old enemies. Who can I trust?" he asked.

"No one. Keep watch. They will come for him and kill him if needed so that they may stay hidden," said Toaaho.

"With any luck, they will be after us anyway," Pile said, wiping the blood from his axe.

The constable's shoulders slumped. "You really think there are more?"

"I doubt they raised everyone on five minutes' notice. I imagine some are still gathering," Pile said. Boruin had not considered that, and he scanned the people creeping out of houses and shops to gawk at the battle's aftermath.

"So let's call this even," Boruin said. "You let us escape, and we'll get out of town."

"Go then. I've got work enough to do," Eloni answered, and pushed the judge across the bridge and out of sight.

Boruin turned to hurry back to Underlund's, but found Wraethe stalking the wounded. He approached carefully as she pushed her knife into a man's breast, her hand slow and gentle. She smiled, watching him gag and then still as his life slipped from her wound.

"Wraethe."

"What?"

"Wouldn't it be best to give rites rather than quicken the dead?"

"We have time for my rites?" Her eyes darted between the dying. Her lips were a tight smile that matched the pain-drawn grins of the dead around them too well.

"I think we'll make time. For your own good."

"My good," she said slowly, as if considering the sentiment. Boruin saw her catch him with the corner of her eye. It gave him a needed second to lean back on his heels as she turned and lunged. He spun aside and slapped her hard on the face as she passed. Wraethe fell to the stone. When she looked up at him her face was pure fury. He knelt over her.

"Remember who your friends are," Boruin said. She sneered, saliva dripping from her lips. She was horrible. It sickened Boruin to look on her like this, but if he broke from her eyes, she would try and kill him. It was the only thing visible in her face. "Your rites, and then we go for Belok and the boy."

The steel went out of her body, and she lay back in the blood. "Sick rutter, I'll take Belok. Have your way with your precious boy."

"Your rites!" he demanded, returning to his feet.

"You're probably tired of Pile anyway," Wraethe said as she knelt before her last kill. Boruin watched her begin the rites that would wash some of the blood rage from her soul. She was hasty and flippant, but it was something. Nurom Misuer was consuming her, and Boruin knew that her soul needed all the forgiveness it could receive.

"What did she say about me?" Pile asked.

"Don't ask," Boruin replied as Wraethe moved from body to body.

"Boss?"

"What, Pile?"

"Your scabbard is smoking."

- 9 -
STONE AND BLOOD

Pile was first to see Belok's huge guard standing on Undurlund's doorstep.

"I told you, Boruin! I told you he was a big rutter! He thought he got an ass-kicking last—" Pile was cut short by the pale woman sliding out of the shadows. Wraethe slipped behind the man and swung her arm around his shoulder to slit his throat. The man fell, gurgling blood, and Wraethe kicked him off the step.

"You at least could have challenged him!" Pile said. "I mean, he was a mean bastard, but a good fighter. He deserved better than that!"

Wraethe's eyes seemed to glow red like a stoked ember. "When I need your advice on how to kill a man, I'll pick it out of your head with my knife," she spat. Pile held his tongue.

As Wraethe rolled the enormous body behind the barrels of a merchant's shop, Boruin took Toaaho aside. They watched her give her rites to the dead man. She knelt, still shaking with the kill. Boruin watched for the calm after the prayer, but it was barely detectable.

"I can't take her in there like this. Can you hold her? Keep her from killing any innocents?"

Toaaho looked as if he'd been asked to swallow the sea or wring wine from stone, but he said the only thing he could. "I'll do what I can."

"This will be quick or it will be over," Boruin added as he headed for the door.

Pile grabbed his arm. "What's the plan?" he asked.

Boruin shrugged. "We turn this over on Belok, or we take the boy and run."

"And the money?"

"Let's see what happens."

Pile groaned. "Don't tell me we might not get paid after six months of work. Don't tell me this might be for nothing, Boruin."

"Maybe you can take down Wraethe. There's bound to be a bounty on her if we don't leave soon," Boruin answered, joking but feeling more truth there than he liked.

A man on the inside turned as the front door opened into the small reception hall. His eyes widened from curiosity to surprise as he recognized the old warrior striding across the floor. Boruin snatched out, grabbing an ornate earring with one hand and shoving him in the chest with the other. The man bounced off the wall. Pile caught him and slapped a palm over his open mouth. The Nefazo merchant held his scream as Pile fondled the other string of gems dangling from his last earlobe.

"Now that you are properly focused on this situation," Boruin said, "I want to ask you something. I want you to take it seriously. Where is Belok?" The merchant nodded over his shoulder. Pile turned him with the earring and headed for a curtained doorway.

"We're wasting time here, Toaaho. The Makua'Moi are getting ready and we're sitting still," Wraethe growled as she paced back and forth in front of the doorstep. "Look at all the people staring. They want to see if you Köpeka are as fierce as legend says." Blood oozed from her palms, her nails biting deep into her skin.

"You just killed a man. They're scared."

"They're not watching me," she said. "Can you see the ones in the shadows? I can see their eyes, Toaaho. They're watching you." Toaaho kept his mouth shut, but Wraethe knew she had a crack started, and she kept chipping. "Haven't you trained for this fight all of your life? Let's spill some more blood, Toaaho. I'm ready."

"Evening," Boruin said as they walked quickly through the greeting room and past a stunned clerk. The man jumped up to follow, halted as he saw the blood dripping across the shoulder of Pile's hostage, then began to stutter.

"St-st-stop. An appointment is necessary—"

Pile shoved the bleeding man on and they moved deeper into the building. Clerks and contract officers leaned out of their doors as Pile pushed the merchant quickly past. The small secretary chased after in silence, having given up his request for them to stop. Boruin watched for any brave enough to step out of their offices; none did. Their job was contracts.

When the weeping Nefazo pointed to the next doorway, the greeter made one more plea for their attention as Boruin kicked their hostage through the entrance. The curtain tore from above as the man fell yelling onto a gravel courtyard. Boruin stepped into the large garden, ornate boulders set evenly across the open yard. Small trees rose from the edges to spread across the Diuntyne sky. Belok and another man sat at a long, central table. Ten men stood with weapons drawn, guarding them. Their job was not contracts.

"You must be Belok, the gentleman Merchant Boruin claims stole the boy," said the man seated opposite the Nefazo merchant. He, like the constable, was of Mana'Olai blood. The Underlund's chief sat with his hands folded, his wrinkled face calm despite Boruin's violent entrance.

"I am Boruin. He's Belok." Boruin replied.

"Well, whoever you are, you owe me a new curtain."

"I don't think this is going to be quick," Pile whispered.

"Where's the boy?" Boruin asked. The boy jumped from behind a large boulder on Belok's side of the table. He waved and climbed up the knotted rock to sit and watch.

"I'm Merchant Oni," said the chief. "I assume you and this gentleman are familiar with each other. If you will have a seat, perhaps we can solve this dilemma."

"As I said before," Belok began, "Constable Eloni validated my identity—though I imagine him dead if these two are free. There is a woman and a Mana'Olai somewhere about, Merchant Oni, and I cannot advise strongly enough that they are most dangerous."

"And yet it is you that I'm most worried about," Oni said.

Belok leaned back in his chair, his face a controlled look of pleasant innocence, but Boruin could sense the man's unease. The guards watched the Nefazo almost as if he might spring over the table and slaughter the Undurlund chief. Boruin had opened his mouth to refute Belok's claim, but thought better of protesting and took a wordless seat at the table.

Oni stared into the garden, watching the boy climb about on the large boulder. "Do you, sir, have any identification that can support your claim?" he asked.

"No, sir, I haven't," Boruin replied.

"Merchant Boruin's papers seem to be in fair order. We hired Merchant Laques," Oni gestured to the man on the floor, "to deliver the contract to Nefazo. He has assured us that Merchant Boruin is our man."

"And one Nefazo merchant vouching for another carries a lot of weight in Easlinder?" Boruin asked. Oni gave a slight smile.

Belok jumped at the opening. "As a slave owner, you are hardly one to judge moral bias. Especially when you own one of the famed Köpeka!" said Belok. His smile was snake-like, wide and tight.

Oni continued on as if the Nefazo hadn't spoken. "The boy seems equally friendly to you both, so how will you convince me that you are Boruin?"

"I have no material proof, but I don't think I need it," Boruin said.

Belok laughed. "Perhaps you could explain that to all of us." Oni raised his eyebrows in agreement and waited with his hands folded.

"You paid a great deal to have the boy brought here," Boruin answered. "You paid a lot *specifically* to have my people do it. You wouldn't have sent Merchant Laques, a Nefazo courier, if you couldn't identify me when I arrived." He hadn't considered that until he saw Belok looking so worried. He bet it hadn't occurred to him, either, until Oni had called his guards.

Oni leaned forward. "So then you can guess my true worry: is this Belok just a swindler or something much more dangerous?"

"I can assure you that he is a dangerous swindler," Boruin answered with a smile at Belok. The merchant was fuming.

"If you think you can deny me, you are wrong!" Belok snarled, showering the table with spittle as his mouth continued flying. "This man has no proof of his claim! What's happening here is a violation of every trade negotiation and contract law! I have proven my personage to the Easlinder customs house, received my visa. How can you claim that he, unproven and untrustworthy, is me?"

"There are signs to be read, Belok," Oni said, wiping his hands dry. "You do not possess them."

"Treason! This is a breach of the highest order, and I demand a hearing before the trade courts! The merchant's jury will never allow such a malfeasance!" Belok roared, rising in his seat though the guards began to surround him.

Oni turned toward Boruin. "I think now that what you said to the constable is proven true, Merchant Boruin."

"You heard that?"

"Of course," Oni replied, "but we could not make judgment at that time. I am afraid our unpreparedness caused you some difficulty. For that, I apologize." He bowed his head until it almost touched the stone table.

"Your apology is unnecessary, but I thank you."

"I demand your proof!" Belok shouted. His face was now red and a vein rose in his neck like a whale about to breach the surface.

"Will you oblige him?" Oni asked. "I'll admit, we are most curious to see your markings as well." Boruin's smile faded with a look of confusion and then dropped altogether as he understood. They sat waiting for his reply as his mind began to run like it was falling downhill.

Who knew of his runes? Few had seen them, and for most it was fleeting glimpse, as if their eyes had decided against it at the last moment. Those usually shook their heads and forgot.

In Ouilainne, a sailor had once followed him through the entire Cabere district, from the docks to the leathers market. The man had actually risen from his whore and followed, proclaiming his devotion and faith. For three days Boruin had quite a little church until Wraethe returned from a moon rage in the swamps and put an end to it. No one but the sailor had really been able to see anything; the other devotees he gathered were addle-brained and half-wits, but Boruin almost had to break the sailor's fingers to keep him from copying his runes in the dirt. No other had seen his secret so clearly—not until the boy. *Someone from before.* That was the answer; there could be no other.

"All right," Boruin said, holding out his arm. The boy was hanging off the boulder, grinning at him, but that didn't mean he had made the right choice.

HAOBRUUM! The sound washed across the garden and passed over them like a gust of wind. Boruin's arm flared blue. The runes cast their light across the garden stones, driving shadows up against the walls. They blazed across his skin, a glowing ribbon of thick swirls and angles. Oni's slight smile returned and Belok's jaw dropped. The light lasted only just longer than the echo, and then Pile was rubbing the afterimage from his eyes. With the blue light gone, Belok's face was pale. Oni snapped his fingers and the guards pushed Belok toward the door. The Nefazo didn't say a word, though his wide eyes stayed locked on Boruin until he was gone.

Boruin's mouth was moving before he could find the breath to speak. "How did you do that? How did you know?"

"That was not in my power," Oni replied, turning his smile toward his companions. "It takes one very studied in rune lore to accomplish such a revelation. May I introduce you?"

Boruin nodded, looking around the empty garden. Oni rose and gestured behind Belok.

The boulder under the boy unfolded from the floor. The rock creature rose from its crouch, climbing to its feet and hauling the boy up off its lap by the back of his shirt. The rilk was enormous, standing taller than the ceiling if there had been one. His body was spectacular, a strange grace in its movement despite its rocky composition. The child held his arms out like wings and kicked his feet as if he were swimming through the air. His giggling filled the awkward silence.

"Your contract was brought to Undurlund by the rilk. Griant is their representative, and the one able to see your runes," Oni explained.

"Griant," Boruin said, repeating it before it was painted over by the astonishment of what he was seeing.

The rilk spoke, his voice a deep rumble like a thunderstorm over the hills. "Boruin, your runes are very beautiful, very brahgheen."

"Brahgheen is dense, though I imagine he means it as strong in this context," Oni said.

Boruin crossed the garden. "Thank you," he said. The rilk seemed to grow larger with each step, and he raised his hand high in greeting. As Griant shook the offered hand, Boruin felt as if his fingers were enclosed in sandy clay rather than solid rock. Standing close, the creature's own runes were apparent; some coarse, some delicate, all hidden among the stone-like grains of his body.

"The man with the open mouth is Pile," said Boruin, attempting the politeness that both Oni and Griant seemed to prefer. "And you've met the boy." The kid swung his feet around, trying to get to Boruin's shoulders. The rilk lowered him there.

"Has he no name?" Griant asked.

"Not one he's told me," Boruin replied. The rilk's laugh reverberated like drums heard through the earth. Boruin wondered how much of the joke the rilk understood, then realized it was probably more than he did.

"What now?" Pile asked, bringing them back to business.

"The contract is completed, but we have been authorized to extend your service a while longer if you are in agreement," said Oni.

"In what capacity?" Boruin asked.

"The same. You would escort the boy and Griant to his conclave a few days north of here."

"The contract originates from there?"

"No, but that is from where Griant can take the boy further."

"To whom?"

Oni shook his head. "That is not information that has been given to us."

"What about the boy? What do you know of him?"

"Only what was outlined in the contract brought to us by the rilk. If they know more, they haven't told us. Further information is not something for which we would ask."

"And our pay?" Pile put in.

"It is here, minus the amount for the curtain. There is also an additional incentive if you travel with Griant."

Pile held back his groan. "Let me guess: more incentive still if we take him all they way to the end," he replied.

"That is up to the rilk," Oni said.

Boruin wandered back around the table, his mind turning and his eyes distracted by the red moon rising. "Can they tell us more about the boy if we continue?" he asked.

"Again, that information is at the discretion of the rilk."

It was all but nothing, but it was enough of a lead for Boruin, and it was a chance to get Wraethe out of the city.

"When can we leave?"

"Immediately," said Oni, gesturing to a wide door at the back of the garden.

"Get Wraethe and Toaaho," Boruin ordered Pile.

"They are not where you left them," Griant said. "They departed some time ago, running yeahun."

"Yeahun means south," said Oni.

"Rutting woman!" spat Pile, his hand dropping absently to his axe.

The rilk was right: the street outside Undurlund's door was empty.

"Yuin's whores!" Boruin cursed. "I knew better than to leave her out here."

"Better out here than inside with us," said Pile, eyeing the spray of blood still slick on the cobblestones. "Belok's?" he asked.

Oni shook his head. "We are holding Merchant Belok until the Guild Council has been informed of his transgressions." Pile drew his axe and followed the trail of blood further down the street.

"Merchant Oni, may the boy stay with you for a little longer?" Boruin asked. "I fear we have business to attend to before we can depart."

Undurlund's head man looked at the rilk and Griant answered for him. "The boy would be best served by your side. I cannot leave his."

Boruin tried to read the rilk's face to guess what he meant, but his stone features held no clues. "Thank you for your service, Merchant Oni," the old man said as he started after Pile. The rilk scooped the boy into his arms. Boruin could feel the ground shake under the massive creature's heavy footsteps.

Pile moved south, changing streets and sometimes ducking into alleys, but always at a fast clip. He was an excellent tracker, both in the wilderness and through crowded streets. The trail here was not hard to follow.

"She's bleeding the poor bastard, dragging him along. Nice of her to leave us a mark, but I'll bet he's begging for a quick death," Pile grimaced. He stopped in a small garden between two main avenues and picked out the signs across the trampled grass. "Ran across someone. They fought along the benches. Look at the blood there alongside Toaaho's track. At least he's kept up with her."

Griant pulled back a glowing hedge of bluestar ivy to reveal corpses. The open eyes of the dead reflected the glow of the small night flowers. "Your friends are deadly," he said.

"If anything, they are that," Boruin conceded as he checked the dead. They carried no purses, no items but their weapons. The blood smeared across their faces was dry, the blood on their bodies fresh. "Makua'Moi. You were right, Pile. They aren't finished tonight."

The trail continued south until the cobblestones began to run past warehouses rather than shops and homes. Fewer people walked the streets here, and so Griant's heavy, hurried strides drew less attention.

"What's at the end of town, Griant?" Boruin asked.

"More warehouses, the old shipping yards, and a gravel pit."

Boruin looked up at the rilk. "At least there will be fewer bystanders that might get hurt." He turned back and almost knocked Pile over. The man had stopped in the middle of the street.

The thin lines of blood from Wraethe's victim split in several directions. Two turned left: one to the edge of a door, the other around the building.

"The rutters figured her out, Boruin. They've added their own blood to confuse us. The trail is shot," said Pile.

"Spread out, see if you can sort hers' from theirs." said Boruin. He picked a trail at random and began to follow it around the nearest building, stopping short as a large man turned the corner with a heavy stone hammer.

Boss?" Pile called. Another line of blood ran further down the street, branching right, and from there came three men at a trot, all with weapons in hand.

"Get the one with the hammer," Boruin said, and started for the trio.

"Hold, Boruin! They are with me!"

Boruin spun to find Eloni stepping from a shop, the doorstep also marked with blood. As he entered Duin's light, they could see the constable was worse off than they'd left him. Half his hair was gone, and a bright pink swath of burn ran down the left half of his face and neck. The left eye was swollen and oozing tears.

"Yuin's mercy," Boruin whispered. "The judge?"

"There are more dark magi than just him." Eloni answered. "They caught me before I could reach the courthouse."

"Who are these men?" Pile asked, still fingering his axe handle and eyeing the strangers. "I thought you didn't know who to trust?"

Eloni nodded at his men. "Family. My father, uncles and brother. If you can't trust family, right?"

Boruin shook his head, "You need a healer, Eloni. Not another fight."

"There are battles best served with planning, and ones unwinnable without the right opportunity," the constable answered. "This night is the latter. The second Makua'Moi magi was Levonae, she has been the head of our trade council since before I was born." He raised his hand and carefully wiped the tears from under his burnt and weeping eye. "No. There are none that I can trust. No way to sort friend from enemy and gain enough hands to fight this plague. The Makua'Moi are too deep set in the foundations of this city."

The axe man spoke up. "We saw your friends when the Makua'Moi taunted them away from Undurlunds. They are unnatural fighters."

"Even so, we're are very few against too many," Boruin said.

"The Makua'Moi have come out from hiding to finish your Köpeka," Eloni explained. "If we can't defeat them now, at your side, they will hide again, and we will not know friend from foe. To wait is certain death."

"Certain death A, or certain death B? Nothing more motivating that a lack of smart choices," Pile said, with a grin made less humorous by the fearful look in his eye. "What do we do with the boy?"

"He must stay near," Griant. "I will keep him safe."

"Alright then," Boruin conceded. "Let's see this through. Any guess where to go?"

The ground shuddered as the rilk lowered himself to his knees, snapping a cobblestone. He leaned down, hands flat on the street, and set the side of his head down. The stone flexed, then the rilk seemed to press into the rock, slipping past its surface like a sweating man dunking his face under the water of a cool stream. They glimpsed it only for a moment before the rilk rose back to his feet.

"Much noise," he said, "sounds of steel and fighting, sounds of hard magiks." He picked the boy back up and hurried toward the industrial district. Boruin counted one rilk stride to his own three. They darted through the warehouses and along the rushing Oriune. The water still flowed faster than their pace. Griant dropped once more and set his palms on the rock. His head snapped to the east, a chorus of cries loud enough that he did not have to commune with another stone.

They turned from the river, Griant leading them into an abandoned block of broken buildings. The walls bowed out like old men, their backs bent from the weight of their time. Fallen roofs let the Diuntyne sky, filled with its huge red and white moons, shine through twisted windows to cast jagged squares of light out on the street. The avenue was empty save for four men stepping out of the shadows and drawing their weapons.

Griant's stride did not break time. He swung the boy behind his head, shielding him in the cup of his wide palm. The heavy thud of his feet continued to pound the ground hard enough that Boruin glanced nervously at the weak walls and the terra cotta hanging over the street.

The Makua'Moi gathered to face the rilk's charge. A sword flashed out and broke across Griant's thigh. The broken half bounced back and struck a second man across the face. He fell, clutching his eyes in the gutter. The three left met a sweeping fist, the rilk's heavy hand crushing skull and breastbone as he passed without breaking stride.

"What do your friends look like?" Griant rumbled.

"Toaaho is wearing plain leather and his face is tattooed," Pile said between panting breaths. "Wraethe's eyes seem to glow red like the envious moon, and she's dressed like… well, let's say she's dressed for warmer weather."

"We will enter from other ends. Give us a moment to get ready," Eloni said. At his gesture, his men split and dashed to opposite ends of the ruined warehouse.

"What is our plan?" asked Pile.

"Yuin knows," Boruin grumbled. "I'd hoped we could surprise them enough to get Wraethe and Toaaho and make a calculated retreat. I think we are past that now."

"Right, talk Wraethe out of a blood fury, and Toaaho from the resolution of a life-long revenge? Wraethe isn't the only one with a mind muddled by the moons. Let's concentrate on the problems present and go from there. First, there's no door big enough for the rilk and he's our biggest advantage," Pile said. "How do we get in?"

The rilk tucked the boy against his massive breast, covering him with his arms. The stone body turned and dashed into a leaning wall. The bricks crumbled as the rilk punched through. For a second, in the great hole left by Griant's passing, Boruin saw the sea of blood masks inside the warehouse, then the rest of the wall groaned and leaned outward.

"Yuin's balls! I'll take a messy fighter over a plan any day!" Pile yelled as he and Boruin peddled back and the wall gave way, falling towards them, into the street. The sound of the fight rushed out with the cloud of brown dust. They stumbled blind across the debris and into the shell of a building.

Boruin tripped on the first body, its shoulder crushed and its jagged ribs jutting through skin and clothing where the rilk's blow had demolished its chest. A man stumbled out of the billowing dust and Pile's axe cut down into his skull. The cloud wavered and cleared. Boruin dropped to his knees just in time to avoid a spark-filled knot of a spell that zipped over his head and smashed against Griant's wide back. A rune on his skin flashed dark grey as the spell sizzled and broke apart across his thick carapace. The rilk pushed further into the crowd, one thick fist swinging, the other wrapped around the boy and pinning him high against the back of his head. Despite the death all around, the boy's face held its usual strange serenity.

"Griant! Get to Toaaho and Wraethe. Give them some room to move," said Boruin. With no roof above, Duin's shine reflected bright from Wraethe's pale skin. It flashed out through a mob of fighters pushing her into a far corner. Boruin spied Toaaho there too, his face appearing as an opponent fell at his feet, only to have the space filled by other angry Makua'Moi.

Griant started across the floor. Blood-masked enemies gave way, already wearied by the fierce energy of Wraethe and Toaaho.

"Perfect. I'll get the tired ones," Pile said and started to follow in the rilk's wake.

"We have to bring down the sorcerers," said Boruin as another spell flashed through the dust-filled air.

"Oh yeah, that would be much easier," Pile scoffed, then shoved Boruin forward. "Get on it then. I've got your back."

Boruin cut through the crowd, pressing for the sorcerer who cast at the rilk. Pile swung wide with his axe at those who tried to close behind. Boruin parried and cut as fast as he could, driving forward and hoping he would not lose momentum. It failed as three men pressed back across the loose rubble of the fallen roof. Boruin felt his feet slip and then Pile's back up against his.

A white-toothed smile split the blood mask of the man before him, as he saw Boruin out of room to retreat. His grin ended there as Eloni's father appeared beside them, swinging down with his heavy hammer and crushing bone from shoulder to lower rib.

"Well met!" Boruin grunted and scrabbled forward again, his sword clearing the weapons of the other two fighters, while the hammer followed behind with two more lethal strikes.

"Where's Eloni?" Boruin asked.

"He was finishing Levonae when I saw you coming across the floor." Eloni's father turned, scanning the crowd. "There. Down at the other end. He's after the other one."

"One sorcerer down?" Pile asked. "Eloni's got more to him bloodied than I do fresh."

"Come on," Boruin said. "He's got to be exhausted."

They drove forward, hacking and cursing into the crowd. The warehouse was strewn with rubble, and Boruin used that where he could, dividing enemies, making them cross through unsteady roof tiles to reach them. Eloni's father split off in the chaos. He crossed their path, flanking Boruin's enemy, with a brother at his side, and then was off again.

At one point, while jammed up and retreating from another knot of fighters, Wraethe flashed past Boruin, the scent of her, mixed with blood and sweat, washing across him after she was already out of sight again. The knot of men pushing him back were dead, or dying, in her wake. The moons had turned her fury into an unstoppable force of nature. *Can she even back down from there?* Boruin wondered.

"Mother forgive me," Pile cried.

"What for?" Boruin grunted over his shoulder.

"That's the third old woman I've killed, Boruin. What are they doing here?"

Boruin ducked under a blow and stood up with a shove as the blade passed over him. His enemy staggered back and Boruin took a quick look around. The Makua'Moi were mixed: woman and men, young and old. They all fought in fury, but they weren't all fighters.

"Eloni was right. They've all come out of hiding for Toaaho. They just didn't know what they were getting into."

"Damn right, they didn't," Pile said with a laugh. "You're Yuin-damned right." The short man ducked, rolled and came up with his axe swinging through a hamstring. The laughter stuck with him as he fought on with renewed interest.

Pile's energy buoyed up Boruin's as well and he rushed the last few yards across the warehouse to where he'd seen Eloni moving in on the judge.

His high-spirits failed as climbed a dais above the general melee and found Eloni pinned to the wall by nails driven through his hands and into the brick. The constable's stomach was sliced wide open and his entrails were lying on the floor at his feet. His eyes met Boruin and a flash of recognition mixed with the fierce pain burning in the constable's gaze.

Boruin's voice rose, as if to cry out, but his dry throat caught and choked it into a moan.

The judge was crouched on the floor, hacking a piece of intestine from the pile. He cupped it in his hand and lowered his face to breathe across the flesh. It swirled into spell, a clotted mess of needles, and he cast it outward before his eyes even turned toward Boruin. Pile turned a man's sword, catching him off balance, and shoved him into the path of the spell. The dark magic burst his skin, shredding it as if the poor soul had been whipped ten thousand strokes in a moment.

Boruin dove over the falling corpse, thrusting his sword forward. The point caught the judge's arm as he was reaching for another handful of meat, shearing through his bicep and catching on the bone beneath. Boruin snapped his knees up underneath himself, though the fall had driven the breath from his lungs. His fist smashed against the judge's face as the man grasped the sharp steel and tried to drag the sword free. The judge screamed, part anguish and part spell. His hands clasped around Boruin's arm and sent magic searing through the old man's skin. The skin boiled under the judge's hand; smoke and the smell of roast pig rose into the air. The sorcerer's mouth opened as if to drink in Boruin's rising cry.

Pile's axe came down with Boruin's scream and severed the sorcerer's spine.

"Bite down the pain, Boss!" Pile yelled. "You can bleed later." He wrenched his steel free and swung back into the crowd of men closing behind.

Boruin pulled himself to his feet. His body shook at the pain in his arm, but he ground it between his teeth to keep from screaming. His pain could be nowhere near the agony of the man beside him.

Peering through the fighting, looking for Eloni's family, someone to come and take the man's pain from him. Boruin searched for the great hammer swinging, but spied it down in the rubble with Eloni's father dead beside it. One of his uncles was near, but the Makua'Moi had split his ribs and were fishing inside as if after trophies.

"I'm sorry, Constable," said Boruin. He turned and mercifully cut across the man's neck before Eloni could again catch his eye. The man's head sunk to his chest as Boruin dove in behind Pile, screaming in pain and hate.

They fought down the wall, keeping one side defended as the Makua'Moi assaulted them from every other direction. Two other mages fell before Boruin, the large crowd to their disadvantage; their spells struck their own men before the Makua'Moi could reach Boruin and Pile. Wraethe flashed past them, her sword cutting so quickly that Boruin felt the wind of it against his skin. She wound back and forth through the mob, cutting across exposed flesh, spinning and turning around their attacks. Her fingernails raked out across faces, plucked eyes from their sockets. There was no fairness in this fight; it was not for honor or peace. Wraethe was an animal, slaughtering those who fought and those who fled alike. With Eloni's death fresh in his mind, Boruin wished there were two of her.

Where Wraethe fought in screaming pleasure, Toaaho worked silently and with the hard focus of absolute will. His blades cut with precision, wasting no movement as he parried and thrust. Each line of sharp steel intersected for a kill and moved directly to the next. His muscles bunched and stretched as he ducked and leaned, lunged and rolled within his fighting measure. Men fell at his feet until there was no solid ground on which to stand.

"I'm spent!" Boruin said. Pile nodded, panting too hard to answer. They worked their way back into a corner and darted out only when approached. From the respite they watched the others raged through the thinning mass of men. The rilk waded as if through sheep, his fist dripping gore as he punched down into the Makua'Moi. They fell in waves as he swung, rose into the air as he kicked. Their blades broke across the hardness of his skin, their magics shattered by his runes.

"I think we're about done now," Pile said, and spat white froth into the dirt. "That was gruesome, though. I didn't care for it."

"You were right," Boruin agreed. "There were some fierce warriors here, but most are simple Kukane'Haku devotees. Fat merchants and old wives answering the summons of their priests."

Pile nodded, "They should have stayed home. No amount of faith is match to Wraethe in her rage."

The crowd now fell, fleeing with Wraethe's claws in their backs. Boruin rested as the enemy had now mustered across the room, trying one last swarm against Toaaho, recognizing the Köpeka's mask of tattoos that had been drawn for them. The final fighters circled him, but died as he danced between them and Wraethe cut at their heels.

Griant walked past the fighters, no enemies willing to try their luck on the stone-like warrior. He stood panting, his chest rising and falling like a blacksmith's bellows. The boy wriggled free from his grasp, sliding out from Griant's cupped palm held behind his large head, and down his back.

The four of them stood in the corner and watched Toaaho and Wraethe break the last of the God-King's worshippers. Those that could still flee ran from the building, and Toaaho dropped, exhausted, on his knees as the warehouse emptied. Wraethe alone continued on.

The woman darted among the wounded, those rising to flee, and those rising to beg. Her steel cut across throats and drove into backs.

"WRAETHE! It is done!" Boruin yelled across the wails of the dying. "Control yourself!"

"Yuin give mercy," Pile whispered as the woman seemed to speed faster now, a whirlwind of death.

Boruin stepped around the dead, trying to get closer. Wraethe fled like a dog, darting in close and then back out of its master's reach.

"Your rites! You must calm yourself or your rage will kill you!" said Boruin.

She turned and stared at him for a moment. It was as Pile described to Griant: her eyes were as dark red as Nurom Misuer. They flashed as she drove toward Boruin, her steel leading the way.

Boruin parried and jumped back, catching her blade jabbing at his side. He turned and circled her weapon, trying to whip it out of her hand, but it was like matching force against the rilk. His sword rebounded, and he dodged a few quick strokes before setting his feet again.

Wraethe's steel beat up under his guard, pricking his wrist and forcing him to drop his weapon. In that moment he felt a small hand wrap around his other arm. Wraethe snarled at the boy as he reached for Boruin's runes.

"NO MAGICS, YOU LITTLE RUTTER!" he screamed.

Wraethe's sword stopped its wide arc toward Boruin's neck and dropped to drive into the child's gut. The point passed clean through the boy and into Boruin's thigh.

Wraethe's burning eyes widened and a flash of blue passed across them. Her face went slack, and Boruin ripped his hand down his arm, pulling at the runes. His rage was now equal to hers, and he would kill–but the runes were stuck on his flesh. He screamed in pain, the characters almost ripping from the skin as he tried to spin them across his wrist. They tugged at the muscles as if sewn down deep into the bone.

The others tackled from all sides, burying Wraethe under flailing fists and solid rock.

The boy fell limply across Boruin's feet as Wraethe's sword came free.

The burdens borne

Whether it was the blood soaking into the floor or the evil glow of Wraethe's eyes as she raged against Pile's and Toaaho's attempts to restrain her, Nurom Misuer's red hue seemed to burn throughout the warehouse. Boruin stepped over the fallen child, infected with the rage that still hung like a thick fog across the room. Boruin fell upon the heap covering Wraethe, digging down through the restraining limbs until his hands clutched the woman's face. He squeezed until her eyes met his own.

"You will stop!" he commanded. She snarled back at him, but she stopped writhing. "Get her up!" Boruin added.

Pile and Toaaho stepped back as Griant took her in his two fists and hoisted her up to face Boruin, her feet dangling just above the floor.

"I share some of the blame for this. I dared bring you out of the jungle even though I know your cycles, but you let your discipline slip in trade for blood!"

"And it is beautiful!" she growled.

Boruin slapped her across the face, smearing the dead blood splashed on her cheek. "'The rites must be served or you must take my life. I will not live as a killer, soulless and feral.' Those were your words. Do you recall?"

"You cannot fathom what I recall; every thrust, every filet of flesh carved by my sword, every scream and choking cry. They sing to me—yours, too." Boruin struck her again, and Wraethe smiled through the wide split of her lip.

Boruin backed away to a sword's distance. "You led me to the jungle on our first cycle of Takata Shin," he reminded her. "You said it would lead you to rage that would be best spent in the wilds. Now I've seen Takata Shin's lust in you, and Nurom Misuer's rage. I will keep my promise if you do not keep your own." He placed the tip of his weapon on her throat.

"The boy, Boruin," Toaaho whispered.

"Yes, even the innocent are not spared in your thirst," Boruin spat at Wraethe. "It is inhuman."

"No, Boruin. Look at the boy," Toaaho said again. The child was on his feet, the ragged tear of his shirt bloodless. His eyes were on Wraethe, his face hard. Boruin's anger drained as if he had been blasted with cold. The boy was never without a smile or some content expression, but now there was no emotion in the strange child's face.

Pile stepped back, crossing hexes toward the boy. His voice shook. "Yuin, he's dead and doesn't know it."

The boy stepped forward and tugged at Wraethe's dress. She squirmed as Griant lowered her to the boy, her eyes like a penned habback's before the butcher's blade. Her head tilted back and she screamed at the boy's blank face. "NO!! DON'T LET HIM TOUCH—" The boy placed both hands against her breast. Wraethe's eyes withdrew as if the sun had appeared out of the black night. She slumped to the floor, and the life left her body as she slept.

Boruin pulled the boy back and examined his torso. There was no puncture through his lung, no rip in his skin where the steel had exited through his spine and into Boruin's thigh. He suddenly felt the pain of his own wound and the wet blood running down into his boot. Boruin sat down hard, drained of everything.

It seemed too dark in the warehouse, and Boruin realized the red moon had finally passed over the horizon.

"You did not tell them she was Ainghid Fas?" Griant asked.

"No," answered Boruin.

"A what?" Pile asked.

"A demon," Toaaho answered. "Murderous wraiths. They drink the world's evil, make it their own."

"A demon today, yes, but one can be made Ainghid Fas through humble sacrifice. It is not always evil to take on another's sin, but drinking in too much will turn one evil. Regardless, her rites have helped her resist well," said Griant. "And the high-born Fae do not degrade to monster so easily."

"High-born Fae?" All three men said together.

"Certainly. An Ainghid Fas can be of any race, but one as strong as this could be no less than a Moir, a queen of the Dreamlands," Griant said.

Boruin scoffed. "How can she be? Look at her face, her fingers. She looks nothing like them."

Griant's shoulders shrugged like two hills rolling. "All the more strange, but it matters not how she looks. She is a Moir, and she is Ainghid Fas—nothing less."

"That's the most I've heard you say, Griant," said Boruin.

"We Rilk do not like Fae," Griant answered. "It stirs my blood and loosens my tongue."

"Rutting Fae! I hate those bastards," Pile muttered. "And this thing!" he said, pointing a hex at the boy. "What is he?"

"Something else," Griant replied as he hoisted Wraethe over his shoulder. The rilk turned and left the warehouse, the boy trailing behind. The others helped Boruin to his feet, and then they followed.

The sun was high above before Griant halted and laid Wraethe down in the dirt. The rilk had led them far north of the city on old logging roads and game trails. It had been a hard march in the dark, but no one had followed. The open valley below them stretched for miles to the south. Nothing moved through the sea of wind-stroked grasses but the occasional black deer. Boruin took another drink from the stream they'd stopped to rest by. His leg throbbed, and he changed the dressing carefully. He had been cut before; he knew the muscle would heal. The pink, hand-shaped scar on his arm troubled him. It anchored the runes to his flesh. For the first time they did not spin across his body in their odd way. He tugged gently, trying to ease the dark tattoos across the burnt skin. The pain was scorching, blood rising from the scar. They were set as stone and not even the rune on his wrist would drop down into his palm. Boruin had always distrusted the runes, feared their power; but now that the magic was out of reach he felt naked, stripped of his last resort.

Griant crouched in the dirt beside Boruin. "I must ask what you know of Wraethe. My warren will not welcome her," he said, still polite but without the gentle tact he'd shown before.

"I know little of her, or of myself. Just the last twenty years—but nothing beyond," Boruin answered, surprised at his quick and open response.

"You did not know she was Fae?"

"No. I don't think she even knows. If she does, she shows extreme patience around Pile," Boruin said as he noticed the young man listening in. Pile moved under a cedar and lay against the trunk, his arm over his eyes against the light.

Griant took a slab of slate from the stream. His strong fingers, which Boruin had seen crush a man's skull not a half-day earlier, carefully peeled the brittle rock into thin layers. The delicate work distracted his hands as he spoke. "My people do not like the Fae. No, that is a light statement." Griant paused, considering, and then corrected himself. "My people despise the Fae. They would crush each one slowly under the settling mountains if given the chance."

"And you?"

"The same, although my responsibilities trump my personal feelings. I am a peacekeeper, one who travels many paths. I do not bend to my inclinations. My warren, however, is different."

"But you are bound by contract, as are they."

The rilk nodded.

"Then I'll tell you of Wraethe if you will tell me of the boy," Boruin offered.

The rilk sat still, examining a sliver of slate as if its grain were forgotten words that concealed the answers he sought. "The boy is different, neither child nor man. He hides as a Duine, but he is not Fae," Griant answered after a long moment.

Boruin stared at the rilk's stone face, waiting for more. It didn't come. "That's pretty thin. No rutting surprise that he's different. Why doesn't he talk? Why can he see my runes?"

"I cannot answer that. I do not know."

"Who hid him in the jungle? Who was his guardian?"

"We don't know."

"Why did you not retrieve him yourselves? Why was that left to us?"

Griant turned to the man. "Left to you, Boruin. And I do not know why, save that to our contractor you are as important as the boy."

"Who is the contractor?"

"You asked of the boy. That is all," Griant answered.

"You've given me little."

"I know little," said Griant. Boruin nodded, disappointed. He had gotten next to nothing out of the arrangement and was about to expose his own past in return—a task he was loath to do.

"My first memory is of Wraethe," he began. "I was lying in the dirt on the highway to Ouilainne. She was wiping my face with a wet cloth. I knew her name and she knew mine. There were no horses around, no overturned wagon, no tracks—no clues as to how we'd gotten there. My head didn't hurt, but I could not remember anything of the past. I only knew her name," Boruin said again.

"When dawn came she seemed to sleep, but it was something more. I tried to wake her and my hand seemed to move through her body like it was shadow, like she was night itself. She rose at my call, walking behind me until we reached Ouilainne.

"When the sun dropped and Diun rose, so did she. Her days pass as if dreams; she's hardly able to remember anything that happens during the sun's watch. She has awakened in the daytime, but it takes too much out of her. She sleeps in the light and wakes with Diun. I protect her days, and she guards me at night."

"Is that why you love her?" Griant asked.

Boruin stared at the stream and let the reflection of the sun hold his attention as long as it could. "I loved her before I felt her touch. Save for her name, it is the only thing I know as true from before."

"And you will not act until your mysteries are solved," Griant said.

"For a man of stone, you are very intuitive."

"I am a good diplomat."

Boruin took to his feet. He hated to talk like this, but it had made his way clear. "She does not know she is Fae. She would not believe it. If your warren is opposed to her, then they are opposed to me. I will travel no further, and the boy will remain with me until the contract is fulfilled," Boruin said, wondering if he had the strength to back such a promise.

The rilk betrayed no judgment with his words. "I will inform my warren," he answered.

For four days they followed the rilk north. His heavy feet thudded across the ground with the steady pace of a bard's metronome. The sun rose and fell and Wraethe slept through it all, carried over Griant's shoulder like a sack of grain. It was as if the boy had folded her up neatly and stored her away. Her dark veils buried her deep, hiding even the usual glow of her blue eyes.

Wraethe's mind was elsewhere, somewhere bursting with light. The sun baked down on her skin, warming the center of her chest. She felt a prickly itch as she began to sweat. Wraethe opened her eyes, staring as long as she could at the sun. Rings of green light danced in her vision as she broke from the fiery glare. Distant rolling hills and a river of white fire danced across the view at her feet. Wraethe sat up as her eyes cleared. The world was so alive in the daylight.

The sunlight fell almost like rain. She felt the drops land heavy and thick, soaking into her skin like oil. Birds and bugs flitted across the land before her. Where night was shadow—the realm of predators and lost creatures—the day was for life. Her soul tasted it all around. It enjoyed the humid flavor and began to drink deep. It was wrong to take without cause, but oh the feeling, so quenching, such mind-numbing pleasure. She was Ainghid Fas and life was hers to take.

Wraethe sat and drank in the life around her while the sun burned and the land began to dry. The grass withered as she drained its spirit. The trees grew brittle and the river smothered. The hot air caught suddenly in her throat, too dry and thin.

The sky was now more white than blue. Waves of watery heat swam across the horizon. The light grew hotter. The animals baked away, the flowers melted into the earth, and Wraethe was on fire. The sun seemed near enough to touch. She screamed as the light pierced down into her darkest points and her whole being burned. She screamed but did not move. There was nowhere to go in all the flame.

No door covered the mouth of Griant's warren, and no sign hung over the entrance. Like all rilk settlements, this one was tucked away under the stone and dirt. The great creatures of rock, while not shy, were not social creatures. The dark realms of the underlands were their wandering grounds. They enjoyed the peace where the only noise was the rush of underground rivers and the groans of aging rock.

"I'm not much of a swimmer," Pile said as Griant led them down the box canyon toward the base of the waterfall. A chasm swallowed the great column of water, a wide mouth drinking open-throated. The river disappeared into the chasm, spearing right through the granite and into the hard crust. Mist rose out of the small valley, brushing across the thick moss and ferns as it drifted up like a grounded cloud escaping back to the sky.

"There is no need to swim," said Griant as he walked along the battered stones. His palm pierced the curtain of water. In the dimness behind the falls, Boruin could make out a set of stone stairs descending into the earth.

They made their way down into the darkness, following the stairway by the scattered ribbons of light that fell through the water. The sun traced the column down and curved across the floor.

"Yuin, look at that," said Pile, awed as the flow of sunlit water seemed to split and rise up the cavern walls. It curved across the floor and into the ceiling, sparkling with pale colors of both water and sun. As their eyes adjusted, Boruin could see the light's source: veins of phosphorescent rock that ran across the cavern. The veins crossed the water and seemed to carry the light of it up through the stone around them.

"Would you say yours is a rich warren then, Griant?" Pile asked. A small, twinkling rock sat on a ledge along the stairway wall. Toaaho caught his arm as he began to reach out to the glimmering stone.

"Hands in your pockets before you make this even more difficult," the Mana'Olai said as the gemstone wiggled off the ledge. Like a small tribe of colored stones, a wave of others detached themselves from the wall to join their companion on the floor. They skittered across the stone, ricocheting about with the clatter of hail on a tin roof. The rocks stopped their play and stood up; the little stone creatures, no larger than a thumb, were jewel-encrusted twins to the giant rilk.

"They are rilka, Pile," said Toaaho.

Boruin didn't think Pile was foolish enough to pocket one of the small rock creatures, but his untethered fingers could be another matter. "The rilk defend them, keep them safe. Do you see?" Pile's fingers answered by slipping inside his pockets where they could do no harm.

When they reached the river where the waterfall hit the bottom of the cavern and shot towards its end, Griant asked, "Would you wait here, please?" He set Wraethe on a bar of smooth sand the water had beaten out of the rock and pushed to shore. The boy, eager to follow, jumped to grab his fingers and hung, swinging until the rilk set him in the crook of his arm. They crossed through the rushing water to the far shore.

"How far are you going to let him lead us without making him pay for our services?" asked Pile. Boruin opened his mouth to answer but was stopped short as an avalanche of sound boomed off the walls. The three clapped their hands over their ears as the sound of rocks breaking and stone grinding beat against their skulls.

Across the river, the inhabitants of the warren had arrived. The other rilk surrounded Griant. Judging from the noise, they had not wasted time in discussing Wraethe.

"What is all the rumbling about? It's their contract, and they asked for us!" Pile shouted over the din.

Toaaho leaned in close and yelled back, "Some people have a higher standard than money. Their hatred of the Fae is deep."

"Bahh," said Pile as he turned to find some moss to wedge in his ears.

After a time, the vocal rockslide settled and came to a halt. Griant and the boy waded back across the river.

"What's the verdict?" Boruin asked.

"We have decided how to decide," Griant replied.

"THAT'S AS FAR AS YOU GOT?" Pile shouted. Boruin plucked the moss from his ears.

"Gynphur will wrestle for the council. If he wins, then the Fae leaves and the boy remains with us."

"But you said I was wanted as well," Boruin protested.

"This trial has no impact on your fate. So you may come or you may leave, regardless."

"I'm not leaving Wraethe. Nor am I leaving the boy."

Pile strained up on his toes to chide the giant stone man. "I thought you rilk were a fair bunch. Not even the four of us together are going to beat that bastard. Some deal there, diplomat."

"I am to wrestle on your behalf," Griant answered.

"You will serve as our proxy, under your free will?" Boruin asked. Griant nodded and set the boy at his feet. "Then we accept your offer, with thanks."

Boruin and his crew stood at the edge of the water. On the other side, the rilka raced around the floor, chalking out a large circle. Inside the ring, Griant's opponent stood ready. The stone creature shifted from side to side, ready and eager to fight his own warrenmate.

Pile cursed. "I thought Griant looked tough." Splintered rock covered the other rilk, Gynphur. It ran in a jagged fault line from the back of his fists to his shoulders then continued down his back like a mountain range. A rune on his chest had been marred by some slamming force that had broken the hard skin and left him scarred.

Griant stepped into the circle and stood beside his opponent. The warren spoke, the sound a low rumble as they set the ground rules for the argument. The two fighters stomped to signal their agreement with the rules and turned to face each other. They slowly circled the ring, eyeing the other's runes and scars of war. They growled their challenges and then stood close, their heads pressed together. After a low final exchange, that reverberated through the hard floor, they stepped back to the edges of the ring.

Gynphur spared no time, turning back at a full run once his foot had touched the boundary of the circle. Griant leaned into the attack. Their heads cracked together, the report bouncing off the walls. They clawed each other mercilessly, grabbing for whatever spines or crevices might offer purchase and leverage.

Griant slipped under the other's arm as the larger rilk pushed forward, trying to drive his opponent out of the circle. The rilka chattered, bouncing on the rock in an odd chittering applause, though it was impossible to tell for whom they cheered. The floor shook as Griant went off balance and caught himself, twisting in Gynphur's grasp and slamming his foot down before him. Boruin took a careful look upward, wondering how much shaking the cracked cavern ceiling could take.

The two stone fighters grappled in the center of the ring while the rilka jumped with each impact like gamblers at the Nefazo dog fights. The rest of the warren stood still, watching without call or cry.

Twice the rilka rolled aside as the Gynphur pushed Griant toward the edge of the circle. Twice Griant slipped free, but the diplomat was growing slower. The larger fellow began to break his holds with less effort, and Griant stood with his arms braced, trying to keep his opponent away. Gynphur forced Griant's knee down. He twisted his opponent, trying to push the stone man on his back. Again, the diplomat tore free, and Boruin saw shards of rock tear from under Gynphur's fingers as the hold broke.

The larger rilk roared and charged as Griant staggered back in pain. Gynphur slammed his huge hands down on the other's shoulders and smashed his chest into Griant's sagging head. Again, he drove the shorter rilk toward the edge of the ring, pistoning his legs and breaking chunks of rock free from the floor as he pushed.

Boruin watched as Griant began to tilt backward. Pile cursed somewhere behind him as their fighter backpedaled toward the chalk line. Rilka scattered out of the way as the two wrestlers battled toward the edge. Boruin's heart sank as they neared the line and Griant's strength started to fail completely.

Griant began to fall, his feet twisting underneath him. Suddenly he turned and his feet bit into the stone before the line. The diplomat tugged his opponent with him, throwing the wrestler off balance and over his back. Gynphur roared as he fell across the line and bounced off the rock and into the river. Boruin's legs quivered as the floor shook, and Pile stumbled into him. The warren grew quiet as the rilka stilled. Gynphur lay for a moment under the water as if cooling the blood that had risen in the fight. When he rose, he placed his head again against Griant's, this time rumbling his admiration.

"You weren't as spent as you looked after all," said Toaaho as Griant escorted them across the river.

Griant's chuckle was like stones rolling around in his throat. "Never let your opponent know your true measure. It is no different in war than in diplomacy." He turned as the leaders of his warren approached, translating as they spoke.

"Griant has won the Fae passage through the Rilk lands and into the Shoro, though it is neither his nor our desire to allow this. She will be considered a mortal enemy if ever she displays a threat to rilk or rilka. There will be no warning and no leniency."

Boruin stepped forward and bowed low. "Understood. She will act as an honored guest. You have my word."

Pile leaned to him. "How are you going to keep that promise?"

"With you and Toaaho holding her down if necessary," he said out of the corner of his mouth.

"You may wake her, child," Griant said. The boy moved toward Wraethe. The rilka gathered around their own rilk, each a measured distance from their giant companions. Boruin knew they all stood on guard and ready.

The boy placed his hands on Wraethe's chest and the life flooded back into her face. It came as agony, a scream of pain ripping from her throat. For a moment, Boruin thought he could see burning flames behind her eyes before they faded to blue and sunk in sleep beneath her cowl.

"Did you see the smoke?" Pile whispered.

"No," Boruin replied.

"Out of her mouth when she screamed. Where did that come from?"

"I don't know, Pile."

"This is getting weirder by the day. Why don't we get them to pay up and be done with it while we are all still healthy and only Wraethe's lost her mind?"

Boruin didn't answer. He knew Pile was probably right, but that had rarely stopped him before.

Belok stepped from shadow to shadow, keeping his head down. The trade council had done him the courtesy of not expelling him from Priyati, but their pigment marked his forehead. The putrid green ink was only a thin dash across his brow, but everyone glanced at it. The shame was almost unbearable.

"Twelfth generation merchant. A seat on the Ouilainne Trade Advisory. Backwoods rutting no-name guild. No respect for my station, no respect for the ways of trade." Belok mumbled his lies, stumbling on a tilted cobble and cursing it. He diverted to the back avenues that wound behind the shops, avoiding the smirks of the other tradesmen.

The Nefazo merchant stopped at the darkest inn he could find, determined to drink himself stupid and then return to the road after the ink brand had faded. He smoldered in the back of the room until the patrons slowly left and his drunken tongue became too much for just his own ear.

Belok weaved across the floor to the one remaining customer and dropped onto the stool beside him. His rant continued in midsentence. K'Juin listened contentedly, though he did not speak Nefazo. The Easlinder nodded where Belok paused and dipped his head to his flagon, his stomach too full of ale to raise it to his lips. Long after Diuntyne, the innkeeper fell asleep by the hearth as Belok complained over K'Juin's snoring form.

"Then out of nowhere the rutter comes in and steals the contract. I mean, I had it in the purse. They were suspicious, but I have a way with the trade. My tongue was smooth like jui leather, a fact I don't have to tell you," he slurred. "Where was I...? Right! So, Boruin comes in with that undeveloped miscreant, Pile, and claims it is his contract. Now that is an outright falsehood! Check the Terre Haute Contract Registry files and you'll see it subcontracted by the honorable Belok Toufoune to Boruin Pig Rutting Shit Eater." He paused for a drink. His fumbling hands sloshed half the ale out of his flagon before slapping it back down on the wet table.

"Where was I...? Right! So, Boruin comes in and this backwoods Undurlund dainty says 'Well I don't care a bit about governmental trade agreements. We're giving the contract to this fellow! I don't care if you brought the boy to us!' as is lettered in the contract mind you, 'or not. Can you give any small bit of proof to make this complete illegality rational to us?' So Boruin raises up his fist, like something out of a bloody Jacques play, and I swear on my father's seal—blue fire! Blue fire springs off his hand and all sorts of runes made of light go spinning around his arm like a bunch of damn trained fleas. A rutting mah'saiid sales trick, I don't need to tell you, and the Undurlund fool goes for it. 'Well you are all fine and good in my book the man says—'"

"Tell me more about this man," a voice dropped smoothly over Belok's shoulder. Belok spun to confront the speaker, but the inn was empty. When he turned back around, he found a finely dressed man sitting across the table. His beauty was a well Belok wished to fall into. The man smiled and filled Belok's flagon from his own. Belok smiled back.

"Who? The Undurlund pig sticker?"

"No, the Pig Rutting Shit Eater and his fiery runes," said the Monarhig.

- II -

REST IN THE CAVERN OF SYAN

That was a hell of a way to win an argument, Griant," said Boruin as they followed one of the glowing veins of rock deeper into the cavern.

"Gudok is a way to settle the most disputed conflicts. The winner is obvious. Sometimes words leave one less certain," said the stone creature.

Pile did not try to hide the sarcasm in his grim laugh. "That's great. You could be proven wrong and dead at the same time."

"If the argument is serious enough, that is possible, but rarely does our anger outweigh our better judgment," Griant replied, stopping at the mouth of a smaller tunnel. "Follow the Guidevein. The passage is too small for a rilk, but I will meet you on the other side." A rune on his chest flared for a brief second as the giant stepped into the wall and disappeared.

"Yuin in the rut! Did you see that?" Pile asked.

Shocked by the rilk's sudden disappearance, Boruin put his full weight down on his wounded leg. He snapped at Pile as he hobbled into the passageway. "We're all standing right here. Did you think we missed it?"

"No, but did you know they could do that?" Pile answered. "What if they decide this is a bad idea after all? They could come right out of the wall on top of us! I don't like it, Boruin. It's too creepy."

"What's creepy is the way you dance after six mugs of strong wine," said Boruin. "Quit complaining about every Yuin-damned thing. Griant isn't going to betray us, and the warren isn't going to jump out and drag us into the stone. They've got a contract to keep—and they will keep it."

Pile was quiet for two steps as he considered this. "You don't think they can do that, do you, Toaaho? Pull you into the rock and leave you stuck there?"

"Quiet, Pile. Sound carries on polished stone," Toaaho whispered as he led the sleeping Wraethe through the lowest part of the passageway. Pile stayed silent for another moment but shouted in fear when the floor before them scattered. The rilka had gathered, awaiting the arrival of the visitors. They bounced and rolled back down the floor of the tunnel as Pile's echoing shout, and the running boy, chased after them.

They caught up to Griant as the tunnel began to widen. He apologized for the trouble. If the echoes of Pile's words had traveled before them, the rilk ignored them.

"The bottleneck keeps our warren well defended. You won't find such an inconvenience further," he said. In another few yards they found the truth of his statement.

The cavern below the waterfall was nothing compared to the warren proper. The skilled hands of the rilk had carefully crafted every surface. Giant columns rose from the floor, their shapes mimicking the chaotic veins of iron ore. They branched out like trees to support the high arched ceiling, so polished that Boruin and his companions could see their own reflections treading above them.

The glowing rock continued in the welcoming hall. Great globules hung from above, like chandeliers, and others rose from the floor like frozen fountains. Rilka danced about the glowing stone, preening under its light.

Boruin turned circles, taking in the cavernous room. "This is tremendous, Griant. Such a work of art! I had no idea the rilk were such craftsmen."

"Our warren has done well for itself. Since we became friends with the Easlinders, we have learned much about business and many goods have moved through our halls. We've established trade routes between Easlinder and warrens from near and far," Griant explained.

The rilk led them into the next hall, a space less decorated but wider and deeper and more amazing than the first. Each column was stamped with another warren's marker and that warren's goods spread under it like a merchant's stall. Dozens of rilk were busy at work between them. Boruin recognized a few from the Gudok ceremony.

"These are goods from all across the Shoro. Other warrens bring them here and we sell them on the Iron Bridge and in the other Priyati markets," Griant offered as he led them down the rows between the stores.

They walked in wonder. There were great piles of black deer antlers, immense racks that spread wider than a man. Griant explained that musicians coveted the hollow bone for its superb tone. Rilka were rolling shards of quartz, taller than themselves, back into a pile that had been dislodged by a dark-skinned rilk. Pile gasped. The rilk muscled about a bleached skull of a rare rabinithair so massive that Pile could have walked into the empty eye socket without stooping. The dark rilk, his carapace scarred from terrible battles, turned the flying serpent's skull to fit its long horns between two wide-spread columns and continued down the row.

A tall pyramid of bright green river rocks caught their eye as a rilka tripped and stumbled into it. An avalanche of green stone tumbled down to the floor, chased by impact waves of orange that rolled across the pile. The orange washed from one river rock to the next as if the color-shifting rocks were one single stone rather than a pile. The boy rapped his knuckles against one and watched the waves of orange bounce about until Boruin dragged him on by the shirt collar.

Leading Wraethe along, Toaaho kept the sleeping woman between him and a crate of cave spiders large enough to wrap all ten legs around one's head.

"Look at you! Afraid of a little bug?" Pile chided.

"Fear and dislike are two wholly different things," Toaaho answered. Pile opened his mouth to dig deeper under the Mana'Olai's skin, but the sight of a mound of silver ore held his tongue. To his credit, and everyone's surprise, the little thief managed to keep his feet in a straight line even if his eyes stuck to the precious metal as they passed.

"What are those large piles in the back?" Boruin asked.

"More ore: iron, bauxite, copper, tin. The biggest is a heap of baker's beetle mushrooms. They're considered a delicacy by the Mana'Olai," said Griant. "They grow off the insect's old compost piles."

"Ugh," Pile grimaced. "Let's turn back. The smell alone will make me sick."

As Griant led them out of the hall, they passed more columns ringed with crates of goods from distant warrens: shells, moss, small glowing frogs, dried cave trout, cages of bats, and stacks of polished marble.

"The Nefazo trade guilds would be quite jealous if they saw the size of Undurlund's operation," said Boruin.

"We are careful to limit our exports to the Nefazo merchants," Griant replied. "The Mana'Olai have been most kind with their trade, and much of our wares pass to them. The Nefazo are consummate dealers. They would fare better by the rilk if buying cheap and selling high were not so close to their hearts."

"I did not realize the rilk were so organized," said Toaaho. "I've always heard that the warrens were small and far apart. How did you manage to bring so much here?"

"Part of what you say is true. The warrens do prefer their space. This may be the largest gathering of rilk in the regions around Easlinder, but it should not be considered a true warren. They only bring their goods and return with what wares they ask us to find for trade.

"In regards to how they arrive, there are many paths hidden beneath the mountains. A great underground river runs below the Oriune, following its track deep into Mana'Olai. The waterfall concealing the entrance we used is a small fork of that river. We ferry most of our goods downstream to Priyati on its back.

"Many other rivers course underground. Lakes and hot seas allow sailing. Cavern highways stretch beneath the crust in all directions. We have ways to move; the lij greatly misjudge the world below their feet. There is much beauty and wonder out of the sun's sight."

Boruin smiled. "You have shown us much already, Griant."

"Hold your judgment yet, for I have one last place I think you will favor."

He led them through dark passageways where no glowing rock flowed. The light of Griant's torch made a small army of their shadows. Soon the flames fluttered as a cool breeze rippled down the passage. Their shadows left the walls as the rock pulled away and limitless darkness surrounded them. A wall appeared out of the gloom, and Griant led them into a small, roofless shelter. Inside, individual rooms surrounded a central gathering place. Griant tossed his torch into the fire pit. The dry wood there began to catch.

"I think you will find this place restful," Griant said, pointing out the beds and the larder. Behind the building, the floor was polished down to a smooth finish, and they could hear the soft lapping of water. As the after light of the torches left their eyes, flickering ribbons of a gentle glow appeared before them.

"This is the river I told you of," Griant continued. "Though it is more like a lake here, very wide and shallow." Air whistled between his teeth as he sucked in air. "GARAZONNE!" Griant shouted in a voice like grinding stone.

Across the water, sparkles of light exploded into being. Above, bright pinpoints winked down at them, and more shone bright beneath the water.

"Those aren't stars," said Pile. "They can't be."

"No, more of the rock we call Guidevein. It runs across the ceiling and through the floor of the lake. We call this the Lake of Syan for its similarities to your Diunless night. Most of our visitors find it a comforting place to rest," Griant said.

Boruin bowed. "It will be very pleasant, thank you."

"I must confer further with the warren. I will return in time. Feel free to enjoy the water. It is shallow for a long distance, and there is no current on this side of the cavern," he added before walking off into the darkness.

Toaaho and Pile disappeared to search the larder, led by the boy's growling stomach. Boruin removed his boots and let the cold water lap at his feet. He felt Wraethe's presence beside him.

"I wondered if you would wake to this, if at all," Boruin said.

"It is a beautiful mimicry, but it has been night above for a while," Wraethe said quietly.

His eyes stayed trained across the black water. "I like it here better, the darkness without the red tinge," he said.

"Can we not talk about it?"

"But the boy. What did he do? Do I still have to worry? Are you done?"

"Please, Boruin. Please let me stay quiet for now. Let me feel the cold," she said. Her voice was rough and so sorrowful that he listened close for the sound of her sobbing. It would be a noise he had yet to hear from the hard woman.

He opened his mouth to say something anyway; to console, to reprimand, to argue. He couldn't decide which was appropriate, so he sniffed against the damp air and stood still instead. They watched the bright patches of Guidevein cast their light up through the water. The ripples turned the light into colored waves rolling across the low ceiling. It was so much like the iceworm lights in the far north that he could almost pretend to be far away from here.

Wraethe stayed beneath her cowl the rest of the evening. The boy fell asleep curled near the fire pit. Despite his hex casting, it was Pile who carried him quietly to a bed and a wool blanket. Only then did Wraethe's eyes appear again beneath her hood. It was near morning, after the others had fallen asleep, that she woke Boruin.

She crouched on her toes as if unsure if she would talk or flee. "I am afraid of the boy. I don't want to travel with him anymore."

Boruin sat up and rubbed his eyes. "I want to see this through. We need to see it done," he answered.

"You don't know what he can do," she whispered with a moan like an upset child's.

"Then tell me. What did he do? Where did you go after he touched you?"

"I'm better. You don't have to worry about me," she continued without answering. "I can go and wait in Mana'Olai. The moons won't cycle again like that for a long time."

"Where has your rage gone?" Boruin asked. Her somber blue gaze drifted aside. His rising voice threatened to break the others' sleep, and he dragged her down the shoreline where the light waves might mask their words.

Boruin waited for her to speak, but her lips remained sealed. He decided to start the conversation. "You killed so many. I know your rites will balance against those evil enough to deserve you, but you gave none. And there were so many, Wraethe. So many that did not require death, did not deserve it."

She was crying now. "You and the boy, too. I know Boruin. I remember it."

"Yes, an innocent and your eldest friend. Your truest friend," Boruin said, his voice as cold as the dark water. "I don't care what he did to you or why you are scared of him. You deserve it twice over," he said, turning to walk back to his bed.

"Fire, Boruin. Endless fire," she said. "The boy set me aflame. I know now it was only a few days, but I swear to you that it was much longer. I burned through without end, ceaselessly, every second for months. I'm scared to death of the boy, Boruin. Don't make me travel with him anymore."

"Cleansed by fire," Boruin said. "Perhaps it was for the best," he added. He walked away to the sound of her sobs drowning in the lapping waves.

He stopped when he felt blood trickling down his thigh. Focused on berating her, he had forgotten his wound and walked too hard on it. He peeled away the dry bandage and dipped his hands into the river. The cold water felt good against the inflamed skin. He dipped the moss pad in the lake, and then Wraethe was there rewrapping the bandage. She pulled it tight, and he hissed, but it was needed. The cool lake had taken his anger, and he held her hands close to him.

"We need this, Wraethe. If there was ever a chance to find our pasts, this is it. Griant says you are Fae—but you know that, don't you?"

"I have always feared it, even after the Monarhig did not believe so. But it is true. The boy has shown me—*is* showing me," she said. She shook her head as if something had come undone in there and was rattling around out of place.

Boruin pulled her chin around to return her to him. "What are you saying? You remember?"

She started and then stopped, trying to find the words. "The boy set something on fire inside me, Boruin. It's like an onion scorched by that hot place. It's still burning, and as each layer crisps black it flakes off and I catch another piece of me etched in ash." Boruin held his breath to keep his tongue silent. Wraethe was chewing her lip, trying to put together what was coming apart in her mind. If he started, the number of his questions would smother her.

"I am a descendent of Polorun, the dead Iraemun. That knowledge is strong in me, like knowing dawn is coming, or that if cut, I will bleed. I've seen bits of my life in his talamh of vision, walking as servant between the dream palace of Obata and Nungisa's nightmare castle. But the Dreaming Lands are so different than what I know now. Each thing I see is so foreign but obviously a part of me... it's like waking to a numb limb. I need time..." She halted, but her mouth would open for a moment and then close as if some image had come around too quick for her to catch and describe.

"What else?" Boruin asked. *Rutting idiot*, he added as Wraethe's concentration broke and the focus of her eyes returned from some inner place. If time was what she needed, he would not press her again. *Better to let it come at its own pace.*

She took a deep breath. "Battle, blood, fighting. So that's nothing new, is it?" she said with a grim smile. The smile stretched tighter, and he could see her teeth clench. "And a betrayal—some hard sacrifice."

"You *are* Ainghid Fas, as we feared. That is certain enough now." She nodded her head, just enough to agree. "You must stay with your rites, and I'll stay close to the boy. I'll make sure he doesn't hurt you," Boruin said.

"With what?" she asked, her fingers tracing the burnt patch on his forearm. "He's strong in ways we don't know, and you're without your runes."

"They are hardly a strength, the way they work," he said, wishing she hadn't seen the hand-shaped wound holding his runes firm in their place. "I have you and the other two. We've always done well together. And the rilk has fought for you against his own. He will stay true to us." Wraethe nodded again, ever so slowly, as if trying to be convinced.

"I can go on," she whispered.

"I know you can," he said, praying to Yuin that he had not lied, praying that he could protect her.

"I am sorry," she added even more quietly.

"I know."

They wandered back to the shelter and found Toaaho meditating by the stoked fire. Boruin lowered himself into bed and watched Wraethe settle down beside the Mana'Olai. Boruin wasn't the only one to whom Wraethe owed an apology. He hoped the others would trust it as well as he knew he could.

Griant returned the next morning, bearing gifts. The rilk had found a mineral salve for Boruin's wounds, a keg of beer for Pile to share, a clean dress to replace the sleeping Wraethe's blood-stained leathers, and two smoked jui deer for lunch.

He rode in on a wave of rilka, a multitude of miniature rilk coming to play with the boy. The little creatures were shorter than the boy's thumb, though quite a few had round bellies that made them look like tiny old men. They swarmed around the boy, chattering and rolling about. They chased the boy around the shelter and stalked him like a herd of tiny thul bears when he hid under Boruin's bed.

"Nothing for Toaaho?" Pile asked.

Griant studied Toaaho. "The rilka have a gift for him, if he chooses to accept it."

"Your hospitality and kindness have been more than enough," Toaaho replied.

Pile frowned. "Don't you even want to know what it is?"

"I suppose it would be rude not to," Toaaho replied with a rare smile.

"Yeah, everyone loves a gift. Especially if it's beer!" Pile shouted, topping off his mug, then Boruin's.

"If I may be so bold as to decipher your mask," Griant began, "I would guess it was for deception, to hide your face from those that brought down your family—the Makua'Moi."

Toaaho nodded at the statement.

"You have defeated those in Priyati, probably the largest group in Easlinder," Griant said, handing the Mana'Olai a small scroll. "Undurlund acquired this from a rider headed south over the border."

Toaaho unrolled the parchment and found a rendering of his face etched on the rough paper. He showed it to the others.

Pile leaned over his shoulder. "Ah, they don't have you right at all. You're far uglier than that," he said with a wide smile.

"The mask is spot on," said Boruin. "Other groups will know you now."

"You've hidden a long time. Your return home has proven your worth," Griant said. "The rilka can remove your mask, if you see fit. You have outgrown its use."

"How can you do that?" Toaaho asked before the same question left Boruin's lips.

"Our people have long studied the power of runes. Your tattoo is similar in a few respects."

Toaaho tossed the parchment into the fire pit. "I would accept your gift," he said. The rilka were already gathered. The boy stood beside Boruin to watch.

The Mana'Olai lay down on the rock, circled by the rilka. The little rock creatures began to move together, their steps tapping at the stone as they walked about the man. In the silence of the cave, Boruin felt their voices as a deep hum that moved through the air. They sang in strange harmonies which sounded like crystals poured from a vat to chime as they bounced across the hard floor. The rock beneath his feet began vibrating as if answering their song.

A rilka speckled with green jade climbed upon Toaaho and beckoned a second, his head and hands plated in silver. The two moved to the man's neck, their voices rising above the loud chorus.

The light swelled in the cave as the Guidevein responded to the song. In the brightness it was clear that the rilka had pulled a piece of Toaaho's tattoo free from his skin. The black line unwove from his neck. They carried it up his jaw and it came free like a strip of bark pulled from a sapling. If it caused him pain, Toaaho didn't so much as flinch.

More rilka joined at his face, taking other edges of the black mask and singing it free from his skin. The tattoo slid away, and then Toaaho's face was there—naked and new.

"I would be honored if you would allow me to carry your mask," said Griant. Toaaho nodded, staring at the lines held in the small hands of the rilka.

"This mask was worn by a great warrior. I am proud that your battle is part of my history. It will make a powerful rune," Griant said as the rilka climbed up his broad back. They lay the mask out over his shoulder blade, and suddenly their song ended. Toaaho's mask was fixed on the grey skin as if it had always been there. Boruin turned to look at the Mana'Olai, but Toaaho had grabbed a torch and moved to the lakeside.

"This beer is stronger than I thought," said Pile. Boruin held out his mug for another.

"I look much like my father," Toaaho said when he returned, his hands feeling the broad smile on his face. "This is more of a gift than I could have hoped for."

"Fight your enemies now in your own skin," Griant said. "Enemies that dare attack me unseen will quake at the fabled face that watches my back." Toaaho grinned again and bowed deeply to the rilk, then again to the rilka.

"What about mine?" Boruin asked quietly after Pile had dozed off and Toaaho had returned to study his reflection in the lake water.

"You want yours removed?"

He rolled up his sleeve and showed Griant the hand-shaped scar on his wrist. "No, just repaired."

Griant's thick fingers gently felt the skin around the scar, but Boruin noticed the rilk did not touch the runes. He scooped a few of the rilka up into Boruin's lap. The small creatures sniffed about the scar but refused to touch his bare skin.

"I am sorry, Boruin. While we can do much with runes, these are something special. I have never seen runes that travel like yours. They are part of you in a way I do not understand, and the rilka worry that realigning them around the scar might ruin the action."

Boruin tugged his sleeve back down. "They've never worked well, but they've worked. I don't like going into the Shoro without them. It will be dangerous."

"Yes," Griant said softly, having no better answer for the man's nervousness.

"What do you want me to say? 'Sure, wasn't a problem, Wraethe. You weren't really that difficult.'" Pile's words pulled Boruin out of sleep, but he lay in bed. There were things here that needed saying, and Pile wouldn't hold them back.

The man paced around the dying fire as if his moving feet helped drive the words through the knot of nerves in his gut. "Yuin's sake, when you weren't picking fights, you were slutting up on every man that crossed your path. It was rutting embarrassing."

"I'm sorry. The moons were at their worst, and I can't help but—"

Pile's finger shot out. "Don't give me that shit. You remember when I drank myself black on that Omman whiskey, destroyed the bar at that inn, and burned the livery? Remember what you said?"

"Yes."

"You said there was no excuse!" he shouted. "It was not the whiskey, but that I was a Fae-damned, spoiled child and no more trained than a dog. Obviously, you are no less an animal, and I don't hold much for your moon excuse." His feet stalled, and he leaned on the beer cask to steady himself. Wraethe put her hand on his shoulder to console him. Pile flinched and ducked away from her.

"Don't touch me! You rutting drove your sword through that boy and stabbed Boruin! You would have killed him outright if Griant hadn't helped us stop you. But now it's fine? You're not going to do that again, huh?"

Wraethe crossed her arms, holding herself tight like a child left alone. "I'm not going to attack any of you again, Pile."

"And I'm to trust a Fae?"

"I'm not Fae anymore."

"Griant sure thinks so, and I figure that explains a lot of shit."

"What do you want me to say, Pile? I'll say it," said Wraethe. Pile looked away, so she continued. "I can't excuse what happened. I can't even explain it. I was Fae, maybe still am—I'm definitely Ainghid Fas, and I kill those that need killing. But this is what is, Pile. This is what I am, but I'll try to keep it from affecting you all again."

Pile collapsed in a chair, his anger ebbing. "I know you've got that rite thing you do. You're tougher than all of us. You're a hard woman, and that's what I've liked about you," he said into his beer. "Boruin is no less a screw-up than the rest of us. You're the one that's supposed to keep us on track, not turn your back on us."

"I see what you mean," Wraethe said. This time when she placed her hand on his arm, he did not move it. "I'll keep it together. We've always made a good team; Boruin said just that same thing. We'll get this job done, get back to Nefazo, and take it easy for a while. Maybe track down Belok and tie him between a couple habbacks. Then everything will be back to normal."

"That would be nice," Pile agreed.

They passed the next few days resting. Wraethe took to meditating alongside Toaaho, and she seemed to be relaxing. Pile taught the boy to skip stones across the lake to keep him at a distance. The young man had seen Wraethe's initial distress at the boy's proximity—the woman tensed when the boy came near—but recently she had allowed him to come close and even touch her again. She was coming out of whatever place had burnt those damn moons from her system. Boruin was glad to have it moving past them, glad to have time to relax and return to some sense of quiet.

Then Griant and three others from his warren arrived in a heavy boat, heralded by the splash of oars and the creak of wet wooden planks.

"We were content to allow some time to rest, but we must go now," said Griant as he stepped from the boat.

"What's happened?" asked Pile.

"There has been a lot of activity above and strange vibrations below. Someone searches for you. The warren does not think we can leave by the northern trails. They will set false marks in the northern passes and along the southern river. The other rilk will travel above ground and below to cover our tracks."

"And us?" Boruin asked.

A sandy rilk rumbled a response, which Griant translated. "All routes outside the warren seem to be watched. Only the eldest of trails remain, and it is a secret to all. It troubles us to allow Fae to know of it, but Griant has won his argument."

"What kind of path are we talking about?" Wraethe asked.

He pointed at the glimmering rock above them. "We will ride the Guidevein."

RIDING THE GUIDEVEIN

The draft of the boat seemed too shallow. Boruin began to sweat as the rilk walked them into the deep water. Ships and sailing were not his fancy. As the rilk climbed aboard and the sides dipped lower into the water, Boruin tried to slow his breathing to the tempo of the shimmering light above. His heart had just returned to normal when Pile stood up and walked to him.

"By Yuin, man! Sit down before you tip us!" Boruin growled. Pile gave him a puzzled look. Then, grinning, he began jumping about. Boruin scrambled to catch his leg.

Pile skipped out of the way, laughing. "Easy, boss! You won't find better ballast stones than these rilk," he said, still throwing his weight from side to side. The heavy creatures that paddled at each corner kept the boat as steady as the cavern floor.

"Well, you shouldn't be messing around," Boruin grumbled, angry at being spooked for no reason.

"As I was going to tell you, Griant's brought the gear we requested. It's up front, if you think you can crawl your way forward," Pile said with a wide grin. Boruin sneered and forced himself to his feet.

They divided rations and supplies, packing their gear in leather sacks, greased and waterproof, at Griant's request. The lights thinned as the powerful strokes of the rilk carried them across the Cavern of Syan.

The next time Boruin looked above, the sparse star-like points of the Guidevein were quickly passing by. "We are in the current?" he asked.

"Yes, the river channel flows along this side of the lake. It exits the cavern further on," Griant answered.

"I thought you said the river was too dangerous, that we might be looked for."

The rilk nodded as he helped Pile and Toaaho lash their bags together. "True, but we will not leave the cavern by the river. Our route leaves the lake by another way."

"And you don't worry about that trail being watched?"

"Entrances to the Guidevein are unlooked for. Often they are hard for even the rilk to find," said Griant.

"But you know of this one?" Pile asked.

Griant pointed to the bow. "The rilka do." Three rilka stood on the rail, looking out across the water. The boy stood behind them, head cocked to the side as if listening to the darkness ahead. "They can hear the Guidevein, feel its branches under the deepest sediment. They can find it where no other can."

"Your children? How can they, if you can not?" Boruin asked.

"Children? What gave you that idea?" Griant snorted a chuckle and the same noise echoed from the other rilk. A chittering laughter rose from the small creatures about their feet. "That they are small does not make them children. They are rilka and we are rilk. If anything, I am the child. My rilka are far older. They travel with me for protection and I travel with them for their wisdom."

Boruin's brow furrowed as he thought through their first rushed days with Griant. "But we haven't seen one traveling with you," he said.

Toaaho guessed it first. "I would expect something that small would not make itself known outside the warren."

"Yes, I keep them well hidden," agreed Griant.

Pile rapped on the stone man's rough shin. "You don't even wear clothes. How does that work?" he laughed. Then he sucked on a knuckle where the skin had been scraped raw.

"We are almost to the whirlpool. I will show you there," Griant answered.

"Whirlpool?" Pile asked. Boruin suddenly felt a little sicker.

The rilk kept them circling just on the edge of the wide vortex. Boruin sat without words, his skin cold and his hands clenched. The sound coming from the dark pit in the center of the whirlpool was a low moan of air, like a great sucking of breath with no exhalation.

"And you guys do this all the time?" Pile asked.

"The entrance is very safe, a short passage you will not regret," Griant assured.

Pile clapped his hands and rubbed them together. "This is nuts! By Yuin, let's do it!" he said, that wide, crazy grin full on his face.

"Come on, old man. We'll go together," Wraethe said, trying gently to pull Boruin to his feet.

Boruin locked his hands underneath his knees. "What do you mean, go together?"

"Over the side. Griant said two at a time."

"Without the boat? Are you rutting crazy! He's a rock, for Yuin's sake!" Boruin shouted. He turned to protest, but Griant was already sliding into the water. The three rilka on the bow scuttled over the rail and down his arm. The small creatures slid into crevices in Griant's back, tucking under his heavy skin like small children burrowing into a winter blanket. Boruin shivered, and Wraethe shot him a look of agreeing revulsion.

The boy climbed on Griant's shoulder. The rilk took a roaring breath that filled his lungs and puffed out his chest like a great wine barrel. He was not a floating creature, and he clutched two large leather sacks filled with air as he pushed off from the boat. He bobbed on the surface, keeping the boy's head above water with frog-like kicks, and wasted no time heading right for the vortex's dark center. His grey head was visible for a moment on the far side as the pool sucked him around, and then he was gone.

Before Boruin could say another word, Wraethe flipped him over the edge. She held his hands to the rail until he quit sputtering and cursing and then climbed over with their packs. The greased sacks floated, and they grabbed hold.

Wraethe chuckled. "Come on, kick your feet! I know you can swim."

"Of course I can swim! It's boats I don't like!" Boruin shouted.

"Good," she shouted back, "because we're done with the boat." Wraethe let go of the skiff and they drifted down toward the shallow bowl of spinning water. Boruin watched Toaaho and Pile, ahead of them on the opposite side. The short man was howling in ridiculous joy, and the Mana'Olai kicked slowly as if it were a soft afternoon swim.

"Am I the only one terrified of this?" asked Boruin.

"Like you said, the rilk aren't going to turn on us. Hold on now!" said Wraethe.

Boruin clutched the sack, holding more than his fair share. Toaaho and Pile dropped out of sight, and then the black mouth of the vortex was a mere boat-length away. It pulled them around in a tight dance. Boruin's yell grew louder with each turn. They fell over the lip, the sack turning them on their side as it floated toward the open center. Instead of falling out into an empty space, they continued to spin down a black tunnel of gulping water.

Boruin quieted when he heard Pile ahead. The short man was hollering back, mocking his cry. In a matter of moments, Boruin felt the sack turning them back up as they rode over another lip.

The vortex had turned itself inside out, now spinning from the center to the outside. The water pushed them up and out to the edge of the churning river. The sight of the shore coming made Boruin bring his feet up under him. His boot skidded along the stone as they swung around toward Griant's outstretched arm. The rilk slung them out of the water, and they landed mid-run in the mouth of a small cavern.

"Whooaah," Pile shouted, running around in circles. "What a ride that was. We get to do that again, right? What do you say, Boruin? You ready for another ride?"

"Can't wait," he mumbled. Even Toaaho laughed.

"Come along, then," Griant said, motioning them toward a brilliant glow.

After the darkness of the cavern, the Guidevein chamber seemed brighter than the sun. Boruin looked at Wraethe, expecting to see her tucked behind her cowl and asleep. She stood blinking, her hands half over her eyes. They all stood with heads down or fingers splayed against the brightness until their eyes adjusted to the glow.

"Oh," Wraethe said once she could finally see. "It's so beautiful, Griant."

"Yes, it is glorious," the rilk answered, his eyes drinking in the sight as well.

Here the Guidevein pooled above them. Sheets of it hung down like curtains of fine lace.

"Almost seems alive," said Wraethe.

"All rock is alive to the rilk," Griant answered, forcing his eyes away from the sight for the moment. "Much of it is just asleep, hibernating. It lies dormant until the world chooses to swallow it up and bring it back to being. The Guidevein you saw in the warren sings even while it sleeps. Here it is awake."

"You're saying it really is alive?" Boruin asked. He pulled the boy back from a low lobe on the edge of the formation. His finger, running along its lip, had sent ripples of white thrumming away from it as if the rock sang out to the beat of his heart.

"The Guidevein is not wholly rock, but it is not wholly creature, either. It grows through the earth's foundations, through the bedrock. It is a living thing like a mountain is a living thing—or perhaps like a tree is more correct."

"Got it," Pile said, ready for the next thrill. "Now how do we ride it?"

"Not like a whirlpool, I hope," Boruin added. Small fissures and folds spread around Griant's mouth as he smiled. "No. This is different, and I won't try to explain it. You trusted me with the whirlpool. Trust me here."

"Where exactly is it going to take us?" Wraethe asked as they slipped their packs out of the greased sacks.

"We head for the Valley of Munier, under the Monahdraichean Range and past the Hetsu Plains. But the Guidevein does not run in a straight line. Its roots spread chaotically, and no single branch reaches all corners of the continent. We will travel this one as well as I can feel our path. The rilka will help us find other veins that will carry us closer."

Pile looked again into his gear. "I've got maybe two weeks worth of food here and you're talking about a damn long stretch of walking," he said.

"We will arrive when we arrive, but time is different on the Guidevein. You will have enough food," Griant answered.

The young man shrugged. "Well, let's go if we're going to go. If this is half as fun as the last ride, I can't wait."

"One last measure." Griant paused as several rilka climbed out of his thick carapace. Boruin suppressed a shudder; the sight gave him chills. The rilka surrounded them, and Griant pointed to a rune on the back of his calf. "This sign is of the Guidevein. You must wear it to enter." Two of the rilka climbed across his broad thigh and began to carve. "This sign will tether you to me. You must wear it so as not to wander." Flakes of stone fell from the rilk as the little creatures worked.

The rilka were kind enough not to carve the sigils into their flesh. Boruin's troupe sat while the little creatures sang the signs onto their skin, much like they had removed Toaaho's tattoo. The rilka set the symbols to match Griant's, one to the calf and one to the thigh. Only Pile's were different; he requested them on the top of each hand. As he waited for the others to finish, he danced around shadowboxing as if the tattoos gave his fists magical brawling power.

"I'm going to be so sick of him by the end of this trip," said Boruin.

"Yeah, we have to send him off for some quiet," Wraethe agreed.

Boruin's rilka dropped down and walked off with only the tether sign on his thigh. "What about the other one?" he asked.

"Show me," said Griant as the rilka chattered to his protector. "Take your shirt off," he told Boruin.

"Why?"

"The rilka claim you are already marked for travel," said Griant. It was where the rilka said, the mark laid in with the long row of tattooed runes.

Boruin was suddenly suspicious that Griant had been keeping him in the dark. "What, are all these rilk?"

"That sigil is used by the rilk," Griant explained, "but runes are a language of their own. It does not mean you have ridden the Guidevein before. It is a sign for passage, though I have not seen it used any other way than here and for this."

"What about these?" Boruin pointed at the ones on his shoulder. "Can you read these?" Griant turned the man around, inspecting the rest of his runes.

"Only a few. This one implies infinite vision. Here is one regarding stones."

"What do you mean 'implies and regarding?'" he huffed. "Do they cause these, make them, remove them—what?"

"Runes are not always one or the other. Without context—without knowing all of them—it is impossible to give an exact meaning," Griant answered. Boruin chewed his lip and thought it over. The rilka chattered; a volley of chirps passed back and forth like a hot rock.

Boruin watched them argue as he pulled his shirt back on. "Any others?" he asked.

"None that I know," said Griant.

"Don't give me that. The rilka aren't discussing ore prices." Boruin snapped. Griant hesitated but gave in as Wraethe nodded to go ahead.

"The rilka know of another," he conceded. "It is too old for my recollection, but I've heard of it. The Ghrunfre is a rune used in resurrection and in deconstruction." The rilka chattered again, and Griant rumbled back in question. He waited a moment, considering their answer. "By itself, it is a very powerful rune, very unsafe. Your Ghrunfre is bordered by sacrificial runes." Griant said. "An unfortunate combination."

"Rutting beautiful," Pile groaned. Wraethe shot a hard look at him, and the man threw up his hands. "What? He's been betting on those runes like a chump at an alleyway cup and coin game. He could have pulled those out, or Yuin knows what else, and we'd all have been blood and bone under the grindstone."

"I would have felt them," Boruin said.

"Like rut, you would have," Pile mumbled, stomping off to the edge of the Guidevein.

"Well, not like I can use them now anyway," said Boruin. He threw his pack on and cinched it tight. "Anything else to do, or can we start this road show?" he asked.

Griant's rilka scrambled into his body for the ride. "We're ready," he rumbled.

Griant led the way, carrying the boy into the curtains of Guidevein. They wove through the maze-like layers, each following the one before. The light was blinding between the lace hangings. It seemed too rich, like something other than light, something thick and coating. Like taking a deep breath in heavy fog, it poured into their lungs moist and cool. Boruin grabbed Wraethe's shoulder, shutting his eyes against the brightness—and then he was in the Guidevein.

Afterwards Boruin would not be able to accurately describe the sensations of the Guidevein. He struggled at first, finding that all sense of his body had left him. Sight fled, and he called out, only to find his voice silent.

Boruin forced himself to calm and felt deep rumblings enter his head. His body was not tethered as he expected; it was his mind that was attached fast to the rilk. The stone man's thoughts danced lightly across Boruin's consciousness like the indirect splatter of dripping water. The sense of the rilk made Boruin feel rilk-like himself: solid, full, and somewhat ageless, or more that age was insignificant. Through the rilk's ears he understood the rumbling of fiery stones deep in their subterranean vaults. The mountains now felt like older brothers.

Boruin touched on the rilka somewhere underneath the sense of Griant. They were silent and listening, feeling the Guidevein and carrying its touch through them to the others.

The Guidevein was all around them, not where they were or where they had begun. They felt it spread beneath the mountains, long roots stretched deep to the core of the world and up high where the peaks cracked under the weathering wind. Each branch tingled like fingers and toes warming from the cold. The system was massive. To feel all the branches at once, one might as well discern every wave on a wind-blown sea. Boruin pulled back his senses and followed Griant's guide as the rilk searched out the Guidevein's wonders.

At the tips of great, thriving veins, Boruin felt living nodes of the Guidevein, like the one through which they had entered. There too the brilliant curtains were expanding with thin lace fingers, growing out into the mountains. He sensed where the veins crossed near other Guidevein systems, their expanses like dim shadows. It was like being the root of a great tree in a forest of great trees—at least that was as close as Boruin ever came to explaining it.

From far off distances, rilk messages found their way through the stone as deep and heavy vibrations. By some talent borrowed from either Griant or the rilka, Boruin could gauge their source, some far north in the Suricles, others close by and loud enough that their bouncing echoes were like stone-voiced singers belting out a round in a nearby room.

As they drifted through the living rock, the sounds of the under-lands sang to them like the wind above ground. Boruin found the feeling so peaceful, so relaxing that when Griant's thoughts dropped into his head it startled him, like being shaken in a deep sleep. The rilk's question came across Boruin's mind in a mix of words and images.

"Where are the other living nodes?" It had taken Griant and his rilka some time to map out the open, growing ends of the far-rooted Guidevein. The structure of it came at him in picture, bright white exits far to the west and back south, but none ahead. The Guidevein seem lopsided. If it were a plant, Boruin would have guessed that a winter freeze had bitten half the roots.

It was against reason, according to Griant's thoughts. They could backtrack, but a feeling of apprehension came from the rilk.

"I feel herded. I do not like that way," said Griant. He offered a lone route to the east with its open end a distant sparkle hanging high like a star above the rest of the vein. The rilka resisted, but Boruin shared Griant's dislike of having a particular direction forced upon them. Boruin voted to follow Griant's choice, though he didn't know if he had been heard. They entered the long path east that climbed into the higher peaks.

The Guidevein climbed into the ranges, riding up the mountains past the trees and goats into a world of snow and frozen rock. Near the top, Griant projected the thought of an unpleasant change. Boruin wondered what the rilk meant and then his eyes teared up at the burst of brilliant white. Then his stomach dropped—they were out of the Guidevein and falling fast from its light. His hand clutched at Wraethe's shoulder as the cold wind began to howl past them in the darkness. This black void echoed the timeless feeling from the Guidevein, but the plummeting descent turned it into terror.

Madness was beginning to simmer deep in Boruin's skull, stoked by the smothering dark, when he realized there was light in Wraethe's hair. He pulled up to look over her shoulder and saw Griant's silhouette plunging down a deep well with the boy riding on the crook of his arm. Toaaho flew gracefully, and Pile turned over and about, fighting the wind.

At the bottom, brilliant sheets of Guidevein were rising fast. From above, Boruin realized the growing node looked like a great white rose. It was beautiful, the center glowing bright and the petals so hard, sharp—and rushing towards him. He buried his face in Wraethe's hair as they fell between the curtains, the lace petals flashing past and the light blinding even behind his closed eyes.

- 13 -
DEAD M'GAGLIND DUUL

The iridescent roots of the first two Guideveins had sprawled wide across the southern part of the continent. This new one was withered and dark. Perhaps it was old, perhaps poisoned, but this Guidevein had shrunken to one root, its only branches too small and spidery to travel upon. It made Boruin nervous; he felt they were in a place that did not want them. He held close to their rilk guide and concentrated on Griant's solid presence.

When they came to the end of the stunted Guidevein, Boruin was glad to depart. The touch of it left a sour stain on his mind. It was hard on Griant, too, and the rilk took them silently out of the chamber. The path was ancient and unkempt. Loose rocks made the steep climb difficult. They exited beneath the roots of a great tree and once again the night sky spread wide over their heads. Everyone felt better after breathing the cool air, but they all felt different.

Pile leaned back against a thick root running across the dirt. "I feel so small," he said.

"That's strange, you don't look any shorter," said Wraethe.

"It felt nice being so immense, you know?" he asked, ignoring the tease. "It was fulfilling."

"A very special experience, to feel another being so closely," said Toaaho, also smiling.

"I'm glad you enjoyed it so," said Griant. "There is more to come if we are to make it to Munier Valley." The boy clapped his hands and then shadowboxed at Pile in glee. The short man raised his hand as though to box the boy's ears. The child danced back behind the rilk.

"Silly kid," said Pile.

Griant had told them right: time and distance were indeed lost in the great expanse of the Guidevein. If the mountains around them felt the heat of the sun, the rocks had said nothing about it.

"Where are we, Griant?" asked Boruin.

"In the Maunua Kuini range, northeast of the Hetsu Plains."

"I can't believe we got here so fast," said Pile.

"It wasn't that fast," Toaaho said. "The stars have traveled far." Wraethe looked up, following Toaaho's gaze into the night sky.

"Spring is coming on," she added.

"A half year? You've got to be kidding me," said Pile. "We haven't eaten since leaving the warren. It's been a day, maybe two on the outside." Wraethe stared longer at the green moon cresting the horizon and the stars nestled around it. A world-tearing storm had whipped Lakshi's blue clouds into a curious eye that peered back at them across the dark night sky.

She was certain now. "No, we've been underground for a year and a half."

"Bullshit."

"I know my moons, Pile."

The rilk attempted to explain. "In the Guidevein—"

Pile through up his hands. "'Time is different.' I know, Griant, but for Yuin's sake..."

"Hey, at least your 120-year exile from Handry's Supper House is that much closer to being served," said Toaaho.

"I do miss their fish and chips," said Pile, kicking a stone down the hill.

Boruin smiled into the sky. "Horseback might have put us here faster, but we'd have ridden from the warren with enemies on our back. I'd have paid a year's time, more than once in my life, for a trail as cold as we've got now." Better still was the clever escape from the moons. His look above showed Nurom Misuer was no longer a worry. The red moon was now a dark star twinkling in the farthest swing of its orbit.

They walked the rest of the night in near silence. Griant seemed weary as he trudged through the forest. He ended their march after an exhausting climb. At the top of the ridge they could see the first smudges of grey growing over the horizon.

The rilk set the boy down. "We'll go no further in the day." A large stone broke out of the dirt where he sat, and he slipped his legs into it like an old woman soaking her sore feet.

Wraethe joined Toaaho in meditation. Pile slept.

The boy sat quietly beside Boruin and scanned the forest around them like a sentry under siege. The woods were silent, and he wondered what the child was looking for, but he did not ask. The boy wouldn't have answered. Instead he let the child curl close when the sun-warmed wind whipped over a distant ridge, sounding like a strangled cry, and the two fell asleep together.

Pile woke Boruin sometime in the middle of the day. Toaaho was gone, and the boy was now curled among the dark folds of Wraethe's robes for warmth. Boruin smiled, rubbing his arms under a shaft of sunlight. He too was a little scared of what the child could do, but it was good she'd remembered that he was still a young boy.

"I want to show you something," the young man said. Boruin yawned and waved him on. They walked up the ridgeline to where an old lightning strike had cleared the crest. Boruin started to step out into the opening when Pile held him back. "Just look from here."

Boruin shaded his eyes with the flat of his hand and peered north through the fire-thinned tree line. It was a beautiful day. They were in the low part of the Maunua Kuini range. White-capped peaks rose in the northeast, but here only a few stunted mountains dotted the land around them. Across the valley two stone columns towered above the forest, rising even higher than the low ridge behind them.

"Watchtowers?" Boruin asked.

Pile shook his head. "No, I don't think so. The bend, high in that right one, is too far over the base. If it were a tower, it would have collapsed. They have to be solid stone."

"It kind of looks like a knee, doesn't it?"

"Yeah, that's what I thought, too," said Pile. "But that's not what you need to see."

Pile pointed higher up the slope. What Boruin had first taken for the path of an ancient avalanche revealed itself as a once-paved avenue. The path had grown wild in large patches, but the great paving stones still kept most of the hillside clear. The road angled between the stone columns, almost wide enough to reach both bases as it passed.

"Now look just below the top of the ridge where the path ends in the trees."

"What am I looking for?" he asked.

"Hold still and just watch."

So Boruin watched, growing tired. He shifted his weight onto his other leg and stood a good ten minutes before realizing that there was no pain where Wraethe had run her steel through his thigh. Come to think of it, it hadn't given him trouble since—

He jumped as something exploded from the shadows, dashing down the distant path. It came crashing into a grove between the stone columns. Birds exploded from the small oasis of trees as the top branches quaked with the impact of that huge thing slamming against their trunks.

A creature dashed back up the hill, a second snarling beast chasing it out of the grove. One brute returned to the shadows at the end of the path. The other turned and walked slowly back toward the forest. It stopped halfway and, like a cat tired of play, curled up to sleep in the sun. It was too far away to make out many details, but Boruin had seen two wide mouths, lots of powerful legs, and the easy way it had moved its great bulk uphill at lightning speed.

Boruin noticed now that Pile was chewing his thumb. The nail was down to the quick, leaving a smear of blood on his lip. "What are those things?" he whispered.

Pile too kept his voice low. "I don't know, but when I first saw it move, Toaaho and I were in the middle of this clearing. It sounds crazy, being so far off, but I swear it dropped out of the tree line to get a look at us. We didn't move for an hour. It didn't either. We stayed here until it turned and trotted back uphill."

"Where is Toaaho?" Boruin asked, even though he already knew.

"Went to find out what those things are," Pile answered. He turned and started back toward camp.

When Boruin again remembered his wounded leg, the sun had almost reached the horizon. Toaaho had returned and was retelling what he had seen up close. Boruin listened to the Mana'Olai with only one ear as he unwound the bandage. The skin beneath the wrapping was healed, and only a faint white scar showed where Wraethe's blade had speared through the muscle.

In a rush of nervousness, Boruin recalled his other injury and cringed, remembering the searing pain and smoke rising from under the judge's sorcerous hand. He turned his arm over. The time in the Guidevein had healed that, too. A slick scar in the shape of a hand remained where the judge had burned him. It was still an ugly pink, but the skin had healed. His fingers quivered for a moment before he brought them to the line of runes. Boruin pulled ever so gently, and the line tensed, trying to shift over his skin. He pulled harder and felt the scar resist, still holding tight to the rune trapped there.

"Kaulths. If they have a name in a lij tongue, I don't know it," said Griant, drawing Boruin back to the conversation. "Probably because they are only found in places lij don't go."

Wraethe came out of her cowl as the sun disappeared. "Like cursed places," she said. At her awakening, Griant rose and started them walking down the ridgeline toward the distant stone columns.

"Yes. Battlefields, fallen castles, or places of plague. The kauolths are drawn to the dead."

Pile stopped when he saw Griant heading for the ancient road. "What are we doing above ground, then?" he asked. "Take us back under and find a way around."

Griant turned to answer, but continued backing down the hill. "There are no passages here. The ground below has been sacked, the tunnels torn down, the caverns flooded."

"The fear we felt from the rilka... it wasn't that Guidevein they thought was dangerous. It was this place." Toaaho said.

"Yes. Now we must hurry. The kauolths are over the next ridge and we need to cross a lot of ground before dawn." He started moving and did not go quietly; the rilk drove almost straight down the ridge. The boy ran to keep up, and the others followed in confusion.

"Those creatures aren't going to hear all his ruckus?" Pile asked as Griant crashed through a thick hedge and onto the ancient highway. No one replied. They were saving their breath as the rilk had hastened his pace now that the ground had cleared. He swung the panting boy up into his arms, and they rushed up the valley toward the stone columns.

"Alright, alright! Unless you want to carry me too, we've got to stop!" Pile cried as they reached the columns. The rilk slowed back to a walk but did not halt. "Look, I'm not going on until you tell me why I shouldn't be worried that we're running right for those creatures," Pile added. Still Griant did not stop, but he did begin to speak, and Pile hobbled along after.

"This once was M'Gaglind Duul, a great warren of the rilk. If we were walking this avenue three thousand years ago, we would pass underneath the figure of M'Gaghulh, who stood watching over the doors to the mountain. This is all that is left of him," Griant said as they passed through the shadow of the towering stone leg.

"The first city of the rilk grew here. It was M'Gaghulh's dream that we should combine warrens, come together and learn from each other. New ideas and skills would rise from our shared knowledge, our traded skills." Griant stopped walking at the top of the avenue, where a great set of stairs led into what Pile had mistaken for the tree line atop the ridge.

They climbed up the stairs toward ivy covered columns and a massive entrance hall. The great columns held the rough stone roof as if the giant statue had once peeled back a layer of rock and propped it up.

Griant turned and looked down the valley as if seeing through the ages passed. "The warren grew slowly at first, but soon new knowledge, songs, and technologies sprang forth regularly from the commune. More rilk and rilka joined, and in five hundred years they had carved the entire mountain into a place of pride for our people. Much of the skill used in creating M'Gaglind Duul has since been lost. The statue of M'Gaghulh was sung from the stone in one piece to stand welcoming those that came to the warren. An amazing feat."

"It must have been very grand," said Wraethe.

Griant grunted in agreement. "I'd think so. I never saw it myself. Too young," he said. "My rilka tell me they've never seen anything like it since."

"You said it was a mountain. I don't see a mountain here," said Pile.

"No. No, you don't," Griant replied as he took the last few steps into the entrance hall. The others followed, expecting darkness, and instead found moonlight deep in the room. There was nothing at the back of the hall but open space. They stood looking down into the shallow valley of a great crater. Broken stone lay scattered among dense groves of trees and brush. Mist rose in twisting spires from a low marsh in the deepest center of rubble. The land looked ruined in the moonlight, and the sounds that rose on the night wind made Boruin's skin crawl.

"The Fae," Wraethe gasped. "The Nai'Oigher of creation—Iys's groundlings fought this war." Her mouth hung open to continue, but the memory had slipped from her tongue.

Griant nodded but did not take his eyes off the crater. "The Feirnann of his talamh are called groundlings to some. Iys sends these low-caste workers to mine the deep earth for ores to aid his projects. They are not beyond trespassing into the Duine lands to pilfer our metals and rare stones.

"At the beginning of our war, when the groundlings stumbled upon our people and retreated with a bejeweled rilka, we thought it was a misjudgment; perhaps the rilka had been mistaken for a gem. We sent emissaries to request its return, and the Fae refused. We sent a ransom, which they kept with the rilka. Then we sent a host that destroyed their mining outpost and all in it."

Griant's hand drifted across his chest where, Boruin had no doubt, his own rilka were nestled deep. "We did not find the rilka. It is assumed to have been taken to the Dreaming Lands, made into a caged attraction or such. We could do no more and hoped to put the incident behind us.

Boruin watched the rilk's eyes light up as if he'd seen something in the valley that pleased him, but his smile was thin and cruel. He turned and looked into the devastation, but whatever Griant had seen was gone. The rilk continued his tale. "The groundlings waited for two hundred years and then returned with an army. M'Gaglind Duul was an open city, not built for war. Its chambers were well connected. Many wide tunnels led into the warren. Little thought of defense had gone into its construction.

"The groundlings swept into the mountain, killing many of my people. They were very experienced at fighting below ground and forced us to retreat onto the mountainside. M'Gaghulh and his conclave flooded the lower chambers, cutting off the underground highways and forcing the Fae up into the mountain. With the city lost and their host chasing us down into the valleys, M'Gaghulh then sung to the foundations of the mountain. The peak collapsed at his request. Most of the Fae army is buried in the sunken mountain below your feet. It is our cursed place."

"What of M'Gaghulh?" Toaaho asked.

"He followed a retreating band into the Dreaming Lands in search of our lost rilka. We have not seen him since. You mentioned once, Toaaho, that the warrens were few and far apart. We returned to isolation following the war and the loss of M'Gaglind Duul. Once the Fae's fear of the rilk is great enough to keep them out of the Duine realm, perhaps we will renew M'Gaghulh's enterprise. It would be nice," Griant said.

The boy pointed down the rubble-strewn slope. Calling for help, a Fae groundling climbed towards them as if the battle had ended moments ago, rather than thousands of years past. Boruin cringed at the sight of the creature; this low caste of Fae was far different from the Monarhig or his servant.

The groundling skittered up the rubble on a thousand boney legs. Its segmented lower body had a hundred thick-fingered hands spread across its long back. They clutched at bits of broken metal and shining stone–still gathering material for its Nai'Oigher. The flat head, bred low to its chest to guide it through shallow passageways, gibbered madly, calling for their help in its strange tongue.

No one had the chance to speak before a dark shadow pounced up the ridge and snatched the screaming Feirnann out of its run. The creature tore the groundling between the terrible mouths of its two heads, each swallowing its portion before dashing back down into the valley.

Boruin's sword shook in his hand. Sweat poured through his cold skin from the adrenaline dumped hot into his veins. He heard the silence of held breath and saw the others in much the same condition. Only Griant had not prepared for the attack. A similar scene, Boruin realized, had brought about his previous wicked smile.

Pile, always superstitious, was the first to understand. "That was a ghost, wasn't it?" he muttered, digging back into his pack for anything he might use as a ward.

"When you said 'drawn to the dead,' I figured they were scavengers, or that they nested among the bones," Boruin whispered.

"They're devourers of spirits, aren't they, Griant?" Wraethe said. "How did so many come to this place?"

Griant's voice carried a tone that was cruel satisfaction. "We brought all we could find," he replied. "They took the rilka and destroyed all M'Gaghulh's warren had built. We were very angry, and these beasts help bring us some peace."

"They have not consumed them all?" Toaaho asked.

Wraethe knew that answer from her long exertion at Toaaho's homestead. "You can't kill spirits," she said coldly.

Pile grimaced. "So they just keep getting eaten every night? That's cruel."

"That's war," Griant said. "While the sun is down and the spirits run, we are safe. We must find the Guidevein before daylight."

"What happens then?" Boruin asked.

"The groundlings are gone, and the creatures look for something solid to fill their bellies," Toaaho ventured.

"Right. So hurry, if you would." Griant started off into the valley. The boy slid down from the rilk's grasp. He came to Boruin and gave a weak attempt at a brave smile as he curled his hand around the man's fingers.

As they started down, Boruin pulled Wraethe behind. "What else did you remember, before your mouth snapped shut?"

"His war was not common knowledge," Wraethe whispered, though Griant was well ahead. "The Court of Twilight forbids such meddling, as Iys does, in the Duine lands. I found out only because the Nai'Oigher came to my lady Dream's palace to show off a prize." Boruin nodded. He knew what she was driving at. Iys had come bearing the jewel-encrusted rilka. Yuin only knew how Griant might have reacted to that piece of knowledge.

"Has anything else come back to you?"

Wraethe's wide smile was a surprise. "So much, Boruin. It is like the Guidevein let it soak and come free. So much is swirling around, and I can almost put it in some order—" They froze, watching another groundling scream as the hunting beasts caught and consumed it. "Let me save it until we're out of here. Then I think I can piece most of us together for you." He nodded and couldn't help but let a smile slip to join hers.

Crossing the valley was as near to torture as Boruin had ever been. The groundlings surrounded them in the dark, some to beg and some to curse the rilk. One taunted Boruin, his broken neck bouncing as the Fae jogged along screaming. Boruin felt the ground shudder and dropped to cover the boy as six legs and two mouths tore out of the rubble field and ripped into the distracted spirit. Fresh blood dribbled down the kauolth's jaw as it devoured its prey. The red faded into nothing, the groundling's blood dry for centuries, and the creature turned downhill. Boruin swore he heard its stomach growling.

That Iys's lowest Feirnann were mostly odd and ugly did not make their deaths any less gruesome to the travelers. The only features they all seemed to share were the armor and weapons that did nothing to protect them against the kauolths. Many bore a mix of parts that seemed traded and swapped between insect, reptile, and crustacean. There were giant claws for moving heavy stone; heads covered in wide, watery eyes made for darkness rather than the bright Diun sky; some had hundreds of legs, others had none. Most moved fast across the ground, and Boruin guessed that there were probably slow ones too, only they survived little past dusk. Ugly as they all were, they were made for digging, mining, and earth moving. Iys had bred them well.

Most of the groundlings had learned to keenly sense the return of death. A look of terror crossed each face, beggar or raver, and the Fae would rush into the darkness. Boruin's crew took cover behind boulder and tree before a kauolth would dash past in chase. Some beasts ran alone, others in a herd, but all were fast and all were hungry. They watched one of the creatures wedge its left head under a boulder while the second head pulled at it with its teeth. It pried the stone out of the ground and found a group of groundlings digging frantically. Some scraped with wide, claw-covered paws, others with heavy bone scoops set into their massive jaws, but Boruin saw no dirt fly from any of them. He almost felt sorry for the spirits. They screamed as the two heads and rows of teeth went to work.

Pile kept his head down, polishing his protective wards with the rubbing of his fingers. The others stared ahead in shock, like invisible guests on a gruesome battlefield. They began to recognize the number of groundlings that would draw the creatures the fastest. The group hid early to avoid being crushed rather than found—the beasts never stopped or turned to pay them attention. Their desire was for the dead Fae, as if only the spirits could quench some awful thirst.

Crossing the sunken mountain proved agonizingly slow as they wound through the rubble fields and dense groves of cedar. Tall grasses camouflaged dark sinkholes. Boruin peered down one only to find more groundlings huddled together. They shushed him away, as if his attention would attract the ravenous kauolth. The ghosts continued to surround them, coming in one by one after the beasts tore off to other parts of the valley. When Diun disappeared over the ridge and Lakshi's half face left only a dim light to travel by, Boruin began to worry. Pile was already frantic.

"How are we doing here, big man? Closing on our exit?" he asked, kicking his way through the persistent begging of a kneeling Fae. "We're getting pretty close to not making it back over the ridge by sunup, if you can't find the vein."

"We've passed that already," said Toaaho.

"Maybe you," Pile almost shouted. "But you ain't finding me here with the sun," the short man added, dropping down to a whisper as another hunting beast passed near.

"Keep calm, Pile. Griant will find the Guidevein," said Wraethe.

Pile's voice broke as it moved up an octave. "Well he's done a fairly po—"

"Calm, Pile." Wraethe repeated. This time it was clearly an order, and her cold tone cut through his rising panic.

"I have lost the entrance," Griant offered at that most untimely moment. "The rilka cannot hear the Guidevein. Perhaps the dead hide it."

Pile's look strained between ironic rebuke and fear, but he held his tongue to a quick sputter.

Boruin, trying to hold his worry at arm's length, took a deep breath. "What do you suggest?"

Griant looked deeper into the valley, toward the swamp now sending waves of white mist into the cold night. "They think we should go lower. The Guidevein is there, and perhaps they will feel the opening closer to dawn, when the spirits weaken."

"That will be cutting it pretty close."

The rilk did not have a reply.

Griant was leading them through the next thicket when the boy started tugging on Boruin's arm. Boruin was stooping to pick him up when Toaaho froze.

"I smell Fae."

"Well they're rutting everywhere," said Pile.

"Those don't smell," the Mana'Olai whispered. Pile leaned in and sniffed a ghostly Feirnann that was gruffly cursing the large rilk from knee level.

Boruin caught where the boy was looking. "Their helms don't reflect moonlight, either." Across a wide ravine, two dozen ground-lings made their way through the rubble of the sunken valley. One of the beasts pounced out of cover. As its mouths opened into a budding flower of sharp teeth, dead groundlings scattered, most leaping over the edge of the cliff. It did them little good as a kauolth bellowed with eager surprise from deep below.

The Fae that hadn't fled stood stock still with their axes out in a thorny cluster. These were bred for more than just mining. Some had two legs and some four. Their arms also varied in number, but all their limbs were banded in thick muscle. These were trained soldiers.

The kauolth swung past them and pursued the ghosts, knowing spirit from flesh. Once it was gone, the warrior groundlings disappeared quickly into a field of large boulders, their shadows leading the way.

"Rutting Fae," Boruin borrowed from Pile's broad vocabulary. "What the rut would they come here for? This isn't a coincidence, is it Griant?"

"No, I think not."

"Either you get us into the Guidevein, or we get the hell out of this valley."

"With the Fae here, the rilka think the entrance must have been destroyed," said Griant, cocking his head to listen. "Not a master singer… perhaps, but it is a great risk," the stone man mumbled as his thoughts to the rilka slipped out loud. "There is a Guidevein below us. We must find it. I don't have much time." Boruin wasn't sure if he was speaking to himself and the others or still to his rilka. The rilk slumped low and pushed his way through the thicket. They followed after him.

When they found the Guidevein, its glow was weak, reflecting off the surrounding stone only where time and weather had not removed the honed polish of ancient rilk hands. It breached the surface in a small cave formed by the chaos of the mountain's collapse. A huge column tipped on its side braced three slabs of granite above their heads. A wall of rubble stood shadowed behind the frozen fountain of pale Guidevein. A broken carving of a wide-mouthed fish had served as the entrance. Wraethe stood guard there now, her bow pointed between the thin stone gills they'd climbed through

Griant went to work as soon as he reached the Guidevein. Boruin had come to recognize two of the rilka, one sparkling with green jade and another with silver sleeves and mask. Seven or eight more poured out of their host as he pulled up the granite floor to widen the base of the small, glowing fountain. A low rumbling filled the cave. Only once the rilka began their own counterpoint did Boruin realize Griant was singing.

"Everyone on the entrance," he ordered. "I'd be surprised if that can't be heard through the rock." They took up their position and watched through the mouth of the fish. The only groundlings they saw were spirits running from hiding place to hiding place, snatched up despite their desperate efforts.

Twice the singing stopped and Boruin looked back to see Griant pacing the floor. Occasionally, the rilka would chatter and the stone man would try a new melody in response. Boruin sent the boy to sit and watch the rilk work, away from the mouth of the cave. The sky at the far edge of the crater was beginning to lighten.

The first arrow came hissing through the fish's mouth as the fletching tore through the air. It ended with a twang as Toaaho caught the iron tip on his knife and deflected it up into the ceiling. When the second followed, Wraethe pinpointed the shooter and sent her own shaft spinning into the deep brush outside the cave. The groundlings moved positions and fired again. A thick black arrow skipped through the gills, ricocheting off Pile's axe. The short man cursed and pressed himself lower to the ground.

"Behind that third boulder on the left," he offered. Wraethe sent an arrow into the shadows. They heard a sharp cry, and then the groundling staggered out into the open. Before the body had even fallen, a kauolth was on it, snatching the spirit right from the dead flesh.

"Yuin's whores," Boruin whispered. "This is not the place to catch your end. Keep your eyes peeled." The thought of death had never frightened him like it did in this place. To die was one thing; to die again every night was more than he wanted to ponder.

The soldiers shifted position after every volley, making it hard for Wraethe to return fire. They made their approach slowly; the tangle of rubble around the entrance was too thick to draw close without stepping into the open. Wraethe caught movement in the shadows. Her bow sang out and her target replied with a hard grunt as the arrow punched through the Fae's stiff leather armor. The rest held off rushing into Wraethe's fire for as long as they could, but not for as long as Boruin had hoped.

Wraethe stopped firing and held perfectly still. "Listen," she whispered.

"No screams," Toaaho replied. With a sudden fear, Boruin could not remember when last he'd heard one of the spirits cry out. In the silence, the boy's clapping made them jump. Behind them, Griant's song grew faster as the bright edge of living Guidevein peeled up around the glowing fountain. The rilka's chanting doubled, and the runes across Griant's body flared bright. Arrows sung through the entrance, and Boruin tucked behind his rock. The iron tips sparked off the gills and the roof of the cave. As he leaned out to look, a second volley followed. He had just enough time to see groundlings silently charging through the thin morning light. Wraethe darted out into the open, firing over the incoming line. She caught some of the snipers covering the charge, but the rest pinned them down until their brothers were climbing over the lower lip of the stone fish.

BROKEN AND LOST

Toaaho retreated from the heavy axe blows of a charging groundling. His knife slipped between the seam of his opponent's helm and gorget, spilling arterial blood. The Fae fell, clutching his neck and tangling the feet of those pressing behind.

Wraethe set her bow aside. Though it was nearing dawn, and wisps of morning shadows were beginning to thicken around her, the woman still fought with inhuman speed and grace. Her sword flashed between the stone gills, spearing through the eye slits of an armored mask fashioned into a wicked sneer. Wraethe pulled the steel free, circled to parry a spear beside her, and drove a heel into the attacker's chest. Pile swung down as the groundling fell, burying his axe through the hardened leather armor and into the groundling's lung.

The Fae charged against the bottleneck of the stone fish, fighting without a cry, without a shout. Boruin caught their worried glances over their shoulders. The light behind them was growing, and the whining cries of hungry beasts interrupted the peace of dawn. The groundlings fought furiously in their silence, the only sound quiet, labored breath interrupted with the sharp tang of metal meeting metal. Even without the battle cries, that rapid staccato beat was enough to call in the kauolths. Boruin saw a blur of claw and teeth as a creature sped past the mouth of the cave, grabbing a rear-guard and carrying him out of sight. The old fighter shoved a Fae to open the measure between them. Instead of charging back, the groundling took another step in retreat. Boruin's fear of the Fae dwindled as the clacking of two tongues against hard teeth caused him to turn.

The kauolth stalked from the heavy rubble behind the great column, its hide covered with dust after worming through the mess of rock. The two heads hung low, the fur of its chins grazing the floor and leaving a trail of wet drool. Boruin heard the groundlings backing over each other, retreating across the ground they had won.

"Toaaho, against the wall," Wreathe said through a stifled yawn. She circled to the opposite side of the beast. Pile drew up beside Boruin, and they braced for the coming pounce.

With a roar, Griant dove out from the bright light of the Guidevein, his fingers intertwined to make a massive club of his fists. The rilk slammed down on the kauolth's closest skull and split the bone wide. The neck dropped, and the beast stumbled to the side.

The stone man shielded his face with his forearm as the other wide mouth snapped out at him. Sharp teeth grated hard flakes from his skin, and Griant drove forward, roaring. With his other hand, he clutched the creature's good throat and wrenched. The beast released his arm and gurgled a harsh cry, its tongue writhing. With both hands on its throat, the rilk snapped the kauolth's neck and it fell, shuddering.

Boruin spun back, expecting a renewed charge, but the Fae were occupied. Outside, the smell of warm blood had infuriated the kauolths. They were swarming the entrance of the cave, tearing at even each other for the chance at live meat.

Griant slung the dead kauolth across the entrance, crushing the skilled carving of the gills and three retreating Fae as he tried to block the opening. Toaaho cut through the shoulder of a fourth groundling as he crawled over the dead body and back into the cave.

"The Guidevein won't hold!" Griant bellowed over the roaring beasts. "We must go!" The rilk pushed into the light like he was wading into a snowdrift. The boy followed in his wake. Pile kicked at a head squeezing beneath a broken gill, then turned and ran for the light. He hit the bright center and slowed.

"Yuin! It's as thick as mud," he said as the light slowly swallowed him. The few white lace petals of the vein that Griant had managed to sing forth were already beginning to shrink. It was clear that this was not a stable gate.

"Come on!" Boruin ordered. Wraethe and Toaaho turned, and the three ran for the light. Wraethe floated through it like air; the morning had come and she was again almost entirely shadows. Boruin drove his open hand into the light, trying to slip in behind the tips of his fingers. The light was hardening, the white stone curtains withering down into dry flakes.

Out of the corner of his eye, Boruin saw the lighted face of Toaaho turn. The man jabbed with his knife. His attacker crashed against a white sheet of Guidevein and snapped it free. The light dimmed, and Boruin saw Toaaho dash away, spinning out of another attack and closing again to drive his knife into an unprotected armpit.

Boruin crossed some invisible threshold, and the Guidevein began to pull at his body. He fought the drag of the light as he saw the groundlings beginning to spill into the cave. The Fae pulled down the broken gills and widened the entrance. Boruin felt the tethering rune tug at him, trying to draw him further in, but he was as anchored to Toaaho as well as Griant and trapped between both.

Toaaho tore into the Fae, keeping them trapped in the fish's mouth. He dashed between the widening holes, trying to plug the gaps with the dead and dying. *He's running out of time. It will take him too long to climb into the light!* Boruin thought. He opened his mouth to cry a warning, but the bright vein of rock squelched his voice. A blade caught Toaaho in the back of the thigh, sending a bright splash of blood across the floor. His attacker fell as the Mana'Olai slipped his knives between four different joints in the Fae's armor.

Toaaho turned to dodge the next attack, staggering on his weakened leg. A heavy mace smashed across his ribs. The owner received a severed hamstring in retaliation, but Toaaho was down. Through the swarming fighters, Boruin caught his friend's eye and then the movement of his hand. The Mana'Olai's knife cut the tethering rune from the flesh of his thigh. Boruin slammed his hands out across the last of the withering petals as the whiplash of being last in the tethered line jolted his body. *Let go!* Griant ordered. *You must enter before the gate fails or it will cut you in two!* The image of his severed body flashed from Griant's mind to his own.

If he dies, he will be trapped here with your Yuin-damned soul eaters! Boruin thought desperately at the rilk in his head. He pulled against the Guidevein and saw an axe come down, severing Toaaho's neck. The strength left Boruin's body. He fell into the light with his mind screaming the anguish that his throat could not. A swelling echo of despair washed across him, and he knew that Wraethe and Pile had also witnessed Toaaho's sacrifice.

The beauty of the Guidevein filled his mind as he slipped into the rock, but it did not outweigh the hardness of his heart. Men had died under his leadership before, but Toaaho had been more than a contracted man. He had bought the Mana'Olai out of slavery when he was little more than a boy. Boruin was often not proud of himself, but he was always proud of Toaaho.

The old man tugged at his head, trying not to think on it more. It needed flailing, wood cutting, or Fae slaying. Being bound up in the rock with no way to purge his anger and shame made the pain too much to bear. Boruin instead clung to the touch of the Guidevein. It was a brilliant maze of tangled roots, pockets twisted together under the Maunua Kuini Range. The more he let the image into his mind, the more the feeling of joining the rock soothed him.

The feeling was so peaceful, so finally distracting that when a long run of Guidevein to the north fell from their consciousness, the impact came as a crushing wave. The violence of the separation softened as it passed through the rilka and Griant, but what intensity it lost was replaced by their rising anger. Boruin felt confusion and rage wrestling within Griant's thoughts. What the rilk tried to communicate came in stuttering pictures of possible earthquakes and other fault line shifts. His hope was nullified moments later when a low taproot of the Guidevein was amputated. Amid the backwash of agony came Griant's image of his Fae enemy.

Griant backtracked down the vein toward a thick cluster of junctions. Thousands of branches spread through the mountains from that sparkling knot. Routes fell around them as they approached, but the tangle of paths would keep them from being cut off. The rilk's voice rose to a rumble that would have been deafening if Boruin's hearing had not been nullified in the Guidevein. The great explosion of sound echoed off the surrounding mountains and spread out across the great bedrocks of the continent.

Griant sung out to the stone, his call of both terror and rage. *A Guidevein is being destroyed!* it said. *Rilk lands are under siege!* The message rippled across the Pilean continent, and then there was nothing but a black void.

Boruin wondered if he were dead. He felt nothing, heard nothing, and his screams were held trapped in his throat. Was this death, trapped with a wandering mind, all his bad deeds done and his good deeds unfinished? If so, it would not be long before madness came. Boruin thought he would welcome the distraction.

The black began to grow cold. It flowed over his body, soaking in. His mouth opened and the black entered, wet and freezing. He opened his eyes and found light filtering through dark water. To his left, more light reached out to him like pale tendrils. His lungs began to empty of air. Boruin clenched his teeth and turned about, searching for the sun, for some sense of which way was up, trying to stay calm. He was deep underwater, but the light to his left seemed dimmer than the light elsewhere. He watched it for another moment, his lungs beginning to complain, and then he was certain: that was the dying Guidevein. It had expelled him as the broken fragment shriveled. Now its beautiful light was fading.

Boruin turned and lunged for the surface. It was like being buried alive, thrashing through the cold water, the light no closer. Fingers fumbling with his scabbard, he felt his lungs hitch in his chest. His sword dropped down toward the bottom, and he slowly breathed out. It stopped the spasm in his lungs, tricked them into waiting just another moment. But once the air was gone there would be no more.

Boruin kicked free his boots. Finally, he was rising faster than the bubbles escaping his lips, but still the light seemed impossibly distant. If anything, the spear-like shafts of light were fading. They begin to thin around him, and he focused on the one thrust down into his eyes. It too dimmed, and his lungs burned with a heat that cried out for the cold water. He ground his teeth to deny it and felt his face break through into a biting wind. His hot lungs gasped at the air, and his eyes filled with light. Boruin lay back in the cold water, the black circles dancing in his vision slowly disappearing back into the lake. He kicked his feet slowly toward the shore, his muscles almost too tired to keep him afloat.

"Rut, I hate the water," Boruin coughed as he dragged himself onto land. The wind was cool, but warmer than the water. He was lucky it was spring. The snowmelt had chilled the black lake, but it left the rocks bare. The old man curled up on a large slab to dry in the sun.

Ting! The sound reminded him of bouncing copper coins into a cup. The bar game was played best by Pile, until he got too drunk. Wraethe missed her shot, and Boruin felt the drink too strong in him. He'd miss this shot, but he was still up four over his woman. Shaking his head to clear it, Boruin bounced the coin and *ting!* the copper ricocheted off the tin flagon. Toaaho was leaning sideways in his chair, too drunk by far to be good at this game. That rarely mattered to the Mana'Olai, whose hands were always as steady as a dead man's. Fumbling the coin at first, Toaaho finally got a hold of it and tossed it side-arm at the table. The coin bounced off a gouge in the wood yet still jumped up to land in the cup. *Ka-ting!*

His head rolled over so their eyes met. "Go, Boruin," he said.

"Other way, my drunken friend. It's Pile's turn next." The short man was sitting back in his chair and whistling. It was a high, piercing whistle with no melody. He wondered how long the kid could go on exhaling.

Toaaho replied with a smile, "No. I think you should go."

"I'm not losing this bet by cheating…" Boruin's tongue stilled as he saw the long gash along the man's neck. It occurred to him that Toaaho never slumped when drunk. He'd pass out sitting up straight, but he never slumped and he never looked so pale. *Ting! Ka-ting!*

"Go, Boruin. Go now!" Toaaho urged. Boruin sat up straight and awake with the dead man's face still in his eye.

"What the—" Boruin looked at the shattered wooden shaft sitting in his lap. The feathers were black. A twang carried over the lake, and Boruin blinked his eyes and stared dumbly about. Pile was still whistling from somewhere in the sky as an iron arrowhead ricocheted off the rocks. *Ka-ting!*

Boruin scrambled off the rock and up away from the shore when he finally came to and saw the band of groundlings across the lake. They stood on shore, two black bearded fellows hauling back on their bows. The arrows arched as high as the Fae could fire them, and they came down just over the shore. Had the banks of the thin mountain lake been any closer, he would have been impaled in his sleep.

Alone, the old man felt exhausted and without hope for the first time in so long. With no sword, no pack, and no food, Boruin sat back down. The Fae had quit firing; his initial retreat had put him out of range. They grumbled and shouted across the lake at him. He wiggled his cold blue toes and wondered where everyone else had gone. Boruin decided it was a thought best left for an hour not harassed by Fae.

With a jerk, his knife came out of its swollen leather sheath. He cut the leather of his pants below the knee, revealing skin almost as pale as Wraethe's. Boruin laughed at the thought, because laughing at this point would ward off his want of crying. Boruin split the leggings down the center as he watched the Fae argue about what to do.

The lake was long and thin in this steep cleft between two mountains. The Fae would have to walk around it or swim. By the time Boruin had carved up his pant legs and tied them tight to his feet, the Fae had turned north. They would come around the lake where the ridgeline dropped low to let the water escape. It would force him to climb higher.

"With any luck you'll be far above tree line before they make it round the water," he said. "Then we'll have a better idea of what to do." It sounded hopeful, but that's what he did. Talking others into working out of a bad spot was the job of the leader. Alone, lying through his teeth was less effective. He pretended to buy into it and set a stronger pace.

The hammering had been echoing across the valley ever since he left the stunted trees behind him. *Tink tink tong, tink-ta-tink tink, tong tong!* He had spotted the signaler as soon as the beating started. The groundling was just above the tree line on the opposite side of the valley. Every time Boruin's path took him a little north, the hammer beat out a new tune. If he turned back south, the tings traded with the tongs. He wanted to fly back down the mountain and pound the drummer over the head with a heavy stone. Instead he drove up the ridge and made it, huffing and puffing, just after his pursuers rounded the far tip of the lake. Boruin smiled as he stepped over the ridge and the signal ended.

"Poor travels to you and yours, rutting Fae," Boruin cursed. It felt good for a moment, and then he took a look around. The distant green of the Hetsu Plains he had seen east of M'Gaglind Duul was gone. The jagged teeth of the Maunua Kuini surrounded him. There was nothing but rock, snow, and a vast, cold sky. Boruin's heart dropped further when he saw the distant specks moving across the plateau below him.

"More groundlings," he muttered, turning north along the ridgeline as a new wave of hammering from the plateau began.

Boruin fled from the Fae, climbing up toward the ugly, flat-capped peak. They swarmed after him, herding him higher until he ran out of rock to tread upon. He sat exhausted for an hour after seeing the third band of Fae climbing through the uneven shelves above him to the northwest. He had hoped to use that ridge for escape. That left only the mountain peak and whatever the gods had thought to create on its back side.

The eggs were an unforeseen gift. He had spooked the bird where the high shoulder of the ridge met the steep climb to the peak. To the mother's dismay, Boruin carried the eggs from her nest between the stones and dragged them up the mountain. The small mountain bird whirled about him, but never close enough to catch. He drew out the meal as long as he could, hoping she'd land close and make his dinner. She finally withdrew, squawking bird curses, and he could not blame her.

The old man ate the last egg while staring down at his death.

The north side of the mountain dropped sharply off the round peak. In full summer, the climb could have been manageable, but in spring the slope still held its snow. The sun began to fall, and the last of his hope was going with it. The thin eggshell crushed beneath his fingers, and the wind carried it down into the valleys where he could not go.

Boruin walked back across the top of the mountain. Its peak was rounded like a bald man's head, save for the scattered rocks and boulders ringed with wind-blown snow. He settled down with his back against a sun-warmed stone and watched the groundlings climb.

"Where the hell did you all come from?" he muttered, panting. The high altitude was making his head swim, and just walking on flat rock stole his breath.

The answer came to him once he quit thinking about it, and a rare warm gust of spring wind traveled up to blow across his face. Traveling the Guidevein was too damn slow. They should not have dropped back into the rock. It had only given the groundlings time to surround and cut them off. Had the others made it out, or were they all separated and trapped, same as he? Toaaho was dead–maybe the others, too. He pressed the heels of his palms into his eyes until white flashes beat in time with his heart. How had so much gone wrong so quickly? He did not like being without Wraethe.

"I always figured we'd have gone together," he muttered, watching the Fae. It was growing so cold now that he had quit moving. He breathed into his hands and cupped his toes. The first group had reached the steep climb to the peak. The others rushed on as if this were king of the mountain and the winner takes all. It would not be much longer until one of them made it.

Diun might rise before then. The thought was pleasing. At least he would know Wraethe would be awake and they'd share the moon. His hands rubbed up and down his arms to quell his shivering.

He paused when he touched the smooth scar of burnt skin on his forearm.

"Left me helpless like she said you would," he said to the strange line of runes. "I should've cut you all out of my skin years ago." Boruin shook his head as the image of Toaaho's last moment jumped unexpectedly into his mind. He had taken his knife and cut the rest of them free, cut the rune right out of his skin. *Maybe you can free the rest,* his mind tempted.

Boruin drew his knife. It had dulled from trimming parts of his leather pants into makeshift shoes, but the tip was plenty sharp. He toyed with it across his skin, tracing a square around the inked design trapped by the hand-shaped scar. Boruin crossed his legs with the offending hand caught beneath the pit of his knee. He pulled his shoulder back, stretching out the skin and taking a deep breath. The extra air went to his head. *This is crazy! But what are my choices?* Boruin brought the tip to bear.

"Don't do that. It will make me hungry." Boruin spun to face the man he expected to find standing over his shoulder, but there was only rock.

"Rilk?" he asked, knowing how he had mistaken Griant for a boulder in the Undurlund garden.

"No. No creature of stone am I, though I have slept like stone for long ages. It has been... peaceful." A shudder went through the granite under his feet. The small quake ended with a loud yawn that made Boruin's mouth open wide in response, though he was now anything but tired. "Why crawl all the way up here just to pierce your hide, anyway?" the rumbling voice asked. "Your blade would serve you better against those Fae, small though it is."

"I am no great warrior that can fight so many. Not with my knife alone," Boruin answered, circling the pile of rocks to see who hid behind. Out of the rubble came the scaled head of a massive serpent, cold green eyes reflecting Boruin's growing silhouette and the sunset behind him. The crown of horns sprouting above its skull was so wide that even Griant couldn't have grasped one in each hand. The old fighter stumbled back, but his instinct to flee was stopped short; the creature's tail had swung around to keep him in place.

"What is your name then, low warrior? And why do you fight so ill-prepared?"

"Boruin," he answered. The serpent's breath was hot and sour as he sniffed about his neck and hair.

"Doubtful. Or at least a half-truth."

The old fighter pointed down the mountainside. "I escaped the mountains by swimming out of that lake. Lost most of my weapons trying to reach the surface." The creature swung away, and Boruin realized the pile of rubble around them was actually more folds of the giant creature. He danced around the unraveling coils as the serpent stretched out in the last bit of sun. The body, large and round as a great Thilan wine cask, still displayed the mottled colors of rock, as if the scales had soaked up the color of the mountain.

"Well, it would have been better if you'd drowned. You wouldn't have minded the Fae then, and I could have finished my nap." The serpent flicked his tongue out, as if tasting the wind moving up the mountain. He tensed to plunge, sliding down the mountain on his wide, snake-like belly.

Boruin stumbled forward. "Wait—can't I hitch a ride with you? Not far. Even the bottom of the next valley would be something." he asked.

"No one rides the rabinithair, lij. We are not horses—but what do you have to offer?" the serpent asked.

"Little but my life, at the moment."

"And a half a life at that, old man," his head snaked around to sniff again at Boruin. "What is your true name? The one people don't call you?"

"Boruin is all I have. Spoken by a friend when I had no other."

"It is dangerous to take a name offered by another. You never know who will call you by it," the rabinithair said. A thick membrane rose over his eye in a slow blink before he continued. "I will know your true name before you leave my company, or I will call in your chit and slake my hunger. Agreed?"

"Agreed," Boruin answered. He had little choice; the sound of Fae armor on stone was rising over the lip of the peak.

The serpent encircled him in its foreclaws and leapt. Boruin yelled as they shot out into the air instead of sliding down the snowfield. Snow and old ice burst upward as the top of the peak continued to unwind into a body long as the mountain streams flowing below. The wingless beast fell until Boruin's scream whimpered out. Then, with a chuckle, the creature rolled skyward in a tight loop that hung in the air until his sharp tail passed through. They raced through the sky like a ribbon caught in a gale.

The sound of the arrow was too slight for Boruin to hear over the roaring wind, but the rabinithair heard. He snapped east, weaving his body out of the missile's path. It drove through the loops and folds of his long body, aimed for the meat of his neck. The serpent twisted and caught the shaft in his teeth.

"Few can shoot my great length. You have more than lowly Feirnann after your blood, unnamed man," he roared over the wind.

"What is your name?" Boruin shouted.

"You may call me Turintou. If I come golden-eyed before you, call me Vestoi."

- 15 -
THE SKYKING

No further," said the serpent. "It has been too long since my stomach has been filled." Boruin had felt the rabinithair slowing, and he was grateful for the respite. They had taken to the sky like it was a long untouched lover. The early winding and rolling had been exhilarating, but worse for his stomach than a ship at sea. Now the creature drifted downward, shifting through the air like a flag in a failing wind.

The two came down atop a rock plateau inaccessible on all sides. The beast sprawled across the rubble, exhausted. Boruin scrambled out of the way to avoid the unrolling coils of tail dropping out of the sky. He hadn't noticed it before, but the rabinithair looked more than tired. The flesh around his face was sunken, the scales dull and tattered at the edges. His ribs were like a heaving steel cage wrapped in thin tissue.

"How long since you've eaten?" Boruin asked. The creature rolled one eye to peer at the sky.

"More than two of your lifetimes," Turintou replied. "And that was just a wandering ram. It's been ages longer since I've had a proper meal."

Boruin peered at the ridges below the peak. "Well, there are bound to be sheep or goats somewhere about," Boruin said.

"They are sufficient during napping, but I will need more than a snack to sustain me. I'll rest for a while, and then we will continue," the serpent said.

Boruin was hungry as well, but it was too late to go searching the unfamiliar peak for more bird eggs. The sun had disappeared, and clouds smothering Diun brought an early Syan. With the wind turning colder by the second, he settled down beside the rabinithair. Though tired and wasted, the beast was still hot to the touch. Boruin wondered, as he pressed against the rough scales, if he could trust the creature's empty gut. He still hadn't decided before the thudding beat of the great heart had rocked him to sleep.

The morning light surprised Boruin, and his stomach set him into motion. The ice melted by the great serpent's nostrils was as sour as his breath, and the old man instead chewed on handfuls of hard snow. The peak was devoid of birds or other animals that might have made an easy breakfast.

He decided to wake the rabinithair. Boruin called to his companion from the backside of a large boulder and was glad for the protection. Turintou did not stir or yawn for three shouts. On the fourth, the rabinithair struck straight from sleep, his eyes snapping open only after his head was moving. Boruin ducked and rolled back as the boulder between them shuddered with the impact.

"Whoa, rabinithair! Easy, easy!" he shouted as great coils of serpent rose about him. The creature sniffed around his body and lowered back to the ground.

"Perhaps you should try a gentler waking. I do not rise well after such a long sleep."

"You woke well enough yesterday."

"I was considering whether or not to eat you," said Turintou. "I probably should have," he added with a snort.

"Then you'd have had the Feirnann to deal with. They probably would have cut me from your belly, given their persistence."

"I must find something to eat," said the serpent.

"Southwest of here there is a place that might hold enough meat for you to fill your belly. The beasts there will fight better than a ram, though."

The rabinithair scoffed and seized Boruin around the waist. "There are few beasts that can match me even after a long rest. None once I'm well fed," he said as he dove off the peak.

Whether the rabinithair was more tired, or Boruin more used to flight, their path seemed smoother. Boruin twisted around to watch the long, wingless body snake through the sky like a kite's tail. Pile's firelight lecture jumped unbidden to mind. "Aiemer moves of its own accord, like tides in an unseen sea," he had said.

"You don't fly through the air. It's the Aiemer. You fly by magic!" Boruin shouted into the wind.

The serpent clacked his tongue against his teeth. "Only the lij think of Aiemer as magic," he scoffed. "I am no more magical than a fish."

"Then the Aiemer carries you?"

"Closer, Duine." The serpent replied, but would explain no further.

They moved gently through the air, conserving strength as updrafts of the invisible Aiemer carried them high above the clouds. Boruin scanned the distant ground until the green smudge of the Hetsu Plains edged west over the horizon. Soon he saw the great crater he was looking for. Boruin shouted to the serpent and pointed down.

Turintou groaned, but his stomach still growled. "M'Gaglind Duul. A foul place, lij, but it will do," he said, floating in broad circles like a vulture coasting down to the dead. The land outside the broken mountain began to stir as the hunting kauolths noticed their descent. Trees shuddered as they tore recklessly through the valleys, chasing the great shadow dropping on M'Gaglind Duul.

"Where are you going?" the rabinithair asked as Boruin climbed down from their perch atop a giant slab of granite. The old man glanced toward the edge of the crater where the kauolths were beginning to scramble over the lip and into the valley.

"You eat; I've got business to attend. If you know this valley, you'll know I couldn't leave it without you. You won't lose what you're owed."

"Yes, but I don't want it owed twice over."

"I think you're distraction enough for these beasts," Boruin shouted over his shoulder. "They won't even notice me. If I'm wrong, you'll hear me hollering."

"So be it," the rabinithair snarled, turning to glare hungrily at the approaching kauolths.

The cave was not hard to find in the light. Twice he'd felt the need to take cover, but the kauolths had thundered past him, their eyes set on a larger meal. Boruin didn't know how long he'd been in the Guidevein, but his nose told him it was more than a few days. The dead kauolth wedged between the fish's stone gills had been stripped almost to the bone by its fellows. A few pieces of rotten meat hung from its shattered ribcage. Gristle and skin slumped to the floor in a wet, decomposing mess. Boruin bit back the bile rising in his throat and held his breath. He squirmed between the bones of the large skeleton and crawled into the dark cave.

Boruin stood, wiping the corpse's clinging filth from his chest and flinging it from his hands. He waited in the same spot until his eyes adjusted. The faint light showed black bloodstains from their fight, but no groundling bodies. Some, then, had survived the kauolths and carried off their brothers. But they had left Toaaho.

In the back of the cave, a dim light like the faintest glow of stars pulsed from the floor. There, over the node Griant had called from the Guidevein, they had laid out the Mana'Olai. The Fae had rent him limb from limb in their frustration. They had hacked his legs and arms free from his torso. His decapitated head was set face down in the dirt. Boruin turned it over and wiped the dust from the blackened and bruised face. What his stomach had held entering the cave it now lost, and Boruin kneeled there weeping for a time.

A tinkle of fine metal kicked across the floor as Boruin rose to his feet. He felt about and came up with a delicate chandelier of fine gold and gems. There was no need to hold it to the light. Boruin could tell it was a Nefazo design just by touch. All the rich merchants adorned their ears with such fancy ornaments. It was a mark of status, a gauge of wealth. He joined Belok's name with every curse he knew as he went to work. His anger boiled away any thought of how Belok had managed to hire mercenaries from the Dreaming Lands.

Boruin tied Toaaho's remains together with the remnants of the deceased's clothing. "No more fitful nights, my friend," he murmured as he carefully wrapped Toaaho's head in his own shirt. He dragged the body out through the cave and slowly made his way up the rubble piled above the cave entrance.

The rabinithair slid across the ground when he saw Boruin. Most of the kauolths stood at a safe distance, watching to see if the hungrier ones would wound and weaken the serpent. The few braver creatures that charged, Turintou had snapped them up in his jaws and flung the broken bodies over the far walls of the valley.

"Filled your stomach, then?"

"Enough for the time being," the serpent snorted. "This is a tough and sour meat, lij. I will not heed your next suggestion so readily," he added. For a moment Boruin thought his wide eye had flashed gold, but then decided otherwise. He was too tired to care.

"Fair enough," Boruin said. "I must take my companion out of the valley. Then you can find something better," Boruin said.

The serpent returned his stare. "I am not a ferryman for the dead."

"Then I will walk," Boruin replied.

"Take your time," Turintou yawned. Boruin cursed the beast and hoisted the wet sack across his back. He staggered west, into the wind, toward the closest lip of the valley.

Tired of defending the slow man from the hungry creatures, the rabinithair slung a wide coil of himself around Boruin, pushing it like a defensive wall before him. They continued in such a fashion until nightfall, when Boruin finally put the wide valley behind him. The wall of scales unrolled, and he heard the rise of screams as the kauolths began their evening meal, an ever-unfinished torment of chase and empty swallows. Boruin waited a moment, half expecting Toaaho to appear and berate him. Part of him desired it. Instead there was nothing, and Boruin wept for the second time that day as he carried his friend to the bottom of the next valley.

Boruin carefully washed Toaaho in a small stream and buried him under soil and rock. He pulled a small rosewood from the ground and replanted it atop the mound to serve as a marker.

"May you find your family well met and proud," Boruin whispered after an apology and a stumbling prayer.

Two days without real food took their toll on Boruin. He woke in the pale dawn light without remembering lying down, slobbering drool down his chin. The smell of raw meat had his stomach in a knot. Boruin tore into the flesh without thinking of fire or asking what he was eating. It was a hunk of meat like boiled leather between his jaws. It tasted little better.

"Thanks for the food," Boruin said between mouthfuls.

"Anything to give you the strength to take a bath," said Turintou. "You smell like a scavenger rolling in its meal."

Boruin ignored the jab. "I need you to take me to Priyati," he added. "The rilk will surely tell me where Griant was headed."

"No," the serpent said, tearing another bite from the carcass he jealously held inside his coils.

"If you want my end of our bargain completed, the boy and the man looking for him are the key," Boruin said, wiping the fat from his fingers across his thighs.

The muffled sound of a distant tree shattering rolled through the forest as the serpent's tail flicked impatiently. "Until our bargain has ended—with you paid or eaten—you will go where I say."

"Look, dragon," said Boruin, jabbing his finger at the great unblinking eye, "you can either help me find them, or I'll find them my—"

Turintou shot forward and snatched Boruin up in his wide maw, a tumbling blur of glistening scales and sharp teeth. Suddenly the bright morning sun was in his eyes, and he felt the wind slow. Boruin made the mistake of looking down and saw the mouth had slung him hundreds of feet into the air like a dead kauolth. The sun disappeared behind the peak as he began to fall back to earth.

Coils of serpent rose as the rabinithair launched into the sky and caught him in his fore claw. They fell together, the tail coming down to absorb the impact and hold them upright above the tree line.

"You will not speak that name to me, lij," Turintou roared, spitting that final word from its tongue with a distaste Boruin had heard only in the voice of the Monarhig. "The rabinithair are an honorable people, and that inference is a crude slang that would have gotten you killed had you said it before another. We are skyborn and once never touched the vile ground. We do not travel the earth by our own choice, and we certainly don't 'drag on' it," the creature snarled, its tongue whipping about as he spat out the words.

Boruin beat on the clawed fist holding him tight, his face dark like a ripened grape. When the rabinithair loosened his grip a few moments later, he sucked in a lungful of air and punched the rock-hard jaw looming before his face.

"Then it would be well for you to remember that I am not your vassal," Boruin roared back. "Neither am I a low man that you can slur depending on your mood. Continue to dangle my debt over me and I'll leap into your mouth myself, dragging my knife down your throat all the way. Then you will be repaid!"

The serpent snorted and then chuckled. Soon his entire body was shaking as the great creature heaved with laughter. Boruin bounced about until the rabinithair finally settled down.

"You are not a low man, indeed. I don't think any creature so small has dared slap me across the mouth," he said.

"It was more of a punch."

"Unfelt, regardless," replied the serpent before sobering. He regarded the lij in his grasp and sniffed him again as if still unsure what he was carrying. "You are right that this boy and your contractor are important. Still, you will not find them by going back into lij territory. I will find you the help you need, but I can not do so without settling my own affairs."

"You've been asleep for ages," said Boruin. "What possible affairs could be pressing?"

"I'm ravenous—my waking meal comes first. Then I'll tend to my lands."

Boruin scoffed. "We are in the wilds of the continent, Turintou. Where would they go?"

"To whom, is the question," the creature said. He rose enough to peer over the tree line and began to worm his way through the forest.

"What happened to flying?" Boruin asked, itching to point out this irony after Turintou's previous outburst. He was glad Pile was not here to speak out of turn.

"The Aiemer shifted while you were hauling that meat—"

"My friend."

"Hauling your friend out of the valley. I must stay on the ground until either it returns or we catch up to it."

"How long will that be?"

"The Aiemer is hard to feel when you are outside of its stream. It should not be long, but I need to conserve my strength and settle my colors anyway. I have decided on my waking meal, and we have some distance to travel before reaching it."

Boruin spent the next five days riding the serpent through the low valleys of the Maunua Kuini Mountains. The withered rabinithair moved like a toothless wolf with no pack, becoming stone when the wind sent an unknown scent his way, darting across open glades only after long, still moments of watching. His long tail followed behind them like a winding stream of flowing scales. The mottled white and brown of the snowy mountaintop had faded, slowly changing to the green and tan of evergreens and dead pine needles littering the forest floor.

When they saw elk on the near slopes or ranging through the bottom of the valley, the sharp horns of the rabinithair's tail snaked before them. Boruin watched an elk sniff the air and return to feeding as its killer crept in from downwind. A quick spear thrust and the animal fell dead in the distance.

In the evenings Turintou chewed on the two bone spears at the tip of his tail. The gnarled points had grown wild in his sleep, curling about each other like long fingernails. Boruin tossed about at night as the creature worked the horns across his sharp teeth. The noise grated on his nerves, and the air smelled like burnt bone.

"Please tell me you'll be done preening soon," Boruin said, stretched out on a beach of soft pine needles. Here the forest had finally halted against an endless sea of grass spread before him on the

Hetsu Plains. The long body of the rabinithair was out there, buried in the tall waves of green to soak up its color.

The serpent uncoiled his tail, removing the wall he had created around the camp. "You wish to sleep somewhere else? With your knife and all, I'm sure you would have no problem with the red wolves. Take my advice and find a place where you can see over the grass, old man. That will help."

"I may be an old man, but I'm all man, you skinny, underfed snake," Boruin replied. The serpent snorted and continued wearing down his tailbone across his front incisor.

"You'll be glad to have this tail soon enough," the serpent said between bites on the bone. "Your archer prince is very determined, and I will not be caught without tail and scale ready."

"If you can handle a valley of kaoulths, I don't think the ground-lings are much of a worry," smiled Boruin. Then the grin drifted off. "Shame you weren't with us on the first crossing."

"Those Feirnann were used to track you through the rilk lands. They are rock-workers, deep-dwellers; the groundlings will not threaten us on the surface." The rabinithair spat out a glob of wet bone dust and shavings before he leveled his eyes on Boruin. "No, your Monarhig has found a better weapon."

Boruin sat up. "What are you talking about?"

The serpent's tongue shook like an old man's finger reprimanding a child. "You spend too much time staring at the moons. It spoils your night vision." Boruin cupped his hands over his eyes until the false-image of Diun faded into black. Still, it wasn't until the full dark of Syan that he could make out the dim light traveling just above horizon like a faint star swinging on a pendulum. "If the Aiemer had not changed course and left this place dry, it would have been bad for us," Turintou said through his chiseling teeth.

The star changed course, rising into the blackness. It shifted erratically, like it was tracing the bloom of some dark thundercloud. Then the light disappeared over the horizon before swinging again north and south. It was like a bee caught under a glass and searching all edges for a way out. "It's waiting for the Aiemer to wash back east, isn't it? It's checking the borders and waiting," said Boruin as he watched the point of light pace across the sky. The rabinithair just grunted and kept gnawing.

"What is it?" Boruin asked.

"A trespasser," Turintou growled. He would answer no further questions. His teeth and tongue worked without stopping as he honed his weapon.

Boruin watched the roaming star and thought of Wraethe and the others. *They had to have made it. The groundlings were focused on me.* The thought was more of a wish than a logical decision, but he held to it.

If they had survived the crashing Guidevein, Griant would have taken the boy to fulfill the contract. It was what Boruin would have done. *Will they come back then and look for me? Or does she think I'm dead?* Chances were they would return to Priyati. If he couldn't pay his debt to the rabinithair, though... *Yuin's whores—it would be a year-long journey and then only if I can travel without Fae or serpent on my back.* The idea was unappetizing and marred too by the fact that as much as he wanted to find Wraethe, he could not let go of the boy. The child's effect on his runes was too much to ignore. *I've got to meet the contractor. If there is nothing there to be found, then I'll be happy to let these go unused and forgotten.* That was an outright lie, but he held to it.

They headed north the moment Turintou finished his tail, traveling quickly enough to leave a wake in the grass like a hull cutting through the ocean. The plains around them teemed with life. Birds burst from the tall stalks as they approached, and Boruin saw strange trees fleeing their passage. Turintou caught one and lifted it out of the grass, displaying a lean, hoofed beast with delicate, branch-like antlers. It made for a fine lunch.

Boruin watched the rabinithair's body follow behind them in long, repeating curves. "How long are you?" he asked.

"It is not polite to ask a rabinithair his length." After a measure, Turintou continued with a slight smirk and a tone found in any darkened bar. "I am long though—very, very long. The meat of the Hetsu Plains and the minerals of the Maunua Kuini have fed me well over the ages. It is a fine territory."

Boruin tried to guess the serpent's length, but the constantly moving tail made it hard to gauge. The sharp horn appeared here and there, peeking over the grass or spearing their meals. Turintou was right: the two curved bones, chasing each other around in a narrowing spiral, did look like a mean weapon. They had been polished smooth on their outside faces. The interior planes retained the odd channels and hollows natural to the bone growth, now cleaned and honed. The tips were sharp and proven deadly. Boruin was glad to have them; they looked like they would pierce the thickest Omman armor.

It was after a week of hard traveling north that Turintou slid to a halt and flattened his body into the grass. Boruin's head knocked against the beast's claw and the sharp pain drove him from his sleep. The rabinithair's tongue darted out, tasting the air. Turintou's body began to vibrate with a low hum coming like the purring of a cat.

"The Aiemer is coming," the serpent hissed between clenched teeth. Instead of taking to the air, he sunk even further against the ground and inched forward through the grass. A heavy wind blew the stalks over them in flowing waves, concealing them like a ship sunk in shallow water. They were hidden, but not well.

"We're not alone, are we?" asked Boruin.

"Climb on my back and see for yourself." The old fighter pulled himself up the rough scales and stood on the rabinithair's wide back. The wind was gusting. With his head just above the grass, the delicate seed heads seemed to crash like foam around him. *It even sounds like the sea*, he thought before a flash of light turned his attention back to the sky. The light winked again, much brighter than that distant, dim star. It disappeared a moment in the blue before brightening again like a cloud of mirrors turning in a long row before the sun.

"It's coming alright, and fast," he said, crouching back into the grass even though he was too small to be seen. "You said there were few that could match you even after a sleep, right?"

"I said there are no beasts that can face me, lij. This is no simple beast. Look how he moves. What does that remind you of?"

"Oh, Yuin," Boruin whispered as he saw what Turintou meant. The light flashed from bright scales as the creature turned across the sky like a ribbon caught in a gale. The sky blue rabinithair snapped around, battered by some unseen violence. He rolled and righted, then dove before snapping back up and rising thousands of feet into the air. The serpent raced on the crest of the Aiemer as the unseen element poured like a flood back into the eastern side of the plains and pushed with an unknown anger toward the mountains.

"He is either a fool to fly on such turbulence or is hard pressed to find us," said Turintou.

"I'd say the latter," Boruin replied as he watched the other rabinithair pass to the south, heading for M'Gaglind Duul. He stumbled as Turintou pushed a few feet off the ground and started forward.

"Stay there. Keep watch," the serpent said as Boruin started to climb back down toward his foreclaw. "There was no hiding my ground-trail in the mountains. It won't be long before he finds it and follows it back. At least with the Aiemer, I won't leave a trail of crushed grass."

Boruin shouted back, digging his hands under the edge of an old scale as they began to pick up speed. "Just take to the air, and let's get out of here."

"Can't risk it," the rabinithair replied. "I can't fly fast for long enough. We've got to make enough distance from our trail to confuse him and then get underground." Boruin cursed and turned his back to the stalks of grass whipping against him. Going back underground was the last thing that felt right.

- 16 -

THE FURNACE OF THE DEAD

S nowcaps from the Maunua Kuini range were distant in the east, hanging high in the air, but their foothills stretched far. They bucked the Hetsu on the eastern border, rising in stumpy mountains that descended into rolling hills to the west. Turintou raced between these, flying through the shallow valleys, dropping below the grass when forced onto the flat plains. He turned circles and changed course like a drunkard who had forgotten where he'd set his bottle.

"If you're looking for something in particular, I suggest you find it right quick," Boruin shouted. The serpent turned his head to confirm what had brought the fear to the old fighter's voice. The trespasser, the eager rabinithair, had turned. The sun betrayed his blue scales when he snaked across the sky, but the flashes were all in one line that followed the crushed grass of their path.

Turintou dropped back into the grass but did not slow. "Come up behind my head," he shouted. Boruin scrambled on his hands and knees, clutching the old scales where they had pulled loose from age. He hugged the left horn of the rabinithair's crown, wrapping his legs around it and wishing he had a rope.

"Your hills have changed with time, but your smell has not," Turintou muttered as he turned and shot forward like an arrow. Boruin had a moment to see a bare glade covered in strange round river stones. There was no pondering it though as they dove into a hole like an open mouth with its throat stretched wide for their passing. Eyes closed, he felt the shudder of Turintou's horns scrapping through dirt. When they hit stone, his teeth smacked against the bone and the taste of blood filled his mouth. The jarring shook him loose from his hold, and he tumbled off the serpent's head.

Boruin rolled away from the rabinithair, afraid of being crushed. "Turintou!" he shouted.

Turintou slowed for but a second. "Wait for me. Defend yourself," he commanded. The serpent snapped up a mouthful of black stones and knocked others bouncing off the walls as he rushed on deeper into the hole.

"Rutter," Boruin cursed as he wiped the dirt and blood from his eyes. Before he was aware of the light, the smell hit him. It was a blanket of rot pulled over his head. The room was a furnace, and he dropped low in search of cooler, breathable air. Mush caked between his fingers and toes. As the last bit of Turintou pushed past, his tail swept across the floor, sending more of the stones rolling deeper into the chamber to crack against the far wall. "It is a wall," he muttered, seeing now great shaped stones stacked to support the wide beams bracing the ceiling. It was an ancient mah'saiid design. Pile would have known what purpose the deep, high-arched room would have served.

The light filtered down from a great crack where one beam buckled, allowing bits of stone to come crashing to the floor over the years. As Boruin wondered how it had held together so long, another segment slipped from its ages-old position and exploded on the floor. The chamber shuddered; Turintou was struggling somewhere below. "Hide deep, you bastard," he growled. The thought of the coming rabinithair sent him searching about for his own hiding spot.

Great mounds of grass piled up on one side of the room. The stink of the place grew as he drew near, as did the heat. As he stepped onto a mound, his feet sunk into the wilted grass and began to burn. Boruin stumbled back and tripped over a river stone. The rock rolled toward him and from it, a feeler, like a leathery feather, lapped across his foot like a kiss. He screamed and kicked out, his heel splitting against the hard shell.

"Rut me," he groaned as a twittering sounded by his ear. He flipped over to find a wide, crushing mandible spread out before his face. Inching out from under the black shell, it snapped shut and then pried open again, like a seamstress testing her scissors before cutting into a bolt. Ignoring the pain in his foot and trying not to slip in his own blood, Boruin danced out from between the shin-high creatures. More stones scurried in from the edges of the room. Looking instinctively down the tunnel Turintou had fled, he saw a flood of the insects scrambling toward the chamber floor.

His foot snapped through bones and caught between a pair of jagged ribs. He kicked free, scattering the ribs among the myriad milk-white bones covering much of the floor. His mind churned frantically at the grotesque find.

Near the entrance, the floor rose in a wide dais. He vaulted a pair of insects and scrambled up the steps. A tall, rusted shield and a broken spear shaft lay on top. There had been another, then, who had made a last stand in this spot.

The insects gathered at the bottom of the steps. For a moment, Boruin thought he'd escaped. The steps were as tall as their shells, and their legs were for scurrying, not climbing. His hope dwindled as the creatures in the back pushed forward like a slow rising tide. Those in the front, caught against the stone, were shoved upward—some flipping over, but others tilting up–and gained their footing on the first step.

Years of battle, bar fights, and wrangling Wraethe had left Boruin with no experience that could possibly help him fight off a wave of bugs. His mind was blank as they bounced and rocked their way up the dais. The spear shaft was bit down to a short haft after he'd flipped just two bugs back down the stairs. The shield made a decent shovel, as long as he kept his toes back from the edge of the step, but still the insects climbed faster than he could knock them down.

Boruin had propped the shield against the edge of the wall and was trying to step up to balance on the rim when a string of rock-crushing pops sounded behind him. Turintou's wide mouth was snapping up the insects. Their gray-green insides sloshed between his teeth and down his chin as he scooped them up by the dozens. The rising wave before Boruin fell back as the serpent snorted in their midst and sent them scurrying.

He brought his chin down low on the last few stragglers. "Pull open these shells," he whispered. "There—those yellow sacks. Crush them and smear that on your body." A low growl rose from the rabinithair's throat when Boruin paused with the wet guts in his hands. "Now get under that shield, lie up against the wall and be dead," he ordered as the old fighter covered himself in the foul slime. "The beetles won't bother you now. You smell as bad as they do."

The serpent slid back through the room. He swept a pile of hot, rotted grass across his body, closing the rear tunnel, and then nosed under the mountains of compost on the side of the room to hide. Boruin lay there, sweat pouring off his skin. He prayed it wouldn't wash off the muck, as foul as it was. He lay like the dead, except for grinding his teeth when more than one beetle snuffed around him.

No matter how close the insects came, the fear was nothing compared to what Boruin felt when the other rabinithair arrived. The light through the cracked ceiling darkened as the great beast sniffed and snorted at the air. A moment later he heard the creeping sounds of scale scraping slowly on stone. *If they start fighting in here, that's it for me*, he thought, envisioning the entwined coils of the two tremendous serpents smashing about the room.

Out of the corner of his eye he saw a wide swath of blue scales. Without moving, Boruin could see little more, except for the muscle that rolled underneath the hard plates as the great beast looked about the chamber. It was like watching iron roll in waves. Turintou looked like an old sock full of marbles compared to this young and healthy rabinithair.

Boruin closed his eyes and held his breath. He felt the air stir as the creature sniffed silently around the front of the room. When his lungs began to burn, the old man breathed out slowly and prayed he'd made no noise. He managed not to gag as he inhaled, filling his chest with the hot air, thick as a black blood clot. Over and over he breathed, deliberate and silent.

When Pile stepped into the chamber, the insects swarmed. The thief was pulling a gold chain from the neck bone of some long-dead woman. He heard the skittering legs coming just in time to cleave the first with his axe. Two more split before a glancing blow sent the steel to the stone floor. It cracked in two. Wraethe had less luck; the creatures dropped from the ceiling, each larger than the last. One, big like a merchant's cart, caught her around the waist. Its mandible was slicing down when Boruin flailed, knocking over the shield and realizing that at some point he had fallen asleep.

"You must swallow that fear and set it away," Turintou said in a low voice. "Your friends are safe, or they are not. Fighting it out in your dreams each night will not change this."

Boruin ignored the advice, still struggling against the vision of Wraethe's surprised look as she… "Where's the other rabinithair?" he asked.

"He's well gone."

Boruin used his hands to straighten out his stiff legs. "Why didn't you wake me?" he groaned.

"Asleep, you don't notice the smell," he replied. The beetles moving across the floor fled Turintou's heavy belly as the serpent slid forward.

"Why is it so hot in here?" Boruin stammered. He was groggy and drenched in sweat. "And why did you leave me with the rutting bugs?"

"I couldn't very well fight with my tail hanging out the door. I had to get turned around," Turintou answered. "And it's hot because they are cooking their meat; they're baker's beetles. They cover the animals they catch in the prairie grass. As the grass decomposes, it heats up and bakes the meat. Then they eat it."

Boruin watched the insects. Some trundled up the piles, rolling balls of grass before them. Others, carrying dissected bits of flesh, burrowed under the mounds. He thought he saw a few of the shells glow a fading red as they scrambled back out.

"This place is rank," Boruin coughed. He tried to breathe shallower. "Still, why couldn't he smell our trail? How'd he not catch us here?"

"I'm a husk, lij. I've spent generations asleep in the mountains. If I smell of anything at all, it certainly isn't dangerous rabinithair," Turintou said.

Boruin wiped the sweat from his face. He suddenly felt so exhausted. "That damn Fae prince was a pompous ass, but this is about more than just pride, isn't it?" asked Boruin. "You rabinithair don't strike me as easily ordered around."

"No," replied Turintou, answering both questions after a pause. "An attack by the groundlings is rare, too. The Courts of Twilight do not allow such incursions into the Dying Lands. They've fought long wars over that idea. No simple Monarhig or Moir would dare break that law without a whisper from some higher authority. Though, if this prince is as arrogant as you say... no, it's more likely you have come under the attention of someone greater. That does not bode well for you," he added, pushing his head underneath a mound. He returned to drop a piece of steaming meat at Boruin's feet. "Now eat and rest. The Aiemer washed in too fast and we can't stay here long. When it thins out we move east."

The cooked flesh wasn't nearly as bad as the old fighter would have thought. Better than raw kauolth meat...

"What if he's hiding over the next hill?" Boruin asked as he checked his feet and made sure that he was still tucked in the shadow of the tunnel entrance. His body kept creeping forward, leaning into the fresh air that was sucked down the passage and drunk by the compost furnace. The beetles, carrying their wares, scurried past him and around the rabinithair's head, lowered to peer out at the sky.

"Hope that he's followed the Aiemer north in the direction of our trail," Turintou answered. "The way he was riding the edge of that flow, he was in a hurry. He doesn't have time to crawl around on his belly to wait and watch." Despite his certain tone, the rabinithair still waited until the sun had burned off the morning dew before they crept from the beetles' lair buried in some long-dead mah'saiid's ballroom.

Boruin watched for the flying serpent, but Turintou was right. Their pursuer had a lot of ground to cover and was not wasting time double-checking this part of the Hetsu Plains.

They moved west at a sharp pace, but slow enough that they got to watch the beetles work. It was amazing, the sheer number. Thousands of the insects moved in long rows, sheering the tall grass like Nefazo gardeners cutting a rich merchant's lawn. They cleared the prairie to stoke their ovens, carrying grass—and whatever creature they found in it—back to their hot home.

When the grass finally began to reach waist high, the beetles evidently exercising proper crop rotation, the rabinithair stumbled onto the Hetsu plainsmen. Boruin had seen in the distance great swaths of the plains charred black by some recent lightning-sparked firestorm. But as they climbed out of the last shallow valley, the old man realized the brown ash hanging above the burnt scars was dust. What from afar seemed scorched, black fields were hundreds of thousands of huge habback. The wild herd was enormous. Its combined mass straddled the hills and filled the valleys, making the colony of beetles seem like a handful of stones. Working habback were common enough in the southern nations, and Boruin had seen plenty, but such a wild herd was something different.

"I've never seen anything like that. It's tremendous!" said Boruin.

"A reasonable herd," replied the rabinithair. "Wait until we take to the air again. Then you will be amazed." They slowed down and crept east along the edge of the herd, finally cresting a steep hilltop. Below, the animals milled through the valley, chewing on the tall grass and trampling it in their wake.

"There is one of the families. We have come at the right time to help," said the serpent. To the north, round white tents dotted the end of a low ridgeline. Looking over the crest of the hill and down the south slope, a small band of horsemen stood in their saddles to peek over the rise. They spied on the herd as it grazed on the hillside.

All at once, in a rush, the horsemen poured down the slope. Their small horses kicked turf high above their heads as they galloped headlong downhill. They raced, hollering, to cut the trailing habback from the main body, turning them up the slope to tire them. The riders slapped the beasts with long sticks when they turned downhill, shouting to steer them back away from the herd.

"Brave riders. Wild habback are pretty dangerous, aren't they?" Boruin asked.

"Quite. They will be lucky to finish their branding season without a death." As if to prove the rabinithair's point, a heavy beast turned, dropped its spiraled horns, and charged back at a rider. The small horse turned sharply and danced around the great animal. Turintou rose high above the grass and slid down the slope.

The riders pulled sharply on their steeds, skidding to a halt. Boruin watched for them to turn, galloping for camp, but they stood still, watching. The habback grunted and turned, driving back to the main herd with no horsemen to stop them. The horses stomped, trying to edge backward, but the riders held them firm. Turintou stopped, giving the riders room.

"We will see if they approach. The plainsmen are too proud to flee from any danger, even from a rabinithair. If they have not forgotten their fathers' oaths, they will come."

"If they have forgotten?" asked Boruin.

"They might be eaten."

Two riders advanced, fighting their struggling mounts. Arrows bounced in quivers at their hips, anxiously awaiting launch from the bows worn across the riders' chests. One hooked his thumb under his bow, and Boruin doubted he could drop to the ground before the man could string an arrow and fire. The smell of their sweat mixed with their horses' preceded them as they rode forward to where a habback had scraped after roots, leaving the ground bare. One struck the dirt with his staff.

"Your tail!" he ordered, peering up with hard eyes at the towering rabinithair.

The serpent growled. "Your fathers never spoke of Turintou?"

"'Never trust a Skyking by his colors!' That's what my grandfathers spoke of!"

Turintou snorted the sharp sound Boruin now knew to be an amused chuckled. His tail came down from behind the hill, and the sharp bones stabbed into the dirt like a greatsword planted for display. The rider waved his younger companion forward. The young man turned his mount around and pulled his shirt up over his shoulders. The shape of Turintou's tail, except with a burning ball of flame suspended between the twisted horns, was etched out in delicate scarring across his back.

"I'm pleased your people have kept their oaths," said Turintou. "It will favor you this branding season."

"Many of the families swore their blood to the newcomer, but not our clan," the rider replied, crooked teeth appearing in a grin. "We watched the eastern skies for our Skyking. Your presence was said to always bless the Swift Horse clan."

"It will again, if I might share from your herd," Turintou replied. "I've slept long, and it has been some time since my last proper meal."

The plainsman's eye grew wide, and he stepped from his horse to lay flat in the dirt. "What herd is ours is so only by your grace, Skyking. It would be our honor to provide your waking meal."

"You have my thanks, horse lord," said the Rabinithair. He motioned the riders on, and Boruin followed after them on foot. He stopped when he'd realized the serpent had yet to move.

"What?" he asked. His head whipped about, searching urgently for their pursuer.

"I did not want to enter camp on my belly. It's not proper form," he added softly as the two riders descended on their band and headed for camp.

"Come on. Your waking meal awaits," Boruin chuckled. He continued walking toward the round tents. "I could ride you in, if it'd help," he added when he'd stepped out of easy snapping range.

- 17 -
RETURN OF THE SWIFT RIDERS

The Swift Horse clan met the rabinithair with ceremony. The women bowed low before their Skyking and his companion. The men laid their weapons on the ground and turned their backs, their lives entrusted to the rabinithair's will. When Boruin tried to refuse their gestures, they insisted, for who deserved honor more than the companion of their lord?

The youngest girl braced a heavy set of tongs against her hips and lowered them into the fire. She struggled with them for a moment, then her sister took one side and together they pulled the shell of a great baker's beetle out of the coals. Steam billowed from it into the cool evening air. A woman dipped a beaten gold chalice into an opening in the shell to retrieve a serving of the liquid cooking inside. She passed it to another woman, who in turn passed it to another, and so on and so forth until it had been touched by every woman in the tribe. The last to receive it, the Swift Horse's oldest crone, poured the liquid across Turintou's outstretched tongue. Boruin tried to take the cup himself, but the woman refused, holding it tipped for his open mouth. His tongue burned from both the heat of it and the fiery taste of fermented milk and grain alcohol. The old man clenched his eyes shut, but he managed to keep from coughing. The riders smirked or held their smiles behind their hands, but they would not yet laugh openly at their new guest for another few hours.

Where the clan's sun-darkened faces seemed so serious and severe before, Boruin could see their wrinkles were born from laughter as much as hard prairie life. Their revelry followed Diun into the evening, and the poor nomads saved no surplus in their desire to celebrate. Chantulp, the fiery drink, poured across every tongue. A young habback calf was spit across the fire. Boruin's mouth watered as the fat dripped into the coals with a hiss and burst of smoke.

The eldest riders sat about the head of the rabinithair and held council while the meat finished cooking. "How many days left in the branding season?" asked the serpent.

The Eldest, named Dark Eye though his pupils were a light green, answered. "Three of the ten, my lord," His hands were clasped, though Boruin saw one toe wiggling from either nerves or, perhaps, hope.

"And how many habback have you marked?"

He scratched cross-hatches in the dirt as he counted. "Seven, to make two score for our herd."

Wind Runner, a man still stout in the legs despite his ancient sunken chest and thin arms, jumped in as if embarrassed at the small number. "We have fine riders, but too few these days. It takes much to ride down the wild habback." Dark Eye shushed the man as if it was a weakness to explain.

"Tomorrow, then, I will eat," said the serpent. "Have your women ready their voices; there will be much branding done. Your clan will have more riders than you need soon enough."

The Eldest's eyes began to well and he shook his head solemnly. It was the promise they'd been hoping for. As word passed quickly throughout the tribe, the celebration fell to uncontainable abandon.

"There are a great number of habback in that herd. How are they counting only forty?" Boruin asked as the elders withdrew to join the festivities.

"This herd is not theirs for the taking. The Hetsu nomads have always adhered to the rule of the plains," he answered. "They must ride for their cattle, sing, brand, and name them. Only those can they keep for the clan. With a small number of adults, there are hardly riders to wear out enough habback to brand. They must live on their own herd until the branding season comes again in the spring. If their habback can't support the clan through the year, then their people starve or join other families."

"What nonsense," Boruin grunted. "I'm surprised they abide it."

"They abide it because it is my rule, lij," the rabinithair growled. "Without some restraint, your kind would ride down all the beasts until there was not but wolves and grass rats. They would kill for hide and back strap, leaving the rest for the carrion. The herd is full because they follow tradition and the branding season. They know this and accept it."

"They preserve the herd so you can have your fill? You were right: the Hetsu Plain is a fine territory," Boruin said, the chantulp leaving his tongue looser than it should have been.

"I eat only what has been branded as well. I cannot expect them to hold to a rule that I would break," Turintou growled. "You should not speak of what you know not."

With that, the serpent wormed off through the grass to watch for the trespasser, leaving Boruin to the clan. They hastened him to the circle around the fire, feeding and watering his tongue until he fell back into the soft grass.

Boruin woke in dim light, naked and wondering where he was. A sweet-sharp scent of light oil was on his nose, and he wondered when he'd washed himself. His hands searched about and found a pair of leather pants. Underneath them he found a shirt of coarse hair along with a leather vest and a fur-lined cap. The boots at the foot of the sleeping mat were tight, but they would wear in. He flexed his toes under the leather and grinned. If his feet were bare he always felt naked, regardless of how well covered he was otherwise. Now clothed in a rider's gear, he remembered the rabinithair's horsemen and the rowdy night before.

Staggering out of the hut, Boruin found the riders bringing in their herd. The day was clear and only the slightest cool breeze stirred the tall grasses. He walked to Turintou and together they watched the riders singing at the edge of the great mass of grazing animals. Their voices were boisterous, the song a lilting march that somehow called their forty habback out of the greater herd one by one.

"Don't tell me habback appreciate the musical arts?" asked Boruin.

"Later," Turintou mumbled. His mouth was a mess of slobber. He turned to Boruin and the man saw flecks of gold rising from the deep green of the rabinithair's eyes. "It's dangerous to watch a rabinithair eat," added the serpent. "They will respect that. I would that you do as well." Boruin nodded, and Turintou shot forward through the grass with a great bellow. He fell on the herd, bracing his tail like a dam across a roaring, running, black river.

One of the spirited ladies from the night before handed Boruin a cup. She laughed at his wary expressions and pushed the vessel toward his mouth. The drink was hot and heavy. As soon as he swallowed it began to wash out the cobwebs from his head, clearing his mind and his sticky throat. As she walked away, with a lasting glance and a smirk thrown over her shoulder, Boruin caught the sweet-sharp scent of the oil on her body.

"By Yuin's blessing," he chuckled as he recalled the late-night washing. Before the memory had finished dancing through his head, the rabinithair was chasing the rest of the Swift Horse's habback behind the hill.

Boruin expected to hear an explosion of roars and animal screams, see bits of bone and entrails flying through the air, but all was quiet. The fire rebuilt for the morning cooking, Boruin took his breakfast near its warmth. He was into his second plate of fried chops when he saw the small, sun-darkened faces peeking through the grass. Three children gazed down at the camp to see if they were missed before ducking back into the grass as they turned up the hillside.

As the riders surveyed the herd, the women prepared the camp for a day of branding. Boruin knew it would be better to let an elder chase down the children, but his curiosity was a bad as Pile's. *I'm more like that short bastard than I like to admit,* he thought as he climbed to his feet.

"You should let the snake handle those kids. It would serve them right," he heard Wraethe's voice chide in his head. He slipped behind the tents and up the hill.

Turning to look over his shoulder, Boruin felt as guilty as if he had led the children to spy on the rabinithair himself. He crested the ridge and looked down the other side. The rabinithair's long tail held several habback in crushing coils. They looked a little like black pearls strung on a woman's necklace. For a moment the old man almost laughed. Then his eyes followed the chain and saw the rabinithair's head stretching to reach the children, who stood higher up the hill. Boruin fell into a dead sprint toward them.

Turintou's head was straining, pulling the weight of his tail and the dying habback up the hill, but he was coming fast. His jaw hung low and loose like a hammock of skin. The rabinithair thrust his chin forward and the disconnected bone fell back into place with a loud snap. The great head weaving back and forth mesmerized the children as it came for them. They stood frozen at the top of the hill, eyes wide and mouths agape.

"Back up slowly! Back up!" Boruin screamed, waving the children toward the camp. They jumped at the sound of his voice, then leaned back on their heels and crept backward through the grass. "Turintou! Get away! What are you thinking?" he yelled.

The rabinithair swung his head around toward Boruin. Thick blood dripped from the serpent's mouth. His tongue shook across his teeth, rattling a warning or an evil greeting. His eyes seemed molten, like liquid gold poured into a cup, bright mirrors in the sun. Boruin squinted, suddenly blinded by the light, and knew the strike was coming. He threw his weight right, felt the sunlight waver as Turintou struck, and dodged back left, diving into the grass. He came down hard on his shoulder. The impact knocked the memory of their introduction into his head.

"Vestoi! Calm, Vestoi!" he shouted as the serpent swung around to catch him flat on his back. The burning reflection from the gold eyes left black disks swimming in the center of Boruin's sight. He couldn't see Turintou's color. Had he calmed? "Vestoi, Vestoi, Vestoi! For Yuin's sake, stop!" The serpent reached down and sniffed, then nudged him with his snout.

"Get up, lij. You are alright. I'm not going to eat you."

"Never trust a rabinithair by his color, especially if gold-eyed. That's what I'll tell my children," said Boruin.

"You've done me a service. I would not have desired to feed on my people," he said, watching the children sprinting back down the hill towards camp. Boruin saw the serpent's eyes flicker a shimmer of gold and then back to a bright green. The ground was turning to mud underneath his drooling mouth.

"Go on and get back to business. You can hardly contain yourself," Boruin said, frightened and already moving after the children. The rabinithair turned back down into the valley. His jaw dislocated as his head struck into the next coil to devour a bull habback.

It was late before the rabinithair floated heavily through the air and returned to the camp. Boruin expected him to be dragging a great round belly, but instead a series of lumps spread down his tail as if the serpent had a stomach for each habback.

"You said not to look at you, out of respect. Didn't mention the chance you'd devour anything that moved," Boruin said after Dark Eye, Wind Runner, and the other elders had driven the children forward to offer their apologies. The boys said their piece and fled, eyes to the ground as their mothers chased after, their own punishment yet to give.

The rabinithair did not respond. "Why Vestoi? How does that pull you out of your gluttony?" Boruin asked after a long silence.

"I gave you that name to protect you from my hunger," Turintou replied. "That danger has passed now. I expect you to forget it and not give it to another."

"Understood."

After another long pause, he muttered further explanation. "My mother called me Vestoi, when I was first from the shell. It was her name of love. I would not strike at my mother." He rolled his stomachs over, trying to get comfortable. His large eyes blinked slowly, and Boruin left him to doze.

The next two days were a rush of work and feasting. The rabini-thair coursed across the prairie, dashing apart the high waves of windblown grass. He wrangled the herd around the valley, cutting out the best habback and driving them through the tall grasses until they were exhausted. The great length of tail surrounded the chosen like a wide corral. One by one, forced down the corridor between neck and tail, the heavy beasts squeezed out where the clan could brand them. The men gave the Swift Rider's mark to each, but it was the women's work Boruin was most in awe of.

As graceful and swinging the pace of the men's song had been the day before, the women's was so much purer. It was like they had stolen their notes from the world around them, taken the wind's playful dancing, the habback's somber hoof beat in the earth, the grass's unending sway, and the sun's perfect time as it marched across the sky. The music enthralled Boruin, but it bound the habback. The great wild beasts settled in the serpent's grasp and took the hot iron of the clan's branding with little more than a snort.

Most of the habback walked back to the great herd wandering the valley, heads raised as if hearing the echoes of the song in the wind. A few others stayed, nuzzling the singers as if love-struck. One singer, a tall woman with the braids of her hair twisted up like habback horns, reached up on tip-toe to whisper into these beasts' ears.

"Silver Song is giving them their names," the sweet-sharp woman explained when Boruin had gotten the nerve to ask her what the whisperer was doing. "Most of the habback only accept our song and their place in our herd. They'll return to us when we sing, but show no deeper duty. Some of the eldest beasts seem driven to pledge themselves to our clan."

Boruin smiled. They were becoming pets. "So you name them."

"And they help us move our camp after the herd."

"Your songs must be magic—or is it just your voices?" he prompted, curious if the rabinithair had taught them how to use the Aiemer.

"It is a song that the habback like. Maybe that's magic. Maybe not," she said before joining her voice back to her clan's melody.

In the evening, they drank and danced and cut meat from the hot spits turning beside the fires. The aroma drew in the red wolves. Boruin watched them line the hills and ridges, silhouetted by waxing Diun. They howled in chorus, a strange prairie song at once wild and beautiful. The rabinithair curled around the camp at night, allowing the riders to sleep off their drink without worry. His bulk would serve as defense enough, and his loud snarls quieted the wolves.

The waking meal seemed to suit Turintou. His mood was lighter and his body certainly was better for it. The skin of his face no longer hung sunken and old. The long rows of ribs now hid under renewed muscle and fat. Absent during the years of fasting, course stubble sprouted over the rough crown of skin behind his head. Soon his horns rose from a white mane that continued down the spine to his tail. The crown looked like flame when the windblown hair caught the light of the setting sun.

"You are not the rabinithair I first met," Boruin said.

"I'd forgotten what it feels like not to be hungry. I feel strong and young," he said.

"You seem new off the merchant's table, except for those scales," Boruin said. "They've yellowed a bit. They probably need some habback fat rubbed into them. I bet you'd polish up real nice," he added with wry grin.

The serpent assented to the jibe with his snorting chuckle. "I'll take care of that soon enough," he replied. "Now that the Aiemer has returned, I'll have the speed for it."

"If the Aiemer's back, why are you still on the ground?" Boruin asked, realizing the creature was still lay ing about in the dirt. "Why aren't we out of here?" he added. He glanced into the sky, half-expecting to see the blue rabinithair crashing out of the dark sky, all teeth and claws.

"In due time," said Turintou.

Boruin struggled to keep his voice low. "The branding is done. You've had your meal. What more are we waiting on?" The rabinithair didn't bother looking at him, just huffed and slid away from the firelight. Boruin cursed under his breath but did not follow. As much as he wanted to find his friends, he'd begun to realize the futility of arguing with a snake longer than a Nefazo caravan. He would wait and continue to tamp down his worry as best he could.

- 18 -
A Trap of worn clothes

It was as the sun broke over the sea of grass that Boruin discovered what the serpent waited on. He drank from his warm mug, watching from the edge of camp as the warming air stirred up the first breeze. Soon the grasses were beginning to rise and fall again in riffles across the prairie. The movement had become so common that when a wave rushed toward the camp like a rogue gust, Boruin thought little of it.

Spilling out of the grass, teeth gnashing, the enemy rabinithair struck. His polished scales had changed from sky blue to the rich green of the grass. Instead of two round horns forming his crown, six flat blades of bone curved back to protect his neck. His mane was a stubbly bristle, like a young man's first beard.

The serpent moved so fast Boruin could do little but spin away and wince, expecting the pain of crushing teeth. He froze there, hunched over his cup, and felt the trespasser's breath hot on his neck. The old fighter's clenched eyes sprang back open to find Turintou's mouth curled into a gruesome snarl, his tongue rattling against his bared teeth in warning.

"I'm taking him," said the trespassing rabinithair. "Will you fight me for the right?"

Turintou answered with his body. He pushed forward out of the grass, the length of him winding into a massive spring ready to strike. The trespasser laughed, and Boruin winced as the heat of his breath baked his skin.

"Old snake," the trespasser hissed. "Do you not think I see your old and ragged coat of scales? You've not left the ground in the last two days. Are you too ancient to feel the Aiemer around you?" he chuckled. "I am Sachuet. I will return for you when my errand is done."

The trespasser's tail had snuck forward while he talked. It whipped out of the grass beside them, seeming to snag the rising sun as it came and smash it against the ground. Light and heat exploded across the camp. Sachuet caught Boruin by the neck as Turintou glanced away from the flash.

Choking, the old fighter felt his body pull away from the ground as the serpent took to the sky. They shot upward and the air grew cold as Sachuet rode high into the Aiemer. He shifted the old man, still dangling by his head and shoulders, into the palm of his foreclaw. "You have some powerful enemies, lij," he shouted through the wind. "There are few mortals that are watched so carefully by—"

The snake shuddered as he was tugged back toward the ground like some invisible wave had broken over him. He spun in a tight loop so fast that blackness rose in front of Boruin's eyes. When his sight returned he saw the blemished green scales of Turintou's body coiling around Sachuet's polished armor. Their scales screamed as they ground together, their bodies constricting. Their heads snapped out and pulled back, circling for a chance to bite down and anchor hard teeth into their opponent.

"Youngling, as much as I am old, you are unwise," Turintou said as he dodged a strike under his throat. "I have slept longer than you have lived. Don't think you can deprive me of my ward. Let him go now and you can leave. I've granted you enough time in my lands as it is."

In the distance a small sun flared where Sachuet tried to untangle his tail and bring it around. The two tails whipped about, knotting and untangling like the swords of two duelers trying to break through the other's defense.

"I will take this lij north, living or crushed in my claw," growled Sachuet. "It matters not how he arrives." Turintou did not respond with words.

The old rabinithair's head ducked down and drove underneath Sachuet's body. Sachuet roared in glee as he dove for the opening, snapping down and latching onto Turintou's neck, just behind his heavy horns. Boruin gulped as the huge head pushed toward him, mouth open. White hair drifted into the wind as Sachuet twisted, trying to secure a tighter hold. Turintou's mane was too thick. Turintou kept pressing on until his teeth snapped down, severing the younger serpent's arm right behind the foreclaw. Sachuet's roar was deafening, but it faded in Boruin's ears as he fell away toward the ocean of grass below.

The old fighter struggled free from the dead claw. It tensed and released, almost breaking his femur before he pushed it away. As it drifted off, he realized fully that the wind in his ears was the last thing he would hear.

Above, the two rabinithair struggled after him, like boys battling over the last table scrap, tripping legs and catching each others' clothes as they raced forward. Their tails lashed and their bodies knotted around each other before slipping free.

Boruin did not look over his shoulder. Counting the moments until death would do no good. He watched Sachuet break free and lunge downward. The serpent was smaller than Turintou by nearly half, but he was faster. Just when he was a body-length away, where Boruin could see the dark blood seeping from the stump of his arm, he pulled up with a frustrated snarl and shot east. Above, Turintou was whipping after, driving through the Aiemer with all his force. Like he was leaping some great chasm, the serpent coiled and shot downward.

Turintou's body went as straight as an arrow, streamlined to pierce through the wind. They were out of the Aiemer! The realization almost made Boruin sick, except his heart was already stuck in his throat. Sachuet had turned, following the current downward. Turintou had dropped out of the strange element, choosing to plummet like a rock, no different than his wingless lij ward.

"What now?" he screamed into the wind as the serpent caught him in his teeth.

"I get rid of these damn scales. They're catching the wind and slowing me down." The rabinithair circled around his tail until he was a wide disk. It slowed their fall as the air buffeted them, but it wasn't going to stop them from crashing into the ground at a terrible speed. "When you hit the ground, lean forward and roll," he added as the grass rushed up at them. Before Boruin could complain, he caught sight of Sachuet following a stream of Aiemer and closing fast. It seemed to matter little whether they hit the serpent or the ground first—Boruin didn't think he'd survive either.

Just before the wide serpent smashed into the rider's camp, they hit the Aiemer again. Turintou lashed out at the current, frantically trying to reduce speed. He managed to slide out from over the cowering riders before his coils crashed into the earth. Boruin fell from the rabinithair's mouth and suddenly he was rolling, his face covered in dust. He wiped it from his eyes and saw Turintou launching back unto the sky before he'd even come to a stop.

The air roared as the great serpent tore upward to head off Sachuet. Just as his tail left the ground, he reversed with such a tight turn that Boruin thought the rabinithair would rip apart. Instead, the air seemed to explode from around his body at the bend, like Turintou was tearing the sky itself into shreds. When his tail reached the turn, it cracked around like a whip. The sound boomed across the valley, the echoes bouncing about the low mountains. It knocked Boruin back down to his knees and his ears rang. The habback started, adding to the thunder as they stampeded across the valley and up the next hill before settling.

Sachuet's tail stabbed forward and a sheet of flame fanned out into the air. Turintou did not stop for it; he lowered his head and drove through the fire. The sound of their impact was almost as loud as his snapping tail. They tore west along the Aiemer stream, a fierce knot of writhing bodies and snapping teeth. Then they were gone.

A jeweled rain fell, glinting in the sun like shards of broken sky. Boruin realized with a start that the strange precipitation was actually the pale green scales of his rabinithair companion. The clan covered their heads and scrambled to collect the pieces, holding plates and furs over each other as the serpent's old armor dropped to the ground. Boruin caught one and weighed it in his hand. It was thinner and lighter than he expected.

"They will make fine armor and tools for the clan," said Dark Eye. Though the elder was ancient, he still pulled Boruin back up to his feet with ease. "The Skyking is very generous."

Boruin scanned the horizon as a distant clash like rolling thunder heralded the continuing fight. "They will be no help if he cannot best the trespasser."

Dark Eye shrugged. "If the Skyking returns, all is well. If not, we will fight. He will not take the Skyking's companion while we stand."

"Nonsense," Boruin scoffed. "If Sachuet returns, I'll leave. No harm will come to me from him," Boruin said, though he did not think that would hold true of his eventual meeting with the Monarhig. Dark Eye shrugged again and watched his people gather up the valuable scales. Either they too knew fighting a rabinithair was useless, or they had greater faith in their Skyking than Boruin.

The Swift Horse Clan began packing the following morning. The habback had been branded and sung to; the season had ended with Diun's setting. The massive herd had wandered west in the night, the clan's habback in their midst. In a day or two the riders would follow. It was impossible to pick the clan's beasts from the wild by sight, but

Boruin bet the rabinithair had almost made them an equal number. Most of the women were still without voices after two days of endless singing. Their Skyking had supplied them with great wealth. Alone, they could never have held and sang to so many. It would not be long until other smaller tribes came to join and follow their herd across the Hetsu. The Swift Horse Clan would be the head of a great family again.

Boruin walked around the camp, trying to loosen up his muscles. Serving as a prize between dueling rabinithair took a toll on one's body. Falling from the heavens and crashing into the dirt had not helped. Looking right was impossible—his neck seized up tight—and his left arm was too sore to raise above his shoulder. The sweet-sharp woman had promised to rub him down again, but it would have to wait until they broke camp.

His back ached, and he reached for his boots again, trying to stretch it out. He held there, feeling the warmth of the sun soaking into his flesh. Under trampled grass, he spied another of the old scales Turintou had shed with his whip-like turn. It had cracked along the middle. He braced it against his knee like a long stick of firewood. Straining, he tried to break it down the fault, but it wouldn't so much as splinter. The rabinithair's scales wouldn't just make good armor and tools; they'd be nearly unmatched.

"It takes some force to split my scales, new or old," Turintou explained. Boruin turned and saw the serpent poised in the air. His new scales matched the Hetsu grass, down to the individual blades. Each was smooth and polished yet unscratched by dirt, rock, or an enemy's teeth. The rabinithair was at his best.

Boruin forgot for the moment that the serpent had laid about, looking old with tattered scales just to draw in Sachuet. His anger at being bait slipped away with the relief that Turintou had won out. "You look like a young girl ready for her first ball," Boruin laughed.

"Joke if you must, but I do look grand," Turintou said.

"Where's our friend?"

The serpent's tongue knocked once across his teeth. "Well west of here, over the Monahdraichean Mountains that rise past the savannas, probably. After you've been driven to the ground and pinned enough times, running doesn't hurt your pride as much," he answered.

Boruin leaned up against the rabinithair as he settled into the grass. The heat coming off his scales started to loosen his aching back. "I thought you would have killed him," he said.

"No," answered Turintou. "I slept long enough for him to grow strong. It would have been a waste to kill him."

"What are you talking about? You said he was a trespasser."

"I was hungry, and even in a good mood we rabinithair are very territorial. We do not get along, even with our children."

Boruin sputtered angrily. "You're telling me Sachuet was your son?"

"Of course. Why did you think I was sleeping while some other serpent fed off my lands? Once he was born, he needed to grow strong. What better place than my territory?"

This was the errand that could not wait? That he'd risked both their lives for? Dumbfounded, Boruin headed toward camp in a daze.

"Wasn't I right? He was quite the fighter, wasn't he? Now he'll stake out and defend his own territory," the rabinithair shouted after him.

"You are rutting crazy, you know that?" Boruin hollered without stopping or looking back. His anger was returning, and he knew better than to let it out near such an irrational creature.

That afternoon a rider came in from the west. The man was tired, though his horse stamped and seemed ready for another day's ride. That evening the Eldest presented Turintou with the rider's news.

"Already the Moon Wolf Clan rides to join us. They are my father's sister's people and have always been steadfast cousins to the Swift Horse," said Dark Eye.

"I'm glad," said Turintou. "You will become a great family of the east Hetsu once more. I will not sleep again until your youngest children are the Eldest of their own clans. The Skyking will watch over you."

"What you asked us for has been found," added Wind Runner. Dark Eye frowned as the man stepped on his own news, but he did not stop him. Boruin guessed this was behavior long established and expected. "A Moon Wolf saw the forest of the sky. He rode under its roots and followed it north to the boundary of the plains. The great moon has made three faces since, he claimed. This was sent as proof." He held out a thick band of leather. The serpent licked the air over it with his tongue, then it was handed to Boruin. The mud-green skin was tough, but thinner than habback.

"I know the lake creature to which that belonged," said Dark Eye. "It follows the windwood. The Moon Wolf speaks the truth."

Boruin frowned and handed back the strange leather. "What is the windwood?"

Turintou answered for the Eldest. "The Imorin Forest. It floats on the Aiemer, same as I. There, among the marii, we may find your name."

Boruin knew of the small, fox-like creatures, but not what they could know of his name. "Will they know of my companions?"

"Hard to say what the marii know. Depends on which way the song blows," the rabinithair snorted absently.

They intended to leave the clan at the first cool breath of Diuntyne, but they delayed until one more calf had been roasted and one last round of chantulp had turned into three. The rabinithair made a lazy pass over the camp before turning northwest. As they sped into the silvery night, a flash of light filled the sky and ball of dark red flame fell toward the plains.

"What is that?" Boruin yelled over the wind. "I thought you two would burn me black as like pig skin." The serpent turned back and chased his tail. Inside the twisted bone, a burning ember spun around in a tight oval like an egg made of fire. The flame licked out over the two twisted tail horns like a living creature searching to escape its cage. Turintou whipped his tail back and threw. The egg slung out into the night and exploded in brilliant fire.

"I told you my tail needed to be ready. It will not draw the Aiemer if not honed," said the serpent. Boruin watched as the bone began to fill again. A spark of red like the distant Nurom Misuer churned into a small pearl, swelling until the egg was reborn and the two horns barely contained the flame.

"Don't tell me that's not magic," said Boruin.

Turintou laughed. "It's just rabinithair," he said. "Each of us are a little different in our own way, but we all have tails of fire, and we all prefer flying to not."

"Why didn't I see it before?"

"I cannot carry this fire outside the Aiemer. So if you want to think of magic solely in a lij's terms, then perhaps my fire and flying are." To avoid talking more theory, the serpent turned into the wind. Boruin buried his face in the fur that had sprouted down the rabinithair's shoulder and around his foreclaw. He was glad for the warmth as Turintou shot for the stars and flew as fast as he could where the air was cold and crisp.

Over the next few days the rabinithair worked west and north, flying into the current of a broad river of Aiemer as it washed back and forth across the land. Where they found small clans following their herds, Turintou dropped down from the heights to circle near.

"When they hear the Swift Horse Clan needs riders, they will know it to be true," he explained.

The Hetsu Plains were home to more habback than Boruin could have dreamed. As promised, the rabinithair showed him the greater herds. Where the tall grass was a sea across the Hetsu, the habback were dark continents. At times they filled the horizon, reaching all sides of the compass. Had Boruin not been floating high with the clouds, he would never have believed it possible.

"There are more beasts here than all the people in Nefazo. Probably more than in the entire south," he said.

"The herds of the Hetsu are mighty again," Turintou replied. "After the Purahd, when the mah'saiid's plague had left all their cities and lands in ruin, I could fly for days without seeing a beast or bird above the desolation. I slept long ages waiting for the return of the land. It took many more ages for its creatures to return."

"And you think they still need saving?"

"Once there were more people than stones on the Hetsu. It will be the same again. 'Kill only what you cull.' You may think it of little use now, but the Hetsu is not far from returning to a place of people. When the wilderness is gone and the land is again boxed by fences and plowed for crop, the habback will still be here to feed their people because of my traditions," he said.

"And feed you."

"Yes, and feed me," the rabinithair said. "You lij survive anywhere, and so I must live with you."

Boruin had watched Diun rise over the horizon. He held it in his eye, thinking of Wraethe, until finally his head sunk into the warm hair of Turintou's forearm. It seemed only a moment before he woke, hands clutched about his ears. The roar was deafening, the rabinithair's body shaking with the fury of it. Boruin peered through the dark but could see nothing. The great serpent dashed through the clouds, breaking in and out of their shadows as he rushed toward what had angered him.

As the rabinithair pounced out of the clouds, his mane of white hair exploded into flame. Boruin threw his arms over his head, expecting the flash of heat against his skin. Instead, the red, fire-like glow raced past him and on down Turintou's spine. The wind played with the hair, flicking it about, to complete the illusion of flame. It burned behind the thick clouds, looking like a fuse sprinting toward an explosion.

Turintou bunched his body into a striking pose, pulling his tail over his head like a spear about to be thrown. The running fire reached the tip of his tail, and heat exploded from the two bones as if it held a small sun. Its light washed like wet blood over the faces of terrified sailors. They stood shaking on the deck of the ship or scurried into the shadows of its sails.

By Yuin! A boat among the clouds! Boruin wondered if he was dreaming. The hull was short and fat, with a large sail that circled the entire bow of the thing. It looked like a cigar with a red tea saucer on its tip. It was impossible that this ship was sailing across the sky. He opened his mouth to shout down to the people, but the roar of the serpent sent his hands again across his ears. He was not dreaming after all.

"How dare you invade my realm!" the rabinithair roared, his tongue rattling across his teeth. His tail jerked as if eager to drive through the wooden hull and set it falling and aflame.

"Skyking!" a meek voice called from somewhere on deck. A furred creature, half the size of a man, worked his way forward to the bow. A lantern swung in his paw, its stenciled brass plate casting a two-pronged sigil, curved like entwining snakes around a flaming sun.

"Turintou! The marii carries your sign!" shouted Boruin. The serpent hissed, his tongue still rattling and his tail still poised to fire. "Vestoi," Boruin dared. "They wish to make peace, Vestoi!"

The rabinithair stilled and pulled his tail back. Boruin knew he could hurl it from any distance and bring the ship down, but his initial rage was cooling and his sense returning.

"I told you to forget that name," Turintou hissed to Boruin.

Boruin growled back. "I'd certainly like too, if you'd just give me the chance."

The rabinithair encircled the ship with his great body. "Where did you get that sign? Why is it not Sachuet's mark you bear?" the serpent shouted to the marii. The small creature held firm, though his hackles stood straight off the back of his neck.

"The Mother Prime heard your song rise again above the Hetsu. She knew it would not be long until you reclaimed your territory. In the daylight, you would have seen the same sign flown above the mainsail." The rabinithair swung his tail again over the ship. The sailors dropped to the deck, and one heaved his supper over the side. The light of Turintou's tail illuminated the signal flag and his sigil embroidered there.

"This vessel flies under the command of the Imorin marii and its Mother Prime?" asked Turintou. His body unraveled from around the ship, lessening the overt threat of a crushing death.

"With her blessing, but under the authority of the eashue who have lived in the Imorin Forest since last you visited," The marii waved forward the captain. He stepped lightly, as if nearly weightless. Where the marii was less than half Boruin's height, the eashue stood a good head taller than the old man. He looked unnaturally thin as though he'd been stretched to reach it.

The eashue bowed low before the serpent, shaking slightly. He seemed green, as if scared sick, but Boruin noticed his comrades shared different shades of the same color. All had darker spots across their bald skulls, and the captain's ran down his bowing back. He crossed his arms as he straightened, attempting a more confidant pose. Boruin realized it was not the eashue's body that had been shaking but a thick band of rough quills that ran from his shoulders to his wrist and rustled in the wind.

"The marii have granted my people a place in the Imorin. In all things we do, we seek the Mother Prime's blessing," said the captain.

"I've never seen a shuen so far from the ocean," Turintou sniffed. "And I've never met a shuen that I liked."

The marii jumped to reassure him. "The *eashue* share your sentiments, Skyking. The captain's folk have long been exiled from the sea. They sail the air now, with your permission," the marii said.

"With my permission," Turintou repeated. "We will see. I do doubt your strange vessel will reach the Imorin before me, no matter how you've deceived the Aiemer into assisting you. If I find the Mother Prime speaks of you differently than you speak of yourselves, you will see me on the horizon. Then you will know only the lightness of falling," the rabinithair snarled before diving back into the clouds.

"Would you knock a bird out of the sky too?" Boruin hollered.

"Of course not. They are meant by the Mother to soar."

"Every one of those sailors had a wing of skin between his arms and his torso. Maybe knocking them off their ship wouldn't be as effective as you think."

"Don't tell me how to govern my territory," Turintou replied, but it was a fading grumble nearly lost in the wind. Boruin chuckled and nestled his head back into the warm fur. It wasn't long before he dreamt of his own rich merchant airships sailing over the Nefazo toll roads and custom houses.

19

WINTER IN THE IMORIN WOOD

Wraethe struggled against the clutches of the Guidevein, but she could not pull free. The stone was dark black, and its sparkling light of life had long since faded to stars before winking out all together. She clawed at the stone with one free arm, pulling at the rock collar around her neck. Her feet were so cold, her body slowly cooling, and her teeth chattering as the stone drew her heat away. *Tic tic tock tock tic* came the sound of an iron pick on rock.

"Griant! I'm here! I'm trapped!" she hollered as loudly as she could.

The excavating of stone grew closer, and she soon smelled the musty tang of powdered rock. Behind her, light trickled through the stone and cast the shadow of her head across the small pocket cave. Tears fell down her cheeks in relief.

"Can you get me free from the rock?" Wraethe pleaded.

"What of you we can, my dear," said the gruff voice. The knobby hand of the groundling reached quickly around, avoiding her flailing arm. The hand pulled back, knife edge in tow.

"Yes, a fine trophy for such a fair chase," the Monarhig purred as he took firm hold of Wraethe's dark hair.

Boruin woke in a strange room with his scream caught in his throat like a jagged bone in a bad soup. He retched, and then the hot vomit came, spilling across the wooden floor as he ran. His feet stopped only when the railing outside the suite caught his body and the morning air replaced the musty smell of powdered rock from his dream.

The old fighter leaned his head against the cool rail and felt the chill wind drying the tears on his cheeks. What a vicious dream. He had tried to take the rabinithair's advice and swallow down his fear for his friends. Awake, Boruin had managed it, but there was no holding back a dream—his mind conjuring them frozen in the dead Guidevein like mosquitoes in a bead of amber.

Dawn was coming early. This high above the earth, the sun peeked over the distant horizon as if bringing a secret to you alone. Directly below, the world was still black. Looking down, he remembered then where he was, that they had reached the Imorin forest. He leaned against the rail and waited for that line of light, the eye of the sun, to crawl across the land. It would creep up hills and mountains and flash across the lowlands and the inland sea. Boruin was used to the erratic dash, a sight seen often while waiting for Wraethe to succumb to her daytime sleep. Sometimes it came so fast that it stole the words from her mouth, and she would slump over with her head on his shoulder.

Now, he'd stay and wait for the warmth of the sun to banish the cold fear of his dream. Until then the cool wind would ease the jittering of his stomach. The rabinithair's Diuntyne approach to the Imorin Forest had soured it, and this foul dream stirred it again.

"That damn snake," Boruin mumbled and spat, more to clear the taste in his mouth than out of anger.

Soon after they'd left the strange airship, the great serpent had dropped to race just above the ground. The Aiemer had become turbulent. The thick currents over the Hetsu Plains spread wide and shallow. They drained like a river delta into the great Aiemer sea which bore the Imorin Forest.

"If it fades, I'd rather be close to the ground than above the birds," said the serpent. He wove around in its tangled streams until they caught up to the tail of the floating wood. Boruin had only a glimpse of the trees climbing like a twirling staircase to Diun when Turintou growled. Out of the dim light under its hovering roots, Aiemer sharks dashed from their hiding places. Theirs was the thin, tough leather offered by the Moon Wolf rider. He wondered for a quick second what fish were doing swimming through air, and then they were dodging blue and green streaks with snapping white teeth.

Turintou spun and leapt like a kite caught in a gale. The sharks turned after them. A pack of hundreds, like one great toothy mouth, spilled out of the last few groves still hanging close to the ground. The serpent flew hard and fast, and Boruin cursed as he tucked his head into the knuckled claw that held him.

The airborne sharks tore after the rabinithair. His tail slapped some out of the Aiemer stream to crash into the earth while his body made impossible turns to avoid the hunting packs. He let the creatures drive him up and out of a long stream of Aiemer that dead-ended in empty sky. The sharks slowed, spreading wide to block the thin avenue out.

Turintou chuckled, sounding amused rather than surprised. "They usually aren't this aggressive," he explained as he backed into the last pocket of Aiemer that held him aloft. "They are scavengers, really, but they do get riled when the Imorin Forest rises for winter. They'll migrate back to the Lakelands on their own. It's a long way across the inner sea, so they'll eat anything that moves to store up fat." His mouth opened to explain further, but snapped shut as the sharks leapt forward for a killing attack.

The rabinithair launched up even higher like an iron spring, out of the lifting stream of Aiemer and over their hunters. He arced through the air as gravity pulled him back into the stream. Hungry sharks driving blindly from behind shoved the leading edge out of the current. With nothing to keep them aloft, they fell struggling to the distant ground. The stragglers below nosed at the edges of the Aiemer, snapping at the best positions and waiting for the current to wash over their downed brethren and deliver a meal. Turintou raced back down the stream and was long lost in the winding Aiemer before the pack realized that he had gone.

"Thinking of last night isn't settling your stomach," he grumbled. Boruin took another deep breath and concentrated on the cool touch of the rail against his head. The thought of that winding chase, more terrible than the worst sea-rolling ship, was almost too much for his stomach. It had been too much at the time, and the sound and touch of Boruin's returning breakfast had cut short the rabinithair's victorious laughter.

He had missed the view of the Imorin Forest as they approached in the night, but now the sun reached the great inland sea below. The forest rose to beautiful detail in the bright light of dawn.

Boruin stood on the foremost grove of a long train of trees spiraling towards the earth below. Far in the distance, still skirting the ground, the tail of the forest was finishing its long arc south from the Lakelands, along the northern border of the Hetsu Plains and back north to the shore of Baszul, the largest of the inland seas.

His first impression still seemed best. At the edge of the shore, the forest rose like a staircase from ground to sky, a long body of trees seeming to spiral up on warm winds. Some sections were like a string of pearls, made from large groves and small thickets. Other parts of the great wood were thick lengths of forest pulled along in that massive line. The roots of the Imorin trees twisted about their fellows, creating a chain a hundred times longer than the rabinithair. Small islands connected by thin anchor lines of root swung outside the main spiral like green moons orbiting their planet.

Far below, a long stretch of Imorin trees suddenly cast off their leaves as if they were a coat that had suddenly grown too warm. The broad leaves, turned pink and white by the cold upper air, hung like mist for a moment, as if surprised, before the wind caught them and whisked them off into the heavens. The bare trees now stood seemingly frosted, their tips pale ivory over the warm red trunks below. They looked like small toys, like edible sculptures of whipped sugar found in the Nefazo delicatessens.

Boruin turned and looked up at the tree in which his room had been built. The trunk rose almost another four hundred feet, so high the white tips of the bare branches were lost in the distance. His head spun slightly. These trees certainly were not toys.

"Our summer falls very quickly to winter, does it not?" came a small voice from behind him. The old man turned to see one of the small, fox-like marii standing on the rail to catch a large white leaf. She pulled it close and opened her hand. The leaf hovered there until a gentle gust of wind spun it back out into empty space. "The leaves will wilt in a few days. They cannot take the cold. Somewhere they will come down like a snowfall and coat the Lakelands in white and faded pink."

Boruin resisted the urge to help her down from her perch. Past the rail were only long minutes of sky, then sea. "I imagine it will be beautiful, though not as grand as this place," he managed after watching her step so gracefully toward him. Far below, another grove of trees released their leaves. The Aiemer and the wind fought over the swirling cloud and drove them up the center of the spiral like a geyser.

"There is no other place like the Imorin Forest. You are kind to honor it so," said the marii. "I will convey your words to the Mother Prime. She has asked to meet you, though she cannot until this evening. I have been asked to tend you. I am Rue."

Boruin flashed an embarrassed smile. "I don't normally need a lot of tending, but I would appreciate being directed to a bath. I could use a mop and pail, too. I had a bit of a rough—"

"No need to explain. I happened to see you come in last evening," Rue said with a quick twitch of her nose and the peeling back of her lip. Boruin hoped that was a teasing smile. Rue leapt down from the rail and looked up at Boruin from just above his knees as she continued. "I'll take you to the baths. Your friend already lounges there in the steam, waiting for you. I'll warn you, though: he seems sour," she said.

"If he's mad at me, then the snake can bite his tail. There will be no apologizing on my part."

The Imorin baths were nestled in a tangled ball of roots deep in what Rue called Foregrove. The water, held tight by the roots that now clenched together against the cold, rose almost scalding as if from a great, beating heart. Boruin lay back in the water and watched the steam rise in thinning columns consumed by the frigid morning air.

The city in Foregrove teased Boruin's eyes. Song molded the buildings from boughs and spurs of the great Imorin trees, Rue explained. The roots held the trees together, but the marii used the high branches for avenues, rather than walking below. It was like a child's fantasy—a city of tree houses, except the houses and trees were one and the same. Hundreds of windows were set into the bark of the towering trunks. Massive entryways opened into large halls. Curls of smoke lilted out of other small, blackened portals as morning cooking fires blossomed.

Far above, the grove was coming to life. Marii on their morning errands moved from tree to tree, crossing the great boughs that reached out to their neighbors. Markets lined these wide avenues. Children raced about, leaping from branch to trunk high above the ground in their attempts to catch each other. Boruin closed his eyes, tired of his heart racing.

"It's embarrassing enough to have to carry a lij. It's worse to arrive covered in his eaten meal," Turintou complained. Boruin continued to ignore the rabinithair's tirade and instead listened to Rue. Her instrument had appeared as soon as she sat to wait on Boruin's bath. The small pipe raced across a variety of scales at once relaxing and inspiring. He opened his eyes when she halted. Rue's ears turned side-to-side as if homing in on some whispering sound, then her teeth appeared again in that sharp smile. The music took on a new shade, as if she were following the lead of a distant conductor.

Come to think of it, music was everywhere in the Imorin Forest. He tuned out the rabinithair and directed his ears about. Voices wafted through the air in song, accompanied by a soft cacophony of piping, drumming, and whistling. Boruin worried that the constant background noise would become annoying, but the more he listened, the more it seemed the different melodies were all part of some great chorus. He was about to ask Rue about it when he was scooped out of the hot water and deposited on a root by the serpent's long tongue.

"Well?" Boruin asked as the serpent stared.

"If you're not going to apologize, then I have other matters which require my attention," Turintou said.

"Go chase some more sharks, you whiny bastard," Boruin muttered. The serpent swept him back into the pool with his long tail as he departed.

Dusk found Boruin back at the railing outside his room, watching the evening winds stir up the waves across the surface of the wide Baszul. He imagined the inland sea a great table of shimmering coin as the waves reflected gold from the setting sun in the west and silver's cool light splashed from the rising Diun in the east. The old man looked left, half expecting to see Pile leaning over the rail, drooling about the mouth without realizing it. Would Wraethe see it at all, with the orbs that judged her waking and sleeping simultaneously in the sky? Boruin chose to imagine she could.

"You look fair in our robes," Rue said, having quietly snuck up beside him for the second time that day.

Boruin answered with a smile left over from his thought of Wraethe. "I'd like to see the marii that would fit these."

"Are you ready to meet the Mother Prime?"

"Is it something that should be prepared for?"

"Not for most," Rue answered.

The answer worried Boruin a little as Rue led him up through the great grove to the crown of the one Imorin tree towering over all the rest. It sat at the tip of Foregrove, the flagship of the Imorin Forest, cutting first through the sky with the entire wood following after.

His worry was for nothing. The Mother Prime was Nemuet, a marii with a smile no less than Rue's and eyes that were kind despite their sharpness. Boruin read her advanced age in her graying mane and wrinkled ears, but that age was diluted by her light step and confident voice. She excused herself from Turintou and the retinue that gathered about him, crossing the wide balcony as soon as Boruin came into sight.

"It is an honor to meet a companion of this rabinithair's," said Nemuet as she fetched him from Rue.

"The more I hear that said, the more I wonder if it is so deserved," Boruin answered as he lowered himself in the best court-bow he could manage.

"I imagine so," she answered. "The rabinithair do not take friends lightly." Nemuet led him across the balcony to the front of the tree instead of back to the small crowd. They stood for a moment looking out over the sea. A storm was building to the north. Lightning crackled up into the sky like a child flailing its limbs from the floor.

"The Skyking says you owe him your name, but it is not known to you," said Nemuet.

"Is that terribly strange?" he asked.

The marii looked up at him, shrugging. "Not entirely. It is true that some live their lives without ever fully knowing themselves, but I think in a way you are different from that. If you like, we will listen to you and see if we can discern what has become of your name."

"When we met, he called me half-man. Do you know what that means?" Boruin asked.

"The Skyking loves to be cryptic," Nemuet said with a laugh. "Perhaps we will learn that as well."

Boruin held out his arm. "And what of this?" The marii took his wrist in her paws, her nails tracing out the scar holding tight to his runes.

"I can do little for old wounds of the flesh," she said. Boruin knew then that she could not see his runes, and his hope for help thinned.

When they turned back from the great expanse, Boruin found many more marii had gathered to watch. Behind the balcony, the crown of the tree had been woven into a small hill. The branches intertwined to create a solid floor before sprouting, as winding columns, into the last few feet above and spreading across the sky. The new growth was so pale Boruin wondered if it was not translucent. The distant lightning made the columns flicker as if stars had been set at the tips. The marii stood one behind another, the raised floor allowing them all a view of the distant horizon. They seemed to watch the storm, ears flicking about as if catching the distant thunder that was silent to him.

Nemuet's small hand took his as she explained. "These are the mothers and fathers of our groves, each wise among our people. They will help me listen for your name and maybe some of the past that has been lost to you."

"What should I tell you?" Boruin asked. "I remember nothing before waking on the Nefazo highway. I don't even have dreams from before."

Nemuet smiled, her eyes sparkling brightly. "You will not have to speak. We will listen for the sound of your soul," she replied. "Some things—the Imorin Wood for instance—sing very loudly to the marii.

The song is bright and clear as the notes of each great tree rise to join the World Song. The sea has its own deep undercurrent, as do the creatures among the roots of our forest, the sky, and the distant stars above. They all sing notes that we marii hold close to our hearts."

Boruin looked again at the group and saw indeed that they were listening to the storm rather than watching it. Their ears flicked back and forth, some with eyes closed, some smiling at times as if they'd caught an especially pleasing string of notes.

"In other things—the rabinithair for one, and in some lij—the song is less clear. It is easier to hear by listening to the World Song around such things, by examining their effect on the notes we are familiar with."

"Do you hear anything of me?"

Nemuet nodded. "Yes, I can hear quite a lot, but it is an unbalanced verse—like a harmony with some parts sung too soft. The World Song here is very strong. We are so high above the land that its notes carry from very far off. They will flush out your song, and we will discover you."

The Mother Prime brought him a few feet in from the edge and then joined the other marii. Boruin felt alone and out of place as the long ears all swiveled to point his way. He was conscious of his breathing, worried it was too loud and that his heart was beating too fast. It passed as he waited, and as the marii continued to listen silently he forgot to be nervous at all. The moon had risen high when Nemuet finally opened her eyes and spoke.

"There is nothing to be heard this way, but there is another option if you are willing," Nemuet said.

Boruin agreed quickly. "Anything, my lady. Whatever you suggest."

They led him to a twisted column of climbing branches at the top of the bowl.

"Hold these branches tight," said Nemuet. "We will sing the song of your heart. It will not hurt, but you will feel the song very strongly. I do not want you to wash away."

The marii surrounded him, and Nemuet began to sing. One by one the marii joined the melody or began a new harmony. The music was unlike a song, more like notes and rhythm gleaned from the world around him: whispers of wind and water, gravel slowly pushed aside by spreading tree roots, the moist sighs of rain-heavy clouds passing. To Boruin it felt like home, like the touch of his own hands, the smell of his sweat after battle, the peace that came just before sunset from knowing he'd not be alone much longer. It was relaxing in a way, and he had to fight to keep his grip on the branches.

The marii had begun singing slowly, but in a rush the last half of the group jumped into their parts with full voices. The song swept Boruin up in its sound and he had to look down to see if his feet were still on the floor. He felt cast off from the world and swirling in a tempest of himself. He squeezed his fists, unsure if he still clutched the branches.

If the marii had found the part they were searching for, Boruin could not tell. He only knew himself and nothing beyond.

Except that's not right, is it? Boruin heard Wraethe say as clear as if she stood shouting in his ear. *What is that right there? That dark root, like a deep well?*

Amid the tumult of his heart's song, Boruin saw the void. His song made it visible by washing around it. He peered closer and knew what it was. The long string, so deep blue it was almost black, wrapped around him in a great circle, binding his flesh. The runes were no true part of him. The sigils were some false construct, some anchor laid on his skin, as foreign as the scarred handprint that held them motionless. They seemed sewn to him, a false limb to fill that void where his name—his first life—had disappeared.

He reached out with his left hand to tear it from his song, as if grabbing it now could remove it from his skin entirely. Boruin strained to reach it, leaning even further out into the flood of song.

"Don't let go of the branches!" Nemuet called, her voice a cold splash of water. The song tumbled to pieces around him, and Boruin fell to his knees. The silence was so complete that it rang in his ears like a thousand small bells. He looked up and saw the branches twinkling, now brighter than the stars. One of those stars fluttered down before his face. The Fae smiled at him as it passed, his face clean porcelain haloed in a yellow moon-corona. Boruin gaped at the little man, his thumb-sized body covered in fish-scale wings that ran down the back of his legs and across his shoulders. The wings rang like bells as they beat together.

"A pflint," whispered one of the nearby marii, obviously surprised. "One of the Feirnann."

The pflint hovered before the Mother Prime. Its voice sounded like snapping sparks.

"We are engaged in a most important matter," Nemuet replied. The crackling voice rose, the tone insistent.

The marii's nose wrinkled. "It is not my decision alone to make, but I will ask if you feel it is of a high need," the Mother Prime added.

Nemuet approached Boruin. He tried for a moment to stand, but was too spent.

"The Fae heard your song and wish to bring an emissary to speak with us. They must be searching hard for you to have picked our chorus out of the World Song as they did. Perhaps they will help us in this matter. Perhaps not."

Boruin shook his head. "I know no Fae that wish me anything but ill. I do not wish to bring trouble to your forest."

Nemuet considered this. "I do not think this is an act of war. Besides, the Skyking is certainly in a position to keep the peace," she added. The rabinithair shook his tongue ever so slightly across his teeth.

"Then let's see what they have to say," said Boruin.

"Alright, Flic-a-wit. Let's have him," Nemuet commanded.

A thousand flickering wings in the treetops descended on their leader. They came like a wash of luminescent dust, swirling in a tightening vortex until it was all one brilliant curtain of bright yellow. Out of the cloud of pflints stepped a man, rather than the expected Fae.

Boruin felt the heat rise across his face. His hand edged toward the bare spot at his side where his sword no longer hung. "Belok," he growled.

The Nefazo merchant's smile was as broad as ever. "Boruin! Glad to see you so well off!"

"Were those groundlings yours?"

"The ones that killed Toaaho? Let's say we have the same employer," Belok answered, pointing off-handedly at the dissipating cloud of tiny Fae settling again into the high branches.

"And what does your new employer want with my crew?" Boruin asked softly.

The Nefazo strolled close and circled him, performing for the crowd as much as for Boruin. "The Monarhig, with whom I believe you're acquainted, wants nothing more of your crew. Save, perhaps, for Wraethe. He has taken quite a liking to her," Belok added with a grin. "The prince wants to know why you dally so and do not search them out." The merchant's lips reversed into a mocking frown. "You're not much of a friend or leader, Boruin. I'd always thought you a more loyal employer."

"Of which Monarhig do you speak?" the rabinithair rumbled. Belok turned, and though his ass of a smile still hung across his teeth, his face blanched noticeably in the moonlight.

"One of the greatest," Belok boasted, "a prince of the talamh of wind!"

The rabinithair snorted. "Is that the one you spoke of, Mother Prime?" Turintou asked.

She considered it, looking about. A few of her companions nodded as she wordlessly sought their opinions. "His song had a strong wind theme. He must be the one surrounding the Munier Valley."

"That is right," Belok interjected. "The Monarhig has your friends trapped, Boruin, and wishes to speak with you. If you continue to flee, he will no longer wait to kill them." He stopped his pacing and stood before Boruin to cast his sly smile full upon him. "Well, all but Wraethe, I imagine."

"So that is your message? Go to Munier to meet the Monarhig?" Boruin asked.

"That is all," said Belok through his taunting, sickly smile. Slowly, rage had begun to replace the strength Boruin lost during the singing of his heart song. Now it had reached his head, and he took to his feet.

"Fine. I will see him, but I will never see you again," he answered evenly.

Boruin walked forward and caught the Nefazo at his collar, twisting it tight about his enemy's throat. Belok grappled at his arms, and Boruin stepped quicker, pushing the merchant before him down the slope. The snapping spark voices of the pflints swelled angrily, but if they were coming down out of the trees, Boruin couldn't see them. His eyes were locked tight on the fear mounting in Belok's.

Belok, feet back peddling, turned to look over his shoulder. A scream tried to slip from his choked windpipe, but he could not stop Boruin's rage. The Nefazo hit the rail at his hip and flipped out into the abyss. Boruin watched him fall, a grin finally rising to his face. A mist of yellow pflints descended on the rail to watch the man fall, but they did not follow him down.

"It is not your place to treat a guest of the Imorin Wood in such fashion," Nemuet said, unphased by his violence. "Skyking, would you be so kind as to return the Monarhig's emissary to Flic-a-wit?"

The rabinithair flashed over the side and down toward the distant inland sea.

"My pardons," Boruin exhaled. "That was impolite on my part. I did not wish to offend the marii."

Nemuet softly blew off a crowd of Fae that had settled on her shoulders. "No doubt he has given you proper cause for your anger, but dealing with the Fae requires strict rules of etiquette. It is more for our safety than out of politeness," Nemuet replied. She placed her hand across his. "At least we know your friends are safe, for the moment. That is one worry from your shoulders."

He took a deep breath, realizing the Mother Prime was right. If Belok was making threats, then at least Wraethe and Pile were not trapped in rock. He looked up at the moon, and it shone for him as if new to his eye.

20

EMPTY ANSWERS

N emuet bid Boruin to escort her from the top of the tree. The World Song this high above Baszul Sea, full with so many miles of singers, was overwhelming. She found it hard to refrain from listening and letting her mind drift away.

"Did you hear what you were listening for?" Boruin asked as they hiked the long stairways down from the high crown of the Imorin tree.

"We will wait on the rabinithair for that answer, if you will," Nemuet replied. "Right now, I'd like to know what you heard."

"I'm not sure what I heard in all that wash of song," said Boruin.

Nemuet grabbed his arm and pulled him around. "Shark shit, young lij. You know very well what you heard. I saw you go for it like a young kit scrambling after his first pipe."

Boruin looked at his scarred skin and ran his finger over the dark runes. They shifted ever so slightly and caught on their snag.

"I saw a piece of someone else bound to my body, as if my early life had been scraped clean away to make room for this falsehood." It was a cold thought, and he shivered without noticing.

Nemuet knew the shiver was of fear, but the cold in the air was growing deeper, and so she led him down into a thick gathering of trunks. The marii's song had taken a burl, like a knotted face peering from the side of the tree, and molded it into a modest home. Nemuet stepped past the door and onto her balcony. She stirred the ash-covered coals of a cooking fire held in a large bowl of stone to keep the heat from the wood beneath. With the fire rising, it was warmer. Warmer still was the view from the old matriarch's terrace.

The marii's homes flowed out through the grove as if Nemuet's balcony was the font head for the village. The fox-like creatures were out in the hundreds, all with either an instrument or their voices raised in song. The sound should have been chaotic, but again Boruin noticed that it all blended into some great harmony. It came to him then that they were singing along to this great World Song that was just outside the edge of his hearing.

"I heard that dark stripe, too," Nemuet said, jogging Boruin back from his thoughts. "You tried to show it to me before we began, didn't you?" She came close and turned his arm about, searching his skin. "Is it something many can see?"

"Only a handful."

"But you can see it. Describe it too me."

"They are thick, blocky runes that twist around my chest, down to my wrist and back again. Before this scar, they moved when I pulled on them. Now they are caught."

"Can you draw them?" Nemuet asked.

Boruin had never tried. Nemuet handed him a stick and he crouched at the edge of the ash pit. He chose the rune at the base of his wrist and started dragging the stick through the ash. The first loop came easily, and then Boruin realized his mind was blank. Checking his wrist again, he saw that even the first loop was wrong. The second try proved the same, and finally he had to draw without taking his eyes off the dark sigil. The sign in the ash was a poor replica, but it was a close as his mind would let him come.

The marii stooped over the sign and quickly wiped it away as if it was not to be trusted. "It is no symbol I have seen. Music is the strongest magic of the lij, but this is certainly no note."

"I am certainly no singer," Boruin replied. Nemuet trilled a chuckle and set a pot of tea to steep over the flames.

The rabinithair appeared suddenly, his body a huge compacted knot floating in the wind. Red light winked out from inside his coils where the fire of his tail was burning bright. Steam rose out of the crevices as he tried to warm himself from the cold.

"All this winter weather makes me sleepy," Turintou said through a great yawn.

"There is no rest for you yet. The lij's debt still stands," said Nemuet.

"That does not surprise me. He is nothing if not difficult," the serpent replied.

"You did not hear my name, then?" Boruin asked. The old marii stirred her tea and served him a cup before answering. She watched his eye as if peering through to see how strong he was.

"There is no other name than what you have given yourself," she said carefully. "Perhaps it is as you said: that part of you has been stripped away and replaced. In that case, it is simply gone. However, I worry more that it was never there. Your song was surprisingly complete, for so much of your past to be missing. It should have been jagged, like singing a song by skipping every third note, but it was not. If your past has been taken from you, by nature or by foe, then it was done in a way I cannot comprehend." Boruin just stared over his cup with clouded eyes. "Drink your tea. It's not the end of the world," she added.

"If it hasn't been taken away—if I just have no past–what does that mean? What does that make me?"

"You still smell like lij to me," the rabinithair said. "Don't get all twisted up," he jumped to add as Boruin's mouth flopped opened and closed, like a fish who overshot a riffle and landed on the bank. "It makes you no different than you have ever been: still a mystery to yourself and to others, but still Boruin, the contractor of all things slightly illegal, and employer to a crew in need of assistance."

That brought things home for the old fighter. He sipped at his tea and his eyes cleared as it warmed his belly. His back straightened, and he looked again like the old Boruin stepping out of the Nefazo wilds, rather than the one trapped, trampled, and chased by Belok and the Monarhig over the last few months.

"You heard the Monarhig in the Munier Valley?" he asked.

"Well, we thought we heard you there first, which was a strange contradiction, as you had just been delivered sick to your room. While listening we came to notice the Monarhig," answered Nemuet.

His smile sprung up before he could contain it. "You heard Wraethe. She said she was piecing her memories back together. Her past must run inline with mine, like we thought."

Nemuet shrugged. "It could be many things. If she has spent enough time by your side, her song could echo parts of yours..."

"It was more than an echo though, wasn't it?" said Boruin as she hesitated.

"Yes, much of it was very close. It was more than an echo. She shares the same blank past, as well as the events hidden underneath. The matching notes probably stem from one or both of those."

"Probably?"

"As far as my wisdom stretches, that is the logical conclusion."

Boruin set down his cup. "Will you come with me to Munier?" he asked Turintou. He was almost ready to jump on the rabinithair right then and there. "Maybe you could hear more if you were closer."

"When we go to Munier it will be for battle," the rabinithair grunted. "If we survive the Monarhig, then we can look deeper into your personal problems."

"I thought without a name, our debt would default to slaking your hunger," Boruin said, shooting a fierce grin over at his friend.

"Trust me, it won't take too much more for that to be true," the serpent shot back with a quick snap of his teeth.

"You will leave tonight?" Nemuet asked.

"His friends will be safe in Munier Valley for a while yet. We can risk another night's wait," the rabinithair said, waiting until Boruin nodded consent, though it wasn't without hesitation. "We will at least stay until tomorrow. I've promised to bless the eashue's harbor."

"Good," said Nemuet. "We will eat and then join the festivities. The marii's Welcoming of Winter is not a festival to miss."

The marii's celebration carried all through the night, and Boruin learned that the festival would continue on in some shape or form until the forest returned from the heavens to drift again across the surface of the Lakelands. By then the Imorin's tiny seeds would be prepared for germination, and Boruin had no doubt there would be a festival to celebrate that as well.

When the rabinithair woke him in the morning, Boruin thought he was walking out into a cloud. The thunderstorm had passed them by in the night and its winds had sent snow, like a gift to a returning friend. The boughs sparkled white in the morning sun. On the spiraling forest below, the powder white of snow turned to the shimmering white of wet winter petals and then a glimmering green where the forest was still warm, just stepping off the land. Boruin looked down over his balcony's rail and sighed in wonder.

Rue danced through the snow as she came. Boruin and Turintou shivered as she sang of the winter's brilliance.

The serpent's body flowed in waves like he was swimming in place. "While it is remarkable, it is cold—and cold is only good for sleeping," he said. "I need to fly to get my blood up."

The marii halted in her pirouette. "I do not mean to impose, Skyking, but shall we go with you if it is haste you require? The shipyards are a considerable distance back along the forest."

"It seems to be my calling of late," Turintou sniffed as he gathered them up.

From outside the forest Boruin was even more amazed at the floating wood, but he was not as ecstatic as Rue. The small marii twisted and turned like a child to see her home from outside its branches and she could not hide her adoration. Her tongue curled to whistle out a few erratic lines, and when he asked her about it, she blushed as if caught talking to herself. Boruin smiled back; there was no avoiding her contagious joy.

Turintou fell along the inside well of the rising spiral of forest, slipping down the updrafts of air that followed the Imorin city. They dodged the snow-covered islands that drifted like icebergs on their thin anchor lines of single-file trees. Marii gathered at the edge of the forest, staring in awe at the great serpent riding the air just outside their doorsteps.

The blanket of snow covering the forest turned to a wet shine as they dropped to warmer climes. Boruin watched what was left of the rain trickle from the roots of the wood and turn to long rainbows as it fell in sheets to the sea far below.

They drifted down through the Aiemer with the forest cork-screwing up around them until Rue pointed to a large harbor encircled in a crescent of trees. It made this section of the forest look fat, like a snake that had swallowed an egg. A tall eashue, his skin the color of polished turquoise, manned the wide entrance. The quills running down his arms flashed silver in the morning sun as he waved at them to halt.

Turintou held a moment as a long ship, more than two hundred feet from bow to stern, glided out of the harbor. The round hull was unmistakable, a bright red Imorin trunk. Its ten masts rose and fell from the hull, five above and five below. It seemed a great sea bird turned to fly on its side. The eashue captain waved as it passed, his sailors staring at the rabinithair in wonder as the serpent stared back incredulously. Turintou's two-pronged sigil flew on a banner from the tallest mast.

The merchant ship unfurled its sails, which snapped out tight as the brisk wind filled them. It tacked around an island grove and slid out of the forest, into the open sky.

"That is quite a sight," Turintou said as the harbor controller waved them in.

Boruin soon found himself looking over the shipyards from an observation deck fashioned in the crown of one of the great trees. Gazing down from that height was like looking into a barrel of fish, though these swimming creatures were molded from massive trees with great red sails for fins. Two more of the long ships sat at dock, anchored where their tall masts would not snag above or below. The rest shared the tea-saucer sail design of the ship Turintou had almost eaten. Their sails wrapped about their hulls, almost like the petals of an unsprung flower.

Boruin whistled at the grand sight. No harbor on the southern coast was as large as the eashue's. He doubted none of the northern ones, aside from Deos, were either. Far below, Turintou wove about the docked boats, his blessings audible as a low rumble in the distance. The marii and eashue crews responded to the honor with the song of their ship, some proud and regal, others as ribald as a chorus from a dark tavern's drunken patrons. Boruin was pleased the rabinithair had accepted the vessels of the strange air-sailing race. Shaped like the marii buildings, the eashue's ships flowed smoothly, and they looked little different from whole Imorin trunks. The rabinithair would find no wrong here; the architecture was natural and respectful as, no doubt, its use of the Aiemer would be. He wondered how they did it.

"They sing those airships into form."

Boruin jumped at the voice that seemed to answer his thought. He stared at the man a moment, realizing it was just chance. The man was not known to him, even if the sharp lines of his clothing and the lilting accent of his voice were.

"The Pileans conquer Thila yet, or have you moved south for your health?" Boruin answered, a little sharp from being snuck up on.

"The Great Wall will stand long after Emperor Pileaus's legend has faded away. We Thilans worry little about that," the man answered. "But I'm here learning about sky trade routes. Quite a fascinating and, I thought, hush-hush venture. I'm surprised they would even allow a Nefazo merchant into the forest, let alone in sight of the airships."

"What makes you think I'm Nefazo?"

"Who else but a well traveled merchant would recognize a Thilan, and who but a Nefazo guildsman would risk traveling this deep into the Shoro?"

Boruin smiled at his quick wit, even if the Thilan didn't quite have the situation figured out. "Independent contractors hold no love for the trade guilds. Besides, I'm here on other matters. Your exclusivity is safe from me."

"Fair enough," the man replied after a long look. Then the trader pointed down, opposite the main anchorages. There a massive tree, its roots pulled in tight like a great ball, was slowly falling down to its side. "They'll spend the next few months on that tree, I gather. It takes quite a few eashue and marii working together, but they sing to it, of all things. The gods only know what kind of magic that is."

"And what? It becomes a ship?" Boruin asked.

"Yes. That's the lay of it. They work the tree into shape like a potter works clay out of a riverbank. The masts sprout up, they give them sails, and the ship is ready to go. Certainly, there's more to it than that, but you follow me, aye?"

"There are big changes coming in the merchant business. Trade routes over mid-continent will cut out the Nefazo-shuen treaties and make some new houses very rich. Lucky you're getting in at the head," Boruin said as the wheels in his head spun up. The money to be made here could match the treasure rooms of most nations. He had no doubt recommendations from a Mother Prime and the regional Skyking would put him in more than fair stead with the eashue.

"Exclusively," the trader reminded him with a testing grin.

"As far as I'm concerned," Boruin said, wondering if he was lying.

The trader didn't give him a second questioning look as then the rabinithair swept up from the harbor. The Thilan grew wide-eyed and made a brisk bow, which was more of a dip, then turned and ran. Boruin smiled, but he could not blame the man. The serpent was generally quite frightening, and now he seemed to be carrying a bound marii for lunch.

Rue looked tangled in the thick hair of the rabinithair's crown. The serpent lowered his head to the deck and the marii untied herself from a harness strung between his two thick horns.

Boruin grinned. "That looks awfully like riding gear."

"Don't make this any more difficult. I'll still be carrying you."

"Right. Not riding, because no one rides a rabinithair. Certainly still carrying," Boruin replied.

"I asked them to make it because it looks odd carrying a lij around in my claws like a pet," he shot back with a snort. "Besides, I'll need them for battle if it comes to that."

"If it comes to that, I hope to be on the ground already," said Boruin. The serpent cocked his head to the side and Rue trotted down a horn to the deck. She handed Boruin a small leather roll with the Imorin Forest ornately drawn in a rising spiral around it. He set the two long edges together, then Rue showed him how to secure the lenses in the ends of the tube.

"A gift from us," the marii said. "So you may see your friends at the soonest possible moment." Boruin smiled and set the farglass to his eye. The distant tail of the forest rose to crisp detail, each tree clear from the rest. Unsure of the proper marii gesture, the old man knelt and bowed his head. He felt Rue press her bristly forehead to his. "You are welcome," she trilled softly.

Boruin wobbled up the rabinithair's horn, resisting the urge to crawl, and finally made it to the harness. Their marii guide waved goodbye as they took to the air. Circling once over the harbor, Boruin saw great green flags with the red emblem of the rabinithair's fiery tail rise at the tops of the highest trees.

"Are you their official guardian?" he asked.

"It is not such a low thing to be blessed by a rabinithair," the serpent snorted. "Besides, if they are to fly in my territory, then others should know it is at my allowance."

It was true: the creature's moniker of Skyking was not wrong. A thought struck Boruin suddenly. "How long are you going to stick with me? Why have you stayed so long already?" he asked abruptly. The questions seemed to catch the rabinithair off guard. He rose up underneath the roots of the next looping spiral and stalled to hang in the air.

"Do you know what makes these great trees float?" Turintou asked.

"Same as you: the Aiemer, I'm guessing."

"You're partly right," said the serpent. "The Aiemer has surrounded the Imorin Forest for so many ages that its power has changed the wood and now the trees ride its currents. But it is the a'shen, small parasites under the bark, which govern the trees. They sense the Aiemer and follow its tides. The a'shen regulate the flow of Aiemer within the tree. They know when to stay low to the ground and when to rise and follow the Aiemer Sea into the heavens for winter."

"I don't follow."

"Often something huge is influenced by something very, very small," the rabinithair answered. "You are something small with a hand in something very, very large. Nemuet heard that in your song. I smelled that on you as I woke on the mountaintop. It was the one thing that kept you from being a mid-nap snack. I'll stick with you until I find out what it really is."

Boruin mulled over this thought as they raced away from the Imorin Forest, watching over his shoulder as it grew smaller in the distance. It looked a great deal like a rabinithair. Foregrove had turned out of the spiral and stretched north, leading a great neck. The tail of the forest had finally left land completely and begun to curl up into the sky. Its leaves were turning white and pink. Boruin wondered what small thing he could possibly be that might move something as great as the floating wood.

The marii's harness was comfortable. When Boruin woke, he was surprised that he had fallen asleep. He blinked against the light of the low sun and looked about.

Turintou was making slow circles above the wave-rocked eastern shore of Baszul. The spray exploded up into the air, a hard evening blow driving the water off the sea in great swells. The thin clouds above ran past as if trying to reach somewhere safe before dark.

"What are we cruising about for?" asked Boruin.

"We're waiting on a friend. It shouldn't be much longer, not with that tailwind," he replied. Almost as if it needed saying, a ship dropped out of the nearby clouds.

The eashue skyboat flew full sails before the wind. Two banks of masts circling the ship sent the vessel racing towards them. Boruin knew that was dangerous on the sea with such a blow. It was not any different in the sky. At that speed, the Imorin hull seemed to almost skip across the Aiemer just before it lost its lift. The ship dropped, the sails luffing as the wind slipped away and the bow nosed downward towards the sea. Boruin's nails dug into his palms as it plummeted a hundred feet before seeming to crash into some invisible liquid. The hull righted itself, and the small boat leapt forward as the wind poured back into the sails.

The rabinithair rose to meet the ship as it dropped its sails to let the wind pass. When they got close enough, Boruin could see a few of the eashue crew still holding tight to the rough bark of the hull. They pried themselves off to check for damage. The captain staggered forward, the spots across his hairless head pale white.

"Quite a bold maneuver, Captain," Turintou called. "You should be more careful over the Baszul, especially with the lowering of the sun. The Aiemer tends to grow choppy, almost as if it is matching the waves below," added the serpent, his tone displeased like that of a cautious father.

The captain bowed, though he had to put his hand on the rail to steady himself. "I will be certain to inform my azh'rei. He is quite adept at sensing the Aiemer currents, but he is new to this vessel and unfamiliar with its abilities."

"He is lucky he drove you off a stream with a second current below. The sea would not have been so forgiving."

"I can not lay all the blame on my navigator. I was afraid we would not find you by dark. The Harbormaster would not have been pleased if I had not delivered my cargo."

The rabinithair dismissed it. "No harm done. I thank you for tending to my request so quickly."

"What is this about?" asked Boruin. The eashue captain glanced his way and back to the serpent.

"I'll fetch him out if he hasn't soiled himself," said the captain.

"Just drop him in the sea if he has," Turintou replied. The eashue smiled at the thought as he disappeared below deck.

"I told you being blessed by a rabinithair was no low thing," Turintou said as they brought Belok out of the round hull. The Nefazo's arms were tied tightly behind his back with thick rope.

"Nemuet told you to return him to the Fae," Boruin whispered, as if mentioning the Fae would summon the pflints upon them.

"Nemuet paid proper face before Flick-a-wit and the rest of the pflints," the serpent replied with a clack of his tongue across the teeth. "What I did with him after was no true concern of hers. For all the Fae know, I missed and he landed in the sea. Then it is on your head anyway."

Belok shook at the sight of the rabinithair's wide, toothy mouth and Boruin's matching smile.

"What will we do with him?" asked Boruin.

"That's a fine question. What shall we do with you, lij?" repeated Turintou. "Will your master deem you worthy of a trade? Perhaps for a withdrawal or treaty?"

"He will certainly pay for my return. But you will pay more dearly after for this breach of conduct. You will pay in blood," Belok replied. He tried his confident grin, but his lips pulled tight white across his teeth, more a death sneer than a smile.

"I'd bet against that," the rabinithair countered. "Perhaps we'll just drop you on his camp as an official response to his parley."

"I like that I idea," Boruin said menacingly.

Belok looked away, not wanting to imagine another plunge downward. Turintou snatched the Nefazo off the deck. It would not be a comfortable ride for the merchant, clutched so stiffly in a claw, but Boruin cared little. He would that the serpent had impaled Belok on his tail like a spitted boar, where the man could bake a little over the bright fire. That would have suited him nicely.

"Thank you, Captain, for your service," the rabinithair said. "Remember about the evening currents. I would tack over land until Diun has quartered its distance across the sky. By then the sea should be calmer," he added.

"We will, Skyking," the eashue replied before ordering the sails back up. They rose short, reefed against the heavy winds, and turned close-hauled to tack south towards land.

"Dangerous bit of work, flying those things," Boruin said.

The rabinithair nodded, shaking Boruin in his tethers. "One in five will be lucky to survive a year, I'd say. The Aiemer currents are no place for those who can't feel it. Maybe with their halfbreed azh'rei they will do better than I suspect, but that remains to be seen."

"What are we going to do with that bastard, Belok?" Boruin asked as they watched the boat disappear in the gloom between the setting sun and the rising Diun.

"I'm not sure what use he might be. We'll leave that to Old Bramble."

"Bramble?"

"It's his valley the Monarhig has surrounded. The man won't take very well to that. One does not threaten Bramble without good reason and a fair certainty of victory. The Monarhig must have some pull both in the Dying Lands and the Dreaming to attack the Munier Valley. If anything, Belok might know his capabilities. If Bramble has no use for him, then I'm sure he'll leave him to you."

"I won't get much of him, then. Wraethe has had it out for him for a long time. I'll be lucky to get a word in before she tears him to bits."

"All the same well-deserved ending," the serpent said. Boruin glanced back and reveled in Belok's wide, distant eyes. They peered down below as if the depth was a great beast rising to bite at his dangling legs.

21

THE VALLEY OF MUNIER

Turintou searched for days before he caught sight of the distant Munier Valley. "Nemuet said she heard them. How could she not know where?" asked Boruin.

"Bramble is not easily found if you haven't been sent an invitation," the serpent explained. They spent another day tucked within the clouds, drifting slowly across the sky. Peering out of the haze, the serpent stayed hidden while they watched the enemy's siege.

Munier Valley was a barren scar, like a great hand had scooped it from the land. Steep hills ringed the valley, forested highlands surrounded by thin grass. The slopes turned to bare dirt as they approached the floor of the valley. The bottom of the valley was lifeless save for a small spot in its center, a smudge of green bracken and a wisp of smoke that Turintou's sharp eyes caught rising from a cottage tucked in a small walnut grove. Boruin didn't need the serpent's vision to know the occasional black clouds drifting from the surrounding hills were volleys of Fae arrows.

"Not much in the way of defense. Why are the Fae hanging back?" Boruin wondered aloud.

"Munier Valley is Bramble's in ways deeper than just possession. Don't take what we see at face value," Turintou answered.

The valley seemed deserted, but the hills around it were not. Boruin caught flecks of movement all across the ridges. More motion appeared at the edges of the trees. At night sentry fires ringed the valley like a burning crown. It was impossible to judge the size of the army, but a large host lay hidden in the cover—and it wasn't just groundlings this time.

Boney, thin-bodied creatures mingled among the deep-mine Feirnann that Boruin had faced in M'Gaglind Duul. Turintou pointed out the pikcs, and Boruin thought he was mistaking a dry bush blown across camp until he put the eashue farglass to his eye.

The Fae rolled in a sloppy ball before leaping out to unfurl itself in the air. Two strips of thin skin, attached at the back of its thick head and again behind both knees, caught the wind and sent it gliding over a trench full of digging groundlings. It landed on the other side and dropped back into its roll. Boruin almost wished the marii hadn't given him the far-seeing glass. The Fae looked like a desert-dried insect, and it gave him shivers.

"They're strange to look at, but don't underestimate their ability in a fight," said Turintou. "Their limbs have about eight bones a piece; they fold up small and then whip out. It's hard to track them, with all that rolling and gliding. They come at you fast, and they don't leave you with much to hack at but bone and tough gristle. You almost have to break them into small pieces to finish the fight."

"Great," Boruin answered. "I'll look forward to that." He shaded the end of the farglass from the sun, trying to get a clearer view. "Are those lij with them?"

"They seem to be Lakelanders, though the Mother knows what the Monarhig offered to persuade them off the inland seas," Turintou said as he scanned the enemy lines. The lij crossed the ground in small packs, either nervous around their new Fae allies, or just by habit bred from the close quarters of their flat-bottomed skiffs.

"Bramble must not have them too worried. There's hardly a skirmish line around the valley. Just enough to keep anyone from fleeing," said Boruin.

"The Fae as a whole are slight in population, but don't underestimate what they can accomplish," the serpent replied. "There's no telling what's hidden in the trees, either. Let's talk to your old friend. We'll need to know more about what the Monarhig has in store before we go rushing into that valley."

Belok was more than willing to talk, once Turintou picked him up with his teeth and shook him like a dog. The serpent tossed him into the air and let him fall out of their cloud before snatching him back up.

"Windwalkers!" the Nefazo was shouting before the serpent's claw had pulled him back from the drop. "He called them windwalkers. I don't know how many." Turintou's long teeth snapped before Belok's sweating face. "It couldn't be more than a handful! He summoned them by name."

"Which ones were they?" the rabinithair pressed.

"He sent me into the cloud of pflints before they arrived. I didn't see them!" Belok replied, flinching again as Turintou snapped his teeth once more.

"And how many groundlings?" Boruin added.

"You saw most of them on the mountain top. We had lost Wraethe and the others at the edge of the Hetsu Plains. Then the Feirnann discovered you slipping from that vein of rock at the bottom of the lake. You came free before we could make it there."

Turintou pulled his head above the cloud, out of the merchant's hearing. "Pflints aren't much for battle; groundlings and pikcs will be difficult. The windwalkers will be the strongest, aside from the Monarhig," he said. "If that is truly the weight of their host, then it seems he's playing war in private; no other princes are helping, and he's certainly got no support from the Courts of Twilight."

"If he's resorted to recruiting the Lakelanders, I'd say you're right," agreed Boruin as they ducked back into the cloud. "Belok, the Monarhig has company enough to attack. Why is he waiting for me?"

The merchant attempted to shrug under his ropes. "He came to me in Easlinder, talking about how you invaded his camp and broke his favorite bow."

"I out-shot him. He broke his bow in frustration. He could have killed us then, but he only blew us back to the trade highway. There is something more. What is it?" Boruin pressed, ready to leap from the harness, no matter the height, and pummel Belok if he didn't spill what he needed to know.

"The prince knows about your magic arm," he answered. "I told him how you fooled those Easlinder idiots. I told him that it was all trickery. He said whatever it was, he'd strip it from you." Belok sneered. "It's your own fault, Boruin! You're a cheat and a robber, and finally I'm not the only one who knows it! The Monarhig will redress the acts against me and his lordship."

"You must have cut his pride pretty good with that arrow shot," Turintou said to Boruin. The rabinithair snorted a chuckle. "Some Fae princes are fair folk, but many are snobby little rutters. I'd rather fight five of those than a cool-headed Monarhig, like Glamhurg, any day," he added.

"What do you know of the Prince of Winds?" Belok scoffed. "He's more powerful than most in the Dreaming Lands. The Courts of Twilight are said to bend to his desires," he added.

"*Are said* by whom? The Monarhig?" asked the serpent. "The Courts of Twilight bend only to the Champion of the Parade, and the Prince of Winds is no champion!" Turintou snatched Belok up with his rear claw and dragged him off somewhere out of sight and hearing. "Enough of that man's mouth," he snarled.

Boruin looked back down at the valley. "We go at night, then? Crawling or flying?"

"At sundown, but we won't make it across on my belly. They'll see me coming too early for that. Flying the Aiemer would be worse. My tail will light this cloud like a beacon come night—there's no hiding that within the currents. Besides, the Monarhig has drained the Aiemer far back from the edge of the valley. I feel some pooled on the other side, doubtless where he makes his camp. The only other stream is a small current flowing out of the walnut grove, and he will have that guarded." Turintou considered how to proceed. "What of that magic arm?" he added after a moment.

"What do you know of it?"

"Only what Nemuet said, and the little bit I could discern from the marii's chorus of your song. The Mother Prime claimed it was strong. The Monarhig seems to think so, too. I'd bet he'll try and take it, arm and all."

Boruin shook his head. "It used to be strong, but it's turned to dead weight under the Makua'Moi judge's hand. You got any other options?"

"Drop from the sky," the rabinithair answered.

"Like hell. You *fly* badly enough, I don't need to see you drop like a rock," Boruin replied.

"It's the last option. Trust me, you'll like it," the serpent said, licking his tongue across his teeth in anticipation.

"Take your tail and hide it from the moons," Boruin cursed as he began tightening the harness straps.

By late afternoon the rabinithair had Boruin convinced a freefall into the valley was their only option. The old man didn't like the idea, but he didn't have anything better. As the sun dipped low in the sky, the serpent watched the eastern horizon and the bank of clouds rising in the last heat of day.

"There's the cover we need," he muttered to himself. "We might just make it unscathed, lij." He began to climb higher into the cold heavens. Boruin's breath felt thin, and it frosted the air before him.

The valley was a distant, pale scar on the dusky blanket of green below.

Turintou turned circles as he watched the sun drop, talking incessantly. It reminded Boruin of Pile before a fight. He suspected that if the serpent had an axe handy, he'd be fidgeting with it.

Finally, the rabinithair stopped turning and went silent. The eastern storms had hidden Diun's rising and the sun now was halved by the dark edge of land. The ground below was black for a moment, an early full night while the clouds obscured the bright moon.

"Alright. I'm going to go fast. You need to hold on for all you're worth. When we get close—" Turintou started, but the whistle of wind cut him off as he began to drop. The serpent tore straight down through the gloom. Boruin felt the air fill his lungs again and his head cleared as they fell into thicker air. Turintou's tail burned brightly behind them as the Skyking channeled the Aiemer to build speed.

Boruin could not see the ground, but he could feel its mass rising eagerly to meet them. As it appeared out of the deep dusk, the serpent pulled up and shot over the trees and hills like a long flash of lightning. The turn forced Boruin back in his harness. The wind roared as if in pain. Boruin could have screamed, and Belok could have been screaming for all he knew, but neither would have been heard.

Turintou hit the edge where the Monarhig had pulled the Aiemer back from the valley. As they left its current, the serpent's flight turned soft like a cart slipping into a deep track of mud. Boruin's fingers tightened down on the harness, waiting for the stomach-turning drop of the serpent crashing to the dirt. The bright star of Turintou's tail winked out behind, and the rabinithair heaved all the air out of his lungs.

The great snake breathed out and sucked his guts up close to his spine. Hundreds of thin rib bones spread wide, stretching the pale skin of his stomach so thin that the dark scales seemed like curious black eyes peering through a lace curtain.

Turintou bounced through the air like a rock skipping across water. Flattened to catch the air, he slithered through the night sky, pushing against the wind to maintain his precarious balance. His glide was fading, the ground rising closer and each hill threatening to reach up and drag them down when the valley appeared before them.

Darkness filled Boruin's head, as if the Monarhig had sent some black fog to cover the Munier and obscure their way. Then he remembered to breathe, and the details rushed back just in time to reveal

Diun breaking through the eastern clouds and moonlight falling down full upon the land. It glinted off Fae helm and sword and the tips of arrows swinging toward them.

The rabinithair was past the Monahrig's rear camp as the first sentries inhaled to cry alarm. Treetops shuddered as the sound of the serpent's passing startled some great beast hidden in the woods. Turintou's tail speared down, spitting a rolling pikc as he drove the hard bone of his tail into the dirt and scraped along to slow his body down.

Boruin looked up again as he felt them pass into the valley. The crossing was palpable, like walking through a curtain of cold water into warm air behind it. Where his eye expected the small cottage surrounded only by walnut trees, instead a dark foundation of rock spread wide. Before Boruin could judge what he was seeing, Turintou rolled left and arched back up into the sky. A wall of black granite passed within reach of Boruin's fingers as the serpent evaded the wide, stumpy tower that had replaced the illusion of the walnut grove alone in the center of the valley.

Turintou managed to flare up into the wind and his glide died out just as they reached the summit of the raw granite tower. The Skyking slipped sideways to avoid crushing the small cottage perched on the wide, flat top of the tower, now without its cloak of trees. A crash echoed between the valley walls as the last half of the rabinithair bounced off the rock. The serpent came down hard, his body latching where it could to the steep stone sides. Boruin tumbled as the harness snapped from the bone horns. He rolled away as the serpent bit the rock next to him like a ship throwing its anchor.

Boruin dug his fingernails into the scree and stopped his tumble at the edge of the cliff. Below, a wild mass of groundlings were running down the dirt walls of the valley. The Skyking's crossing had incited a charge.

"I think my tail is stuck in the thorn wall," the rabinithair growled through a mouth full of rock.

"When you come crashing blind into someone's home you get what you get," said a rough voice, its tone as gruff as the serpent's. Boruin turned and found a short man standing at the edge of the flat-topped rock tower that was somehow not a walnut grove. He surveyed the Fae's charge as if he were watching cows graze.

Under his crossed arms, the man splayed out his fingers. Far below, a section of the thorn wall encircling the tower's foundation twisted its points away from the last bit of the serpent's body. The tail crossed over into the thin fount of Aiemer rising around the tower. In the dim glow of its returning fire, Boruin saw the long thorns snap back outward toward the Fae.

"I hope you are ready to fight," Bramble grumbled. "Look what you caused, big rutting snake vanishing into the thin air of my valley. Now those deep-grounders have got to waddle down and see what's really here."

"Bramble, this is Boruin," Turintou said. "Boruin, unless I'm mistaken, this is your contractor. Best known as Old Bramble here in the Shoro."

The man was short of stature and thin, but his muscles stood out like iron cords wrapping his bones. His bare scalp glistened silver in Diun's light. The way he stood, feet set apart and shoulders square, made him seem anchored like a deep-rooted tree—but when Bramble turned away from the tower's edge to greet Boruin, he moved as smooth as water breaking around a stone. This man was a fighter as sure as Wraethe was a killer and Pile a thief.

His dark eyes took in Boruin quickly. His rough face was stern, but Boruin could see there that some of the lines had been wrought by laughter rather than just hard days.

"Fine to meet you, son. I'll say your crew will be glad to see you've finally arrived, but let's hold all other pleasantries for the moment," Bramble said as he turned back to the cliff. Boruin's heart, calming from their entrance, leapt again at the mention of his friends. He started for the cottage, eager to set his eyes on them, but stopped as a cacophony of Fae screams unleashed their battle cry.

The first of the charge reached the bottom of the dirt embankment. The groundlings shuddered as they ran, their short legs pumping furiously to keep from tumbling at such a speed. The pikcs rolled after, springing out into short glides and back to their odd tumble. Some simply loped along with their long arms pushing the ground between their legs like dogs at full sprint.

The ragged line of excited infantry hit the edge of the valley floor and had but a moment to skid to a stop before the thorn wall. As it had for Boruin, the false view of the lone walnut grove and cozy cottage vanished as they crossed onto the valley floor. Standing in its place was a squat tower of hard rock rising higher than the siege army's lines. Black Fae arrows, fallen far short of their intended target, ringed the earth around the tower's base like a miniature of the outer defensive line.

Unable to stop their charge, some of the Fae plowed into the high wall of thorns. A loud cry of pain, rather than war, rose around Bramble's promontory as the creatures tried to tear free from the barbs. The long thorns drove between armor plates and linked chain. It gouged at the eyes of the tall pikes and pinned their wide feet to the ground. Only dark blood crept past the wall and neared the base of the granite tower.

Turintou spat the last rock from his teeth now that his long body had found purchase in the crags around the rock tower. "I told you the Munier was Bramble's in more than just name."

"The Monarhig doesn't control his army well," Boruin observed. Bramble chuckled and ran a callused hand over his sun-darkened scalp.

"Gorsmelt has never been much of a soldier. A fair hunter, but not a general by any means."

"Gorsmelt?" Turintou asked with a chuckle.

"Gorsmelt, Gotsmock, Gumsmut, something ridiculous like that. I can't ever remember all the Monarhig's names, and this one doesn't pass his around much. Insists on being called Prince of the Winds, not that I can blame him."

"Why didn't he use those pflints to scout out the valley?" Boruin asked. "It would have paid to at least know of the wall."

"They're too small to penetrate into the valley. Gusmolt could have used anything else, since he pulled back the Aiemer, but hasn't. He yelled from the ridge a few times, but he won't come down himself. The rutter knows there's trouble to be had. Soon Gobsnot'll know the trouble up close—" Bramble stopped and turned finally to the snorting and sneezing of the rabinithair. "What in the two realms are you going on about?" he shouted as the serpent chortled and heaved in his strange laughter.

Boruin kept silent, trying to hide his own grin.

"You've always been a strange bastard," said Bramble, his fierce face softening at the serpent's infectious state.

"Captain! Griant says they've stopped delving, but they're still too far out to have reached the line. I'll bet they're up to..." Pile halted his run from the small cottage. His eyes grew wide at the great face of the rabinithair, and seemed somehow to grow wider seeing Boruin standing beside it.

Suddenly Boruin forgot how to speak. Long weeks of worry dissolved and left nothing, save for the tears he tried to blink back.

Pile solved the issue, returning to a run and an embrace that almost knocked Boruin off the edge.

"Good to see you, boy," Boruin managed to say. "Don't you know Nefazo law against improper working relationships?" he added as Pile continued to hold on tight.

"Good to see you too, boss," said Pile, keeping his own wet eyes lowered from Diun's revealing light. "When you disappeared right after losing Toaaho—Yuin's whores, I think of him every time the sun drops."

Boruin squeezed Pile's shoulder, knowing what made the young man's voice crack. "Don't fear that. I got him out before I left the mountains." Pile looked up as if needing to see Boruin's face to believe his friend was no longer stalked by those spirit-hungry kaoulths. He wiped his eyes and smiled.

"That's good then."

A pikc's coughing cry, eerie like the sound of some strange laughing dog, sounded north of the valley.

"You brought their full charge on earlier than I would have liked," Bramble interrupted. "They're bringing those churstamps out of the forest now. We'll have to save this little reunion for another time. Pile, tell Griant to take Sergeant Dharl and half his Ommans to the south face. I'll need the rest," he shouted as Pile raced back into the cottage.

"Where did you get Omman fighters?" Turintou asked.

"I'm training Sergeant Dharl to be our champion in the coming parade," answered Bramble. "He offered his men for our little situation and snuck them in before the Monarhig closed us off." He paused a moment. "Any more time-consuming questions?"

"Where do you want me?" the serpent asked with a snort.

Bramble led Boruin into the cottage at a trot. "You're almost longer than the valley itself," he called over his shoulder. "Strike that which needs striking."

Bramble's cottage could only be called such from outside. Like the valley itself, the face of it was illusion. The main door opened upon a wide hall with delicate woodwork from floor to beam. Numerous doors led from the hall, servicing too many rooms to fit in an actual cottage. On the left, a bank of windows showed the distant fires along the Fae lines. Further along, the view was from the bottom of the valley walls, the long Diun shadow cast by the tower in the center of the frame. It was obvious that the strange valley's rules applied to the cottage as well.

Boruin looked to the dark windows on the right. "Those windows show outside, but why are these black?" Boruin asked.

"Those window ways should view the Dreaming Lands." He shook his head in irritation. "That damn rutter. He claimed he was cutting off all escape routes. You can't move anything between realms across a window way but Aiemer. This prince is a dimwit, I'm telling you," Bramble answered, though that explained little to Boruin.

They stepped from the welcoming hall through a small door and into a menacing weapons cache. Racks of sharp instruments lined the walls. Boruin's mind, filled with joy at finding his team, narrowed down to the prospect of killing.

"I'll need you by my side on the north line. Watch the west flank," Bramble said as he dove into a thick leather chest plate and pulled it over his head. Boruin scrambled to do the same, choosing a thick short sword from a rack and a brace of long daggers. "How's your arm?" the short-haired old soldier asked bluntly. "Still mucked up?"

"What do you know of it?" Boruin snorted, suddenly tired of his long-kept secret being thrown at him like questions about the weather.

"I know plenty. Don't forget I pulled you out of that dark womb and laid them across your body." Bramble hefted a long mace and shouldered open a door at the end of the room. Boruin hurried to finish strapping on his bracers and raced after him.

The rut you did! ran through his mind but missed his tongue as Boruin stepped through the doorway into blinding daylight.

22

DUINE FIGHTERS

Boruin found himself standing on an open desert plain in full sun. He squinted, trying to understand the wedge of day driven somehow through the stretch of night between tower and thorn wall. It was impossible, save for Turintou's words. Bramble's valley was his own, and it was above all laws of nature.

"HOO HOO HOO HOO HAHAAAAA!" The deafening sound made Boruin spin and drop into a defensive crouch. The Omman infantry at his back stamped their feet and rattled their spears against their wide shields. The ranks of rough looking fighters, women and men both, stretched back an impossible distance. Boruin shielded his eyes with his hand as they adjusted to the blinding light, but still he could not see the back of the ranks. What had been a short walk between tower and thorn wall, Bramble had more than doubled. It was as if the valley had swelled to accommodate a larger host than Bramble had invited to attend.

"A lot of men under the Omman rank of Sergeant," said Boruin.

"Eyes forward, son," Bramble commanded as the churstampts began to thunder down from the ridge before them. Boruin fought the urge to step back by grinding his heel into the dirt and bracing his foot.

The churstampts were heavily armored, their six thick legs wrapped in scale and their feet spiked, some naturally and some augmented by Fae blacksmiths. The dead-gray beasts from A'Batassi's talamh were twice as large as a bull habback. The thick mists of their home had soaked into their flesh, turning their skin a sickly, mottled color. It hung like rotted curtains about their bodies, sagging in rolls down the front of their faces and obscuring their white, unused eyes. The eight wet chambers at the ends of their snouts snuffled at the air, scenting out the fight before them. Between their legs, a breastbone dropped low like a misshapen stalactite. Cruel iron barbs were bolted into the thick bone. Underneath a churstampt was not a place to get caught.

As the beasts lumbered off the ridge, the skin across their faces and necks pulled tight and rose into wide fans over their heads. The fans bowed in like a sail catching air before snapping out with a thundering crack. The booms rolled across the valley floor and rattled loose pieces of Omman armor. Each fighter felt the weight of it strike their chest like a carpenter's mallet. Closer, the blow would be enough to knock a man off his feet.

Boruin envisioned the focused sound knocking him on his back, and those spiked feet and barbed bellies grinding down on him. He found himself picking up the infantry's war chant to ramp up his courage. His blood was pumping hot and heavy as the beasts lowered their knobby snouts and drove thick, brass-capped tusks into the dirt before the thorn wall.

The air filled with earth, root, and trunk as the weight of the churstampts uprooted the barrier. The creatures bellowed as they hit the unexpected light of day. Their eyes, rendered useless by the thick mists of home, were treated with a hot flash of white and gusts of hot, dry wind. Most dropped their fans, pulling the skin back over the eyes that had let a burning fire into their small brains.

Boruin danced to the side, slashing uselessly at an armored leg as one plowed past. The infantry caught their charge with upraised spears digging for joints in the shell plate. Fighters were thrown far by the bucking legs, while others were jerked about horribly as they were impaled upon the spiked feet. A skin-fan boomed and knocked a knot of warriors across the dirt. They scrambled away, save for one unlucky man who stabbed at the hard bone chest as the creature knelt, driving its barbs into him.

A few of the churstampts continued their charge deep into the Omman ranks, but many vomited blood and fell thundering to the side as the spearmen found openings in their armor and drove their sharp blades high into pumping hearts and panting lungs.

Boruin almost froze, confused as one creature bucked and kicked far to the side, digging with its tusks through soldiers that stood like ghosts formed from the blowing dust.

Illusion! How few then are real? Bramble had manufactured more than the landscape.

There was no more time to consider what else Bramble may have prepared. The pikes and groundlings reached the gaps in the thorn wall and pounced on the Omman line. Turintou was right; they came in a scramble, a gliding pounce that tormented the eye. The serpent had neglected to tell of the thin blades of bone that ran down their spines. One rolled up an Omman soldier as his spear missed its thin body. The blades cut a line deep from gut to brow and down the fighter's back.

Boruin's parry shuddered under the attack of the first pikc that reached him, its eight-jointed, whip-like arm swinging a sword around much faster than a man could. Bramble stepped forward and his heavy mace crushed the pikc's thick skull. The mace continued on its wide arc to send a groundling helm, head inside, flying back into the darkness beyond the valley floor. The sunlight somehow clung to it, turning the helm to a shooting star that crashed into the hills above the enemy lines.

Boruin bellowed as he cleaved through the enemy with his short sword, slipping his dagger where armor parted or flesh was unprotected. His blood rose in rage as he recognized an etched breastplate from a groundling in M'Gaglind Duul. Boruin tore through the Fae warriors pouring in between the thorns and fell on the creature in fury. A spearwoman leapt into his wake, protecting his flank and shouting for the others to push forward and close the breach.

The groundling fell as Boruin's sword parted the head of his axe from the shaft and continued to beat down until the creature's head parted likewise from its body. The Omman infantry roared their approval. With Boruin at the lead, they pressed into the thorn hedge and filled it like a clot against the flow of pikc and groundling.

It was a small gain, though; more Fae poured down the valley walls. For each breach the Ommans held, two more had been ripped open by the trampling churstampts.

A one soldier rear-guard, the rabinithair ground the churstampts in his teeth. As the Fae tried to flank from east and west, he swung around the tower, stabbing his great horns into the groundling packs and snatching slow-gliding pikcs out of the air, but he had only one mouth with which to protect the four sides of the tower.

On the south side, Sergeant Dharl faced an equal wave of attackers. The Omman leader fought in the dark; either he preferred the cool Diuntyne, or Bramble was unable to spread the sunlight any further. The pale light favored the churstampts, and they rolled through Dharl's ranks, their ear-breaking booms thundering out of the darkness.

Bramble pulled his Ommans in close behind the thorn wall and the breaches they held. The Fae had discovered the boundary between the real Omman fighters and Bramble's illusionary ranks.

Boruin stepped back from the thorn wall, a husky woman with a tremendous greatsword sliding into his place. "Bramble, we've got to pull back to the tower—get the stone to our backs!" he shouted.

"Another moment," Bramble replied, driving into the ranks of Fae behind the wake of his mace.

Before Boruin could protest, two great whirlwinds spun into the hot air of the flat plain. The black tower vanished as a cloud of dust bloomed out of the cracked soil. It stuck to some unseen gate, an arch that was only visible by the dirt blowing across it, jamming stuck in the joints of its heavy stonework. For a moment a long avenue appeared behind it: a road rising into the Diuntyne sky and out over the hills. Down its back came something long and probably terrible.

Damn you, Yuin, Boruin cursed as he saw movement at the mouth of the gate. Over the clash of iron and Omman steel sounded the heavy rumble of the coming creature. Clouded by dust, it seemed one great body, like an insect with a thousand legs supporting some devastating Fae-bred creature. Scales glinted where the sunlight pierced the cloud. Boruin's breath caught as the creature split into two, one racing for him and the other spinning south toward the dark side of the tower. As it galloped out of the dust, a choking laugh broke from his lungs.

"Swift Riders!" Boruin roared over the din of battle. The last rows of Fae turned, frantically bracing for the horsemen about to trample through their line. Instead, the Hetsu Plainsmen swung aside at the last moment, running down the Fae flank. Their arrows screamed through the air as they galloped past. The light flashed across their new rabinithair scale armor.

The riders circled and returned, their keen aim knocking pikc out of the sky like sparrows and filling the groundlings with feathered shafts. The Fae line rushed forward to catch them, but the riders danced their horses back out of reach, the staccato twang of their bowstrings as sure as a musician's metronome.

A churstampt braved the light and pulled tight its skin. As the fan spread and bowed, the horsemen fired their arrows. The shafts plowed through the fan as it snapped tight. The devastating boom turned to a rip as the tightened flesh split around the wounds. The spread of skin exploded, sloshing dark blood down the churstampt's neck and leaving useless rags of flesh hanging around it in tatters.

Suddenly pinched between the wild Omman fighters and the cloud of Hetsu arrows, the Fae held out only another breath. The churstampts, confused still by the light and sudden heat, retreated back through the wall as they fled for the safety of darkness, some opening new holes in the thorns and some plowing blindly through the avenues held by the Fae.

"HOO HOO HOO HOO HAHAAAAA!" The fighters, real and illusory, began to scream again as the heavy beasts retreated and the rabinithair turned his maw to pikc and groundling stragglers. They held silent a moment and heard the victorious echo of Sergeant Dharl's men from the opposite side of the valley, still curtained in Diuntyne. The Ommans roared with the pleasure of war.

The tide of Fae had reversed. The enemy struggled to climb the loose scree of the valley walls, their eyes blind again as day turned back to night. The Hetsu horsemen, the Swift Riders at their head, rode up the slope after the routed Fae. The Ommans gave chase, laughing as battle now turned to sport. They laughed even as the horsemen galloped back behind the wall, clouds of arrows finally falling to cover the Fae retreat. Omman shields filled with black shafts until they withdrew to a safe range.

"Hail, friend of the Skyking!" Boruin turned to find Dark Eye cantering past. The old rider sat tall, his back straighter in the saddle than it had been out of it. His armor was a tight weave of Turintou's scales. There was as much joy in his sun-wrinkled face as Boruin had seen among the plainsmen. The man opened his mouth to speak.

"The Swift Riders are a host again!" Wind Runner shouted, as always close behind the Eldest and finishing his words.

Boruin grinned as Dark Eye frowned and spat in the dirt before his fellow's horse. He jogged beside them as they trotted along, the horses too riled to halt completely. "How did you come here? How did you know to?"

"The Skyking commanded a boat to sail on the winds!" cried the Eldest. "It came out of the sunset two days ago and told us of his road across the sky."

"But I for one will return south on my own, even if I ride into camp dead on my horse!" said Wind Runner. "Blessed by the Skyking or not, that road is unnatural. A man should not sit that high above the world. It is an unsettling sight, one not meant for an honest plainsman!" Dark Eye shook his head. Being borne hundreds of feet over the land had not bothered him, even if it had frightened his friend. He grinned a farewell to Boruin and waved his riders toward the base of Bramble's tower.

"That ancient road is not the rabinathair's doing," Bramble said, stepping up beside him. "The Sescha runs across the entire continent. It is one of the few working mah'saiid wonders still left in the land. It was nice of the rabinithair to think to call in reserves. Finally using that huge head of his for something other than eating everything in sight."

"Good thing it runs over this valley," added Boruin.

Bramble tapped at his temple. "No, that was just smart planning."

"Well, it was sure a needed turn. How'd you know they were so close to arriving?"

"I didn't, until the Sescha appeared and they rode out of the gate," Bramble answered. Boruin clenched his teeth and crossed his arms to keep them from fidgeting on his sword pommel.

"If you didn't know, why weren't we pulling back? Those Fae bastards were ten-times these men, and your little illusions weren't fooling them anymore."

Bramble sniffed and started the hike toward the tower. "If it was such a concern, maybe you should have used some of those runes," he said over his shoulder. "I didn't give them to you for decoration. I thought you knew that."

With Fae blood drying across his body and his heart still pounding, Boruin snapped. If the runes hadn't been trapped under scar tissue, he would have pulled them all into his palm. "I don't know that. I don't *know* anything," he shouted, stepping up to try to shove the man into the dirt.

Bramble turned, grabbed Boruin's arm and continued around, pulling the arm with him. Boruin's weight was thrown forward and his body checked hard on Bramble's hip. He tasted dirt and blood on his lip as he hit the ground. By Bramble's whim he bounced not in the dirt, surrounded by laughing Ommans, but on the hard rock of the tower's summit.

Boruin jumped back to his feet, his eyes blinking at the sudden darkness. White light flared as Bramble struck him across the face and he crashed back onto the ground. Boruin's ear caught the scuff of Bramble's boot against stone as it pulled back to kick him in the gut. He grabbed it and kicked out at where the man's other knee should have been. Instead, Boruin found it coming down on his throat.

Boruin gurgled and choked under the man's weight. He arched his back, but he could not buck Bramble off.

"Calm down, Boruin," said Wraethe. "He's no enemy of ours. Bramble gave you those runes to keep them protected." Her face lowered to fill his vision. She seemed a twin sister to the pale moon beside her in the night sky.

"He tell you that?" Boruin coughed.

"No. I remember, Boruin. I remember it," she answered. Wraethe sat beside him and began her story, beginning with the day of his birth, fifty year past.

- 23 -
SOULS UNWEAVING

Wraethe read the crowd packed in the stands in a short second. No Fae missed the Parade of Champions. The bicentennial, hand-to-hand battle decided which of the two courts would rule the Dreaming Lands. Now, it seemed finished. Some Fae were crying. Some roared with victory. Others looked aghast, many smiled smugly, and more than one hand was already turning over its betting chits. Her eyes scanned the Nai'Oigher's platform hoisted above the gathering and settled upon her sponsors, the son and daughter of Polorun. Obata, called Dream by those blessed by her warm hand, had her ear cocked to the blather of some high-ranked, fawning Monarhig, but her eyes were keenly tuned to what was about to pass. Nungisa, cursed as Nightmare by any who'd felt his terrible touch, was a shade in his throne; the dark king's brooding spilled across his body in tangible blackness. His eyes, crimson in the shadows of his face, also watched the field closely.

Wraethe's gaze finished its circle and came back to the young man crouching over her, the hot sting of his blade biting into her neck. Despite an hour-long battle, the champion of the mortal realm was as steady as when they had begun.

"You will yield, or I'll take your life," said Smallmuss. Wraethe glared at the man. She did not see the future emperor and God-King of the north in his face, only the grim resolve that would get him there. He pressed the sharp edge harder against her pulsing vein. "A death is not required in this challenge. Take my offer. I am the victor, regardless."

A lij was beating her—that was no small humiliation—but what energy left to Wreathe was draining from her hard stare and jaw-locked sneer. She nodded and rolled away as he climbed off her. What jibes and curses would come in the future she thought she could ignore. The boy was a champion, mortal as he was. Wraethe gave a silent thanks to the sleeping Iraemun, the firstborn, that she would not face the young man from Pileaus again. She spat blood and whispered a prayer for any that would.

The city seemed to quake under the erupting roar of the Moir and the Monarhigs. Boos and cheers rose between the opposing courts as if their discord could bring the battle back to life. The noise rolled out of the city like a trumpet's blast and spread into the Dreaming Lands. In the wilds, Feirnann perked their ears and forgot for a moment their cattle and crops as the sound streamed across the valleys and knolls. The hermit-like scholars and secret keepers, the Riddari, noted the time as the din filtered down into their hidden dens, their quills crossing parchment furiously as they charted the sudden shift of power. The Sidhe'Lien court, with their agenda of acceptance and subtle assistance toward the Duine, had won the Parade of Champions and would wrest control of the Courts of Twilight from the isolationist To'Sidhe'Lien. Change had arrived, and the Dreaming Lands listened as the noise passed to hear what more was coming.

"What now?" Smallmuss asked with a grin. "If this is their best, I'll take on two more."

Bramble smiled at the young man's arrogance, but he understood the pride that was swelling in the boy's chest. It welled there too for the old trainer. Exiled from the Dreaming Lands, the old Fae had trained many a mortal warrior for the Sidhe'Lien court. This one was unsurpassed, and glancing about he relished the shocked look of the To'Sidhe'Lien members that both feared and hated the mortal realms so much. The boy was a born fighter, but Bramble had cut away the loose meat and made him a true champion. That was his talent, as much as conquering a continent would later become the boy's.

"Stand, if your legs can quit shaking," said Bramble. "Fessi will present you as champion. Accept the stand of roses, which officially turns the court leadership over to the Sidhe'Lien. After that, you can rest or you can celebrate. I for one will celebrate," he added as he led the boy forward to the center of the field.

The old man then pulled Wraethe to her feet, despite her refusals of help. "Nonsense. You fought like few I've witnessed in past parades. I had forgotten what a true Fae champion looked like." He helped her steady herself and then returned to his fighter's side.

The noise from the stands quieted as the officiate approached. Children of the first Iraemun, the Nai'Oigher siblings Gemab and Fessi presided over the parade as they had for millennia. Gemab,

Lord of Action, had initiated the event, and now Fessi, Lord of Consequence, would order it resolved. The booing faded—there would be no changing the results—and the cheering hushed as those gathered held their breath at the sight of the court leadership changing hands.

Fessi shuffled forward on his thin legs. White scars showed where his skin peeked out from his long robe. The thin lines covered his face as well, though his long black hair concealed most of it. His swollen knuckles cracked as he placed his hands together and bowed before Bramble and Smallmuss, then to the Fae champion and the To'Sidhe'Lien trainer, who stood apart from his court's fighter as if Wraethe now was some loathsome sewer Feirnann. Though Fessi seemed a beaten figure, the victim of all the damage of his sibling's inherent love of action, the lord's voice boomed with ancient authority.

"Have you both fought to the best of your abilities?" the Nai'Oigher asked. Smallmuss smiled, and Wraethe nodded and dropped her head. "And your name again, lij?" Smallmuss smiled as their word for "short-lived, pathetic mortal" finally carried with it some respect from the mouth of a member of the Fae's highest caste.

"Roderick Smallmuss of the continent of Pileaus," he answered. Fessi motioned the rose-bearer forward and turned to the crowd.

"As Lord of Consequence, I call an end to another Parade of Champions. The Sidhe'Lien will lead the Courts of Twilight until Gemab calls the next parade into action. Celebrate your victor—Pileaus!!!" he shouted. His voice rolled over the stands, through the great city and out across the Dreaming Lands to reach every last Fae with his official ruling.

Wraethe watched the flowers pass her by, ending her career as champion. The roses were a brilliant red against the white gloves of the bearer. She watched the young winner draw the bouquet from the gloved hand, watched them slide free of the leather without snagging. *Why is he wearing gloves if there are no thorns?* she wondered, raising her head. The rose bearer had turned, his shock of white hair crossing his face before she could get a look at him. He walked off the field like a man stepping away from a bull habback, his calm betrayed by the jittery bounce that was a barely reigned in sprint.

Smallmuss raised the bouquet over his head in victory. The Sidhe'Lien court roared in deafening approval. Wraethe blanched—deep in the stack of stems, a dark cloud bloomed like a cloud of mold spores. Smallmuss's fingernails stained first, then cracked as a black like the murk of dark water rolled up his fingers.

Wraethe was not pleased with her loss, but she would suffer it. There were greater humiliations than losing—being deemed a cheat was one she could not weather. She stumbled forward and grabbed the boy's wrist. His grin fell to confusion and then sudden agony as his eye met hers. She dragged his arm down from its victory salute as the drying flesh of his hand began to peel and roll up toward her grasp. Wraethe held him firm and searched around her for help. Fessi was turned to the crowd, his announcement still echoing off the stands. The rose bearer was nearly gone, his mane of white hair disappearing from the field. Old Bramble was drawing his knife and stepping toward her.

Rose petals fell around them and caught in a sudden wind that swept the dying flowers into a tightening vortex of blood red. She looked down and saw the blackening flesh had passed under her grasp. The muscles of the boy's hand were detaching from the bone, coming unwoven like a wool shawl run backward through the knitter's needles. Bramble's knife passed by her head as he buried it in the young man's elbow. Smallmuss screamed in pain, but Bramble's iron arms wrapped about him and held him tight.

"He's cursed!" Bramble cried above the rising wind. "Help me!"

Wraethe grabbed the blade and cut through the muscle. If she could cut the curse free, he might have a chance. She drove the blade deeper into the gristle, trying to take the arm at the joint. The black motes jumped the span just as his forearm came free; the illness spread faster up his shoulder as if knowing it was under attack. Smallmuss's jaw bobbed up and down, stuck between screams as the black curse swam into his mouth.

Wraethe heard Fessi's cry for the healers but she could not see beyond the petals whipping around them. The red was turning darker, and Wraethe raised the amputated arm to see the unwoven muscles dissolving into dust and whipping away in the wind. No Monarhig or Moir healer could keep him alive against such a curse.

The rose stems lay spread across the ground, and from them the curse had latched onto the fighter's legs. Wraethe saw the black dust of his corrupted flesh falling out the bottom of his leather cuffs. This was an evil fate for such a fighter. Her gut cramped at what needed doing. She bit her lip, letting the pain drive her decision into action.

Wraethe reached down and took the roses, even as Bramble cried out against it. The Fae champion, a Moir of the realm, sunk her teeth into the black, rotten stems and inhaled. The curse diverted into her lungs, and she felt her throat parch and crack. Her body soured as the ancient rules of sacrifice dictated; her tan skin paled and her hair blackened as she took in the evil engineered for the boy. The rule and consequence of her sacrifice would hardly matter, as the rot of the curse was much faster. Wraethe would be undone before she could become Ainghid'Fas, bearer of other's sins.

Smallmuss withered under the attack, but the curse was slowing, diverted into two hosts. His body failed, and as he fell back into the dirt, some part of him stayed standing. Pain wracked Wraethe's mind, but she knew she was seeing true, as Bramble too stood awe-struck. The curse did not just separate bone from muscle and sinew; the young man's essence seemed to remain on its feet, a soul spirit writhing as the curse probed at the form and tried to unravel it as well. It began to separate, two beings splitting above the waist as an act of self-preservation, risking division rather then dissolution by the curse. Bramble moved forward quickly as if to grab hold of the raw spirit, its intensity building like a rising tide as it struggled to get free.

"Stand back!" Wraethe heard her lady patron's command through the roar of the wind and the ringing of her dissolving ears. From somewhere outside that swirling cloud of lij dust and red petals, Dream was headed their way in an odd show of assistance. If she would pull them into her realm, there was a chance. The early-born Dream was all-powerful in the land of sleep.

A red petal froze just before Wraethe's eye. The world skidded to a halt, as if the god-like Iraemun had wakened and called on the world to still. Out of the corner of her eye, she spied Bramble alone moving, his motions a maze of complexity and his voice a muttering of spell work. His fingers cupped around an imaginary bowl. With his right hand he scooped at the air, pulling the dust of flesh, and petals, and what scrap of ruin he could grab hold of down into that unseen void he held in his shaking left hand. Into the small hole made by his encircled fingers, Bramble dragged in one of the twin souls that had split from Smallmuss's body. Then it was all gone; darkness swallowed Wraethe, leaving her no time to wonder if she was saved or just undone.

The door to the cottage slammed shut, and most of them jumped at the sharp noise. Wraethe paused in her story as the boy trotted over to Bramble, detouring slightly to pat Boruin's leg in passing. The old fighter leaned down as the boy cupped his hands around his small mouth. Bramble nodded at whatever he heard.

"Tell Dharl to prepare his best bowmen. Have him man the walls; the Ommans won't survive now on the field. I'll see to Griant myself," he answered. The boy walked back to the cottage, stalling at the door to give Boruin a little wave before slamming it again. It was as if they had never separated.

"He was the only one not worried about losing you," said Pile. "It was strange, like he knew you'd be along. Calm even after Griant thought you had been…"

"Trapped in the Guidevein?" Boruin finished for him.

"Yeah."

Boruin squeezed Pile's shoulder. "I had that same fear about you. Didn't happen."

"What did he say, Bramble?" asked Wraethe.

"Hey, how come he talks to you?" demanded Pile.

"Because I listen instead of talking out of place," Bramble answered. Surprisingly, Pile blushed. "He said the windwalkers are here," he added, pointing one-by-one at each of the four corners of the compass.

All turned to the edges of the tower and looked out to the horizon. For a moment the Fae were unseen in their immensity, Boruin's crew scanning too close, at the hills above the valley or at the thorn wall.

"Mother of Yuin," Pile cursed. Suddenly Boruin saw them too.

Four creatures, wardens of the winds of the Dreaming Lands, strode out of the dark horizon beyond the valley. Clothed in cloud and rain and wind, they towered above the land like living thunderheads. Lightning shot through their bodies and leapt out of their misted forms like angry snakes writhing. Inside, the exploding light gave edges to their swirling masses. The dull rumble of thunder rolled before them like a war cry as the windwalkers approached, carrying the unchallengeable force of weather as their weapon.

Boruin turned to Bramble. "What do we do against that? You going to build a rock dome over the valley to keep them off?"

"I will prepare our last defense as best I can, but it will not be much. I've used what Aiemer I had at my disposal, save a reserve for the rabinithair's tail. Unless we can reopen the window ways to the Dreaming Lands, the Monarhig has us starved. We will fight with the valley as constructed—and we will win," Bramble answered.

Pile scoffed. "How are we going to fight against cloud and wind?"

"It would do you well to trust Bramble," chided Wraethe.

"The windwalkers are fearsome, but remember the Monarhig's love of flair," Bramble answered. "In his attempt to frighten us, he has given us time to prepare. Finish your story, Wraethe. Do so while I check on Griant. The groundlings have been tunneling and are probably near our foundations," he explained before disappearing into the small cottage.

Boruin began pacing. "More great news."

"Naw. We've got a surprise for them," said Pile. "If it's time to drive the groundlings to the surface, I'd rather that task then fight wind and rain," he added, heading after Bramble. The short man turned at the door and shot them a wide grin. "Besides, if Boruin's history is as strange as Wraethe's, I might not want to know it."

A deep rumble rose from the rock like a mountain clearing its throat as Bramble made his last adjustments to their defenses. They moved to the edge and watched great shards of stone fall from the tower, leaving covered terraces and stairways for the fighting. The Ommans started taking their places even before the last rock fell away.

"Perhaps you should continue on the parapets below," Turintou suggested. "This sheer top will provide no cover when the wind comes."

"Thank you, Skyking." Wraethe curtsied deep, a court gesture Boruin had rarely seen from her.

The rabinithair cocked his head. "For what, Moir of the Realm?"

"For keeping my friend safe and out of trouble."

"Pah," Boruin scoffed. "If you only knew." The rabinithair snorted a laugh and turned to watch the four walking storms approach.

"That fire you told me of in Griant's warren, has it burned out? Did it reveal everything?" Boruin asked as they climbed down the rock stairs and onto a rough parapet carved into the split rock. She avoided his eyes a moment by watching the northern windwalker. Lightning struck from its raised foot, destroying tree and rock where it fell. Rain doused the fire as the foot settled amidst the destruction, almost as if the creature were clearing a path for tender feet.

"I don't know what that fire was or how the boy put me inside of it," she said, shuddering, "but it did burn everything free. Things started coming back, bits and pieces rising to fill what the fire had gutted. It was all convoluted, like piecing together a reflection from rippled water. What I hadn't pieced together before we arrived, Bramble helped me put back into place. He knew everything I did not."

"So tell me the rest. Where do I fit? What of the boy?" he asked, turning her now to force her eye to his, demanding the answer. She took his hand, but she could not hold his gaze, turning instead to watch the destruction of the approaching windwalker.

"I don't think you will like the answer, Boruin, but I can finally give you one."

24

A BIRTH OF TWIN SUNS

Dream saved Smallmuss with a pocket dream of timelessness, holding the curse still for the healers' working fingers. After years and fortunes in gold and favors spent on the Riddari, with their pale bodies and contemptuous stares born of secret-hoarding, Bramble pulled out of his own void something other than he had gathered out of that mess on the parade ground.

Four long months Bramble waited, and a hundred miles deep into the Nefazo jungle he'd waded, before using the magic he'd bought from the Riddari. Most of their kind were bookish snobs salivating over even the least of secrets, clutching them close for fear of their arcane knowledge becoming common and mundane. It had cost him dear to cull the secrets he needed from so many of that pride-swelled caste of Fae. It was like haggling with one's own blood to buy a few pieces of puzzle board when the picture was still beyond his comprehension. He could have dealt with fewer—there were at least two that would have known outright how to coax his strange womb into fruition—but then they might have guessed what he was up to.

It was hard keeping secrets from secret hoarders. They could coax lost knowledge out of powdered bones and stale air. But two decades of careful work was worth it; as the Moir crawled out of the void, he was sure of it.

"Breathe, my lady," Bramble said. He did not move to help as she dragged herself out of the tree, its bark split open and sap still welling from the wound he had made. The fire oak had taken root long ago under the wall of a mah'saiid ruin smothered now by the jungles of the deep south. The great tree had cracked the stone and risen up through the building. Sun-searching branches poked out the windows in moss-covered walls, the tree's crown replacing the long-fallen roof.

He shifted his weight slightly, fingering the club in his left hand as she grabbed at the tired stone and pulled forward. His right grazed the scabbard that felt so foreign on his hip. A sword gave the master fighter too great an advantage on the field, something that bruised his honor, but he had strapped it on, thinking he might need it here.

With a thud, her feet slid last out of the black womb he had woven into the heart of the great fire oak. Her pale hands slapped at the dead leaves on the jungle floor, and she coughed. Thick phlegm rattled out of her throat before she finally sucked in a great draft of cold Diuntyne air. The jungle, its night creatures chattering as loudly as an Ouilainne tenement moments before, had completely stilled. They could feel the creature worming out of the mah'saiid ruin and were either fleeing or frozen in hiding.

"Ainghid Fas, are you well?"

Wraethe pulled her feet up underneath her in a crouch. Her face rose to meet the pale moon, and she pulled her hair free so its light could fill her eyes. The change that had begun twenty years past on the parade field had completed in that dark void Bramble had scrapped together in quick haste and nurtured over the years. In sacrificing herself, choosing to take the evil aimed at Smallmuss, the Moir had become Ainghid Fas, an agent of balance sworn to rules older than even the Iraemun's will and songs of power. She was leaner now, the color of her skin faded to ivory and her hair jet black. Her face was gaunt, maybe hungry. It was smaller too, shortened to a shape closer to lij than Fae. Her fingers and feet had also shrunken. Either her change, his void, or something stronger had made her Fae no more.

Diun's light seemed to cover her naked body in brilliant radiance, her skin alight as if burning with cool flame. She clutched her knees, breathing a sigh as if the moon's glow were a drink of water to a long-dry throat.

Bramble tried again. "Moir, do you remember who—" She exploded out of her crouch, slapping his club out of his hand.

Bramble twisted, avoiding the weight of her body coming down, but still caught a rake of her claws across his neck. An inch higher and she might have hooked into his jugular.

Fear rose in his head for the first time in centuries. It drove his heart into a drumming frenzy, and he pulled too hard on his sword hilt, tearing the scabbard and all free from his belt.

He rounded on her and found the Ainghid Fas low and sweeping at his feet. Her calf caught him in the ankles, and he fell back into the jungle brush. Blazing blue eyes filled his vision as she pounced. He jammed the palm of his hand between her teeth as she went for his throat. Her fingers clawed at him, her toes raking at his stomach and thighs as if she were an animal.

Tearing flesh free from his hand, she spat and snapped forward again for his neck. This time Bramble rocked forward too, his hard forehead smashing against her face. She screamed as blood burst from her nose. As she struggled back to her feet, he rolled her, trapping her under his frame. He punched into her temple, but it was unnecessary. She tried to raise a hand to strike, and it fell back into the mud. She was as weak as a child—all her energy burned out in that quick flash of Ainghid Fas hunger and rage.

"I didn't know if you'd be strong or not," Bramble said as he climbed off her. "Glad you weren't stronger." He dragged her back toward the void by her feet. She moaned as the tree approached, unwilling to return, but unable to fight. "Hush, lady. I have another need for you. If the Riddari are right, we can help each other. You're still a virgin— no kills since your change—and that makes a difference. I'll give you peace if you will lend me your strength."

Bramble looked into her eyes, curious if she was hearing anything he said. The moon drowned out the blue and seemed to hypnotize her. He bound her arms and legs in chain anyway.

Returning to the fire oak, he stared at the black void that sat in the hollow trunk like a soft, slick egg. In its darkness he glimpsed a petal, still red, and grains of dust. They swirled in a slow eddy. What he thought was his reflection softened, grew younger, and he realized it wasn't his face at all. The void had one more to give, as he'd expected. The face watched him a moment before slipping back into the darkness. Bramble sealed the trunk around the ripening womb, calling too for the old cracked stone to close about the fire oak and hold it hidden within the ruin.

Bramble knew the horrors Wraethe would consume as a sin-eater, the evils of others that would rot her body and mind. The Ainghid Fas were fated to balance evil and good just as the sun and moons would constantly chase each other's tails. She would kill those that deserved it. She would kill, too, some that didn't; such was the balance the Great Mother had entrusted to these frightening creatures. With each act of violence Wraethe would sour further, soaked in rage and sin, until she could no longer keep the balance. She would become more monster than Ainghid Fas, and then finally someone would kill her. Bramble required more from her than that.

The old man forced her to memorize a series of rites purchased at further cost from the Riddari, secret prayers that would help balance her soul if she were to stay a protector of the man still congealing in the void. She would kill, but perhaps she could resist the cruel slide into feral brutality that came from layers of sin stacked upon one's shoulders. Maybe she could slip out from under that weight until her task was done.

It was another decade before they returned to the fire oak deep in the Nefazo jungle. Bramble felt the surface of the void finally being pushed against, finally cracking. He stood in the same place with the same stance as when he'd watched Wraethe struggle out of the void. Now she stood beside him, cool and eager as ever for a fight.

"I feel it coming," said Wraethe. "I think it feels me."

"That's alright. It's time, and we're ready." Bramble replied. He had skipped the sword this time—Wraethe was weapon enough for his safety—but bought and brought further protection against what might spill out. He feared stronger ties than chains would be required, and he hoped his words of binding would be enough.

The tree shuddered as the womb began to swell. It bulged out of the hollow trunk, pressing against the stone walls. They gave to it, old joints cracking and mortar exploding into dust. Just as the wall was set to topple, the thick, black flesh sucked back inward and imploded. The incorporeal mass of soul and body finally solidified, like an exploded sun collapsing back from dust and burning gas, into a recognizable form.

A man, germinated like a seed from the motes of Smallmuss, stumbled from the void. Bramble nodded his head, pleased at the way the man looked him over. His eyes sized up Wraethe as well and assessed his surroundings with quick, furtive glances. The man looked nothing like Smallmuss, but his core, his instinct, was one and the same.

"Born of ruin," Bramble muttered under his breath.

Wraethe misheard. "Boruin?" she asked. "I kind of like the sound of that." She looked at him easily; her always tense frame softened for a moment, the temper that rode the back of her tongue, always waiting to jump forward, added no harsh edge to her voice. "What is he?"

Bramble relaxed in his stance as Boruin, naked as Wraethe had been, lay out to stretch on the jungle floor. "He is Smallmuss—or at least some central essence of him. Like a traced shadow of the champion. More than that, I'm not fully sure."

"Shadow of the champion," Boruin mimicked, grinning like a toddler. Bramble chuckled, but his own smile fell away in disappointment. There was something missing here. The curse on the parade field had shucked away the layers of Smallmuss, and he had seen something there that was pure power. He had scrambled to hide it, risked more than death by sneaking his small void away under both Fessi's and Dream's noses.

Dream had watched him closely as she protected Smallmuss while the healers worked. The powerful Nai'Oigher had glimpsed something too, searched quietly for it while they wove him back together. He could see some touch of that split-soul attached to the man; it sparkled on him like mist across his skin, but it was residue. *A vessel emptied*, he thought.

Bramble stepped over Boruin. "Bind him just to be certain." Wraethe laughed. The man could've been twice her size and she wouldn't have worried. Still, she pulled him to his feet and smiled again as his fingers grazed her face, drawing her black hair over her shoulders.

He sniffed at the air. "I can't smell the sea. I don't like that," Boruin told her.

Wraethe bound his forearms behind him, careful not to chafe his skin. "We're far from the coast, but maybe we can visit."

The fire oak was dying. Bramble could hear the fine cracks as the grain withered and contracted. It had fed his womb for decades, and that final push had drunk in the last of its life. He ducked his head into the hollow trunk for a quick peek, certain that he was missing something. The child's face, inches from his own, made him holler and stumble back.

"Bramble?" Wraethe cried, rushing forward.

It was not the closeness or surprise that had made him jump. It was how this thing was hiding in a child's form. The boy was something wholly not lij, not young, and not innocent—it frightened the old man. It stepped free from the withering skin of the womb still more soul than body. Its storm of raw power was so visible, wrapped about by the thinnest layer of skin.

Like Boruin, the first thing the child did was look about its surroundings. Bramble knew Wraethe could not see what he was seeing or her sword would have been drawn and she perhaps would have already been dead.

Bramble saw under the thin shell of the boy's body the staggering amount of what the child was gleaning from the world. It was judging not Bramble and Wraethe, or even the new man, by how strong they appeared, or how fast they might spring from their tense stance. Instead it examined the ties between the Aiemer and the matter constructing their bodies. It read the intersections between life in the jungle around it and the energy of the Great Mother. That raw, powerful soul, wrapped in the guise of a child, gauged the Duine realm like a carver examining a block of wood. Its awareness was deep, full of wisdom and heavy thought. In the ideas that flashed too close to the surface of its skin, Bramble did not see malevolence, but neither a particular sense of good. *This is a being not fully tempered*, he thought.

As the boy looked up at him and began to speak, Bramble clapped his hand over its mouth. The child held still, unafraid as Bramble reached into his throat and stole his words before they could be spoken and unknown energies set upon the world.

The ancient language burned across Bramble. He realized his mistake too late. It was like expecting the last sip of a cup and finding a bucket poured down your throat. He'd been prepared for the short vocabulary of a boy, but the words washed over him in a tide—words enough for a thousand voices. He went to his knees, his mind crushed underneath the weight. For a moment Bramble was almost buried.

It was what he was trying to avoid, casting free those words, those combinations that, once spoken, could open this boy-thing like a puzzler's box. Only the Mother knew what the words would do when murmured by the running brooks or whispered by the wind. But with his last choking breath Bramble vomited them out, rolling aside like a man stepping out from under a heavy stone. The jungle burned under a wash of blue light as the words spilled out like entrails from a busted gut. Instead of reeling out into the darkness, spreading thin like a silk sheet across the world, the words of the boy snagged across the skin of the new man. Boruin began to howl as the ancient tongue stuck, smoking in a line of runes across the surface of his flesh.

Lightning began to crackle in a constant river of light dancing about the windwalker's nebulous head like a living crown. The creature roared, vomiting snow and ice from between its black teeth. The sentry fires on the enemy lines whipped under the cold wind like bright flowers scrambling to flee but rooted too deep to escape. The windwalkers would douse them shortly, their rain-swollen feet treading the last few miles outside the valley.

"So I am a man unmade? Just a living parchment to carry these damn words?" asked Boruin. He stabbed a finger at Wraethe in anger. "Were my feelings written on me as well, something to help you keep me close?"

"Those came from before," Bramble said as he stepped out of the tower and onto the parapet. "Something cultivated while you both healed in that sunless womb. Do not think you were the only one affected," he added. Boruin looked to Wraethe and knew it was as the old man said.

"It's not easy for Ainghid Fas to show," Wraethe explained. "It's a foreign concept, like an eashue grounded or a tuneless marii. But I have tried." She reached out to him, and he did not shy away from her touch. Even when he had dismissed them, Boruin always knew by her sharp words and constant chiding that their's was a shared love.

"So you've discovered what this boy is, then. That's why you bought us to bring him here? Brought us together?" asked Boruin.

"No," Bramble countered, "I contracted you because the boy would wait no longer. His will on the matter was greater than mine. Any discovery to be made about this boy, I've come to accept, will come from him alone."

The first gust of wind reached the valley from the west and drove the dry brown dust into the sky. The crash of thunder rang from behind them as the southern windwalker stepped over the ridgeline and howled a torrent of floodwater.

"Then for now, we fight. If I live, we'll ask the boy what he wants done," said Boruin. He placed his hand on his sword hilt but did not draw. The windwalker to the north bent low like a falling tree and his crown of lightning scattered across the thorn wall, setting it aflame. "How again do we fight these?" he added with a questioning look for Bramble.

"You will leave that to the bowmen. I don't need you struck down by lightning for waving your sword uselessly," Bramble answered. He leapt down to the next parapet to command the Ommans.

Boruin felt slighted, but he was glad to take cover behind the rock. The rain hit then like a barroom blow to the face. The four windwalkers dashed against the tower at once, leaning down to plow forward with fists of hail and brows of lightening. They broke upon the rock spire like a great ocean storm. Fault lines cracked and rock shards exploded from the walls, sending terraces and Omman fighters crashing to the dirt plain below.

Lacking the power to fly, Turintou snapped out into the sky like a striking snake, punching through the giants of cloud and mist. He delved their centers, lightning cracking against his scales as he searched for some soft heart in the creatures. His tail attacked their fire with his own, sending bright spheres of flame rocketing through the unflinching bodies of the Fae. Then the eastern windwalker seemed to duck, his shoulders hunching down to let the ball of the serpent's flame pass through his head.

"Look to the neck!" the rabinithair cried from somewhere above, his voice faint behind the rolling thunder.

Boruin wrung the water from his eyes and peered into the rain. The neck of the storm creature was a thin mist cast like a veil between the great head and the thick body. Something dark shifted in the cloud, hands clenching and beating down toward the tower in a pantomime of the towering storm.

"Like a puppeteer," he muttered. He cupped his hands around his mouth and shouted at the terrace below. "Aim for the throat!"

Bramble relayed the order. The Ommans raised their bows against the impossible winds and fired. The windwalkers exhaled in disgust, sending the shafts spinning like dandelion seeds out of the valley. Boruin heard Wraethe's bow creak; he smiled at her as she patiently held the heavy draw. As the northern windwalker inhaled deeply for another blow, the twang of the released string sounded sweetly in Boruin's ears. The windwalker stumbled backwards as the shaft arced through the hollow in the wind and found its mark. The cloud slumped, inanimate, until the wind of its fellows tore it apart. The puppeteer struggled through the air, its long, thin body limping toward the earth on gusts of wind, like tumbling down some unseen flight of stairs.

On the south face, the rabinithair dove between boulders of hail and long arcs of lightning to snatch the windwalker from his commanding perch in the clouds. The Fae screamed as Turintou's long teeth snapped down once and again before the serpent spat the bloody remains to the field below.

The skies cleared as the last two windwalkers withdrew under waves of Omman arrows. Pulling back from the field, their storms dissipated to reveal a charging infantry that spread almost completely across the weather-pounded plain. To break the strong lines of the hard Omman fighters, the Monarhig had positioned his pikcs into wedges, with three heavy churstampts serving as each point. The last of the snow and rain fell from the sky as the pikcs and churstampts bounded towards the tower.

"Why aren't we forming on the field?" Boruin asked as Wraethe set her bow aside.

"This is Griant's time to fight. The rilk have been waiting patiently to serve punishment for the destroyed Guidevein. Bramble would not thin their enemy's ranks."

A low rumble Boruin had mistaken as the last echoes of thunder ground through the stone at his feet. Bubbles of rising dirt littered the base of the tower like great eggs swelling to hatch. When they exploded, shafts of stone propelled frantic groundlings out from the earth before the charging Fae line. Behind the shafts came rilk, pouring from the ground like cold lava.

"The groundlings have been digging toward our foundations since they arrived. Luckily, Griant's call brought out the rilk first. They've been sitting quietly in the rock, listening for the chance to pounce," Wraethe said with a cruel twist of a lip that served as her satisfied smile.

The infantry stumbled, their momentum broken by the sight of the routed groundlings running wide-eyed toward them. The giant creatures of rock, trotting in chase, furthered their confusion. From atop the tower, Boruin could feel the rilk war chant, a heavy *"Hump Hump Huoaur Hump!"* like a symphony of hammers pounding deep in the earth. He followed along with the Ommans as they began to stomp their feet to the heavy beat. The song seemed alive to Boruin; it lightened his spirit, warmed his heart, and strengthened his limbs. Perhaps it was his relief at the beaten windwalkers, or the sight of Griant and hundreds of his rilk racing across the field, but the song made him feel prepared for any enemy.

No infantry can charge into stone and remain intact. The pikcs smashed against the rilk and were driven down into the dirt. The churstampts stumbled as the massive rilk tackled their legs. Boruin could feel the impact in the air as the rilk's heavy stone fists pounded against the hard plate scale of the beasts.

The runes of a few rilk glowed as their rilka worked beneath their thick skins. One obsidian rilk began to burn brightly until his carapace was smoldering like molten stone. He grabbed hold of a churstampt racing past him. His hands melted through the creature's armor and cooked its heart between clutching fists. Another stone man shifted the mass of one arm into his other, creating a great spiked hammer that devastated the enemies around him.

A warren of rilk stood back from the rest, singing to the stone beneath the plain. When the Monarhig, shocked at the chaos across the valley, drove his reserves of frightened Lakelanders and low-caste Feirnann down the valley walls, they reached the level plain to find the earth crumbling. The floor of the valley turned under their weight, upending in great slabs. The Monarhig's reserves slid down into the crevasses, buried somewhere deep and dark.

Boruin matched Wraethe's cruel smile at the destruction wrought by the rilk. Griant alone had proven a powerful fighter, but Boruin would match this band against the Pilean Empire's entire army and navy at once.

The Prince of Winds stepped off the ridgeline and, like his living storms, walked down gusts of wind toward the tower. His white hair blew like a banner of surrender, though his words were hardly so humble. He halted, standing before the tower on a hot updraft. "Quite the show of tricks, Bramble." The Fae prince snapped a finger out as an eager Omman fired his bow, and the shaft went wide in his summoned blast of wind. They watched it spin up into the sky and turn, driving back down into the archer and pinning him to the rock. "I would that I'd paid more attention to your band when we first met," said the Monarhig, once again talking to Wraethe and ignoring Boruin.

"Unless this is an offer of surrender, we have little use for your conversation," Bramble said, climbing up the parapet stairs to stand beside Boruin.

"It is indeed an offer, but not for your terms, Bramble. Where is that darling little lij child you were toting around last time? I'd have him and this old fellow. In exchange I'll leave your valley intact. The Moir should come along willfully if I ask. She has a lost bet to pay—time in my baths, was it not?"

"I think I resolved that bet," Boruin said through a wide, goading smile, "just before you broke your bow."

"What did I say about talking to me, lij?" the Monarhig growled, his lips thin and white in furious anger. Boruin stepped forward to the edge of the parapet, his own jaw rippling with hatred.

"What you want is here," Boruin said, slapping his forearm. "If you want any chance at it, I'm the one you'll deal with." The Monarhig stepped slowly down toward the stone shelf, his eyes trying to burn through the man.

"Then let's deal. Come with me and bring the boy. I'll withdraw from the valley and leave your lady friend behind," the Monarhig said bitterly.

"If not, what will you do? We've beaten your infantry and your windwalkers. I doubt you have anyone left, except maybe Churly. You going to send that fat man down here to finish us off?"

The Monarhig leaned down until his face was almost touching Boruin's own. "I will tear your painted skin from your body and leave you drying in the sun. This valley will become a land of death as I draw each of your men's lives from their bodies in the slow length of two full moons. The boy will become a thrall to my groundlings, and if you don't know of their appetites, I can certainly arrange a display to entertain you while I work on your skin. The Moir, I will satisfy myself, and perhaps leave her pieces with your Mana'Olai to be further devoured by the kauolth."

"Fair enough. Let me consult," Boruin said, turning to look at his crew. Their hard eyes, and the rabinithair's turning gold, confirmed his answer.

Boruin turned back with his hand whistling through the wind. It struck the Monarhig's beautiful cheek and mouth, leaving an imprint of five spread fingers in a red blush of rising blood. The smack rang through the air, echoing off the stone for a moment before being swallowed by the Ommans' howl of laughter. The Prince of Wind's face swung between disgust and fury. Bramble did not wait for the Fae's next reaction.

"Archers!" the old fighter yelled, hurling his mace as the Monarhig began his spell work. The prince side-stepped the metal club and then ducked Wraethe's whistling arrow. His lungs filled for a great roaring breath but were forced to blow early to disperse the first wave of Omman crossfire. The rilk threw stones as big as barrels from below, and the rabinithair's long body snapped out after the fleeing Fae prince.

Boruin opened his mouth to congratulate himself on a parley well refused, but the thunderous crack of breaking rock and the shifting horizon distracted him. Below, rilk ducked or turned their backs, rocks ricocheting off them as the northern foundation exploded across the field. Without its support, the tower leaned forward like a drunk forgetting to bring his feet.

Boruin caught the lip of the parapet just as he tumbled over the side. Wraethe grabbed his forearm as another earthquake rocked the stone tower.

"The window ways!" Turintou yelled as his body again took to the air atop a flooding bloom of Aiemer. "The Monarhig has torn them open!" He shot upward, dodging the lightning of the last two wind-walkers as they came for the Skyking. The serpent chased them into the high clouds, where his tail fire and the Fae's lightning exploded against each other in flashes of light.

"Only the Aiemer passes through the window ways," Wraethe grunted between clenching teeth as she dragged Boruin back over the rail.

"No," said Pile, wiping the streaming blood from his brow. He glanced back down the dark hallway from where he'd run. "Monsters too, bigger than the churstampts and meaner than the rilk. And did I mention there are thousands?" the short fighter added, face bright white under a smear of blood.

25

THE UNMADE MAN

I can't hold the tower," Bramble said through clenching teeth. They turned to find him straining with his hands flat, his shoulder bracing against some invisible wall. "Grab on to something," he whispered as his feet began to slide. They felt the stone begin to tip forward.

The top of the tower leaned out over the valley and its crippled foundations groaned. The rilk had already begun to run out from under its shadow, their great legs loping in pounding strides after the galloping Hetsu Plainsmen. The stone shifted too far over its base, and with a crackling rush the hard rock splintered apart in great sheets of jagged granite.

Bramble, sweat pouring from his face, held their vein of rock together. The crown of the tower hit the earth shaped like a great needle, with Boruin's crew and a few lucky Ommans huddling on top. The tip shattered and broke apart as the stone came down, slowing their descent to a teeth-jarring crash that sent them sprawling across the dirt. They rose to their feet at the edge of the destruction.

The Hetsu Plainsmen had ridden clear of the collapsing tower, though a few fallen horses screamed where massive shards of exploding stone had chased them down. Most of the rilk had also made it free, but much of the tower had fallen, with the Ommans at its face. Boruin saw Sergeant Dharl climb from the rubble, then turn to pull survivors free. He came up with one arm missing a body before he caught sight of some terror rising from the ruins of the tower. Dharl grabbed the nearest wounded man and roared for the others to follow him to defensible ground.

The tower had broken open on impact like a giant beetle, its hard exterior splitting wide to reveal not an oozing mass of gray and green guts, but horrid creatures from the sour places in the Dreaming

Lands. The things that had wormed through the window ways and cracked the tower's hard foundations clambered over the rubble, snatching up the dead and dying where they lay.

The Monarhig is not alone, thought Boruin as he watched the survivors and monsters alike freeing themselves from the mountain of rubble. *Something greater ripped open those window ways. Someone stronger has invested in our destruction.*

A great worm, slick with muck, darted over a boulder and snagged a rilk by the foot. Its hard beak tapped on the rilk's thick skin like a bird hammering through tree bark in search of soft meat inside. The rilk's great hands tried to find purchase on the worm's slippery head. Neither combatant saw the dark fog moving toward them. Something sparkling whipped out of the blackness and beat the pale worm aside. It dragged the rilk into its formless mass and Boruin heard the snapping crunch of crushing stone. Tiny rilka rolled out of the dark as they fled the monster that had consumed their protector. They were too slow; tendrils reached out for each one and yanked them back into the darkness.

To their credit, the Ommans screamed in rage rather than fear. Great corded centipedes, with hundreds of tiny mouths under their bodies like hungry open sores, raced over the rubble and pressed their weight down on the fallen. Their mass muffled the fighters' screams, which faded into silence as their blood soaked into the dirt.

A tall ghoul, limbs disjointed and guts tied about its waist like a skirt hiked up over its hips, leapt high out of the broken tower. It came down in the crowd of Dharl's retreating fighters. Boruin saw its mottled skin was made of hundreds of faces stitched, or molded, or grown across its body. The mouths roared curses and obscenities as it tore into the surrounding fighters. A spearwoman dashed forward and drove her weapon through its side. It grabbed the woman, drawing her weapon deeper through its torso as it clutched her close. The mouths whispered sing-song rhymes which Boruin could not quite make out, but which made the woman begin to scream. The creature held her tight as she rotted in its grasp, her howls turning to vomit and blood running from her eyes. It held her in its embrace even as two rilk grabbed the creature and woman both and tore them in two. The evil thing laid still, mouths giggling and snarling and drinking from the dead woman.

"Form up! Make a line, you sons of whores, or we're all finished!" Bramble shouted over the din of the creatures. The living, heeding Bramble's call, backed out of the scattered rubble and onto the open plain.

Boruin found Pile and trotted to him. "Son of Yuin, what are these things?"

"Nightmares," Pile said calmly as he drew his axe. The short thief had turned off all emotion, a trick Boruin had never seen him use, and he realized Pile had come to accept his certain death.

High above, explosions of lightning and rabinithair fire spread across the sky. Turintou battled on against the windwalkers; there would be no help yet from him.

Boruin tripped over the boy as he backed into the last line of defenders. He came down with a crash, kicking out in fear.

"Son of a—where have you been?" he asked, grabbing the boy and clutching him tight. The boy pulled him toward the back of the line. "I've got to fight, boy. You need to hide. Get under a rock and don't say a word." The boy just stared in his simple way, and Boruin wondered if he should slap him.

"Go with him, Boruin," ordered Bramble. "You aren't going to increase our odds that much."

"I'm not one for running. I'll stay here."

A great sheet of rock shifted as something big began to pull itself out of the earth. The earth shook as a two-fingered, claw-like hand slammed down on the earth. Cracked and yellowed spines, like burnt porcelain, rose as the thing pulled itself up from below. Flame licked about the root of its spines and oily smoke poured out across the plain, hiding everything below their hips in shadow.

The Hetsu Plainsmen, using their quick horses to avoid the creatures and pull the wounded from the rubble, turned back for the open plain as the black smoke blew under their stirrups. A few horses made it, but something under that black smoke had a taste for horse flesh. Men tumbled as their steeds were pulled out from under them. They ran for their lines, as whatever hungered under the smoke dragged the screaming steeds back into the darkness.

"For rut's sake, Boruin, go!" Wraethe yelled, her temper snapping. "Maybe the boy's not running, but if he is you've got to go with him." His crew turned their backs to him as the rilk again began their fight song.

Boruin picked up the boy and ran, trying to ignore the cold looks of the Ommans as he fled.

"Where are we going? The Monarhig has us surrounded," Boruin asked as he sprinted for the thorn wall with the child on his hip. The boy fought his hold and scrambled up, trying to climb on Boruin's shoulders. "No horsing around, for Yuin's sake!" he yelled, angry at having to flee, angry at leaving his friends to die, angry at the kid's games. The boy wriggled free, pulled himself over Boruin's shoulder, and braced his feet on his back.

"What the—?" Boruin had no time to curse as small hands seemed to dig under his skin and grab hold of raw muscle. The boy pulled with all his might.

The old fighter went to his knees, like a galloping horse reined in too hard by its rider. Like he had with Toaaho's parasitic tongue, the boy grunted with the effort, tugging on his flesh with more strength than his small body should have held.

Boruin stretched out his left arm against the boy's pulling, grasping for the sky as if praying for help. The boy reached over his shoulder and took another hold on the long line of blue runes tattooed across Boruin's body. They would not move, held firm by the hand-shaped scar across the old man's forearm. The skin had melted under the Makua'Moi priest's spell, setting a rune deep into his flesh. Then the skin on Boruin's wrist stretched. It felt like fire racing up his arm, and he saw through tearing eyes the rune outlined in welling blood.

"Huuuuggghhh!" the boy grunted as he pulled. Boruin leaned against the child's weight and grabbed the rune above the scar, adding his own strength. Two deep breaths and he tugged—then screamed.

The skin of Boruin's arm ripped, sending the boy tumbling off his back and the runes spinning about his body with a high-pitched clatter. Blood flung from the tattoos and splatted across the ground as they ran through the opened scar. Boruin, still yelling, turned to face the smiling boy.

He bit down on a scream in order to speak. "What now? I still don't know what to do with them."

The boy took his arm and pried his hand from the torn flesh. Blood pulsed from a split vein and trickled down his árm. The boy set the runes into motion. Boruin hissed as each one passed the wound and drew more blood, until a rough circle made the loop and slid down successfully into his palm.

"This is the first rune in the spell that can save them?" Boruin asked. The boy shook his head. Boruin looked closer, recalling Griant's words.

By itself, it is a very powerful rune, very unsafe. Your Ghrunfre is bordered by sacrificial runes, Griant had said. *An unfortunate combination.* The rough circle was the Ghrunfre, the rune Griant named for resurrection and deconstruction. It was the origin rune in the long line that wrapped up his arm. Flanked on either side were the runes of sacrifice—one to start the spell, and one to end it. One for both of them.

Boruin struggled to his feet. "It's one spell...one long spell," he said in disbelief, "and you want me to pull the whole thing."

The runes were dangerous; Wraethe had always said as much, though he hadn't needed her judgment to believe it. He had felt the strength of just two runes and the pulsing beat of intense power in five. The wrong runes could tear him into pieces and destroy the land for a mile about him.

"And that's just with a few," he said, starting to laugh. "You want all of them." He found it strangely funny, an old man brought to an end by such an odd boy. "But you're not a boy, are you," he said, pushing back the strange hysteria.

The boy shook his head.

"I'm scared."

The boy smiled, and Boruin wished he saw more comfort there than pity.

Boruin turned and saw the Monarhig's gruesome host driving Bramble's dwindling army just shy of a rout. The flanks were retreating too fast and would shortly circle around and turn them into an island on a sea of death. He flipped the second rune down into his palm and felt the warmth of the magics combining. The boy took hold of his numb fingertips, though Boruin's blood ran down his small arm.

The fire in his hand burned hot, fiercer than the wound of the priest, as though each rune were a sun beginning to explode. Boruin began to flip the line of runes faster, trying to get them into place before the rising pain became too much. He had not taken his eyes off the battle, searching for Wraethe's fighting form. The old man had some fancy that he would lock eyes with her once more across the distance. It would not happen; light welled up from his hand, a deep blue that obstructed his vision and made him feel suddenly like he was falling feet first into the sky.

Boruin felt the last rune pass his finger and fall into his palm. *I wonder what I look like without all that ink*, he thought just before his hand imploded. Boruin fell into the spell, dragged into the depths of its power, and for the second time in his strange life he was unmade.

The long line of the boy's words, containing more wards of deconstruction and resurrection than just the Ghrunfre, unraveled the two beings in a heartbeat. The creature, mostly man, and the being, mostly soul, returned to a cloud of carbon and energy, spinning in a tight vortex on the dry plain of Munier Valley. A bright sparkle of lights exited the sphere like tiny falling stars thrown back to the heavens. One pierced the Monarhig's eye, causing his vision to dim as if he had stared too long at the sun.

The Prince of Winds took to the air, circling wide around the host of nightmares he had unleashed on the field, and stepped to the dirt as the swirling mass of blue motes slung its last spark of light out into Diuntyne. The vortex slowed and stilled. As the wind pulled the last of it apart, the Monarhig struggled against shock and hurriedly called his spell down on the naked man lying where Boruin and the boy last stood.

Stepping from that dark, moist womb and out into the wind and hot jungle sunlight, Boruin had felt himself harden to his new form like a late-winter seedling pulled from the window ledge and set out in the spring morning. The first days were hard sailing, his senses a constant distraction and his mind unfettered and always wandering. It was not long before bits and pieces of Smallmuss solidified, and though he was missing any true memory, Boruin felt real at last. He knew what he smelled and he could name what insects made the chirping sound in the grass. The sun rising was no longer a surprise to him. The constellations he knew perfectly, though somehow knowing also that they were too far south for Smallmuss to ever have seen himself. That helped him understand too that he was not Smallmuss, not in any real sense of being someone. His pieces were the same as the Duine champion's, but somehow, they made a different whole. Trying to figure it out made his head throb. He took the name Boruin then as a measure of comfort; that was something solidly his own, at least.

The boy's form settled as well, better covering its dense center mass. He took to dancing with the wind and contemplating flowers. The boy was doing that very thing when Boruin propped himself up on his elbows and found Bramble again, standing at the edge of the wide glade and watching him and the boy. He laid back into the tall grass and closed his eyes to the hot jungle sun, listening to the muffled steps of the child as he ran in wide circles for the joy of it. He was tired of the man's watchful eyes, but he knew why Bramble kept him and the boy close. It was the same reason he had yet to make up his mind what to do. The boy was too dangerous to be possessed by any in the Dreaming or the Dying Lands.

It was hard to look at the child, dancing around in flowers and catching bugs, because if he closed his eyes Boruin could feel him. The boy was dense; his small form concealed something vast. It was like the child had managed to pull a doll's dress over a mountain. Worse, that hidden mass pulled at him. He felt the tug even in his sleep, a constant dragging that churned up dreams of falling into a bright star.

When Bramble paced a bare spot in the grass at the edge of the glade, Boruin decided to weigh in. "You want to know how I see it?" he asked.

Bramble smiled, and it annoyed Boruin, knowing that he'd seen something familiar, some trait of Smallmuss's in his approach. "You're wondering about Smallmuss. The man has spent the three decades since winning the Parade of Champions, conquering Pileaus."

"He was the Duine champion, and now he's an Emperor. He's obviously something special." Bramble replied.

"And you saw that when you chose him for training, but you didn't see him—that boy, the one out there chasing butterflies. Where was he, in that man?" Bramble didn't nod outright, but Boruin caught the slight rise at the corner of his lips. He was on the right track.

"The power of this child is too bright—it should have shown out of Smallmuss like a bonfire wrapped in cheesecloth," Bramble replied.

They watched the boy fall backward, arms spread to see how much grass he could flatten at once. "If this boy had been part of Smallmuss," said Boruin, "someone buried that diamond deep."

Now Bramble nodded in agreement. "Hidden from and for what?"

Boruin turned to him, shaking his finger. "Don't know—and right now, I don't care. What matters is that you separate us; at the moment we're one big prize, all standing in a field of flowers. That child-thing will wait patiently. Tuck the boy away. Until you can find out what you've uncovered, you'd best lay it in shadow."

Wraethe wiped the sweat from the back of her neck. Even in Diuntyne the jungle was hot. She knelt beside Bramble as he carved the sigil on the clay man's forehead, and used her wet fingers to smooth the rough edges he'd made. "If the boy is so powerful, is it wise to let Boruin use him?" She spoke as if Boruin wasn't there, the way she had a couple months back when his mind was still floating loosely in his head.

Bramble shrugged. "I certainly don't have the power to do it, and we have to hide them well. If a Riddari found them out or, Mother's mercy, the Nai'Oigher? If Dream gets a hold of these two, I can't imagine the price the Duine realm might pay." He breathed into the mouth of the clay golem, and a warm glow, like blown-over coals, rose from the body. The golem inhaled and stretched before waking fully.

As the guardian stood, rising out of the grass in the middle of the jungle glade. Boruin gauged the golem next to its creator. "A fair twin."

"A sibling, perhaps," Bramble answered, as he looked over the clay man fashioned as his double. The golem nodded a greeting, or perhaps accepting the statement as a compliment. It would care sufficiently for the boy while they were gone, Boruin thought. If the boy needed caring for at all.

The boy grabbed at Boruin's hands, and he opened them to reveal more seed heads plucked from the tall grass. The boy gathered them from his palm and blew each, one by one, up into the Diuntyne air. As they rose into the night, the boy giggled at the night hawks snapping them up, mistaking them for fluttering insects.

"You know which runes to use?" Bramble asked, pointing to the black tattoos riding like a snake around the man's arm and over his shoulder. They were powerful, but not like they would be if he'd left them to the boy.

Boruin flipped the line across his body, watching them spin. It was an action that was quickly becoming an unconscious habit. "Yeah, I've got a pretty good idea. You've got nothing to worry about."

"Wraethe and I should be far enough away by Syan. Cast your spell then."

Wraethe stepped to the new man's side. "I'm staying with Boruin. If he is as important as you say, he'll need protection."

Bramble nodded. That had been his desire as well, but he was curious how deep that odd connection the two shared went. Whether it was their shared time in the womb or her sacrifice on Smallmuss's behalf, she was bound almost as close to Boruin as Boruin was to the boy. "You know what that will mean?" he asked. Wraethe nodded.

"Keep her to her rites," Bramble said, poking his finger into Boruin's shoulder. "If you carry any one memory out of this spell, let it be that."

After Bramble left, Boruin and Wraethe watched without speaking until Diun slid down to slip under the dark line of the horizon. "All right?" he asked.

Wraethe pulled her long hair back and tied it in a tail. "I'm ready."

When he looked away from Wraethe, the boy was already at his side. The wide smile attached to his face like hardened plaster had given way to a blank look of serious concentration.

"You know what is needed? You remember what we talked about?" Boruin asked the child. The boy's small hands reached up and started pulling on the line.

In the dark of Syan, Wraethe's blue eyes seemed to burn extra bright. "You told Bramble you knew which spells to use."

Boruin held her gaze, even though the heat of it made him want to blink and look away. "I don't have any better guess what these are than you do. The boy though...he knows them perfectly." Wraethe dropped her raised eyebrow as the boy pulled the first rune into Boruin's palm.

"You're going to get yourself killed playing around with what you don't know," she said as he took her left hand with his right.

The boy stacked runes into Boruin's palm until he thought he might have to stop him. The power swelling in his fist was like a grain of sand unfurling into a towering dune. It bloomed out of his hand in radiant sheets that lighted the jungle around them in false day. The boy clapped his hands in glee twice before the spell exploded.

The wake of it lashed out, not through the air but in a wave of Aiemer that first pushed against the jungle and then dragged it back in like a high tide pulling the shoreline deep out to sea. The firmament itself shifted, layers of jungle broke apart and tacked back together in the shape that pleased the boy. The valley forming around the jungle glade, and the simple cottage, would house him well. Bramble's golems would keep watch for intruders, and his clay double would keep the child company, but the valley itself was protection enough. There was Aiemer pent and poised to defend against a Nai'Oigher—one alone, at least. The boy had done what was asked.

As for Boruin and Wraethe, they were cast out into the world on the tidal edge of the spell, both their memories set aside to better wrap their secret from prying eyes. Wraethe, with her ward, tumbled out of the boy's spell onto the Nefazo trade highway. Boruin woke with dust in his mouth, no past, and the voice of another tattooed in runes across his body.

26

DREAMS AND NIGHTMARES

B oruin woke in Munier Valley, again with dust in his mouth, but this time he was complete. The words once tattooed upon him had returned to raw thought and knowledge. They flew about his mind like leaves swirling in a windstorm. He felt the boy's mind call out to the Aiemer and cast a spell in a voice that he could barely discern from his own.

Boruin opened his eyes and saw the Fae's binding winds straining to surround him, saw the Prince of the Winds grimacing under the pressure of the boy's counter spell.

This time, Boruin spoke himself, choosing a few of the boy's swirling words as they settled, drifting down into piles like tired, falling leaves. He whispered out into the wind, and the Aiemer heard him. *That shouldn't work. Only Fae use the Aiemer directly.* The thought was smoothed over by a rising calmness. Confidence borne of the sheer volume of power at his fingertips steadied his breathing. Boruin let the feeling soak into him; after the years of torment the unexplainable runes had given him, for a moment he let them be the gift he needed now.

Whoever had broken open the window ways for the Monarhig to bring his monstrosities through had made a mistake. The Aiemer pouring into the valley came now at Boruin's call. At his request, a web of sorrowful prayers wrapped around the Fae prince, breaking his spell work and pinning him to the thorn wall. The Monarhig's tears ran down his face as the sorrow poured into his body through clenched eyes and bitten lips. It soaked through the pores in his skin, and the prince shook with pain and grief. Boruin reached forward and, with careful hands, pressed the Monarhig deeper into the wall; more thorns caught in his flesh, their barbs holding him like fishhooks. When he was certain the prince would not struggle free, he turned back into his mind and found it a mess of words cast in mountains of parchment.

"Who's going to clean—" The boy plucked a book from the floor and set it into a shelf. Rings of bookshelves rippled out from Boruin, like his wish had been a stone dropped into water. When it stopped, he saw that the library housed the vast collection of rune combinations once written across his body.

His fingertips ran across the wood shelves and the leather spines of ancient tomes. "What are these?" he asked, his voice strangely echoing through the cavern.

"All of me; all of you," the boy answered from somewhere in the stacks.

Boruin turned a corner, looking for him, and he shuddered at the way the stacks just kept on into the distant gloom. "And we are what, exactly?"

"We are as we should be, as it was."

He shook his head. The hope that the boy now talking would make him easier to deal with was fading. "I don't think I like the idea of you traipsing about in my head."

"There is no me, now," the boy said, giggling. "I understand your need to imagine me, though. In time you will realize you are whole, and maybe then I'll be gone."

"Until then?"

"Until then, I'll be traipsing about in your head."

"What are you?" Boruin asked. The boy was silent, letting the echo serve as his answer. *What are you? What are you?*

A brutal scream from one of the dark beasts dragged Boruin back from his mind. It was a cry of bloodlust; he had heard the sound from Wraethe's mouth often enough to know. From somewhere, still browsing through the stacks in Boruin's mind, the boy pulled ideal suggestions from the library as though picking his favorite flowers from a summer field. The Aiemer breathed life into the complex constructs, and Boruin waded into the field naked, armed only with the boy in his head.

The tower had fallen to the north, its rubble spread across that half of the valley. Only at its furthest tip was there open ground, and that was covered in smoke and prowling beasts that hunted Bramble's men as they tried to retreat. Their flanks had indeed failed as the men fell back too fast under hard fighting. Now they stood back-to-back, a small island of hard fighters crowded about by these horrid nightmares from the Dreaming Lands.

The beasts in the back of the encircling host snapped at each other, squabbling for their chance at live meat. An eyeless salamander, its pale skin still glowing from the fire of his bed, first smelled Boruin approaching. It turned, leapt, and fell impaled on a shaft of hardened moonlight.

The old man felt the Aiemer fill another spell and he cast it into the center of a snarling pack of rock trolls fighting for an Omman's ribcage. They ignored the small spinning ball of spores until it exploded and drifted across their hard skin. The silk cap mushrooms that swelled from their flesh grew noxious, fed by the foul blood of the beasts. When their prey had been quickly drunk dry, their silky heads burst and spores drifted with the wind further into the Monarhig's ranks.

As the shore of Bramble's small island of fighters, the Omman spearmen jabbed blindly into the dark, oily smoke that lapped about their waists like water. Unseen beasts had yanked down too many of them. Even several rilk, heavy and steady on their feet, had fallen and been dragged away. Where the smoke rippled, as water does when fish rise, the Hetsu Plainsmen fired the last of their arrows, striking at the unseen horrors under its surface.

At Boruin's whispered call, a water cheon, hair blue like the sky and hooves of shimmering pearl, trotted out of the hills and down into the valley, and raised his long trumpet. The creatures squealed, chittered, and roared at the shrill noise; the small circle of fighters held tight to the rilk as the wind from the cheon's horn blast blew dust and shattered rock across the plain. At the windstorm's passing, they opened their eyes to find the smoke gone and a carpet of knotted hands and teeth surrounding their island, reaching out to pull the fighters back to the nightmarish hordes. The gruesome things retreated on splayed fingers as the spearmen went to work, driving their iron blades through the mouths and pinning the hands to the ground. The rilk stomped and swung their hammer fists as the larger beasts lunged in to attack. Even with their belting war song and their powerful strikes, Bramble's ring of fighters were falling back, and falling in number.

"I need something bigger, son," Boruin said as he lashed a ring of circling wraiths with a shimmering flail of dismay. The creatures slunk away, cowering under rocks and fallen bodies. Their black eyes closed tight in fear as he continued past.

From deep in the library of Boruin's mind, the boy carried his choice forward with both hands, staggering a little under its weight.

It swelled as Boruin called the Aiemer to it, and for a moment he was again afraid of the power he wielded. But unlike the runes, the spell took form without the burning pain singeing his palm. It flowed out of him in a rush, like the exhalation of a breath held too long.

From the sky a whistling cry preceded a mass of black wings pulled back in a dive. The dark host turned upward with tooth and claw as the flock of giant falcons plummeted toward the living nightmares.

"Down!" Bramble yelled over the tumult of battle, and his fighters dropped to the dirt. Just above the plain, the birds snapped their wings out to catch the air and slow their attack. The speed of their descent was too great, and the wind tore feathers and skin from their bodies. Left were great birds of stone, gargoyles of red-laced obsidian that crashed into the Monarhig's dark army and their outstretched arms. The brittle stone exploded, and jagged shards, sharper than the finest iron blades, ripped through the lines. The hard armor plate of deep earth insects turned to sieves as the rock shot through. Fat skinned brutes exploded in mists of black blood. The larger shards tumbled, rolling across the dirt, halving any bodies that stretched before them.

Silence stood as the only victor for a brief moment on the field. Then Wraethe's voice, hoarse with rage, cried out her battle roar. The Ommans leapt to their feet and shoved into the dismembered battle line.

Though much of their army had fallen, the creatures roared in return. The greatest beast, some deep rock urchin with hidden fire pulsing between its thousand cracked porcelain spines, rolled over its own to meet Boruin. Bodies of the dead and living, squirming beasts rode pinned on its spines, like riders on some hellish festival wheel. Their screams served as the monstrosity's challenging bellow. Limbs clasped together into a barbed war hammer came slinging over from behind its rolling mass. It whistled as it came down, the shadow leaving Boruin blotted in dead night.

The spines drove deep into the plain as the fists crashed into the dirt. The heavy body rolled on top, its towering weight pushing the barbs deeper into the earth until Bramble's fighters felt the bedrock cracking like the thud of distant trees toppling.

The oily smoke poured anew from the urchin, spilling down its sides and over the fallen. Its inner fire flared up between its spines, driven by a heaving breath that huffed like a smith's roaring bellows. Flame licked up to the urchin's sharp tips in a heat that made the whole field stumble back under the burn.

As it threatened to ignite all left in the valley, the flame, now a great ball of fire, suddenly winked out with a woof, leaving only the ping, tap, tap, ping, tap of cooling stone. The noise grew as the cooling came faster, the popping turning to a tinkling of racing cracks. Great fractures ran through the urchin's body, and its spines began to fall with the singing crash of tumbling ice.

The urchin fell in upon itself, and its frozen pieces spilled out in an avalanche of unearthly cold. Those beasts quick enough fled from the tidal wave of tiny ice crystals, and the rest slowed in their retreat and froze as the cold sunk deep into their flesh.

Boruin swam out of the sea of ice, his skin blue and his teeth chattering from his outpouring of cold. Bramble's fighters swung around to envelope him as they unfolded back to a tight line and reformed before the confused enemy with the steep valley wall at their backs.

"You're naked, boss," Pile pointed out with a grin.

"Takes a confident fighter to battle unclothed," Bramble answered.

"Well, he's got no cause to be timid," Wraethe said, her wandering eyes above a growing smile.

"Give me your cloak, for Yuin's sake," Boruin snapped, stamping his feet as the cold came off him like waves of smoke. Wraethe handed it over slowly, but kept his eye.

"What is all that?" Pile pointed to where the silk caps were still spreading across the dead and swarms of jewel-horned hummingbirds attacked in bright swarms. A gray stag charged through the enemy ranks, its rack a storm of green fire and its coat a writhing mist as if it evaporating under the trailing flame. Its herd followed in its tracks, driving the dark creatures before them or crushing them under hoof. The enemy was routed for the moment—a frantic mess, harassed by Boruin's spell work.

"Dreams to counter the Monarhig's nightmare creatures, Pile. Some might be nightmares in their own right, but most, I think, are dreams," Boruin answered.

"Where's the boy?" Bramble asked.

Boruin tapped the side of his head with his fist, and in some auditory hallucination, heard the rapping through the giggling boy's ears. "Climbed in my head," he answered.

Bramble smiled. "And your runes?"

"Stacked in here, too. The kid ran them all in one long line to open me up. He's tending some great mausoleum of arcana stored away up there. The boy says I'll get used to it, but I can't see how."

Bramble opened his mouth to answer, but a torrent of wind raced down the hillside and slammed them to the ground. They tumbled, clawing at the ground for purchase, until they washed up against the rilk, kneeling with their heads in the wind and their arms interlaced. The few beasts that Bramble's band had not dispatched rolled and tangled in the thorn wall. The low-laying creatures, like the crawling hands and teeth, crept against the wind, still determined to taste blood. The Ommans and Swift Riders lay in the windbreak of the great rilk bodies, and Sergeant Dharl pried the beasts up with his spear where the wind caught them like kites and spun them up into the air.

"That damn Fae!" roared Griant. His rilka echoed his hatred, the noise like a mountain splitting in two.

The last two able windwalkers had escaped Turintou's wrath and now flanked the Prince of the Winds. Eyes still red from sobbing, the humiliated Monarhig inhaled and blew harder. His gale, augmented by the windwalkers, drove the topsoil from the plain, digging down into the earth. The dark host disappeared behind the storm as dust, hard chunks of clay, and uncovered rock began to pelt the stone men.

The rilk took the assault with lowered heads, driving their fists into the earth to anchor themselves. On the end, a wide-bodied rilk, rough and knobby, caught a boulder in the chest, knocking him upright. The wind grabbed him and tossed him up into the sky to fall far outside the valley.

Boruin, the shock of the attack over, climbed slowly to his feet. A bright line of light, like the lining of a cloud or the reflection of the sun from a wave crest, wavered before him. The storm of dust and debris broke around it.

The wind tilted, coming down from above to flank the light. The Ommans scrambled under the hard bellies of the rilk, who crouched on their hands and knees. Boruin raised his hand and pointed at the top of his lighted line. His finger traced up over his head, and the line followed, creating an arch over Bramble's defenders. He splayed his fingers above and dropped them down at his sides. Ribs of light fell about them, and the wind broke across the ward of protection. The haggard army stood, looking like weary captives gathered in a tall birdcage as the dirt swirled about them.

Lightning rattled against the shimmering light, and Boruin felt the boy propose another spell. Boruin called it out of his mind, and water stuck to the light, covering the ward and deepening. The lightning broke against the water to spill its energy in blinding cascades down to the earth. Boruin heard the boy's gleeful clapping and turned to find Pile in an unknowing, near perfect imitation. The young man laughed and pointed at a school of fish darting to chase another lightning bolt.

"Where do you get this stuff?" he asked.

"Like I said, the runes were dreams, Pile. Must be somebody's. Maybe the boy's," he answered as he walked to the edge of the wards.

Bramble stepped beside him, his finger dimpling the light where he touched it. "But who is the boy?" he asked.

"*Who are you*?" Boruin heard again the faint echo through his head.

Water exploded from one side of the cage as a great slab of the broken tower drove into the ward. Boruin stumbled as the light flickered. He pulled more Aiemer in to reinforce it, and a second crushing blow brought him to his knees. Dim moonlight fell from above, and they looked upward through a tunnel of swirling dirt. As if they were in the bottom of a great well, the wall of dark wind rose hundreds of feet into the air, twisting and writhing above them.

"A Finger of God," Pile muttered, in awe of the great tornado. The spinning column swelled until it filled the wide valley, tearing everything within to pieces.

"No, Pile," Boruin mumbled, feeling the Aiemer under the Monarhig's command driving the great cyclone. "Not that big, but big enough."

Boruin did not know what to cast. A whole library of spells lay before him, but none the boy brought seemed to penetrate the winds to reach the Monarhig. A fury of lightning dashed against them again, knocking Boruin onto his back. He saw a few of the Ommans wisely climbing back under the rilk and wished he could do the same.

The eye of the tornado washed over them again, and the distant starlight darted down to him. He let the world slip from him a moment as he dashed into the cavern in his head and tore through the tomes. Then Boruin struggled to his knees, the weight of the wind made the wards almost too much to bear. He called to the Aiemer, begging it to come, and the force rushed in through the window ways. The cage of light still flickered and darkened; a breeze rose inside the hollow chamber and began to howl in tune with the outside gale.

Boruin pulled a leg up under him, and Wraethe ducked beneath his arm. Pile climbed out from under Griant and took the other side, hauling Boruin to his feet. The old man's head snapped back, and his clouded eyes searched the dark cloud above. Something whistled through the dust like those stone birds, and the three bounced on their feet but remained standing. The ground shook as another impact rocked the valley floor. Boruin put all of his will into channeling the Aiemer against the wind, and Pile gasped as the earth broke apart around them. The ground at their feet quaked, the thunder of it drowning out all noise of wind and voices. The eye of the storm above them thinned.

"The stars!" Wreathe cried out. All looked above to see them coming. Unlike the Makua'Moi judge's spell, where the stars came fast and small like a child's thrown rock, Boruin's stars came thundering down like burning kul whales. They roared as they fell, their trails bright clouds of fire-filled smoke. The earth was crushed under their impact, and debris shredded the tornado. The fighters held their hands tight over their ears, but the rilk reveled in the drumming noise, adding their own counterpoints to form a message even the furthest warrens would hear: *The Fae fall under the rilk!*

The massive cyclone spun out as the windwalkers were smashed under the falling stars. The Monarhig huddled under the last twisting lick of wind, shaping it for protection as one final star broke across the valley floor.

Boruin, standing again on his own, kept his head turned upward to watch Diun turn red as it caught fire in the upper atmosphere. Down it came at last, the heavenly body slipping from orbit and plummeting toward the valley. The Monarhig's wind failed in fear, and he held his hands above his head, screaming as the moon came, its cry a whistling shriek as its silvery gas stripped away under so much heat.

Pile grabbed his boss's arm. "Boruin! This is too much!"

Bramble shouted over the moon's cry. "You can't kill a prince of the realm! Not here, Boruin! The Courts will not abide it, and their army cannot be held back save by the combined might of every nation of Pileaus. Do not risk this!" he said, but Boruin seemed to hear nothing. He stepped down from the small dirt hill protected under his ward from the hammering stars. The Monarhig stood on the battered bedrock, panting as he mixed his spells and murmured incantations of protection.

"No! Don't you touch me!" he screamed, wide eyes still latched on the falling moon. Boruin stepped through his wards as if they were whispers and hauled him up in his fists. He held him up for the falling moon.

"Are you ready to accept terms?" Boruin said.

"What terms can there be? You have killed us all!"

"The moon comes only for you, Monarhig. Die under its weight or be bound to my command for three-times-three years," Boruin answered. The Monarhig's face curled in disgust, but fear still reigned in his eyes.

"Yes," he whispered. "I'll do as you command."

"Swear," Bramble said, coming up from behind and nervously eyeing the great weight of the moon bearing down over his shoulder. "You know what to swear—and hurry, for the Mother's sake!"

The Monarhig snarled but assented. "I swear on the Great Mother and her first born, the sleeping Iraemun. May my rank and place in the realm be forfeit if I do not hold to our agreement!" swore the Monarhig.

Uncovered by the excavation of the falling stars, the window ways lay about the battered valley floor as five pools of green water. Boruin led the Monarhig by his hair, muddied and tangled by bits of rock and meat from his dead army. The Fae leaned toward the water, struggling to cross to the Dreaming Lands before the moon crashed into its green reflection.

"You will come when I call," Boruin commanded. The boy strode forward from the gloom of the stacks and, using Boruin's finger, traced a rune behind the Fae's ear. The Monarhig was bound.

"I will come, lij," he spat, the word even more full of hatred and disdain than usual, if that were possible. Boruin dropped the Monarhig into the pool, the water taking his body without wave or ripple.

"Will he hold the bargain?" Boruin asked.

"Long enough to register the deal with a Delledeir. Then the bargain will be unbreakable," Wraethe answered.

Boruin thought of the rune behind the prince's ear—he'd bound him tight enough.

"The moon, Boruin?" Pile reminded. Boruin kept his eyes on the pool, its flat sheen mirroring the sky full of the burning orb. Before their eyes, the rilk's upturned faces, the Ommans' fearless grins, and the Swift Rider's drawn bows, the fire withdrew from the moon. Its bright light wavered and its center faded, leaving only a wide ring of falling rabinithair, his tail in his teeth to complete the circle. The Skyking slid to a stop as he fell back into the Aiemer pooled above the valley.

"I apologize," said Boruin, "you do fall as well as you fly."

"It's a handy skill in this realm," Turintou answered with a snort.

"I have your answer," Boruin said to the serpent. Turintou's tongue rattled once as he waited. "My heart is that of a Duine champion boy; my head a boy that is too powerful to be Duine; I was born of ruin, and so my name remains."

Turintou shook his mane and grinned wide with his mouth full of teeth. "If you say it is true, Boruin, then I accept it. Our debts are even."

"I'm hungry," said Pile, rubbing his stomach.

Bramble snorted, shaking his head. "My cupboard has been beaten into the earth," he said. "Once I've set that straight, perhaps we can consider your stomach."

"You can take the repair cost out of Boruin's share of the contract," Pile offered.

"What now, boss?" Wraethe asked. The man stayed silent; the Dreaming Lands had caught his eye. Below the green surface he could see the roads which all led to the one great city, Maeda Criacao. Aside the paths were the wilds of the talamhs, which could trap a soul and keep it from finding the roads ever again. The Dreaming Lands were at once beautiful and frightening, immense and yet all inside the horizon. There was an enemy there, someone hidden behind the brazen tongue of the Monarhig, and part of him wanted to flush him out while their victory was still fresh. Instead, Boruin finally wrenched his eyes up from the window way and looked at Bramble.

"It's time to meet Emperor Pileaus. If I'm a piece of him, some root grown without him, I have to see if he's the same."

Bramble grinned. "And swallow him as you did the boy?"

Boruin didn't return the smile. It was something he hadn't considered. *Who would swallow whom?* "I hope not. Maybe just meeting him will answer enough questions."

"We go north to the Empire, then," said Wraethe, her face smooth and pale under the restored shine of Diun, crossing high above the land.

"Not before we get a beer someplace," Pile said, "and a day at least to relax and spend some money. I know I, for one, deserve it."

"A day at least," Boruin agreed.

"Do you now know what you are?" Wraethe asked, as the others followed Bramble and the soft grass rising to his feet as he walked toward the center of the valley.

Boruin wiped his hands across his face, tired all of a sudden. "I am dreams, and nightmares too, I think, wrapped in the guise of a mortal champion. I am the boy and he is me—at least that is how he thinks. I had hoped Bramble would have found out more before it came to this. I feel like a great machine built with no obvious use."

"Whose dreams? Whose nightmares?" she pressed. He took another inward glance towards the back of the library, the gloom where the torchlight failed to penetrate.

"I dare not guess. They are too frightening to be of men; too great even to be Moir or Monarhig. I dare not guess," Boruin repeated. In his mind though, he had guessed. The boy had marked the Prince of the Winds with a sigil. A rune of Polorun, the murdered brother of the sleeping Iraemun, had obeyed the boy's command by adhering to the Monarhig. It would not have done so for someone without the authority to summon it; Boruin felt that with a deep certainty.

His eye dropped again to the window way, holding it like one's distant view of home. Wraethe pulled him away before he sank too deep, and they followed the others to the cottage nestled under willows in the center of a plain of broken bedrock. Boruin walked without seeing it, instead wandering the stacks of his mind, peering down the long shelves and not yet daring to venture the depths hidden in an oily darkness that swirled like smoke and breathed like the living.

EPILOGUE

"Tuck the boy away. Until you can find out what you've uncovered, you'd best lay it in shadow," Boruin said.

Bramble stared at him, considering how much of his mind he should speak. With one more look at the boy bouncing around in the jungle glade, he sighed.

"You're right, but it's not just him I've got to hide." Bramble said. "He's certainly a force—I've seen nothing like him and frankly it scares me—but the truth is I don't think he's capable of anything." His feet carried him back to his pacing, and he made two strides across the dirt patch before checking himself and turning back to Boruin. "He's like a great boulder perched on a hilltop. Alone, it can do nothing..."

Boruin finished for him. "You think I'm the one the one to give it a shove. I'm the one that scares you."

Bramble shrugged and ran his hand across his scalp, as if he could wipe away the heat pouring down from the sun. "You're definitely two parts of the same...something. Surely you've felt that?" Boruin ignored the question.

"Two parts of how many?" he asked, his fingers, whether he knew it or not, splitting a stalk of grass into fine threads. "Is Smallmuss a third? Does a fourth run around his gardens?"

"I've heard he's assumed the god-head of the Yuinite religion—named himself Pileaus, the God-King," Bramble answered. He watched the boy weaving through a patch of thistles, his fingers tapping each one as he passed. "It's possible that he's got something like the boy in him already."

As Bramble turned his eyes on him, Boruin caught where he was going. "You really think that's the answer? Somehow the boy and I will stitch into one soul?"

"I think it's inevitable. If I could have kept you in the womb longer, I think you would have come out on two feet instead of four," Bramble answered. He took the new man's hand and turned it palm up. "These runes could have gone anywhere, but they latched onto you. You and the boy are orbiting bodies of the same material—twin suns that will crash together sooner than later."

"I have a hard time believing that."

"You will, son. It's only a matter of time."

ACKNOWLEDGEMENTS

When asked to work on what was originally the *Baeg Tobar* project, I knew only that we would be fleshing out a rough draft of a fantasy world. I could not have conceived the sheer volume of words that would be written by so many talented authors who would go on to great things. Jeremy Mohler rounded up an equally talented group of illustrators so the world of *Baeg Tobar* (and now *Pileaus)* would live through both prose and imagery.

The Unmade Man is one of many good things that came from that project, and while I'm grateful for everyone I worked with, I will especially thank Jeremy Mohler, who led the process; Scott Colby, fellow writer and primary editor for this book; and Jeffrey Koch, whose illustrations gave me what few beginning authors receive—a chance to behold the world spun out of his head.

At the moment, *Pileaus* is still veiled by the enormity of the internet. I have no doubt it will soon be plucked out of the waves and recognized for the jewel it is. In fact, it could be your hand, right now.

DTG

ABOUT PILEAUS

Pileaus is an ambitious transmedia project set in a sprawling dark fantasy realm. It's the story of a world in chaos as told by a diverse group of creators.

The emperor is dead. What's left of the once proud Pilean Empire is under siege from threats both internal and external. Ommany, Thalia, Ud, and the pirates of Brailee's Steps have all set their sights on the empire's land and resources. It is a time of war and strife, but also of discovery and opportunity. The race to control the north has brought with it major steps forward in science, technology, and sorcery, all of which are contributing to the chaos in their own unique ways.

Meanwhile, there's a whole wide world out there many of the northerners have forgotten about. A race of aquatic zealots plunders the seas and coasts. Far to the south, a small cluster of younger, more progressive nations grows more powerful every day. Dark secrets and ancient ruins await discovery in the untamed center of the continent. More and more musicians learn to weave amazing magic with their songs. Immortal demigods in a wondrous parallel dimension endlessly debate the fate of those chaotic mortals—and occasionally intervene. Life on the Pilean continent grows more interesting by the hour.

ABOUT THE AUTHOR

Daniel Tyler Gooden was born and raised outside of Kansas City. He spent too short a time in New Orleans, but picked up a wife and a persistent southern twang, then brought them both back to midtown Kansas City.

His writing ranges between literature, fantasy, and horror, and is at the moment preoccupied with a novel of personal apocalypse, a hundred-years war, bicycle cavalry, and Google-overlaid reality causing magic to swell again into the world as man forgets to believe in physics.